AMISH SPRING ROMANCE

JENNIFER SPREDEMANN   JENNIFER BECKSTRAND

RACHEL J. GOOD   KATHLEEN FULLER   DEBBY GIUSTI

MOLLY JEBBER   PATRICIA DAVIDS

BLESSED PUBLISHING

Compilation Copyright © 2022 "The Arrangement" © 2022 by Jennifer Spredemann, "Love Blooms" © 2022 Kathleen Fuller, "Finding Her Amish Home" © 2022 by Debby Giusti, "A Match for the Teacher" © 2022 by Patricia Davids, "The Cedar Box © 2022 by Molly Jebber, "Ivy's New Beginning" © 2022 by Jennifer Beckstrand, "Hope Blossoms" © 2021 by Rachel J. Good

Published in USA by Blessed Publishing

Cover design *iCreate Designs*

All Scripture from the *King James Version* of the *Holy Bible*

ISBN: 978-1-940492-69-8 (paperback)

ISBN: 978-1-940492-70-4 (hardcover)

LETTER TO OUR WONDERFUL READERS

Dear Reader,

Our hearts are overflowing with gratitude for you. You are the reason we write our stories and the reason we can get through the long days and the hard times. This collection of stories is our heartfelt gift to you.

Each of the authors in the *Amish Spring Romance* Collection comes from a different background and has varied and plentiful experiences with the Amish. Our stories feature Amish communities from around the country, so the customs and rules you read about in one story might be different from those in other stories in the collection. And while we all try to be as accurate and true to the Amish way of life as possible, we all use some artistic license to tell our stories.

May these stories lift your spirits, brighten your days, and touch your heart through laughter, tears, and heart-stopping romance. Above all, we pray that you will feel the love of the Savior and experience the miracles of Spring through our stories.

May God's love and hope bloom in your heart as you read these stories, and we pray for the Lord's choicest blessings upon you this spring and for the rest of the year.

All our love,
The *Amish Spring Romance* Authors

THE ARRANGEMENT

JENNIFER SPREDEMANN

CHAPTER ONE

*L*ucy Bontrager's fingers trembled as she held the plastic device in her hands. She stared down at it in disbelief. Two blue lines. *Ach,* this could not be. It couldn't. She was the bishop's *dochder.* She couldn't be in the *familye* way. Especially not with an *Englischer's boppli.*

Nee. Tears rushed to the surface, threatening to spill over her lashes and onto her cheeks. *Take a deep breath,* she told herself. *It's going to be okay. It'll work out.* Somehow.

But would it, really?

Her father had been watching her again this morning as she'd completed her chores. He had to know something was up when she'd retched after entering the barn two mornings in a row. Her stomach couldn't handle the offensive odors that accompanied farm life, even though she'd been around them her entire eighteen-year existence.

Dat had asked her what was wrong, but she couldn't bear to tell him what she'd suspected. Now, the truth had been confirmed. Now, she would *have* to tell *Dat.* Now, her life would be changed. Forever.

For sure and certain, she'd need to get a message to Trey. Somehow. How would he react? Would he offer to marry her? Would he become Amish? *Nee,* she didn't think so. He still had three more years of service to the military, which was something he couldn't get out of if he wanted to. At least, that was what he'd told her before he'd been deployed overseas two weeks ago.

Ach, she should have never given in to his pleas. He'd wanted to be sure she was his girl, he'd said. He'd wanted to have something to remember her by when he was away, he'd said. He'd wanted her to commit to him with her whole heart, he'd said.

And she had. She'd given him everything. But now that she had time to think, *he* hadn't given *her* everything. After he'd promised his love and said he'd think of her every day while he was away, he'd gone and broken up with her. What had she expected, dating an *Englischer*?

She had no promise that she wouldn't end up carrying his *boppli* while he was thousands of miles away. He hadn't promised to marry her. He hadn't promised her a happily-ever-after.

Nee, this was anything but. This was terrifying. *Dat* hadn't even known she'd been dating an *Englischer*. As far as her father knew, she'd been faithfully attending the Amish youth gatherings on the weekends. Not meeting in secret with her *Englisch* beau.

Ach, what had she done?

A knock on the bathroom door startled her.

"Lucy, are you okay in there?" *Mamm* asked.

Nee. No, she was not okay. Not in the least.

"*Jah*." She lied. "I'll be out in a minute."

She hurried but fumbled with the pregnancy test. What should she do with it and the box it had come in? She rifled through the bathroom cabinet and found an empty plastic grocery bag, then she wasted several squares of toilet paper to wrap around the test and hide any evidence. She would close the plastic bag tightly, then chuck it into the trash can.

The evidence was now gone, but her predicament remained the same. She, the bishop's daughter, had become pregnant out-of-wedlock with an *Englischer's* baby. What on earth was she going to do?

～

The last thing Lucy expected as she entered the barn was to find her father standing between the stalls, his arms crossed over his chest, his lips turned downward, and holding her positive pregnancy test in his hand.

His steely gaze fixed on hers. "I think we need to talk."

Ach, she couldn't breathe. She couldn't move. Without permission, tears and a sob escaped her, and she hung her head in shame. "I'm sorry, *Dat*!"

In a split second, her father's arms were around her. In all her life, she couldn't remember her father ever pulling her into an embrace. "We will take care of this, *dochder*. We will find a solution."

After her tears had dried, her father released her.

"I don't know what to do, *Dat*." She brushed away a stray tear.

"You must marry the *bu*. Who is it? One of the Stoltzfus boys?"

"*Nee.*" *Ach*, it pained her to even utter the words. Because, in reality, her situation was much worse than her father had imagined. "It was an *Englischer.*"

At the proclamation, her father stumbled back, eventually falling onto a bale of hay.

"*Dat*! Are you all right?" If she'd caused her father to have a heart attack, she'd never forgive herself.

"What have you done, *dochder*? When...? How...?" He shook his head and swatted the air. "*Ach*, I guess it doesn't matter now. What's done is done."

He rubbed his forehead. "Is there any chance he would become Amish?"

She wasn't sure why he'd even asked, since their district didn't readily accept *Englischers* into their fold. But perhaps they'd make an exception since she was the bishop's *dochder*. Or maybe for her situation? "He isn't even in the country. He's a soldier, *Dat*. I have no idea when he will return from wherever they sent him."

"A *soldier*?" *Dat* covered his eyes. "Did you set out to defy *every* rule our community has put forth? Everything our people have stood on for centuries? Lucy, I am the bishop! Do you have any idea how this will look to our people? Why didn't you think first?"

Ach, she hated hearing her father's reprimand, but he was one hundred percent right. She had not been thinking about the consequences her choices would bring. She hadn't thought about any of it. All she'd thought about was loving Trey and making him happy. She'd never dreamed she would end up alone and in the *familye* way.

"What are you planning to do?" he demanded.

"I don't know. I haven't had time to think about it yet."

"We will send you to my *Englisch* brother's to—"

"*Nee, Dat*! Please. Don't send me away." Her entire body shook now. She couldn't bear enduring an entire pregnancy alone.

"It is better if you give this child up."

She adamantly shook her head. "*Nee*. I could never. Please, *Dat*. Let me keep the *boppli*."

"I...I need to pray. I must seek *Der Herr's* will in this." He marched to the tack room, then turned before shutting himself inside. "You will mention this to no one. Do you hear me? No one."

She nodded. "Okay."

"You must pray too."

Ach, she was too ashamed to go before *Der Herr* now, but she nodded, nonetheless.

At that, her father closed the door. Chances were, he'd lock himself inside until *Der Herr* provided an answer. She only hoped it would come soon.

CHAPTER TWO

When Justin Beachy heard footsteps approaching his shop, he turned his head toward the entry door. He slid out from under the buggy he'd been working on, then wiped his hands on a shop towel. His grin widened, and he stretched out his hand as his friendly bishop approached. "Hello, Jerry. What brings you by today? Need a new buggy?"

A frown etched deep into the bishop's face. "If only it was as simple as that." He glanced around the quiet shop. "Do you have a few minutes?"

"*Jah*, sure." Justin sensed unease in the bishop's demeanor.

"Could we go somewhere more private?" Jerry asked.

Justin gestured behind them. "Is my office okay?"

"*Jah*, that should do."

Justin led the way and motioned to the chairs across from his desk. "You may have a seat, if you'd like."

Jerry nodded. "*Denki*."

Justin sat in his leather office chair, as unease crawled through his veins. What on earth could the bishop have to discuss that required privacy?

The bishop's hands clenched and unclenched, and he blew out a breath. "I'm sure you're wondering what has me all worked up."

"Have I done something wrong?" Usually, it would be the deacon that confronted such matters. For the life of him, though, he couldn't come up with any rules he may have broken.

"*Nee*. At least nothing I'm aware of." Jerry drew in another long breath, then expelled it. "Before we begin this conversation, I need to know that I can trust you. Nothing that we say can pass these four walls."

"You have me worried, Jerry."

"It is a very personal matter that I have been praying about. Every time I do, *Der Herr* brings you to mind, so I'm thinking you're the one."

"I'm the…?" Justin shook his head. "You're being quite vague."

"This is very important to me. Until I have assurance you will not utter this to anyone—"

"You have my promise."

"You're sure?"

"If it's that important to you, then yes, I will keep it to myself. I'm just wondering, why me?"

"And that is the matter I am getting to." The bishop wiped his hands on his pant legs.

Ach, Justin had never seen their district leader so vulnerable.

"My *dochder*…she…" Jerry's words came out as a sob.

"What is wrong with her? Which *dochder*?" Not that he even knew Jerry's daughters by name.

He wiped away his tears. "The youngest. Lucy, she's…*ach*, I can barely even say the words. She's…in a situation."

Justin's brow furrowed. "A situation?"

"A predicament, actually. She just found out that she is expecting a *boppli*. With an *Englischer*." Jerry hung his head at the words.

Justin understood good and well what it meant when someone left the Amish church and became *Englisch*. In the Amish community where he'd grown up in Pennsylvania, they'd believed that leaving the Amish doomed one to certain hell. He wasn't sure about all the rules in this Indiana district just yet.

"*Ach.*" What was he supposed to say to that? He had no idea. "I'm sorry."

"*Jah*, me too."

"What…I mean, why are you sharing this with *me*? I'm confused."

Jerry raised his eyes to meet Justin's. "I was hoping you would agree to briefly court and marry my *dochder*. Soon."

A punch in the gut would have been more expected—and welcomed—than the words the bishop had just spoken. "You…" He scratched his chin, attempting to wrap his mind around the bishop's ludicrous proposal. He shook his head. "Listen, Jerry I—"

"I'm *begging* you, Justin." The bishop's eyes evidenced his words.

All of a sudden, Justin's throat felt dry. "Why *me*?"

"You're a *gut* Amish man. I trust you. You are older. You are already established with a place of your own. And I know you would treat the *boppli* as your own and treat my *dochder* well."

It was true. He was all those things, but… "I'm honored that you have that

7

much faith in me. Truly." He squeezed his eyes shut. "May I have some time to process this? To think? And pray?"

"Of course." The bishop seemed visibly relieved. Was it because he hadn't outright rejected the crazy notion? He'd certainly wanted to.

"Okay, let me think for a minute here." Justin rubbed his forehead. "Your *dochder* Lucy is in the *familye* way. With an *Englischer's boppli*." He stood up and paced behind his desk. "What about the *Englischer*?"

"He doesn't know about the *boppli*. No one does. Right now, it's me, you, and Lucy."

"Her *mamm* doesn't even know?" He felt like his eyes might jump out of their sockets.

"I thought that if the two of you courted...and then she was in the *familye* way..." Jerry shrugged.

"So, you'd want me to pretend the *boppli* is mine." He said flatly. "Do you know how much I've wanted to redeem my family's name after my *brieder*...? *Ach*, Jerry. I don't know if I can do this. Maybe if I wasn't a Beachy, but—"

"Don't you see? That's what makes you the perfect candidate. No one would think twice about a *boppli* if a Beachy is involved."

Justin palmed his forehead. *Candidate?* It made him feel like he was running for public office. "How old is your *dochder*?"

"She just turned eighteen."

"Eighteen!" He hadn't meant to shout the word, but for goodness' sake. *Eighteen?* "No way."

"I know you're—"

"Past thirty. Can you imagine how people would talk? I'd be labeled the worst Beachy yet. A cradle robber."

"I hadn't considered that, really." Jerry sighed heavily. "All I know is that when I prayed for a solution, *Der Herr* brought you to mind. More than once."

"You think this is something *Gott* wants me to do?" He hadn't considered *Der Herr* asking him to sacrifice his reputation. Wasn't a *gut* name rather to be chosen than great riches? "But pretending the *boppli* is mine would be dishonest."

"I would never ask you to lie. And I'm pretty certain most people aren't going to ask."

"And if they do?" Because *he* was pretty sure his family would have something to say about it.

"Like I said, how you respond will be on you. Just, if you *do* happen to tell someone, ask them to keep it a secret."

"What does your *dochder* think of all this?"

"Lucy has no idea I'm talking to you. But I told her I would help her find a solution."

"Well, that's great. She'll probably take one look at me and flee for the hills."

"Nonsense. She will do as I advise her. She really is a *gut* girl; she just doesn't always make the best decisions." Jerry grimaced.

You think? Thank *Gott* he'd had enough sense to keep that comment to himself. *Barely eighteen?* That meant she had two years of being a teenager yet. *Ach.*

"I know I promised you I wouldn't tell anyone, but—" He left off talking at the bishop's frown. "It's just that I *really* need to talk to Sammy Eicher. I tell him everything, and he advises me. He's not even in this district, and I know he wouldn't tell a soul if I asked him not to."

The bishop seemed to be contemplating his words. "I know Sammy Eicher. He will offer sound, Godly advice. You may share it with him *only.*"

Just hearing those words lifted about ten pounds off Justin's shoulders.

The bishop tapped the desk. "When do you think you can have an answer for me?"

"I'm not sure. But I would want to speak with your *dochder* as well. I don't know her at all. Honestly, I'm not even sure which one she is."

Jerry nodded. "I can bring her by tomorrow, if that suits you."

"Tomorrow." He blew out a long breath.

"If time wasn't of the essence, I wouldn't be rushing this. Or encouraging it." Jerry's eyes pled with Justin's. "I'm desperate."

"I'll speak with Sammy tonight, then." He moved around his desk to walk the bishop out.

"I appreciate it." Jerry clasped Justin's shoulder. "I realize this is a great sacrifice for you. I'm confident *Der Herr* will reward you for it, *sohn.*"

Sohn. Ach, the word made him think of his folks. Just the thought of his parents discovering that the *maedel*—the very young *maedel*—he would be courting was in the *familye* way, and them believing it was his *boppli*, sent him reeling. The thought of their disappointment was a heavy burden he didn't even want to think of bearing.

Why me, Gott? *What have I done to deserve this?*

Ach, he should be ashamed of his thoughts. Who was *he* to question *Der Herr's* will? If it were someone other than the bishop who'd approached him, he would have outright refused. But the fact that Jerry had spent time in prayer and *Gott* put *him* on the bishop's heart...who was *he* to say no? How *could* he say no?

Whatever he decided to do, he knew he needed to talk to Sammy. Perhaps Sammy would help him see another side. Another solution. Talk him out of it.

One could only hope.

CHAPTER THREE

*W*ell, it's an interesting situation for sure." Sammy, Justin's wise elderly friend, rubbed his wiry beard. "Can't say I've ever encountered anything like this before."

"Sammy, I honestly don't know what to do about this." Justin's hand slid through his hair. "I mean, I *do* feel bad for the girl."

"Have you taken any time to get to know her?"

"No, I can't even... This really isn't what I planned for my future. It's not how I thought my life would go."

"Maybe God has different thoughts than you do." Sammy's eyebrow arched as he sipped his lemonade. "Why don't you allow GOD to write your life story? He's a better writer than you are. Have you ever considered His hand might be in this?"

"I did, but...How can that be?"

"You know, this might sound funny, but your situation kind of reminds me of another one I've read about." Sammy's head bobbed.

"Okay." Justin wondered where his friend was going with this. "The thing is, I hate to drag the Beachy name through the mud. Again."

"I see. Well, this other situation that I was thinking about, it was similar to yours in a way."

"Do I know these people?"

"Personally? *Nee*. Not yet, anyhow."

"Are you planning to introduce me to them? Because I don't really have a lot of time. The bishop was hoping for my answer tomorrow. He was going to bring his *dochder* by."

"I cannot introduce you because I have not met him either. But I do know His Son." Sammy's eyes met his. "I believe you do too."

Justin wrinkled his brow. "Who is it?"

"Jesus."

"Jesus?"

"*Jah*. Just think about the circumstance of His birth. Joseph found out that Mary was pregnant with a *boppli* that wasn't his."

"But he was going to divorce her, right?"

"It would have been like a divorce. In that day, to break up after you were betrothed was a pretty scandalous thing." Sammy lifted a finger. "But Joseph didn't 'put her away' as the Bible says."

"*Nee*, but an angel spoke to him and told him it was okay to marry her. Her child was conceived by the Holy Ghost. *This* is hardly the same thing."

"That is true. But have you thought of Joseph's reputation? His intended being with child, although they were not married yet? I assure you, it was a bigger deal back then, and in that culture, than it is today. If Joseph abandoned her and claimed she was expecting another man's child, there was a *gut* chance she could have been put to death."

"So, do you think people believed Jesus was Joseph's biological son?"

Sammy chuckled. "I reckon that would have been easier for them to believe than a virgin birth. Remember when Jesus spoke and those around Him were amazed at His wisdom? They mentioned Him being the carpenter's son. So, *jah*, I think there's a *gut* chance they thought Joseph to be His father."

Justin contemplated Sammy's words. If what he said was true, then just like Justin, Joseph might have pretended the child was his own. And just like Justin, Joseph would have sacrificed his reputation—not only for the *gut* of Mary and her *boppli*, but for good of the entire human race. "My sacrifice wouldn't be as noble."

"Maybe not, but it is admirable that you're considering it."

"What would *you* do, Sammy?"

"Well, first I'd pray and seek *Der Herr's* will in the matter."

"I don't think I've stopped praying since the bishop left. That's why I'm here."

"Other than your reputation, is there a reason why you wouldn't agree to it?"

"I feel like there are a hundred reasons. It's not my *boppli*. What about the other guy?"

"You said he's not around, right?"

"Correct. But is it right on her part not to tell him? If I had a *boppli* coming, I'd want to know."

"Even if it was by an *Englischer*?"

"*Jah*. It would be my responsibility."

"But you said the father was far away, ain't not? Can she contact him?"

"I'm not sure. Jerry said he's in another country and she has no idea when or if he'll return."

"It's a predicament indeed." Sammy played with the condensation on his lemonade glass.

"Another thing. She's only eighteen. Practically a *boppli* herself. Wouldn't it just be wrong?"

"If she is in the *familye* way, I assure you she is not a *boppli*. Eighteen is considered an adult in the *Englisch* world. She may just be more experienced in some things than you are." Sammy's brow arched.

Justin's face ignited in warmth. "*Ach, jah*, you're right. I haven't...I mean, I've never..." *Jah*, he'd just leave off talking right there.

"Have you thought about what you have to offer the *maedel* and the *boppli*? Perhaps you can be a blessing to them. And what about you? Have you never considered having a family of your own? Don't you want to settle down?"

"*Jah*. I just thought it would look...*different*."

"Love seldom looks the way we imagine."

Love? He hadn't really thought about *loving* them, just meeting their needs.

Sammy continued, "It might be awkward at first, but before you know it, life together will become as ordinary as waking up to sunshine. And then when the two of you have *bopplin* you've created, you'll wonder why you stayed single for so long."

Ach, he hadn't thought about the future. He could only think of the here and now. But Sammy was right. This part of his life might be difficult, but it wouldn't last forever.

"Sammy?" Justin took a deep breath. "Would you pray for me? For us?"

"I will."

"I'm just so scared I'm going to mess things up."

"And how would you go about doing that?"

"I don't know." He shrugged. "But the fear is there just the same."

"Remember, it is not *Gott* who gives the spirit of fear. That comes from the evil one."

"I'm just wondering, why me?" He lifted his palms.

"Why *not* you?"

Justin rubbed his forehead. "I don't know. I just know everyone's going to flip when they hear the news. My *brieder* will give me a hard time for sure and certain."

"*Ach*, that's what brothers are for." Sammy waved a dismissive hand. "Besides, they have no stones to throw."

"Right." He sucked in a calming breath. "What do *you* think I should do?"

Sammy raised his hands. "I will not tell you how to decide. That has to come from *Der Herr*. But know that whatever you decide, I will support you."

"Denki. I really appreciate your friendship." With Sammy's support and the bishop's, would the situation really be that bad?

All he could think of was to pray it wouldn't.

CHAPTER FOUR

I've found a solution for your situation, *dochder*." Had Lucy ever seen *Dat's* demeanor so serious?

She swallowed hard as dread filled her. Who knew what "solution" *Dat* may have found? All she knew was that she didn't want to have to go away by herself and live with strangers and give up her *boppli*. Anything would be better than that, wouldn't it? "Wha…What is it?" Her hands trembled.

"I found a *gut* Amish man who I think will take you as his *fraa*." *Dat* nodded in satisfaction.

Oh no. She combed her mind for who it might possibly be. "Who?"

"Justin Beachy."

Lucy couldn't help her sharp intake of breath. *Justin Beachy?* Oh my. She needed a fan. How on earth had *Dat* managed to rope their community's most eligible—and handsome—bachelor into marrying *her?*

"I realize he is quite a bit older than you, but he will make a *gut* husband. You'll see." He patted her hand.

"He agreed?" She squeaked out the words.

"He said he would pray about it. I'm certain he will agree." His eyes searched hers. "We will go see him later today. He is expecting us."

~

Lucy had been lost in thought since she and *Dat* had begun the journey to Justin Beachy's homestead. She'd tried quelling the butterflies swarming in her belly, to no avail.

If she were honest with herself, she would admit that she was nervous about speaking with Justin Beachy. If she were honest with herself, she would admit she used to have a secret crush on Justin Beachy. If she were honest with herself, she would admit the possibility of Justin Beachy courting and marrying her brought a measure of comfort and excitement to her soul.

The thing was, when she'd met Trey, she'd all but forgotten about her fanciful musings of the older handsome bachelor. Justin Beachy had been way out of her league—someone to be admired from afar. When he first arrived in the community, she and her friends would tease each other, dreaming he would ask one of them if they'd like a ride home. He never had.

Come to think of it, she couldn't remember him ever taking anyone home. He'd mostly hung out with the guys and kept to himself.

In all fairness, though, he may have considered Lucy and her friends too young. She thought she had caught his eye a time or two, but to her disappointment, nothing ever came of it. She hoped the reason wasn't because he didn't find her attractive. Because, if she ended up married to the man, she'd want him to find her irresistible.

Although he'd attended the youth gatherings for a while when he'd been new in the community, he eventually stopped going. That was around the time Lucy had met Trey at one of the local stores. Trey was friendly and charming and good-looking, and Lucy was immediately attracted to his plentiful smiles. No doubt, his *boppli* would be handsome as well. She'd thought she loved him, but somewhere deep inside, she'd known a relationship between them wouldn't work out in the end. Thinking back now on her gut feeling, she wished she wouldn't have given herself away to him. A part of her was saddened that Trey would never know his child. And even though her father insisted on keeping her *boppli* a secret, she felt guilty not entertaining plans to tell Trey about his *boppli* when he returned home from overseas. He had a right to know, didn't he? The *boppli* was his too.

But she knew *Dat*. He was terrified of losing her—or any of his *kinner*—to *der welt*. Like he'd lost his older *bruder*. Once *Onkel* Lawrence had left the community, her father had never seen him again. As a matter of fact, Lucy had never even met her uncle. Which made her wonder why *Dat* suggested sending her to his *bruder's* house, if he hadn't heard from him in years. Had he hoped to reconnect? Did *Dat* secretly keep in touch with his fence-jumping *bruder*? Or had *Dat* planned to track his brother down, somehow?

Whatever the case may be, it sparked Lucy's interest.

"Are you ready to meet your soon-to-be husband?" *Dat* asked.

She stuffed her fingernail between her teeth. "I don't...what if he finds me...lacking?"

"He is a *gut* man. I'm sure you will suit him *chust* fine, *dochder*." He shot her a sideways glance from his perch behind the reins. "I will leave you there for a while so you can get acquainted."

Ach. But she was nervous. "What should we talk about?"

"Whatever you'd discuss with any beau, I reckon. You likely know nothing about each other, so you will have plenty to talk about."

~

Justin blew out a breath and paced the shop floor. Again.

He'd attempted to work on his buggy orders today but found himself daydreaming. And when he hadn't been daydreaming, he'd made inexcusable blunders. Like trying to attach the back wheel to the front axle. Or cutting the canvas wrong. *Jah*, that mistake had been costly. He decided he was better off not doing anything at all when his brain was all *ferhoodled.*

Never in his life had he been this nervous about seeing a girl. *Nee*, a woman. Because this wasn't just any woman. *Gott* willing, this woman was to be his *fraa.* Soon.

That meant they'd be living together. Working together. Eating together. Sleeping together. He'd never allowed himself to fantasize about having a *fraa.* But now that the scenario would very likely become a reality, he couldn't help but dwell on the thought. Truth be told, he was crazy with anticipation. But what he *wasn't* anticipating were all the rumors that were sure to soon be flying around the community, nor the disapproving looks aimed at the "Beachy bachelor who took advantage of the bishop's teen *dochder.*"

What was, in reality, an act of sacrifice and heroism, would be perceived as an act of selfishness and gratification. He was willing to put himself on the line for the bishop and his *dochder*, though. *Der Herr* knew the truth, and that was what mattered. He just needed to keep reminding himself of that fact.

A rattling sound commanded his rapt attention, and his head snapped to the buggy pulling into his driveway. *Ach*, she was here. He briefly closed his eyes. Gott, *please help me.* The short prayer was all he could manage.

He swiped his sweaty palms down the pant legs of his broadfall trousers and then realized his *mamm* would soon be relieved of her pant-making duties. *Jah*, having a *fraa* might be a blessing.

He took another calming breath, then stepped outside to greet his guests. The moment the buggy came to a stop at the hitching post, the *maedel* glanced his way. *Ach*, she looked familiar. While he'd never spoken to her, he remembered their eyes connecting on occasion. He'd thought her pretty from the moment he saw her but never considered pursuing a relationship with her because he figured she would think he was too old. But if he had the bishop's full support and his *dochder* agreed, could they make a relationship work between them?

He attempted what he hoped was a smile. His pounding heart had him all *ferhoodled*. His attention never strayed as she exited the buggy and exchanged words with her father. Then the two met him halfway between the hitching post and his shop.

"Justin Beachy, this is my youngest *dochder*, Lucy."

Ach, what should he do? Hug her? Place a holy kiss on her cheek? Offer a handshake? *Nee,* he wasn't thinking straight at all. Instead, he simply nodded. "*Gut* to meet you."

She dipped her head. He hoped she wasn't afraid of him. Or was she just nervous like him?

The bishop looked back and forth between the two of them. "Well, I'll leave you two to get acquainted." He turned to Justin. "I trust you'll bring her home later."

"*Jah.*" Justin nodded.

"Very well." The bishop made eye contact with his daughter, then returned to his buggy.

They both watched in silence as he drove out of Justin's driveway.

CHAPTER FIVE

*S*econds ticked by in silence… Well, this was awkward.

Justin finally cleared his throat. "Would you like to see my place?" *Soon to be our place.*

"Sure." Lucy's chin trembled. "Um, I…I'm sorry to drag you into my mess." She looked up at him through glassy eyes.

Ach, his heart went out to her. This situation wasn't going to be easy for either of them. "It's all right. I just hope that I can meet your needs. And the *boppli's.*"

A stray tear rolled down her cheek. "You are kind in saying that."

"I mean it." He pivoted and held her gaze. "If your *vatter* prayed and *Der Herr* brought me to his mind, who am I to question *Gott*? It must be His will, ain't so?"

She shrugged. "I suppose."

"I aim to make the best of this situation. I told your *vatter* I wouldn't outright lie, because I know *Der Herr* would not approve of that. With that being said, I'm okay with people believing this *boppli* is mine. Ours."

Her head lifted. "You are?"

"*Jah.* And I expect people to judge us. That is just how people are. You can't really blame them. We know the truth and *Der Herr* knows the truth, so that is all that really matters to me. I just want our lives to be pleasing to Him."

"You are a *gut* man, Justin Beachy."

"I try, but I often fall short."

"Do you truly think *Der Herr* will bless us? After what I've done?"

"That is the beauty of *Der Herr's* grace. It is called amazing grace for a reason. His grace transforms our frailties into our strengths, our failures into our triumphs, and our biggest mistakes into our biggest blessings. With Him, we can conquer anything."

She ducked her head. "*Ach*. I am not worthy to be considered as your *fraa*."

He lifted her chin and stared into her eyes. "Apparently, *Gott* thinks otherwise. And His thoughts are higher than our thoughts. Whatever doubts you have, place them in *Gott's* hands, Lucy. *Kumm*."

When he held out his hand, she placed her delicate fingers into his palm. *Jah*, he was certain *Der Herr* would guide them to the future He had planned.

~

Lucy felt like hugging her father. Had he already known how *wunderbaar* Justin Beachy was? As terrible as her situation was, this was probably the best possible outcome.

But she felt horrible that a *gut* man like Justin would bear the blame for her mistakes. And he would. Especially with their age difference. *Ach*, she really didn't even know how old Justin Beachy was.

"How old are you?" she blurted out, as they meandered toward his house.

He grimaced. "Thirty-three."

"Fifteen years between us then."

"I would have thought your *vatter* would've chosen someone closer to your own age." He glanced in her direction.

"He trusts you."

"*Jah*. It will cause us grief, though."

"Like you said, people will talk. It's really only our business, ain't not? If we don't mind the age difference, they shouldn't either."

His eyes widened. "*You* don't mind our difference in age?"

She couldn't hide her smile. Who would have thought that tall, strong, gorgeous Justin Beachy would have vulnerabilities? "Did you think I would?"

"*Jah*. Maybe." He shrugged.

"Truth be told, Justin Beachy, I've had a crush on you since the first time I saw you." Her cheeks warmed at the admission.

His jaw dropped. "Truly?"

"*Jah*."

Disbelief accompanied his stare. "Why?"

He couldn't be that clueless. "Have you looked in the mirror? You are every girl's dream."

"I only look in the mirror when I shave." He chuckled. "And I confess I have no idea what girls' dreams consist of. But I never..." He shook his head. "You're not pulling my leg, are you?"

Lucy laughed. "The Beachy men have a reputation around here."

"*Jah*, I know." He frowned. "It's unfortunate."

"Not that, *bensel*." She shook her head and grinned. "A reputation for being handsome."

"I hadn't realized. Really?" He eased into a smile.

"*Jah*, really. But don't let it go to your head," she teased.

"Too late. I think my head may have just exploded." The lines around his eyes crinkled. *Ach*, she loved seeing this less serious side of Justin Beachy.

She stopped and stared at him, then made a show of examining his head. "*Nee*, still there. And still quite handsome, I might add."

"If you keep talking like that, you are going to have a *hochmut* husband."

"You are the furthest thing from proud I've seen. And I mean that in a *gut* way."

He held the door open to the house. "This will be your new home soon. I hope you find it tolerable."

Tolerable? She wanted to laugh. "What is wrong with it?"

He shrugged. "It's just that it used to be an *Englisch* home." He pointed across the road. "And don't tell anyone I said this, but the neighbors tend to be a little nosy."

Now she did laugh. "The Millers? Aren't they kin to you?" She glanced toward the neighbors' new quilt shop. Nathaniel scored major points with the women in the community when he'd built the shop for his new *fraa* last year.

"Two of my *brieder* married Miller girls, *jah*."

"But it's only Nathaniel and his *fraa*, Amy, and his folks there now, right?" Her eyes meandered to the property next door again, where one of the Miller women worked in the garden. Just as they stepped inside Justin's house, Amy, she guessed, glanced in their direction.

"*Jah*. I'm just worried our relationship won't be believable to them."

"Why wouldn't it be?"

"Because they've never seen an eligible woman here. And trust me, they watch." He glanced through the window.

"Well, then, we're just going to have to make it believable. *Dat* thinks I should come over every day. He suggested you taking me for buggy rides to places other people in the community go. Like Millers' Country Store and Bakery. Make our relationship obvious."

"Your *vatter* said your *mamm* doesn't know about the *boppli* yet?"

"She doesn't. She'll be surprised for sure. *Dat* said we can date like normal, but you should stay at the house longer in the morning so people will 'catch' us together."

His Adam's apple bobbed, and he nodded. "Well, that might make it more believable."

"We wouldn't do anything inappropriate, of course." Her hands twisted.

Pink mottled his neck. "*Ach,* I wouldn't. Not until we're married." Then there would be nothing inappropriate about it.

"But we *should* kiss."

His eyes practically jumped out of their sockets. "We should?"

"*Jah.* And maybe let somebody walk in on us."

"I don't—"

"It has to be believable, remember? That will have people talking for certain."

"You're right." He nodded and rubbed the back of his neck, which inadvertently brought her attention to his muscled arm. "Should I show you around the place now?"

She smiled at the thought of someday being the recipient of Justin Beachy's kisses. "Sure."

CHAPTER SIX

*J*ustin eyed Lucy as she sat across the porch from him on one of his hickory rockers. From what he had come to know of her so far, he liked her. He enjoyed their easy conversation. As he'd shown her around the property, she seemed pleased and offered welcome suggestions on how to improve things. He enjoyed hearing a woman's perspective. If she were to become his *fraa*, this would be her place too, and he wanted her to feel at home.

He leaned forward. "Will you tell me about the *boppli's* father?"

She moved the condensation on her tea glass around with her finger and twisted her lips. "What do you want to know about him?"

"How long were you dating? How did you meet?"

"I met him at the dollar store. He put on one of those silly pairs of glasses with the big nose and bushy mustache. He made me laugh." Her smile told him she was probably reliving the moment.

Justin hoped he'd be able to make her smile that way. "I see."

"We were dating for about six months before we broke up. Trey's a soldier." She frowned.

"Your father said he was in another country, but I hadn't realized he was a soldier." He leaned forward. "He didn't say when he was supposed to return?"

"*Nee.* I guess he was going on a secret mission. He said he didn't know where he would be, and if he did, he wouldn't be able to tell me anyway. He didn't know how long he'd be gone, but he guessed it could be a year or more."

Justin blew out a breath. "So, what will happen if he shows up?"

"Maybe I'm naïve, but I really don't think he will. We broke up before he

22

left. He said it would be best that way." Sadness momentarily flashed across Lucy's features, and Justin's heart went out to her. "He doesn't know where I live. And if I'm living here with you, he'll have no idea."

"Has he seen you in Amish clothes? Would he be able to recognize you?"

She nodded. "The first time we met, I was wearing Amish clothes. And he saw me after that in my dress and *kapp*."

"Hmm. We'll just have to hope he doesn't come looking for you. And if he does, we'll trust *Der Herr* to show us what to do." He met her eyes. "Did you love him? *Do* you love him?"

She twisted her hands in her lap.

"You can be truthful." He encouraged.

"*Jah*, I thought I did. We made a *boppli* together and all." Her voice was barely above a whisper. "But I don't know how he felt for sure. He said he loved me, but maybe he only said it so I would share the marriage bed with him. Or not. I don't know."

"I'm not sure if this is the right thing to do." His finger motioned between the two of them. "Do you?"

"I don't know." She lifted a shoulder. "Trey did end our relationship, so I'm not even sure if he would welcome a *boppli* or want me back in his life. Even so, I could never be *Englisch*."

Justin sympathized with her words, but he didn't understand how any man would not want his own baby. "I want to be honest with you, Lucy. I feel like I'm moving in on another man's family. If I were in his shoes, and I found out my beloved married someone else while carrying my *boppli*, I'd be very upset." He shook his head. "*Nee*, I'd be heartbroken."

"Trey and I had already talked about the possibility of getting married. But neither of us were willing to leave our home and culture to be with the other. It's an impossible situation." Her hand moved to her abdomen, and a tear slipped down her cheek. "I thought somehow we could make it work, but now I know I was living in a dream world. After he broke things off and left, I knew there'd be no hope for us. He told me he'd probably return a different person. War does that to people. I should have never shared the marriage bed with him. I don't know what I was thinking."

He refrained from reaching out a hand to her. "We all do things we aren't proud of."

"*Nee*, not like what I've done." She hung her head.

"No one is perfect." He frowned. "It's just...if he *does* come back and he wants to continue the relationship..." He sighed.

"He won't. Trey and I were a mistake. I can't imagine being apart from my family and friends. I have no desire to become *Englisch*." Her eyes lifted to his. "If you're worried I would leave you, you don't need to be. I would never do that. If we're married, it will be for life."

"I'm not worried about myself. I know *Der Herr* will be with me. I just want you to be sure about this. I want you to be happy. Satisfied."

"My biggest fear is being sent away to have this *boppli* on my own." Her chin trembled at the words.

"You will not be sent away. I won't stand for it." He reached over and touched her hand now. "You are not alone, Lucy. I will help you in any way you need me to."

"You...you will still marry me, then?" Her gaze was hopeful.

"If *you're* sure that is what you want."

She sighed, and he noted the relief in her mien. "It is. *Denki.*"

"How long did your *vatter* want you to stay?" He leaned back. "Not that I want you to leave or anything."

"He didn't say."

"We could go for a drive so people will see us together. We can stop a few places, if you'd like. Timothy and Bailey's greenhouse, Millers' store, Emily Troyer's roadside stand. Do you want to make a list of things we can use for the house? I'm hoping one of these days you might want to make me supper." He winked.

"*Ach*, for sure. I'd be happy to. Probably many suppers, and other meals too." Her expression lightened. "I like to cook."

"I don't keep much stocked, so we can get whatever you think we'll need."

"If you get me a pen and paper, I can make a list."

"Pen and paper coming up." He shot up from his chair and snatched their empty glasses. "Would you like a refill?"

She smiled up at him. "Yes, please."

∿

Justin Beachy was a dream, Lucy decided. A very lovely dream. Although they would likely be married within the month, she wouldn't allow herself to fantasize about lying in his arms. And he had really nice arms. Among other qualities.

What kind of man would agree to an arrangement like theirs? Only a sweet, selfless, and thoughtful one. Only Justin Beachy. With each moment that passed, she was learning Justin was so much more than a handsome face. He was truly a gift from *Der Herr*. In a way, he was her savior.

And the more she dwelled on Justin's qualities, the more she compared him to the true Saviour. His kindness alone was enough to make Lucy's heart run wild.

Lucy was looking forward to spending time with this man, who would become her husband. Spending the day with him pleased her in ways she couldn't describe. She desperately hoped he felt the same way about her. She didn't want to be a burden to him. Did he truly enjoy her company? The last thing she wanted was to be an annoyance. Of course, he hadn't implied she might be. But she wanted him to desire her.

"Here you go." Justin stepped outside carrying a glass of tea and a notebook and a pen.

"*Denki.*" She received the items from his hands.

"*Ach.*" He swept his hair out of his eyes. "It looks like I need to visit *Mamm* soon."

"Because of your hair?" She'd noticed it seemed a little long.

He nodded. "I'm overdue for a haircut, but I've been so busy in the shop lately."

"I could cut it for you." She offered. "We have plenty of time. I've done my *brieder*'s hair many times."

"You'd really do that for me? That would be *wunderbaar.*"

"Do you have a towel and sharp scissors?"

"I do."

"If you fetch them, I can trim your hair before we leave."

"I will. That would be *wunderbaar.*" His smile stole her breath away. "*Denki.*"

From now on, she determined to bless him any way she could.

~

Justin fumbled around in his kitchen drawer, searching for the sharp scissors he kept handy in the house.

Ach. What had he been thinking?

He hadn't, plain and simple. The more he thought about his future *fraa* trimming his hair, the clammier his hands became. *Mamm* clipping his hair was one thing. But an attractive woman with her gentle hands roaming his face, his neck...her soft fingers feathering through his hair?

He swallowed. *Jah*, this might be a bad idea.

But he couldn't back out now. That would just be silly. And he didn't want Lucy to believe he lacked confidence in her abilities.

He headed outside, then realized he'd forgotten the chair and towel. If he was already this *ferhoodled* now, what on earth was he going to be like during the actual session?

When he finally stepped out of the house, his eyes collided with hers. Her bright smile had his heart tripping all over itself. *Ach*, she was a pretty little thing.

He handed over the scissors but couldn't help his trembling fingers.

"*Ach*, are you nervous, Justin?" His name sounded heavenly on her lips.

All coherent words had escaped him, so he nodded.

25

"It's okay. I won't botch it. I'll do a *gut* job. You'll see." She gestured to the chair. "You may sit."

He admired the confidence in her voice. How could she remain so calm at a time like this?

She opened the towel, draped it over his chest, and brought the corners around to meet at the nape of his neck. Her deft fingers brushed his skin as she tucked the towel under his collar, causing a prickling sensation to shoot through his entire being.

"I should have asked you to get a few more things, it seems." She tapped her lovely pink lips, unwittingly drawing his attention to them. Again.

He stared up at her, mesmerized. Had he ever been this *ferhoodled* in his life?

"I'm going to need a comb and a glass of water," she said.

He began to rise, but her warm hands on his shoulders encouraged him to stay put.

"*Nee*, I can get it. Just tell me where you keep your comb."

His comb. Where did he keep it? His mind drew a blank. *Ach*, he needed to be knocked upside the head with a two-by-four. "The bathroom." He cleared his throat. "In the cabinet."

"I'll be right back. Don't go anywhere." She spun around and hurried into the house. His eyes trailed her until she disappeared out of sight.

He momentarily considered bolting from the chair and locking himself away inside his buggy shop. But then what would he do? He still had to drive her home. He still had to stop by Millers' with her. He still had to pretend like he was madly in love with her.

Pretend?

"All set. You ready now?" Her cheerful voice commanded his attention.

He nodded and allowed her to commence the most frustratingly delicious moments he'd ever had to endure.

CHAPTER SEVEN

*A*s Lucy sat beside Justin in his spring buggy, she couldn't help but notice his warm arm brushing against hers as he guided his driving mare along the road.

His new haircut looked *gut,* despite her getting distracted by his nearness. At one point during his trim, he'd stopped her by catching her hand in his. He hadn't said a word as his thumb had roamed the top of her hand, but his mouth had opened slightly, and his gaze had strayed to her mouth. Had he been thinking about kissing her?

Her heart had hammered so hard in her chest that she was almost certain it could be heard not only by Justin, but by the neighbors across the street too. And maybe Nathaniel Miller *had* heard it. Because when they'd glanced in that direction, he'd been staring at them. She hadn't minded, though. The Millers' seeing them together would aid in their faux courtship.

But Lucy was beginning to realize this courtship might not be fake at all. If she was fortunate enough, perhaps Justin would pleasure her with a kiss at the end of the evening. One could dream.

"What are you thinking about?" His deep voice captured her attention and drew her back to the present. Had there been a hint of huskiness in it, or was that just her imagination?

"I...uh...Nathaniel Miller," she blurted out. *Jah,* that probably hadn't been the best thing to say. But what was she supposed to say? *I've been daydreaming about you kissing me before the evening is over?*

"If my memory serves me correctly, he's already taken."

Lucy heard the teasing in Justin's tone, but she took the bait anyhow. She feigned offense, then lightly rubbed her shoulder against his. She wouldn't miss the opportunity to flirt with her future husband. "Not in *that* way. You should know I'm already taken." She gave one quick matter-of-fact nod.

A smile danced on his lips. *Ach*, he had a nice smile. And lips. "Is that so?"

"Uh-huh."

"Would I happen to know this fellow?"

"I don't know. Do you?" She arched an eyebrow and set a bold hand on his knee.

"*Ach!*" He quickly removed her hand. "Don't do that." His voice was gruff.

Her cheeks warmed. "I…" She swallowed hard. "I'm sorry. I didn't mean to upset you. I was just teasing."

He turned his head, and his wide eyes snapped toward hers. "I didn't say I didn't like it. It's just that…I don't want to dishonor you. And touching me like that…well, let's just say that it makes me think about things I shouldn't." His gaze slowly swept over her, then he turned his eyes back toward the road and gripped the reins tightly.

~

When Justin walked into Millers' Country Store and Bakery with Lucy at his side, sisters-in-law Kayla and Jenny Miller were busy behind the counter. The confused looks he and Lucy received when the Miller women looked up almost made him laugh. *Jah*, he guessed seeing the two of them together would spark a bit of controversy. They were an unlikely couple. A Beachy and the bishop's *dochder*.

After greeting the two ladies, he followed behind his future *fraa* as she perused the grocery aisles. Compared to the big-box stores, their offering of consumable items was small, but it was enough to throw together some decent meals. And he didn't know anybody who could stop by the store and not pick up a few delicious treats from the bakery, like Kayla's famous potpie or Jenny's heavenly cinnamon rolls.

He added a few extra items to the basket he carried that hadn't been on the shopping list. Lucy's eyes widened. "You're not going to buy that sugary cereal, are you?"

"Well, I was going to, *jah*." He scratched his cheek, then shrugged. "I'm a bachelor."

"Who desperately needs a *fraa*, I see." A shy smile formed on her lips.

He loved when she teased him. But he hadn't realized how heightened his senses were around her until she'd touched him in the buggy. How was it that he was aware of every little move she made?

He reached over and twisted her *kapp* tie around one of his fingers, then released it, purposely brushing his fingers against her cheek in the process. "I found one." His brow quirked.

Lucy's eyes searched his. "She must be one lucky woman," she whispered.

"*Nee*, I'm the lucky one. But 'blessed' is probably a better word." He lifted his head toward the front of the store, his hand on the small of her back gently encouraging her to walk toward the checkout. "Get whatever you want," he whispered.

Kayla's gaze bounced back and forth between them. "Did you find everything you need?"

Justin's eyes slid to Lucy. "*Jah*, I did." It appeared that neither Lucy nor Kayla missed the insinuation in his words.

Lucy lightly bumped him with her shoulder. She was good at this whole faux courtship thing. "We wanted something from the bakery too, ain't so?"

"I can get it for you." Jenny Miller offered.

"What do you recommend?" Justin examined the glass bakery cases.

"Today's pretzel day, if you like soft pretzels. Paul loves them." Jenny smiled at the mention of her husband's name.

Kayla chuckled beside her. "Paul loves *everything* Jenny makes."

"He likes your potpies, too," Jenny said.

"Everybody likes Kayla's potpies," Lucy remarked. "They are very *gut*."

Justin eyed Lucy. "Would you like to get one? We could have it for lunch tomorrow."

Lucy nudged him again. Was he giving too much away? He'd never been great at nonverbal communication. "*Jah*, that sounds *gut*." Lucy nodded.

"Lucy," Kayla said, setting a potpie on the counter. "Shiloh and Sierra are up at the house if you'd like to stop in and say hello."

Lucy studied Justin, a question in her eyes.

"It's fine with me." He nodded. "Whatever you want to do."

"I'd like to say a quick hello." She grinned at Justin, then looked at Jenny. "Could we get a couple pretzels, please?"

"And a loaf of zucchini bread," Justin added. "I think that'll be it."

Kayla rang up their groceries and goodies and handed over several bags.

"Would you like some cheese sauce for your pretzels?" Jenny offered.

"None for me, *denki*," Lucy said. "I like them with just salt."

"Me too." Justin winked at Lucy before the two of them bid their goodbyes.

CHAPTER EIGHT

*a*ch, I can't believe your boldness!" Lucy said, the moment they stepped out of the store. The windchimes' songs caught her attention as a gentle breeze wafted through them along with the hanging flower baskets that carried the sweet scent of spring.

"We want to be believable, ain't not?" His eyebrow arched. "Besides, I have the Beachy reputation to uphold."

Lucy giggled. "You're certainly doing a *gut* job. Just wait until Shiloh and Sierra see us together. They're going to flip."

"Did you go to school with them?"

She smiled, thinking of their school days. "*Jah*, they're both *gut* friends."

"Should we put this in the buggy and walk up to the house, or would you rather drive?"

"I'm a little tired, actually."

His brow creased and concern blanketed his features. "Tired?"

"It's common when you're in the *familye* way. Nothing to worry about." She squeezed his hand.

Justin set the groceries in the back of the buggy, then offered her a hand into the carriage. "How do you know that? Have you already seen the midwife?"

"*Nee*, I was looking through one of *Mamm's* books. I smuggled it up to my room. It's under my mattress." She admitted.

"I see. Maybe I should read this book too."

Lucy nibbled her fingernail. "*Ach*, I don't think so."

"Why not?"

"There are pictures in it." Her face warmed. "A man probably shouldn't see them."

His eyes widened. "*Ach*, okay. I don't think I'd want to read it then."

"I could read some of it to you."

"*Jah*, that might be a better idea. The only woman I want to see is my *fraa*." The side of his mouth twitched.

Ach. "We should…uh…eat our pretzels." Because if she dwelt on his words too long, her face was sure to catch fire.

Justin chuckled. "That sounds like a *gut* idea."

Ten minutes later, Lucy forsook the second half of her pretzel and knocked on the door of the Silas Miller residence. Justin had said he was going to stop in and say hi to Silas and Paul in their metal shop, so she had several minutes to visit with her friends. Lucy knew Justin was anxious about showing up at her home with her, since her father was the only one who was privy to the situation. She wondered what *Mamm* would think when she saw the two of them together. Lucy had already invited Justin to take supper with them. It would be an interesting evening, for sure.

She glanced back to see Justin entering the shop, just as the door to the house flew open.

"Lucy! What a happy surprise." Shiloh beamed. "Sierra, Lucy's here!" She called over her shoulder. "*Kumm* in."

Lucy stepped into the house. She heard sounds coming from various areas and guessed the others were likely playing in their rooms or doing chores.

"I'll go get us a drink and snacks." Shiloh disappeared before Lucy had a chance to decline the offer. She really wasn't hungry after eating the pretzel.

Sierra strolled into the living room, wiping her hands on a dish towel. "Lucy." Her friend radiated happiness as she engulfed Lucy in a hug.

Shiloh joined them, and the three of them took a seat on the living room couch.

"Don't tell me that was Justin Beachy I just saw going into the shop!" Shiloh grinned.

"What? Justin 'too-hot-to-handle' Beachy?" Sierra's jaw slacked.

Lucy laughed. She'd forgotten all about the silly name they'd given him when he'd first shown up in their community. What would Justin think about that?

"Well?" Shiloh bounced.

"*Jah*, it was Justin Beachy," she admitted.

"Lucy Bontrager! You've been holding out on us." Sierra braced her hand on her hip.

"So, *that's* where you've been disappearing to after the singings!" Shiloh gasped. "And here I thought you were thinking of jumping the fence or something."

"Never." Lucy asserted, but she didn't correct Shiloh's assumption.

Shiloh lowered her voice. "So...does this mean something?"

Lucy's cheeks warmed. "Maybe. Probably. We'll have to see."

Shiloh squealed. "*Ach*, I'm so happy for you!"

"I can't believe you've been keeping this from us. Justin Beachy. Out of all the men." Sierra shook her head. "Oh man, Judah's going to be heartbroken."

"Judah?" Lucy's eyes widened.

"He has had a crush on you for forever. Didn't you ride home with him once?" Shiloh said.

"*Jah*, I did, but..." Lucy shrugged. "I guess there just wasn't a spark. Maybe it was because I knew he was your *bruder*."

"But there's a spark with Justin Beachy." Shiloh's white teeth were nearly blinding. She almost seemed more excited about Lucy and Justin than Lucy was. Almost.

Lucy rubbed her hands on her dress. "*Jah*, there's definitely a spark with Justin."

"You are the luckiest girl alive." Sierra's hands clutched her heart, and she practically swooned.

Lucy sipped her tea and nodded, not able to hide her own grin. "I know."

A knock on the door caused Lucy's heart rate to quicken.

"Is that him?" Sierra's eyes flew wide.

"Probably." Lucy shot up from the sofa. "I guess I'd better go."

"I'll get the door, just in case." Shiloh winked before opening the door.

Justin stood in the opening, filling most of it with his masculine presence. Man, he had to be the most handsome man Lucy had ever known.

His warm gaze appraised her. "I just wanted to let you know I'll be in the buggy. Take as long as you need." His words were smooth as fresh-whipped butter.

"I'm ready now." Her excitement tumbled out.

He nodded, seemed to realize three young women had been staring at him, then he turned around and headed for the buggy.

Sierra giggled. "I think I'm going to give you the nickname Lucky Lucy." She teased. Fortunately, Justin was already out of earshot.

Shiloh pointed at Lucy, caution narrowing her gaze. "You better be careful. And you know what I mean."

Heat crawled up Lucy's neck. If her friends only knew the truth of the matter.

"*Jah*, he's a Beachy." Sierra nodded. "The last eligible one, unfortunately. What I wouldn't give to have Justin Beachy look at me like that." She sighed.

Shiloh elbowed her younger *schweschder* with a warning. "He's already taken."

"Well, I better go. I don't want to keep him waiting." Lucy smiled.

Lucy's friends waved their goodbyes as she and Justin traveled down the Millers' driveway. No doubt, they would be the subject of conversation in the Silas Miller household for the remainder of the evening.

CHAPTER NINE

I'm guessing that went well?" A smile slipped across Justin's lips.

Lucy nodded. "Even better than I'd hoped."

"How so?"

"Shiloh thinks I've been sneaking out with you after the singings. I let her assume it was true."

He was unable to keep a frown from forming. "I wish it was."

"Me too." She shook her head. "This would be so much easier."

He shrugged. "Don't beat yourself up about it. It is what it is. You can't go back and change the past. You just have to deal with it the best you can. Learn from your mistakes and move on."

"You're right."

"Besides, I'm glad in a way. I don't know if I would have ever had the pleasure of knowing you otherwise." When he glanced her way, he noticed her eyes shimmering. "*Ach*, what's wrong?"

"You're so sweet. I don't deserve you." She brushed away a tear with a shaky hand.

"I am nothing."

"*Ach*, Justin Beachy. You are more than you'll ever know. I've only known you a few hours, and you've already captured my heart."

He reached over and squeezed her hand. "Likewise."

The closer they inched toward the Bontrager residence, the more nervous Justin became. Since he hadn't lived in this district very long, he'd only been there a few times for Sunday meeting. How would Lucy's family react to his presence? "Who do you think will be there?"

"Probably *Dat, Mamm*, Linda, and Marcus."

"Your *bruder* and *schweschder?*"

"*Jah*. Do you know them?" She glanced at him.

"*Nee*. I don't think so."

"Are you nervous?"

"A little."

She blew out a breath. "Me too. I just don't want to have to lie."

"You don't have to. Just be vague."

"What do you mean?"

"Well, if someone asks how long we've been seeing each other, I plan to say a little while." He shrugged. "They can determine what that is in their own mind."

Lucy tilted her head.

"Another option is to just say it's none of their business. Of course, you wouldn't want to say that to your *mamm*." Justin chuckled.

"*Nee*. She wouldn't like that." She nibbled her fingernail. "What if she asks me if I'm in the *familye* way?"

"Tell her the truth. She will likely assume I'm the father since we'll be there together. And because I carry the Beachy name, of course." He shook his head. "You know, the Beachys really do have a much better reputation in Pennsylvania."

"Your *brieder's* behavior is not your fault, you know." Lucy's forehead wrinkled, then she became teary-eyed again. "I don't...I'm sorry I'm ruining your reputation too. You're a *gut* guy, and you deserve much better than me."

"*Ach*, I didn't mean that."

Her chin quivered. "You can still back out of this, if you want to. No one would blame you. Especially not me."

He slowed his driving horse and brought the buggy to a stop on the side of the quiet gravel road they'd been on for the last few minutes. "Hey, now. *Kumm* here." He beckoned her close with his hand.

She leaned toward him, and he brought her head to his chest, wrapping her in his arms. He didn't say anything but allowed her to cry for a minute. If her hair had been down, he imagined he'd be softly combing his fingers through it.

"I'm sorry. I shouldn't have said anything. Honestly, I don't mind. I like us together." He rubbed her back. "And I like you in my arms," he murmured and pressed his lips to the side of her traveling bonnet. She likely didn't feel a thing.

She pulled back and stared at him. Her eyes searched his. "Do you mean that?"

"Wouldn't have said it if I didn't." He smiled and thumbed away her remaining tears.

"*Denki.*"

"I meant it when I said you've captured my heart." He squeezed her hand. "Should we continue to your folks' place now?"

"*Jah.*"

~

Lucy didn't know who was more nervous, her or Justin. As they pulled into their driveway, she directed Justin to the hitching post just outside the barn, where he could tether the horse. Although, if he ended up staying long, it might be better to put the mare in a paddock.

"It looks like *Dat* is in the barn. You could go say hello to him."

"Just me?" His brow arched.

"*Jah,* that way I can answer any questions *Mamm* and Linda might have. And it'll be less awkward for you if you walk in with *Dat,* I think." She lifted her chin toward the barn. "My *bruder* could be in there too."

"That's *gut* to know. I wouldn't want to say anything I shouldn't."

"Wish me luck." She shifted to descend from the buggy.

"I'll do one better. I'll pray." He hopped down and hurried to her side. "Wait. Let me help."

She took his hand as he assisted her exit. "*Denki.*"

His hand lingered on hers, then he brushed the top of it with his thumb before reluctantly letting go. It might have been a small gesture, but it was enough to stir her heart. Was he oblivious to the sparks he was igniting, or did he feel them too?

Her eyes studied his. "You'll never know how much I appreciate you."

His mouth opened slightly but snapped shut when her father approached.

"Lucy, I think your mother and *schweschder* could use some help with supper," *Dat* said.

Lucy took that as her cue to get scarce. She shared one more longing glance with Justin, then headed toward the house. Before stepping into her home, she caught *Dat* and Justin walking out toward the field. No doubt Justin was filling *Dat* in on their goings-on today. Would they be speaking of a wedding date too? Oh, she hoped so.

CHAPTER TEN

I didn't expect you'd stay at Justin Beachy's all day, *dochder*." *Mamm* eyed Lucy suspiciously. "Is there something going on I should be aware of?"

"We're dating." She admitted, then turned at her *schweschder's* sharp gasp.

"*You're* dating Justin Beachy?" Linda's eyes bugged.

Mamm's head shook. "I should have known. *Kumm, dochder*." *Mamm* led the way to her room, then closed the two of them inside. No doubt her *schweschder* was eavesdropping on the other side of the door.

Ach. Lucy suddenly felt queasy. Was it the *boppli* or nerves?

Mamm pulled out the pregnancy book Lucy had hidden under her mattress. "I found this today. Would you mind explaining what you were doing with it?"

Lucy hung her head but didn't answer.

"Are you in the *familye* way, *dochder*?"

"Oh, *Mamm*!" She burst into tears.

Mamm's hand planted on her hip. "What were you thinking, dating a Beachy?"

"Justin's a *gut* man, *Mamm*."

Mamm snorted. "*Gut* men don't do this sort of thing. You should have known better."

Lucy hated the fact that Justin was being blamed for her indiscretion, but she kept her mouth closed.

"Do you realize how this is going to make your father look?" *Mamm* shook her head. "I can just hear people now. *He shouldn't be bishop if he can't even keep control over his own household.*"

There was so much Lucy wanted to say, but she'd learned at a young age when to keep her thoughts to herself. This was one of those times.

"I'm guessing this means there will be a wedding soon?"

Lucy nodded.

"Is that what Justin Beachy and your *Dat* are talking about right now?"

"Probably." How she hated the wariness in *Mamm's* eyes. It was a grief she'd caused.

Mamm sighed and handed the pregnancy book to Lucy. "Go ahead and take this, then. You're going to need it." *Mamm* steeled her resolve.

"*Denki, Mamm.*" She'd stuff it into her bag upstairs and take it with her next time she went to Justin's, which she suspected would be tomorrow if *Mamm* allowed her to.

"Put that away and help your *schweschder* set the table," *Mamm* suggested, before slipping out of the room.

Lucy took a deep breath, wiped the wetness from her face, then straightened her dress. She hadn't expected a hug or any type of affection. That wasn't their way. Truth be told, it hadn't gone as bad with *Mamm* or *Dat* as she thought it would.

"*Denki, Gott.*" She breathed out the nearly inaudible words.

～

"By the looks your mother was giving me at supper, I'm guessing she knows?" Justin's brow arched as they strolled toward the barn.

"*Jah.*" Lucy glanced back to make sure they weren't being followed. "*Mamm* found the pregnancy book in my room and asked me about it. I had already told her that you and I were dating, so she assumed the *boppli* was yours."

"That explains it."

"What did you and *Dat* talk about before supper?"

"The wedding, mostly. He said he'd talk to the leaders this week and get back to us."

She nibbled her fingernail.

"You know, if you're wanting me to kiss you, you might want to ditch that habit."

"*Ach.*" She yanked her finger from her mouth.

He chuckled. "I was teasing you. If I had in mind to kiss you, I reckon there'd be very little that could stop me."

They rounded the corner of the barn, now out of view of anyone who might be watching from the house.

She swallowed. Did he plan to kiss her before he left? *Ach*, if only it were so.

"Did you have a *gut* time today?" he asked.

"I did."

His smile reached his eyes, crinkling the skin at the corners. "Me too."

"Do you think we make a *gut* match?"

"I do. Do you?" His voice dipped. *Ach*, he had the most amazing voice.

She nodded and smiled. "The best."

"I know we just officially met today, but I feel like I've known you my whole life. Is that even possible?"

"I think so." She tapped her lips. "It's strange how much your life can change in just a day, ain't so?"

"It is." He stopped walking and stared into her eyes.

"I was so nervous about meeting you this morning."

"If it makes you feel better, I was nervous too." His fingers brushed her forearm. "And I honestly hate the fact that I have to say goodbye to you tonight."

Her breath hitched as he took a step toward her. Could it be that Justin Beachy was falling in love with her?

A squeak from the screen door distracted them.

"But I should probably go and let you get some sleep," he said.

Lucy took a small step backward and found herself against the barn. Justin's left arm pressed the metal wall beside her. His chest rose and fell, and desire burned in his eyes. Her heart pounded even more as his right hand moved to cradle her face. His thumb slowly roamed over her cheek in a gentle caress, then he dipped his head to brush his lips against her forehead.

"*Guten nacht, schatzi*," his hoarse voice whispered.

Then she watched, dumbfounded, as he abruptly turned and headed toward his buggy.

As he drove down the driveway, he lifted his hand in a small wave. She stared until he drove out of sight, then allowed herself to swoon.

Nee, it hadn't been a lip kiss, but it had been every bit as romantic and amazing and *wunderbaar* as one.

She was certain she'd never forget it for as long as she lived.

How Justin Beachy had managed to stay single for so long, she'd never understand.

CHAPTER ELEVEN

*J*ustin tapped his leg, waiting on the porch for his driver to show up. Saturday morning was the day Justin met for men's fellowship with his *brieder*, Sammy, and some of the other guys in the two neighboring communities. Although he was looking forward to it, he was nervous. Today, he'd divulge his plans to marry Lucy. The news was certain to be met with hesitancy and possibly discouragement from some, but he'd already mentally prepared himself. Having Sammy on his side was a great comfort.

Last time he'd spoken with Lucy's father, he'd said the leaders would stop by Justin's home tonight. Which meant he'd probably receive a reprimand and be assigned a wedding date. To say he was anxious would be an understatement.

After spending the last few days with Lucy, he was ready to begin the rest of his life with her.

They'd shared so many things: their favorite colors—they both loved green; their favorite foods—his was barbequed ribs and hers was spaghetti; their favorite animals—he liked horses and she liked squirrels. Squirrels! Of all things. He hadn't told her he used to hunt them with his *brieder*.

They both enjoyed all kinds of games, and the two of them assembled a jigsaw puzzle the day he'd stayed at her place till morning. They discussed favorite Bible verses and songs—just about anything they could think of. He truly felt they had formed a solid friendship.

And their first kiss? *Ach*, their first kiss had been amazing. He could recall it vividly.

Lucy had been in her folks' kitchen, rustling up yummy snacks for the two of them, when he'd walked in with a wrapped box.

"What is that?" Lucy's smile could've hung the moon.

He'd shrugged. "A little something I picked up for you. Open it," he urged.

She pulled the ribbon off, then tore the wrapping paper, her smile not leaving her face. When she opened the box and pulled out the gift, she giggled at the "Kiss the cook" message on the apron he'd chosen. It had been absolutely perfect.

"Should I help you put it on?" He offered.

She nodded.

He took his time tying the strings behind her neck and around her waist, lingering on purpose. Then he stepped back. "There you go."

"I love it."

"Me too."

She stared at him, fighting a smile. "Well?"

He took a step closer. "Well, what?" he murmured, leaning close to her ear. He loved teasing her.

Instead of waiting for him, she'd hooked her fingers around one of his suspenders, wrapped her other hand around his neck, and brought his lips down on hers. From there, he took over and pulled her into his arms. His mouth blissfully moved over hers, then momentarily left to explore her delicate jawline and neck. His hands ached to explore as well, but he forbade them to do so. His lips returned to hers, and he deepened the kiss. Her heart beating against his chest sparked a desire that coursed through his entire being. When he could hardly stand it, he forced himself back.

"Ach, it's so easy to get carried away." He finally caught his breath. He glanced toward the entrance to the kitchen just to be sure they didn't have an audience. Because, if they did, well, he might be receiving a reprimand. Fortunately, they were alone. As a matter of fact, he was certain he heard snoring wafting from her folks' bedroom.

"I can't wait to get carried away with you," she murmured, her cheeks flushed.

His fingers caressed her earlobe. "Soon, lieb. Very soon." He indulged in one more brief kiss before commanding himself to refrain.

Lucy grasped his hand, her eyes searching his. "I love you, Justin Beachy."

The passenger van pulled up, ruining his lovely daydream. *Jah*, their wedding couldn't come soon enough as far as he was concerned. He'd managed to behave himself, even when they'd spent several hours alone, although it hadn't been easy. Today would be the only day this week he wouldn't spend with her, but he'd hoped to visit after the leaders left this evening. Even so, he'd miss her.

~

Fellowship with the men had been *wunderbaar* as always. Time with his brothers in Christ always lifted Justin's spirits. As usual, Sammy's Scripture readings had been on point. The verses he'd read today centered around fleeing temptation and allowing God's Spirit to lead them. A couple of verses had jumped out at Justin specifically. *But put ye on the Lord Jesus Christ, and make not provision for the flesh, to fulfill the lusts thereof.* And also, *Walk in the Spirit, and ye shall not fulfill the lust of the flesh.*

Jah, walking in the Spirit and putting on the Lord Jesus Christ was certainly something he needed to do more of. Because spending time alone with Lucy bred more temptation than he cared to admit. He knew it was a temptation for her too. The last thing he wanted to do was cause Lucy to sin.

Sammy cleared his throat. "Justin has something he'd like to share with everyone."

Justin took a deep breath and released it. This was it.

"I thought y'all should be the first to know. I'm getting married." Justin smiled at the thought of taking Lucy as his *fraa.*

"You're *what?*" His *bruder* Jaden rocked back in his chair a little too far, sending it sliding out from under him.

The other guys chuckled, and Sammy offered Jaden a hand up off the floor.

"I didn't even realize you were dating anyone," his older *bruder* Josiah remarked, scratching his beard.

"*Jah,* Lucy Bontrager," Justin admitted.

"*Lucy Bontrager?* You don't mean the bishop's youngest *dochder?*" It was Paul Miller this time.

"*Jah,* he sure does," Nathaniel, the youngest Miller brother, said. "Saw the two of them together. They're definitely...*involved.*" Nathaniel raised a judgmental brow. According to Justin's brothers Jaden and Joshua, Nathaniel had never been much of a Beachy fan.

"I forgot to mention Justin stopped by the shop the other day when you were out, Paul," Silas Miller said. "Justin and Lucy were all the *maed* talked about that night." He chuckled.

Gut, so they *had* been believable. He'd have to tell Lucy.

"How come you're planning on getting married, and we're *just* finding out you've been dating? *Wait.*" Jaden held out his hand. "You're not...she's not..."

Justin frowned at his *bruder* with a warning attached, and his eyes begged Sammy for help. *Ach,* he really didn't want to have to explain himself in front of everyone.

"Let's not accuse anyone of anything," Sammy said.

"Innocent till proven guilty. Even so, it's none of our business," Silas Miller chimed in.

"Right. We have no right to say anything, Jaden," Josiah said.

Michael Eicher held up both hands. "I know I don't."

Nathaniel's mouth opened. "Wait. Are you saying—?"

Sammy thrust out a hand. "He isn't saying *anything* except that he is gettin' hitched. Besides, like Silas said, it's none of our business." Sammy tossed Nathaniel a reproving look.

"I didn't know you and Lucy were dating, either. I'm sure Susan would have said something," his youngest *bruder* Joshua remarked.

"Only a few people know. We haven't said anything to anyone *on purpose*." Justin's gaze slid to Nathaniel.

"Well, your secret's safe with us." Sammy examined each of the other men in the room. "Right, guys?"

"Is it a secret?" Timothy Stoltzfoos spoke up.

"Just until the *banns* are published," Justin said.

"And when will that be?" Joshua asked.

"Not sure yet. Next Sunday, probably." Justin didn't make eye contact with anyone because their mouths were probably agape. He was sure and certain his *brieder* must have a few questions right about then. "I'm not getting any younger."

"Congratulations." Titus Troyer, who'd kept silent, offered his hand.

Justin smiled and shook it. "*Denki.*"

"Me and Emily are a *gut* number of years apart too." Titus grinned. "It's not really a big deal."

Justin appreciated Titus's words.

The men fellowshipped and discussed the Bible verses they'd read, but Justin was aching to get home and get his meeting with the leaders over with so he could see Lucy. He'd hadn't even been away from her all that long, but he missed her like crazy. Was this what love felt like?

"It looks like the driver's here." Timothy remarked.

Justin, Joshua, Paul, Silas, Timothy, Nathaniel, and Titus all rode over to the neighboring district together. Sammy, Michael, and Justin's older *brieder*, Josiah and Jaden, all lived there in Detweiler's stricter Amish district. Justin had heard that Sammy had been reprimanded on more than one occasion for hosting their inter-district men's Bible study group. But one thing Justin knew about Sammy was that if he knew something was *Gott's* will, he wasn't going to let the leadership—or anyone—stop him.

"We ought to obey *Gott*, rather than men." Justin had heard Sammy assert.

"Hey, Justin, wait up," Jaden called as he headed toward the van.

Justin stopped and watched as the other men entered the waiting vehicle. "*Jah?*"

His *bruder* leaned close and whispered, "Is she in the *familye* way?"

Ach. Justin grimaced and stared at his *bruder* but didn't offer an answer or an explanation. He guessed Jaden received confirmation in his silence.

43

"Justin. How long have you two been seeing each other?" Jaden's countenance was riddled with sympathy. *Jah*, his *bruder* would understand.

"Long enough," Justin replied, then continued toward the vehicle. He stopped and turned before entering. When he caught Jaden's eye, he made a gesture zipping his lips.

His *bruder* nodded and waved goodbye.

Justin hoped Jaden wouldn't share the news with his *fraa*, because if he did, the entire district would likely know prior to the wedding. If Nathaniel's *fraa* didn't let the cat out of the bag first. Because Justin was certain Nathaniel would share the news with his family. And news of a sudden wedding would surely set the rumor mill on fire.

CHAPTER TWELVE

*I*t seemed to Justin he'd been pacing the floor more over the last week than in his entire life prior. Of course, he'd never had so much to be concerned over. Being a bachelor evoked so much less drama.

Would he miss the quiet calm he'd felt up until this week? Or would things settle down once he and Lucy were hitched? He surely hoped so. Because now that he'd met and fallen in love with Lucy, he couldn't imagine doing life without her. He'd be downright lonely. If he had to choose a quiet life alone or a hectic one with Lucy, he'd choose her. Every time.

Now, if he could have her *and* a quiet life, he reckoned it would be close to perfect.

After he'd returned from his men's group, he stopped by Millers' and picked up some fresh cinnamon rolls to serve the guests he was expecting. Maybe they'd be less harsh if they were eating something sweet and delicious? One could only hope.

It wondered him how Jerry would act among them. Would he be playing the part of bishop keeping a rigid stance? Or perhaps, since it was his *dochder* who was involved in the transgression, he'd be lenient amongst his peers.

All Justin knew was that he hoped they didn't require a kneeling confession in front of the church. Because if they did, Justin would be required to lie about sinning with Lucy. And who in their right mind would kneel before the *Gott* of the universe and confess to a sin that they didn't commit? That would be like lying directly to *Der Herr*. It was something he wasn't willing to do.

Ten minutes later, he was serving his guests cinnamon rolls and coffee. They'd all settled around the dining table. Justin had insisted the bishop take the head seat, then took his place after everyone else was seated. Jerry had motioned for Justin to sit next to him.

"Let's pray," the bishop said. Each one bowed their heads while Jerry said a silent prayer. Jerry looked to the other leaders. "Thank you all for joining me today to address this very serious matter."

The other leaders nodded.

Justin folded his hands, then unfolded them, then folded them again. *Jah*, he was nervous.

"Justin Beachy, is it true you've been courting my *dochder* Lucy Bontrager?" Jerry looked him straight in the eye. Something in his mien told Justin he could trust him to lead the meeting in an appropriate way.

"*Jah*." Justin agreed to what they both already knew was true. He guessed the bishop said what he did for the sake of the other leaders present.

"And is it also true that Lucy is in the *familye* way?" Jerry couldn't hide his disappointment. No doubt, his *dochder's* behavior had been a grief to him. Or perhaps Jerry counted the transgression a failure of his own.

"*Jah*, it's true." Justin hung his head. *Nee*, it wasn't right to deceive the other leaders, but nothing Justin had agreed to was untrue.

"Since you have confessed before the leaders today, we had already determined amongst ourselves that a public confession won't be necessary." The bishop looked to the other men. "With that being the case, we have also agreed the two of you should marry as soon as possible. Because of the nature of the sin, you will not be allowed to have a formal wedding. You will marry during the next meeting."

"*Denki* for your grace." Justin nodded to the men.

"It is the grace of *Gott* that cleanses from all sin," the minister added.

Jerry looked to the other leaders. "Do you have anything to add?"

The deacon, who was also his neighbor Nathaniel's father-in-law, spoke up. "I think it might be a *gut* idea for the two of you to abstain from contact until the wedding."

Ach. An entire week without seeing Lucy?

"They will need to confer on wedding preparations." The minister set his cinnamon roll on his plate. "How about they refrain from seeing each other till Friday? I think that will give them enough time to prepare."

Justin could kiss the minister. But what on earth would he do with himself all week? There went his plans for the evening. He'd have to ask Jerry to apologize to Lucy for him.

After they'd polished off their cinnamon rolls and coffee, the men headed out together. All the men, except for Jerry, had come in one buggy. He lingered a few extra moments after the men headed down the driveway.

"I am greatly indebted to you, Justin Beachy." Jerry shook his hand.

"I'm beginning to think it's the other way around. I've fallen in love with your *dochder*."

The bishop's eyes widened. "You have?"

"I'm going to miss her something wonderful next week. Will you—?" Justin pivoted and headed to the kitchen. He grabbed a notepad from the drawer and jotted a message on it, then bagged up one of the cinnamon rolls and handed them both to Jerry. "Will you give this to Lucy, please?"

"I will." Jerry smiled.

Justin accompanied the bishop as he strolled out to his buggy.

Jerry rubbed his beard. "If you happened to show up at the library in town, say around ten on Tuesday morning, to check out a book or something..."

A sly smile formed on the bishop's face, and he shrugged.

"*Ach, jah.* I don't think the leaders would have a problem with me checking out a book." His grin widened.

Jerry picked up the leather reins. "Welp. It's about that time. I expect I'll be seeing you on Friday, then?"

"Lord willing."

CHAPTER THIRTEEN

*L*ucy stepped into the library and immediate inhaled. *Ach*, she'd always loved the smell of books. Perhaps Justin would build her a few bookshelves for their home. That would be *wunderbaar*. As it was, the small bookcase she had in her bedroom could hardly hold her collection. Did Justin like to read too? That had been one thing they hadn't discussed yet.

She knew exactly which section she wanted to explore today: Pregnancy and Marriage. She needed tips on both. If she could accomplish a healthy pregnancy and a happy husband, she was pretty sure she could accomplish anything.

"Lucy?"

She slid the book back into its place on the shelf and turned at the male voice.

"Trey?" Her eyes widened at his approach. "What are you doing here? I thought you were out of the country." Trey was the last person she expected to see at the library, but there he was, the biological father of her *boppli*, in the flesh.

Before she knew it, he'd grasped her hand and swooped in and stole a kiss on the cheek. She stepped back and gasped. It was a *gut* thing they were back in the corner out of view and hopefully earshot of other patrons.

"It's great to see you too, babe." He wiggled his eyebrows.

"I'm not your babe anymore. We broke up, remember?" She pivoted. "Why are you here?"

"Unfortunately, I was wounded during a training exercise, and they sent me home to recover. I had surgery last week, but I'm healing up pretty good.

I'll be back on my game soon. I've been bored out of my mind, which is why I'm here."

She frowned.

"Don't worry, I'm all right. You want to meet up for dinner one of these days? We can hang out at my place afterward." His smoldering gaze hinted he had more than hanging out in mind.

"No, I can't."

He glanced around them, examining the titles on the shelf. "Are you looking at pregnancy books?" His mouth gaped, and he stared at her middle section.

~

"There you are." Justin stepped around a bookshelf, moved beside Lucy, and snaked his arm around her waist. It wasn't their way to show affection in public, but he thought it was necessary, considering the circumstances. He hadn't meant to be eavesdropping, but when he'd heard Lucy's voice in conjunction with a male voice, he'd paused, waiting for the right moment to show himself.

"Justin?" Lucy's pleased expression widened. Had her father not informed her that he'd be there?

The young man, whom he assumed was Trey, stared at him. His confused gaze bounced back and forth between Justin and Lucy.

Lucy recovered from her surprise. "This is my fiancé, Justin Beachy." She smiled up at him, relief flooding her features.

Trey frowned. "Wait. You're engaged to an Amish guy?"

"*Jah*, she is." Justin nodded.

"I thought…" Trey's eyes shot from her flat abdomen to the bookshelf in front of them, then lifted to Justin. He huffed. "Never mind. So, you were cheating on me when we were together? Or were you cheating on him with me?"

"Uh…" Lucy's eyes pled for help.

Justin frowned. "Who are you?" He figured it was the *boppli's* father, but he needed to ask anyhow, to change the subject, if for nothing else.

"I'm her ex-boyfriend." He frowned at Lucy.

"Well, she's getting married to me on Sunday," Justin asserted.

"Seriously, Lucy? I thought we could pick up where we left off. We had a good thing going. Boy, was I wrong." Trey shrugged as though it were no big deal, but Justin recognized hurt in his expression. He truly felt sorry for the guy.

As soon as Trey walked off, Lucy fell into Justin's arms. "*Denki.*" She released a sniffle. "I didn't know what to say or do."

He pulled back. "Your father didn't tell you I was coming to the library?"

"*Nee.* Now I know why he suggested I come."

"We can't be seen together by anyone in the *g'may.*" He glanced around, thankful for their seclusion.

"*Jah*, I know." She reached up and touched his cheek. "I've missed you."

"So that was Trey, huh?"

She frowned. "*Jah.*"

"Well, I don't think he'll be coming around again, since he knows you're getting hitched."

"*Nee*, he won't."

He held her at arm's length and stared into her eyes. "I love you. You know that, right?"

She nodded.

"I wish we'd met before you and Trey got involved."

"I know. Me too." Her hands twisted. "I'd always hoped you'd ask me home from a singing."

"Really?"

"You probably thought I was too young." She shrugged.

"I did. Apparently, I was mistaken." He sighed. "Unfortunately, there's nothing we can do to change the past."

"Maybe there's a reason for all this. Maybe *Der Herr* wanted this *boppli* to be born. Maybe He has something planned for her."

His brow lifted. "Her?"

She smiled. "I have a feeling."

CHAPTER FOURTEEN

$\mathcal{E}$arlier in the week, Justin had made a trip out to Titus and Emily Troyer's place to see about Titus crafting a special wedding gift for Lucy. He had a talent for woodworking, and Justin had been impressed by some of the items Titus had shown him in the past.

Justin already had in mind to hire Titus to craft a cradle for the *boppli* once Lucy's time got closer, but he wanted something special as a wedding gift. Something personal. Something big. He had no clue what, though, so he'd asked Titus for ideas.

His friend had suggested a few different things, and they all sounded great to Justin. But Titus only had a week to complete the project, so Justin chose something simple but intimate. He couldn't wait to see it once it was completed.

While Justin was there, he observed their precious family. An irrepressible desire filled his heart, and he suddenly couldn't wait to hold his and Lucy's *boppli* in his arms. Of course, the *boppli* wasn't his biologically, but he would love and care for it—*nee, her*—just the same. He was certain becoming a *dat* would be natural to him. He'd always loved *kinner*.

Now, to get through their wedding.

~

Lucy had chosen a special green fabric for her wedding dress, since she and Justin shared a fondness for the color. She guessed he was probably expecting her to wear a blue hue, since that was more common in his former Amish district in Pennsylvania. They hadn't discussed her dress, and she hoped he wouldn't bring it up when he stopped by today, because she wanted it to be a surprise.

She'd loved sewing it and the white apron she'd wear with it. She couldn't help but imagine their wedding day. *Nee*, it wouldn't be a fancy ordeal with several hundred guests. It would simply be their *g'may* and a few other friends and family members from the neighboring district.

Justin and her family would be transforming their barn into a reception area. The church and the wedding ceremony would be held down the road at the Henry Troyer residence. Their district owned two church wagons for special occasions, such as this. Since the extra wagon stayed at the bishop's house when it wasn't needed, they'd be able to prepare without disrupting preparations for Sunday's church service. *Dat* planned to make an announcement for the reception after their vows were spoken during church.

Lucy already had in mind to ask Shiloh and Sierra to be her impromptu sidesitters. They wouldn't have special-made dresses, but they'd be wearing their Sunday best. Now that she thought of it, she could sew each of them a new white apron. *Jah*, she'd have enough time to do that. She only wished she could give them each a little something special to remember the day by. She'd been to many weddings over the last few years, and the bride and groom always provided a personalized gift for their attendants. Maybe she'd ask Justin for ideas.

Lucy didn't know if Justin had anyone in mind to ask to be his attendants. Since his *brieder* and most of his friends his age were already married, he'd likely choose someone younger. Maybe Shiloh and Sierra would have some ideas. After all, they would be the ones accompanying the young men throughout the event.

As soon as she heard Justin's carriage traveling up the driveway, she squealed and hurried out to meet him. To her surprise, he'd brought several helpers with him. *Dat* would be grateful Justin's brothers Joshua, Jaden, and Josiah had all come along. *Jah*, she was certain the Beachy brothers could be on the covers of those magazines at Walmart.

Only one of them stirred her heart, though. Justin's long legs striding toward her proved that fact. She moved toward him, closing the gap between them. *Ach*, if only they could steal away for a kiss or two.

"How are you feeling?" He briefly brushed her hand with his.

Did he have any idea that his slightest touch, the timbre of his voice, his masculine scent, sent her heart galloping into next Tuesday? *Ach*, their wedding couldn't come soon enough.

"*Gut.*" Her hand instinctively moved to her abdomen.

"No sickness?" He'd seen the effects of pregnancy the couple of the days she'd spent at his house. On one of their excursions, he'd had to stop the buggy and let her out. She was fine when she remembered to drink her ginger tea, though.

"A little yesterday."

"I'll have to stock up on that tea your *mamm* buys."

Just the thought of his caring ways prompted tears. What kind of man would ruin his reputation, take in a virtual stranger *for life*, and agree to raise a *boppli* that was not his own? Justin Beachy was beyond any dream she could ever conjure up.

"Hormones?" He fetched a handkerchief out of his pocket and handed it to her.

She wiped her tears with his hanky and smiled. *"Jah."*

"Want to say hello to my brothers?" He reached for her hand.

"Sure."

Within a couple of hours, they had everything set up and ready for their big day. Everyone had headed into the house for a snack, but Justin and Lucy lingered in the barn.

Justin took her hand in his as they stood in front of their wedding table in the corner. "Can you believe we'll be sitting here in just a couple of days, celebrating our marriage?"

Ach, did she see tears shimmering in his eyes?

She stared up at him in amazement. How was it possible she could be so blessed with a man of such great character?

Justin drew her into his arms. "I'm so glad *Der Herr* chose you for me, Lucy Bontrager."

At his last words, he lowered his head and bestowed the most beautiful kiss she'd ever experienced. *Jah*, she was certain being married to this man would be like one of those fairytale books she'd read when she was young. Because he definitely treated her like his princess.

CHAPTER FIFTEEN

*J*ustin figured their wedding day was every bit as exciting, and just as nerve wracking, as it would have been if they'd married during a normal wedding day. Part of him was relieved they didn't have to stand before many hundreds of witnesses, some of whom he wouldn't have known. He was glad for the intimacy that being surrounded by close friends and family afforded.

The preaching had seemed to take forever, and he'd been so lost in his own thoughts he wasn't sure he'd heard most of the sermons. He'd guess that was typical for a bridegroom. How could one focus when they were standing on the precipice of "till death do us part"? Gott, *I'm doing the right thing,* jah?

When Bishop Bontrager called him and Lucy forward, Justin froze. Instead of rising from his bench, he stared up at Lucy and the bishop. Lucy's brow furrowed, and she frowned. The bishop moved his head ever so slightly, motioning for him to join them. But he couldn't move, and he was unsure why.

The bishop approached and leaned down to his ear. "Do you still want to marry *mei dochder?*"

His eyes found Lucy's, where tears shimmered. He looked up at the bishop. "*Jah,* I do."

The bishop expelled a sigh of relief. "*Kumm* then."

"I can't move." He frowned.

The bishop summoned Lucy over. "Help me get him up," he whispered.

"Justin, what's wrong?" Her voice was soft.

He grimaced.

54

The bishop gestured for Lucy to grasp his arm, and he took Justin's other one. "It's just cold feet, *jah*? Happens to the best of us. Do you think you can stand?"

"*Nee*, not yet." He stared at the bishop. "May I have a minute to speak with Lucy?"

Jerry's eyes widened. "Now?"

Justin nodded.

"*Ach*, okay. I will stall for you." The bishop stood before the congregation, indicating that it would be a few moments, then preceded to lead the congregation in song.

Lucy sat next to him and took his hand in hers. "Tell me what's wrong." She spoke in a hushed tone, although those around them wouldn't be able to hear over the singing anyway.

He stared at her, hating the doubt he was feeling. Hating the fear surrounding his heart. Hating that his next words might hurt Lucy. "Are you *sure* you can remain faithful to our marriage?"

Her chin trembled. *Jah*, he'd hurt her. "Justin...you don't trust me?" She wiped away a tear. "I wouldn't be standing here if I wasn't ready to commit to *you*. For life. I love you more than just about anything, Justin Beachy. Do you not feel the same about me?"

"I do." He shook his head. "I'm sorry."

"You are nervous, ain't so?"

"*Jah.*"

She squeezed his hand. "It's almost over. Just a few more minutes, and it will be done."

He nodded.

"We can do this."

He attempted a reassuring smile.

Several moments later, they stood before the *g'may*, pledging their lives and their love to each other. Justin had finally come to terms with reality. Even if his *fraa* left him in the future, he would survive. Even if the *boppli's* father came and took her away, he would survive. Even if all his worst nightmares were realized, he would survive.

It would only be by the grace of God, but he would survive. Because God was all he truly needed.

~

The reception following the wedding had been everything Lucy hoped it would be. Shiloh and Sierra had been thrilled the day before, when she'd presented them with their aprons and an invitation to join Lucy and Justin at the *Eck*. Shiloh suggested Mikey Eicher as one of the side-sitters for Justin, and he'd liked the idea. It made Lucy wonder if maybe Shiloh had a crush on Mikey. Justin's other attendant was Lucy's older *bruder*, whom Sierra knew as a friend. Both girls seemed satisfied with Justin's choices.

The food, the games, the laughter…everything had been wonderful. But as wonderful as everything had gone, a single thought niggled in the back of Lucy's mind. Was her husband all right?

CHAPTER SIXTEEN

*B*eing married to Lucy was a *wunderbaar* dream, Justin decided. He hadn't known what he'd been missing out on until he met her. He made sure to thank *Der Herr* for her every day. He hoped he would always see her for what she was—a gift straight from *Gott*, something to be cherished.

Although he figured some people in the *g'may* viewed him as less than proper, he found his comfort in knowing the truth of the matter. Fortunately, he knew nobody would ever say anything to his face. And if anyone ever did, he wouldn't care. He'd do it all over again to have Lucy as his *fraa*.

Unfortunately, being married wasn't *gut* for his concentration. Justin had been lying under this buggy way too long, when he should have been finished by now. He slid the creeper out to work on the wheels. Maybe something that took less concentration would help his focus.

He couldn't help the curse word that slipped out of his mouth when the tool slipped from his hand and landed on his toe. He picked it up and flung it across the shop.

"*Ach*, Justin. Are you all right?" His *fraa*.

"Sorry, I didn't know you had come in."

"What's wrong?" Lucy frowned.

He jumped up and drew her into his arms. "I'm a mess. That's what's wrong."

"I don't understand."

His lips captured hers until he got his fill. "Mm…now I know why people used to take a year off after they got married. I'm useless in the shop today.

You make my mind all *ferhoodled*. I lose my concentration, then I make *dumm* mistakes."

Her hand slid up his suspender, and a smile formed on her lips. "It sounds like you might need a break, husband."

His heartbeat quickened when he caught desire in her eyes. "I think you're right."

He lifted his *fraa* into his arms, then proceeded to the house, not caring if the neighbors were watching.

Upon entering their bedroom, his gaze caught their special bookcase headboard with their names carved into it. Lucy had loved the gift he'd commissioned Titus to make for them. She'd given him a quilt she'd made a couple of years ago for the occasion when she had no clue who she'd marry. Since they both shared a love of the color green, the quilt suited them both perfectly.

Jah, their union was truly a match made in Heaven.

CHAPTER SEVENTEEN

hree years later
Lucy snatched her reusable shopping bags from the pantry. "Abby, do you wanna go shopping with *Mamm*?" She eyed her daughter and husband, sitting at Abby's little table Justin had made for her. Justin looked like a giant sitting in the child-sized chair with his knees near his chest and long legs folded in two. It couldn't be comfortable, but he wore a smile none-theless.

"Not right now, *Mamm. Dat* and I are having a tea party." Abby's grin stretched across her face. She always loved her daddy time, but she'd likely get less of it in a few months when her little brother or sister arrived. Their daughter looked adorable in the tiara Justin had insisted on buying for his "little princess."

Justin lifted a tiny ceramic cup between his thumb and forefinger and took a pretend drink. Lucy laughed when she discovered his pinky finger extending up in the air. "We can finish our tea party when you get back from shopping, Abbs. I've got plenty of work in the shop to keep me busy."

Abby sighed overdramatically. "Okay."

Lucy and Justin hid their amusement. Having *kinner* was *wunderbaar* indeed. Surely, they were *gut* for the heart.

***

"Hey, Lucy! Wait up." *Oh no. Trey.*

59

She'd seen him in one of the aisles and tried her best to avoid him so he wouldn't notice her and Abby. Because if he did... She closed her eyes and briefly prayed he wouldn't see his *dochder*.

She had almost made it out to her driver's van. If she could just get Abby strapped into her car seat before—

"Lucy, didn't you hear me calling you?" Trey caught up.

"I was in a hurry to get home." *Ach*, why wasn't her driver at the van yet? She needed to leave. Now.

He stared into the vehicle, his eyes not leaving Abby. "I knew it. Something in my gut told me when I saw you at the library. I knew something was off."

Lucy frowned. "What are you talking about, Trey?"

"That little girl is mine, isn't she?" He pointed at Abby.

Lucy had never been more thankful that her young *dochder* only understood *Dietsch*. "What?"

"Do *not* lie to me and tell me that is not my kid! She looks exactly like me when I was her age, and I have the pictures to prove it. I don't even need a DNA test."

Lucy's mouth opened then closed.

"I am so angry right now." His fists clenched tight as they hung next to his thighs. "Why didn't you tell me you were carrying my baby?"

"Not now, Trey. This isn't the time or the place." She looked around, desperate for a way to escape this situation.

"Yes. Now is the perfect time. You've kept me in the dark long enough, don't you think?" He stuffed his hands in his pockets.

"Trey, please. When I found out, I couldn't tell you. You were away. You'd said you didn't know where you were going, remember? We'd already broken up."

"You could have told me at the library." His voice rose a notch.

"Why? What good would it have done? I was already engaged."

"You can get out of an engagement, you know? They're not permanent. And that's another thing." He shook his head. "I'm guessing you only married the Amish guy because you were pregnant, right?"

She shrugged. "*Jah*, at the beginning."

"Did your father make you marry him? Because if he did, that's considered marriage under duress. You could get it annulled, you know."

She rubbed her belly. "I don't...I'm not going to leave Justin. I love him."

"Get her car seat out of that van, and tell your driver you're coming with me." He hitched a thumb over his shoulder.

Lucy's heart rate sped up. *Can he do that?* "No, Trey. Justin's expecting me home. I'm not going with you."

"Do you think I give a rip about *Justin*? We're talking about *my* baby! You do realize what you've done borders on kidnapping, right?"

"What?" She could hardly breathe. Were his words true? Would they try to send her to jail? *Ach.*

"You hid my child from me for—what's it been?—three years now?" His hand raked through his hair. "Don't you think my parents would have liked to know they have a grandchild?"

Was this really happening? If only Justin were here with her. He'd know what to do. *Please help, Gott.* "I can't go with you right now, but maybe…maybe I can meet you sometime."

"Tomorrow. At my house. Ten thirty."

Her hands trembled as she fiddled with her collar. Was she doing the right thing, agreeing to meet with Trey?

"No, let's meet at the library instead. The last thing I need is your husband or father showing up at my house." He arched a brow. "I'm assuming you'll bring one of them along?"

She nodded.

"It's too bad you went and married that Amish guy. We could've had a good life together. I know I'm being a jerk, and I'm sorry. You just have to know how upset I am about this whole thing."

"But you said you wouldn't become Amish, remember?"

"Tell me something. Does *everyone* in your Amish community think Justin's the father of *our* baby?"

She nodded. "Except my *dat.* He knows the truth."

"I will never understand the ways of your people. If your father thinks it's better to sweep things under the rug, than face the truth, he's dead wrong."

"He was just trying to protect me and the *boppli.*"

"Protect the baby from her rightful father?"

"No, from being gossiped about and from the ways of the world."

"So, what happens in the future when I want to take *my* daughter somewhere special, like to an amusement park that's out of state? Or to the beach?"

Horror filled her heart. "You want to take her away from me? Away from the home she knows? She'd be terrified."

"You are not understanding me. That little girl is *my* daughter too. I have a right to spend time with her and to get to know her. If we have to go to court so that I can have access to my daughter, then so be it."

This was turning into a nightmare. "Please, Trey. She's happy now."

"She'll be happy with me too."

"Please don't do this. I beg you." She couldn't help her tears.

"Lucy, are you all right?" Her driver, Betty, rushed toward them and threw an arm around Lucy.

Trey stepped back.

"Yeah, I'm fine." Her gaze warned Trey not to say anything.

Trey waved, acting normal. "I'll see you tomorrow, Lucy."

When he walked off, Lucy sighed.

Betty stared at her. "Is there something you want to talk about? Was that man harassing you?"

"No. I'm fine. Can we just go home, please?"

CHAPTER EIGHTEEN

*J*ustin paced the living room as Lucy recounted the goings on in the store parking lot. They had put Abby down for bed early because his *fraa* had told him she had something important to discuss. He closed his eyes against the words he was hearing as worry seeped into his bones.

"We will take Abby to your folks tomorrow, speak with your father and ask him to pray, then go meet with Trey." It was hard to sound confident when the world around him was falling apart. He crouched in front of Lucy and reached for her hand. *"Der Herr* will be with us."

She gasped and pointed to the window. "A car just pulled up."

Ach. Did Trey follow Lucy's driver home, so he'd know where they lived?

"I'll go see who it is." He rushed to the door and flung it open, then sighed in relief. "It's Sammy." Just who he needed to see. *Gott's* timing was amazing.

He opened the door wide and ushered Sammy inside.

"I couldn't be this close and not stop in and say hello." Sammy's smile creased around his eyes. "And I brought a potpie for your *fraa*."

"It's *gut* to see you. Your timing is perfect."

Sammy must've read the angst in Justin's eyes. "Shall we go for a short walk?"

"Jah. That sounds *gut."* Just the older man's presence produced a calming effect for Justin. He turned to Lucy. "Do you mind?"

"Nee. Take as long as you need," she encouraged.

As soon as they were away from the house, Justin unloaded his burdens on Sammy. "To tell you the truth, I'm worried. My family is *everything* to me. I love them with all my heart. Now that Trey is back in the picture, I'm afraid I'll lose them both."

"You think your *fraa* would leave you?"

"It has been a fear of mine. I mean, she once loved him enough to create a *boppli* with him."

"But she's created a *boppli* with you too, ain't so?"

Justin couldn't hide his smile. "You can tell."

"She *chose* to marry *you*. She could have chosen him. Take heart in that fact." Sammy scratched his beard. "The bonds of matrimony are strong. I don't think there's much that will take a woman away from the man she loves."

"I hope you're right."

"Don't give her a reason to leave you, and she won't. I think many more marriages would stay together if men took heed to the Scriptures and loved their *fraas* as Christ loved the church."

"I'm trying my best."

Sammy patted Justin's hand. *"Der Herr* will work it out. You'll see. Do not fear, but have faith. *And we know that all things work together for good to them that love God, to them who are the called according to His purpose."*

"*Denki*, Sammy. I needed to hear that."

"Should we go inside and enjoy some of that potpie now?" Sammy waggled his eyebrows.

Justin chuckled. "That sounds *gut*, my friend."

CHAPTER NINETEEN

*J*ustin recited the verse Sammy had quoted over and over again in his mind. He'd encouraged Lucy with it too. No matter what happened during their meeting with Trey today, *Gott* was in control. He would work things out according to His will and purpose.

Justin prayed *Gott* would give Trey patience and understanding, but most of all, he prayed Lucy's former beau would come to know Jesus. Because really, that was Justin's main concern. If Trey knew Jesus, even if he did spend time with Abby, he could guide her down the right path.

As Trey pulled up and stepped out of his car, Justin held his breath. He brushed Lucy's forearm, attempting reassurance. "God's got this," he whispered.

Trey joined them in the small park across the street from the library. He frowned as he neared them. "Where's my daughter?"

"She's not here." Justin's arms crossed his chest.

"Why not?"

"It's better to discuss adult matters with just the adults." Justin insisted. "We need to figure things out, first."

Trey eyed Lucy. "I've already told Lucy that I want to spend time with my daughter."

Justin rubbed his head and sighed. "We don't want to disrupt her life, to cause unnecessary stress and confusion."

"Well, maybe you should have thought about that *before* you swooped in and married my pregnant ex-girlfriend."

Ouch. Justin frowned. "Lucy wasn't willing to marry an *Englischer.* And you weren't willing to become Amish."

"Right. But we still created a life together. And, honestly, I still love Lucy." Trey's gaze moved to Justin's *fraa,* a sad half-smile forming on his lips.

Ach, this was not a *gut* situation. "We need to come to a solution that will work for all of us."

"My intention isn't to disrupt her life. But at the same time, I want to know my daughter. I want to see her grow up."

"And how would you do that without disrupting her life?"

"I could be an *Englisch* uncle." Trey shrugged. "Unless you have a better idea."

"*Nee,* that wouldn't work. The community would know. And it wouldn't be truthful," Lucy spoke up.

Trey snorted. "Truthful? Really? *Now* you're concerned about the truth. Well, then, let's just tell her I'm her real father. How's that for truth?"

Justin stepped forward. "Maybe we didn't go about things in the perfect way, but we can't change the past."

"Right. I'll never get back the first few years of my daughter's life." His lips pressed together in a flat line. "How about just a friend, then? We could meet once a week."

Justin looked at Lucy. "That sounds reasonable."

"But when she's eighteen, I want full disclosure. She has a right to know too."

Justin grimaced.

"I want her to have a choice. If she decides she wants to become *Englisch,* she can. If she wants to get her high school diploma or go to college, she can. As a matter of fact, I will probably encourage her in that and put money away for it."

Lucy started to protest, but Trey held up his hands.

"Those are my terms. Take them or leave them. If you choose the latter, then I will pursue custody through the courts. It's up to you to decide which you prefer."

Justin squeezed his eyes closed and briefly sent up a silent prayer for wisdom. "Trey, may I ask you a question?"

He shrugged. "Yeah, sure, go for it."

"Do you know Jesus?"

"Jesus? As in Jesus Christ? We celebrate His birth at Christmas, and He died on the cross for our sins? Yeah, I know Jesus. I grew up in church."

"Do you know Him as your Saviour?"

"I accepted Jesus in my life when I was a boy. I've been baptized, even." Trey's brow lowered. "Why do you ask?"

"That's *gut.*"

"I know I haven't done everything right. Obviously." Trey rolled his eyes. "I'm probably not the world's best example of a Christian, but I *am* saved."

Justin raised his shoulder. "Would you mind if I spoke with Lucy in private for a minute?"

"No, go for it. I wanted to run over to the library anyhow." Trey jogged across the street.

When he'd gone inside, Justin turned to Lucy. "You're probably not going to like what I have to say, but I think we should just let Trey spend time with Abby."

Lucy's eyes flew wide. "What?"

"The *g'may* is eventually going to find out anyhow. How is Abby going to feel if she grows up thinking we've lied to her? She's going to resent us. The Bible says the truth will make you free." Justin frowned. "Besides, I couldn't imagine being in Trey's shoes. He obviously cares for Abby. Do you think we can honestly keep her from her *dat* who wants to know her and be in her life?"

"What about my *dat*? It would ruin his reputation as a bishop."

Justin wished he could kiss away the worry that wrinkled his sweet *fraa's* forehead. "*Nee*, it won't. They might put him in the *Bann* for six weeks, but it won't be the end of the world. People realize that he isn't perfect. They'd know he was just trying to protect his *dochder*, whom he loves. And I don't plan on confessing for him. Just our part. It'll be up to your father if he wants to admit anything."

"Okay. If that's what you think is best."

"If Trey was okay with spending a day of the week with Abby, he'll be fine with every other weekend, ain't so? Especially if he can tell Abby he's her father. Or, maybe we should tell her first."

"*Jah*, I think *we* should be the ones to tell her."

"Can we just pray about this right now? If it's *Gott's* will, He'll give us peace, right?"

She nodded, and he took her hands in his.

A few moments later, they lifted their heads.

Just then, Trey trotted across the street. "What did you decide?"

Justin examined his *fraa* and raised a brow.

She smiled her response.

Justin explained everything he'd just told Lucy. "What do you think?"

Trey's mouth hung open. "You're serious?"

Justin and Lucy nodded.

Tears surfaced in Trey's eyes, and he hugged both of them. "Thank you so much. You don't know what this means to me." He nodded. "And I'm going to start going to church again. I'll take Abby with me. My parents will be floored."

After they exchanged phone numbers and arranged a schedule, Trey drove off. No doubt, he'd be on cloud nine for the rest of the week.

Justin turned to Lucy and grinned. "I think we just made his day."

She smiled. *"Jah."*

"Let's go visit your folks and pick up Abby. We have some confessing to do."

CHAPTER TWENTY

*J*ustin decided he'd rather share the news with his men's group first, instead of them finding out secondhand after he and Lucy confessed before the *g'may*. Sammy had been supportive and had even encouraged him to invite Trey to their men's group. Having an *Englischer* join them would sure stir up controversy with the leaders in Detweiler's district.

His older brothers had been surprised, but Joshua had already suspected something. Justin and his younger *bruder* had always been close and not much happened with one that the other did not know. Most of the men understood their plight and didn't fault them for their deception.

Even Nathaniel Miller had been surprisingly amiable. He'd approached him after his confession. "Well, I've got to hand it to you, Justin. It appears you have redeemed the Beachy name."

Justin's jaw slacked. "What? What do you mean?"

"I'm not sure any of us would have done what you did. Stepping in to raise another man's child is a big deal. What you've done is admirable."

Justin couldn't have been more shocked. "It is?"

"One hundred percent."

"Wow. *Denki* for saying that."

God's ways never ceased to amaze him. Sammy had been right. *Gott* had worked everything out, not only for Justin, Lucy, and Trey's good, but for *Der Herr's* good as well.

Perhaps He had a special plan in all this.

EPILOGUE

*L*ucy stared down at their brand-new *boppli*, and her heart filled with an overwhelming joy and gratitude for *Der Herr*. She couldn't help the tears trailing down her cheeks as she examined her and Justin's tiny new miracle.

"*Ach*, she's beautiful just like her *mamm*." Justin leaned on the bed and kissed Lucy's lips.

She gazed into her beloved's eyes. "I will forever be grateful to my *dat* for arranging our marriage. If he would have left it up to me, I probably would have chosen someone else."

"*Ach*! You wouldn't have chosen me?"

"*Nee*. I thought you were way out of my league. I probably would have settled for someone like Enos Stoltzfus."

"Nothing wrong with Enos."

"I know, but he isn't you. He's not a Beachy brother." She teased.

Justin's eyebrow lifted. She loved it when he did that. "So, being a Beachy is a *gut* thing?"

"Well, I took the name as my own, didn't I?"

He leaned in for another kiss. "*Jah*, you did. And you can't give it back."

"I'll never want to."

Justin glanced up at the clock. "Trey should be bringing Abby over soon. You know she's probably dying to see her new little *schweschder*."

A knock on the door confirmed his words, and he left the room. Lucy made sure to cover herself properly.

Abby bounced into the room. "I have a sister?" She'd spoken the words in

English. When they'd agreed to let Trey spend time with her, they realized she'd need to learn English quickly. She'd done a great job at picking it up, as most young *kinner* did.

"That's right. Would you like to come close and see her?" Lucy waved her near.

"I wanna hold her too!" Abby reached for the little one.

"I think *Dat* is going to have to help you with that." Lucy glanced up at Justin and set the *boppli* in his arms. *Ach*, he was such a *gut* father.

"But Daddy wants to hold her too. Right, Daddy?" Abby looked at Trey.

Trey glanced back and forth between Lucy and Justin. "Do you mind?"

"No, of course not." Lucy said.

Justin handed their bundle of joy over to Trey.

"I've never held one this little." Trey's eyes glassed over. "This is a beautiful experience. Was Abby this small when she was born?"

"She was a little smaller yet," Justin said.

"Really? This one hardly weighs anything."

"About seven pounds."

Trey handed the *boppli* back to Justin. "Thank you for letting me hold her. We should probably go soon, Abby."

Justin let Abby hold her tiny sister. Lucy could hardly believe how big their little Abby looked next to their newborn.

Trey leaned against the doorframe. "I wanted to let you guys know. I met someone a while back. We've only been dating a few months, but I think she might be the one. How would you feel if I brought her over to meet you in a few weeks?"

Justin's gaze shot to Lucy.

"That would be wonderful." Lucy nodded.

"Abby, are you ready to go get that ice cream now?" Trey chuckled. "I had to bribe her. Otherwise, she'd want to stay and hold the baby till evening."

"You're probably right." Justin smiled.

"And I'm sure Mom could use some rest, right?" Trey smiled at Lucy.

"*Jah*." She nodded.

Abby gave both Lucy and Justin a hug and a kiss before Trey hoisted her onto his shoulders.

Lucy watched fondly as father and daughter made their way out of the bedroom. She sighed in contentment.

"Who would have thought all of this could turn out so well?" Lucy stared at her husband and *boppli* in amazement.

"*Der Herr* knew the plan all along." Justin planted a kiss on the little one's cheek.

"Please remind me of God's goodness next time I start doubting."

Justin lowered himself onto the bed with the *boppli* in his arms and sidled up to her. "I will, my love."

The more Lucy considered everything that had happened, the more convinced she became that it hadn't been her father who'd arranged her and Justin's union. It had been *Der Herr* all along who had made The Arrangement.

THE END

ABOUT THE AUTHOR

USA Today Bestselling Author **Jennifer (J.E.B.) Spredemann** seeks to pen compelling stories that captivate readers and bring glory to GOD. She has penned more than forty Amish fiction titles in her "cant-put-down" writing style. She resides in Indiana Amish Country with her family on a former Amish farm where the documentary *Breaking the Silence* was filmed. "...Spredemann weaves a thread of love and intrigue into a quilt of faith and values." — reader review

You can find a list of Jennifer Spredemann's books at www.jennifer-spredemann.com or contact the author at jebspredemann@gmail.com

Jennifer Spredemann ~ Heart-Touching Amish Fiction

If you loved **The Arrangement**, you'll enjoy the other books in the *Amish Country Brides* series! Find the entire series here: www.amazon.-com/dp/B08525F1YT or at your favorite online retailer. Available in both paperback and ebook.

LOVE BLOOMS

KATHLEEN FULLER

CHAPTER ONE

*G*atesville, near Holmes County, OH
Ah, Spring.
Lorene King clipped a damp pillowcase to the laundry line, breathing in the fresh morning air and sunshine. After a long Ohio winter, her favorite season had finally arrived. Rich earthy scents surrounded her—freshly mown pastureland, the pile of black mulch Samuel Miller had dropped off next to her front flower beds, the small beads of dew glistening on the green grass. She smiled. Although the official beginning of Spring had occurred nearly two weeks ago, today's mild weather truly ushered in the season.

She quickly finished hanging the wash. Growing up as an only child, she'd never found laundry to be an arduous chore. The task had been even simpler during the past five years, after both her parents had passed. Doing laundry, cooking, and cleaning was easy when she only had to look after herself. It was grieving her parents that had been difficult.

Entering the back of the house, she dashed down the stairs to the basement, placed the basket next to the wringer washer, went back upstairs, and opened every window in the house. Balmy air filtered through each room, and the powder blue curtains she'd made almost twenty-five years ago fluttered against the window sashes. *Oh, how I love Spring!* Not only did the mild weather bring her joy, but she could also start selling her plants and vegetables again at the small farmer's market opening this Saturday. Her parents' nest egg was enough that she didn't have to work as long as she carefully managed her finances. But she wanted to support herself. She couldn't imagine having to completely depend on anyone else.

Lorene whistled as she watered her indoor plants—all twenty of them. "Good morning, Celia." She added a small amount of water to the baby rubber plant on her kitchen table before going outside to tend to her greenhouse. Her father had built the structure more than twelve years ago when they had moved to Gatesville from Maine, and with little maintenance on her part, it was in good shape. Greenhouses weren't necessary like they were back home, but she enjoyed having a garden, even during the most brutal days of winter. "Look at all the flowers; look at all the trees," she sang. "Our God is amazing. He created all of these."

When she went inside, she grabbed the flat wicker flower basket from the small table near the door and headed for the back of the greenhouse. She stopped at a long table covered with a variety of leafy plants and eyed a robust flat of spinach. "Don't you look healthy and delicious?" she said, picking a few handfuls. "Thank you for sharing." People would probably think she was crazy if they heard her constant one-sided conversations with her plants and flowers, but after decades of gardening experience, she knew talking to them had a positive effect.

In addition to the spinach, she added four carrots, two onions, a turnip, and a few sprigs of thyme. The rest of the plants looked vibrant and healthy. On her way back to the house, she wondered what she would make with her bounty. Mashed turnips and carrots for sure, and maybe a vinaigrette to pour over the spinach leaves.

"*Gut Morgen*, Lorene!"

She turned to see her neighbor, Rebecca Beachy, waving. Two clotheslines full of laundry flapped behind the tall, thin woman as she walked to Lorene's. "*Gut Morgan*, Rebecca." Lorene smiled. "Lovely day, *ya?*"

"*Ya.* It always is when Spring finally gets here." She glanced at Lorene's basket. "That all looks nice," she said. "You're blessed with two green thumbs."

Lorene glanced at the ground but appreciated the compliment. When she met Rebecca's gaze again, she said, "I've got some lovely cucumbers ripening on the vine. They should be ready in a day or two. I'll bring some over when they are."

"Danki. Ben and the *buwe* do love fresh cucumbers. By the way, did you remember that you're supposed to take a casserole to Jonas today?"

Uh oh. "*Nee*, I forgot. *Danki* for reminding me." She and several women in their community, including Rebecca, had signed up to take food to Jonas Stoltzfus this week. The middle-aged widower had sprained his ankle last Monday, and they had jumped on the opportunity to bring him fresh food, which would be a change from his typical menu of olive loaf sandwiches and canned soup. But after one of the women had taken a meal to him, they'd started to wonder if they'd made a mistake. Not only didn't he appreciate the food, but he'd acted more curmudgeonly than usual, something Lorene hadn't thought possible.

"I made him an egg and sausage casserole yesterday." Rebecca grimaced. "Guess who doesn't like sausage? I thought every man in the world loved sausage."

"Count on Jonas to be different." Despite her words, Lorene brightened. She wasn't going to let Jonas or anyone else spoil her day. "Hopefully he likes turnips," she said, deciding that she'd double the meal she planned to make for herself.

"Don't count on it." Rebecca headed back to her house. "The only things he likes are olive loaf and Campbell's Chicken Noodle soup. You know he eats that right out of the can? Disgusting."

Lorene shook her head, wishing Rebecca hadn't revealed that tidbit about him. Lorene couldn't imagine eating food full of preservatives. She turned to go back to her greenhouse for another turnip and some more spinach leaves. Jonas was getting a delicious meal straight from her garden—whether he wanted it or not.

~

Jonas's stomach growled, but he ignored his hunger as he sat on his front porch in the hickory rocker he'd made as a wedding present to Mary thirty years ago. The warm spring breeze that had started this morning continued until evening, but he couldn't enjoy it or the approaching sunset. This was the blackest day of the year for him, and it didn't get any easier or better, despite the passage of time.

He closed his eyes, fighting to remember her beautiful face. Since Mary's death, he'd lamented the Amish tradition of not taking pictures. He could barely recollect what she looked like now, making today so much harder. How could he forget the face of the woman he loved? He couldn't even recall what she sounded like, and he never thought he'd forget a single thing about her. But nine years was a long time, and his memory wasn't what it used to be, even though he was only fifty.

When he opened his eyes, he pushed up his glasses and squinted at the plump figure walking up his driveway. Great, another woman bringing him food. He should be grateful for their thoughtfulness. Instead, he found them intrusive. Not a single woman could simply drop off their meal on the porch and leave. No, they had to come inside, chattering the whole time, explaining how to heat up and eat their food like he didn't know how to feed himself. And now the chattiest of them all was nearing his house. Lorene King. Maybe if he hurried inside and shut the door quietly, he could fool her into thinking he wasn't home.

"Yoo hoo! Jonas!"

Too late. He grabbed the cane near his chair, having ditched the crutches two days ago. At least there was one a thing to be grateful for. He touched the brim of his straw hat as Lorene bounded up the stairs like she was sixteen years old instead of…forty? Forty-five? He wasn't sure. He'd never asked her how old she was. In fact, he didn't interact much with Lorene at all.

"What a lovely day it's been, *ya?*" She held a huge basket in front of her rounded belly. For as long as he'd known her, she'd been on the heavier side. A far cry from Mary, who, like him, had always been thin. But the weight seemed to suit Lorene's bubbly personality. She grinned, her full cheeks apple red from the mile walk to his house, her green eyes sparkling with delight as she waited for him to answer. When he didn't, the sparkle dimmed, but her smile remained.

"I brought you some goodies," she said, holding out the basket. "Mashed carrots and turnips, fresh spinach salad, baked chicken with thyme and rosemary, and a plum tart for dessert."

"I don't like turnips," he said, looking her straight in the eye. "Or carrots. Or plums."

"That's because you haven't had *my* turnips, carrots, and plums. You'll love them after you've eaten what I've prepared. Let's *geh* inside, and I'll dish it out for you."

"*Nee.*" He let his cane hit the floor and crossed his arms. "I have plenty of food already." Food he'd barely touched. He hadn't had much of an appetite lately. Not only had he been in terrible pain from his ankle, but he'd also been furious with himself for spraining it in the first place by stepping into a muddy hole in his driveway. It was his own fault since the gravel drive had needed repairing for years. It wasn't the only thing on his property and in his house that needed some TLC.

Her gaze narrowed. "What do you mean, '*nee*'?" She looked him up and down. "You're going to waste away if you don't start eating properly."

Would that be a bad thing? He was too gloomy to push the idea out of his mind, even though deep inside he knew it was wrong for him to think so. God had numbered his days, just like he'd numbered Mary's and everyone else's. It was up to God when it was his time to go. But when Jonas found himself grieving over his late wife all over again, especially on the anniversary of her death, he couldn't help but wish he was with her instead of here.

"Humph." Lorene moved past him, opened his screen door *and* his front door, and walked inside.

He glared at the closed door. Who did she think she was, barging into his house with her mashed turnips? Well, she could set all that healthy stuff on his table and leave. He turned and stared at his bumpy, hole filled driveway for a few minutes. More minutes ticked away before he glanced at the door again. What was she doing in there? It didn't take long to put a basket on the table. He was just about to get up and go inside when she burst onto the front porch.

"Supper's ready," she said in a sing-song voice.

He scowled again. Lorene was always singing or talking or making noise. Even now, as she picked up his cane, the sound coming out of her mouth was a combination of whistling and humming that sounded…a little pleasant. His scowl deepened. He didn't want pleasant, and he for sure didn't want hovering. He wanted her out of there.

She handed his cane to him. "Your chicken is getting cold, and it's more appetizing when it's hot. The thyme and rosemary came straight out of my greenhouse this morning. So did the turnips and carrots. I bought the plums from the Yoder's. Those were a little sour, but with a pinch of sugar, they sweetened right up. I also got the butter for the tart from there too. I prefer their butter to the butter at the grocery store. It's much fresher tasting, especially on yeast rolls right out of the oven—"

"Don't you ever *shut up?*"

Lorene froze, her mouth still open, but no sound coming out. Guilt appeared, but not enough to apologize. Hurt entered her bright eyes, and she took a step back.

"I don't need nothin' from you, or anyone else," he said, throwing the cane on the front porch. Anger coursed through him, and even though she wasn't the cause of it, she was going to get the brunt. "I didn't ask for turnips or chicken or pie or gravy or anything else you *frau* keep bringing over here. I want to be left alone. Got it?"

She ran her palms over her apron, not looking at him. "*Ya*," she said, her voice softer than he'd ever heard it. "Got it." She turned around and walked down the steps, her back straight as a newly sawn board.

He half expected her to run off after his tongue lashing, but her steps were measured as she walked down the street, as if she was already over any hurt feelings his outburst caused.

He blew out a breath when she disappeared and dropped his head into his hands. She didn't deserve his scolding. But he was tired, so tired. Every year this day came around, and he dreaded it for weeks, with everything coming to a head when the date arrived. Pain squeezed his heart. "Why did you leave me, *lieb?*" he whispered, as dead leaves skittering across his porch. *Why does this still hurt so much?*

CHAPTER TWO

$\mathcal{O}$ne month later
"You're going to be so happy in your new home." Lorene gently mounded dirt around the small tomato plant at the end of the last row in her garden. She had two rows of tomatoes, all grown from seed in her greenhouse. She patted down the dirt, started to stand, her knees and back cracking. There was a time when she could kneel for hours without pain or her joints complaining. That was a few years ago, and now she had to rest her knees on a foam pad and shorten the time she spent close to the ground.

She brushed off her hands and surveyed her garden. Every row was perfectly aligned, every plant carefully placed and given a few words of encouragement to grow. It had taken her the entire day, but it was a day well spent. Glancing at the sun hovering over the horizon, she had one more task to do. "Now you all get a *gut* long drink." She wiped her forehead as she walked to the well. Most of her neighbors had hose hookups to their wells, but she preferred to pump the water and carry the buckets to her plants. Not only was it good exercise, but she didn't have to worry about the hose touching or knocking over her new plantings.

After she picked up the large bucket near the well, she pumped it full of water. Grabbing the handle with two hands, she turned around to head back to the tomato plants.

Splash!

Jonas's eyes were round with shock as a large dark spot appeared on his sage green shirt. Water soaked through his shirt. "You should look where you're going," he snapped.

"Me?" She dropped the bucket, barely noticing when it tipped over. "You shouldn't be sneaking up behind people!" She took a step forward and poked him in the chest. "Especially on their own property."

"I thought you heard me," he said, looking down at his chest through his silver-rimmed glasses. Her finger remained in place.

"Well, I didn't." She dropped her hand and stepped away, her pulse slowing down. She started to put her hands on her hips but stopped, fighting the urge to chide him. Instead, she forced a smile. "Can I help you with something, Jonas?"

He stared at the ground, pushing against the grass with the toe of his boot. The pair were old and worn. She also noticed the hems of his pant legs were frayed. When was the last time someone made him new clothes? Surely, he hadn't been wearing the same clothing since his wife died nine years ago. Or was it ten? Even the best cared-for clothing would show wear, and she doubted he was meticulous about his outfits, or anything else.

Since the day he'd bitten her head off because she'd brought him something to eat, she had only seen him at church services. They were cordial, nodding hello to each other in passing after the services were over. No one observing them would know there was anything amiss. But Lorene couldn't forget his harsh words or that he hadn't apologized for them.

"I, uh…" He shoved his hands in his pockets and kept his head down.

Something about the sad state of his clothes and his discomfort with her made her month-long irritation with him melt a little. "Would you like something to drink?" This time, her smile was genuine. "I have some iced tea cooling in the pitcher. Fresh made this afternoon."

He lifted his gaze and nodded.

"I need to water the tomatoes first. It won't take but a minute." She glanced at his shirt. "I'm sorry about that," she said, gesturing to the spot where the well water had landed.

He waved off her apology. "It'll dry."

She started to pick up the bucket, but he grabbed it off the ground and walked over to the well without saying a word.

He filled the bucket, handed it to her with one hand, picked up another bucket, and started pumping again.

Odd. The last thing she expected was for Jonas to assist. But she wasn't going to refuse an extra set of helping hands, so she hauled the water to the rows of the tomatoes. Together she and Jonas made short work of the task, and when she finished pouring the last bucketful on the end of the rows, she said, "All done! *Danki*, Jonas."

He grunted something unintelligible, and she almost laughed. He really was the epitome of a cranky old man, even though he wasn't that old. His dark brown hair had a few strands of gray threaded throughout, and he looked like a typical forty-something Amish man. His attitude aged him, though. There had to be a reason he was so irritable all the time. *But that's none of my business.*

Lorene motioned for him to follow her inside. After she washed up at the sink, she moved so he could clean his hands. When she handed him a towel to dry off, she asked, "Are you hungry?"

Jonas shrugged. "I could eat."

She grinned. "How do potato salad, ham slices, and creamed corn sound?"

Finally, he met her gaze. "It sounds *gut.*"

She tried to move, but she couldn't, realizing she'd never been this close to him before. Behind his round glasses were brown eyes, the color reminding her of milk chocolate, with tiny lines at the corners. His olive complexioned skin was tanner than it had been since she'd last seen him, as if he'd spent a lot of time in the sun, despite being a woodworker with his own shop behind his house. Her gaze dropped to his strong jaw. She'd never thought of Jonas Stoltzfus as handsome before. Now that he wasn't scowling, she realized he was. *Definitely.*

Her heart skipped an unexpected beat.

"Something wrong?" he asked.

"*Nee,*" she said, stunned at the breathlessness of her voice. She whirled around and hurried to the pantry to get the loaf of bread she'd made yesterday. When she opened the door, she pressed her hand against her heart. She'd never had this reaction to a man before. What was this reaction, anyway? *What is happening?*

"Mind if I use the facilities?"

His request pushed her back into reality. "Of course. The bathroom is to the right of the kitchen." She grabbed the loaf of bread and the butter dish and closed the pantry door. When she turned around, he had already left. *Gut.* She had some time to get started on supper, and to gather her wits.

A few minutes later, he walked into the kitchen again. The creamed corn was heating on the stove, and she was scooping the potato salad she'd stored in her large camping cooler into two small bowls. She didn't keep much in the cooler, just a bag of ice with a small carton of milk, the potato salad, a jar of mayo, and a wedge of cheddar cheese. "I hope you don't mind peach tea," she said as she set the bowls on the table, calmer now than she'd been before. "I forgot I'd added peach syrup. Normally I like my tea plain, but Rebecca and her *buwe* had gone peach picking last year and brought some delicious ones over. I couldn't resist making some syrup out of them, after I canned a few jars, of course." When she turned and looked at him, he was standing at the sink, staring out the kitchen window.

"Jonas?" She walked over to him. "Are you all right?"

He didn't answer her right away. He simply stood there, staring. Eventually, he whispered, "*Nee.* I'm not."

~

Jonas was lost. He'd come over to apologize to Lorene for his behavior last month, something he should have done sooner. But he kept putting it off, wishing he could sweep the embarrassing incident under the rug. Yet the times he'd seen her at church, he could tell she was still hurt. Oh, she hid it well, giving him a quick nod and a false smile when they couldn't avoid each other. But he knew he was in the wrong.

When he'd woken up this morning, the guilt he'd had in his soul since that day had become unbearable, and he couldn't put off his apology any longer. The task was simple—go to Lorene's, say he was sorry for being a dolt, and return home to his empty house, his unfulfilling work, and the last can of chicken noodle soup in his pantry.

The plan had changed when he arrived at Lorene's. He'd gotten there in time to see her finish planting the last tomato plant. He should have announced himself, but watching the sheer joy on her face as she worked in her garden had halted him in his tracks. Mary had possessed a green thumb, and her garden had always been full of colorful flowers and healthy vegetable plants. But his late wife had never considered gardening fun or talked to the plants the way Lorene did. The woman was probably a bit off her nut, but there was something endearing about her he hadn't noticed before. *Maybe I'm the one off my nut.*

He had to admit it had been nice helping her water the garden, and since he hadn't managed to apologize to her yet, he couldn't refuse her invitation to stay for supper. But seeing her in the kitchen preparing the meal reminded him of Mary. She had loved cooking more than gardening, while Lorene seemed to enjoy both. His memory of Mary in the kitchen faded, and all he could see was Lorene...and it had shaken him to his core.

"What's wrong?" she asked. "Is there anything I can do to help?"

He stepped away from the window, wishing he hadn't said anything. If he'd apologized in the garden and left like he'd intended to, he wouldn't be so confused and irritated with himself right now. "Stop being so nosy."

"I'm not being nosy," she snapped. "All I did was ask a simple question."

He peered down at her. She was a few inches shorter than him, but not too short that he couldn't see the fire in her eyes—fire that in some bizarre way made his pulse race. Mary rarely lost her temper, even when he had trouble controlling his. She had softened his hard edges, and those edges had returned when she died.

"Why are you staring at me?"

He blinked. He hadn't realized he was. Stepping back, he mumbled, "I shouldn't have come here...I shouldn't have stayed." He turned and rushed to leave.

"You are the strangest, most perplexing man I've ever met!"

Jonas couldn't help but turn around and look at her. Her hands were on her hips, and she was still glaring at him, her round cheeks redder than he'd ever seen them. But even through her anger, he could still sense her warmth and kindness, and he almost changed his mind about leaving.

She took one step toward him, her hands dropping to her sides, confusion entering her eyes. "Jonas?"

He whirled around and ran out of the house. By the time he was half a mile from her house, he slowed his pace, slapping his forehead with the palm of his hand. Not only did he owe Lorene two apologies, she for sure and for certain had to think he was certifiable. *Maybe I am.* Although he knew he should turn around and go back to her house, he couldn't bring himself to do so. There was *definitely* something wrong with him. He had no idea what that was, or how to fix it.

Lorene paced in the kitchen, attempting to cool her ire. While normally she was slow to anger, Jonas's weird behavior had brought out the worst in her. Well, maybe not the worst. There was the time she'd blown her stack when she'd visited her cousin back in Maine last summer. His eight-year-old son had put not one, but three frogs in her bed, so losing her temper was justified. But today...ugh. How could she had ever thought he was handsome? Or nice? "He's *seltsam*, that's what he is," she said to Celia.

Or maybe he's just hurt.

The creamed corn started bubbling on the stove, and she jumped up from her chair. She removed the pot, barely in time to keep the bottom from burning. She turned off the gas burner and flopped down on the nearest chair by the table, her anger disappearing. She didn't want to sympathize with him, but she couldn't ignore the glimmer of pain she'd seen in his eyes before he snapped at her, and later, when he paused at her kitchen doorway, as if he couldn't figure out which end was up.

She rested her hand on her chin, considering Jonas more seriously than she ever had before. She thought about the times he spent alone, although that was mostly his fault. His bitter disposition had driven a lot of people away, even in a tight community like Gatesville.

But why? Why was he so grumpy all the time? An even bigger, more baffling question floated in her mind. *Why do I suddenly care?* Of course, she cared about everyone in the community, and she didn't like seeing people upset. But her sudden interest in his feelings went beyond the Golden Rule. While they'd worked together in her garden, she had caught a glimpse of the real Jonas, the way he probably was before his wife died. Thoughtful. Helpful. And although he was quiet, she had appreciated his steady company. It was nice to work alongside someone after so many years of working alone.

Lorene sat up and smiled. Maybe there was a way to bring Jonas back to the land of the living. *It's certainly worth a try.*

～

Jonas dumped the last shovelful of manure into the wheelbarrow and pushed it outside to a larger pile several yards away. After emptying the dung, he looked out into the pasture, annoyed and baffled by his earlier behavior.

When he'd returned home from Lorene's, he'd headed straight for Nick's stall, let the horse out in the pasture at the far side of his property, and thrown all his energy into cleaning out the stall and the rest of the barn. The work had been strenuous. He was sweaty from head to toe, and he needed a shower. But all he could do was watch Nick as he munched on the growing spring grass. *At least one of us is happy.*

He glanced up at the cloudless sky. *Lord, what is wrong with me?* Usually, these intense depressive times only lasted a few days. The loss of appetite, the insomnia, and his irritability were off the charts during those periods. But this time, he couldn't shake off his paralyzing grief. It seemed to consume him. Today he'd had a moment of relief when he was with Lorene, and for once he hadn't minded her constant chatter. The respite hadn't lasted long, and the guilt over enjoying her company still sat in his chest.

He'd always been introverted, and so had Mary. Often, throughout their marriage, they would tell each other, "You're all I need." And they both meant it. They liked being by themselves and enjoyed each other's company. But after spending so many years alone and separating himself socially from his community, something shifted inside him when he was with Lorene. For a fleeting moment, he'd had a glimmer of something he thought he'd lost forever. *Hope.*

After letting Nick eat a little while longer, Jonas motioned for the horse to go to the barn. He fed him some oats, filled his water trough, and made sure Nick was settled for the night before he went back to the house.

But when he walked out of the barn, he stopped. Lorene was knocking on his front door. Her blue scooter lay against the railing near the bottom step leading up to the porch. A jolt of anticipation ran through him, only to vanish quickly. Was she going to yell at him for being rude to her again? She had a right to, but he wasn't in the mood for a dressing down. Frowning, he walked toward her. "What are you doing here?"

She turned around and gave him a surprised smile. "Oh, there you are. I was just about to start looking for you."

He moved to the bottom of the steps. "You're not answering my question." He tried to hold back the usual bite in his words.

"I'm getting to that," she replied, not sounding bothered at all. She walked down the steps until she was standing on the bottom one. They were eye to eye now, and she didn't flinch as she looked directly at him. "I'm here to cheer you up, Jonas Stoltzfus."

"I don't need cheering up." He brushed past her and went to the house.

She followed him. "I think you do. You've been down in the mouth long enough."

He ignored her and walked inside the house. She caught the door before it closed and slipped in behind him. "My goodness, look at this room." She put her hands on her hips. "It's almost as messy as you are."

He rubbed the back of his neck. "Cleaning the barn is messy work. Besides, I was on my way to shower when you came over here *uninvited*."

"Don't let me stop you. I'll tidy up around here while you're gone." She glanced around at the piles of discarded newspapers, empty soup cans, and dust bunnies surrounding them. "This place needs a few plants," she said. "And some light." She flipped on the gas-powered lamp in the corner of the room by his old recliner. "There, that's better." She looked at him, her nose wrinkling. "Well? What are you waiting for? *Geh* get your shower."

He had to stop himself before he said, *Yes, ma'am.* "I'm going," he grumbled, knowing it was useless to snap back at her, despite the fact he disliked being ordered around. He hurried upstairs, took a fast shower, threw on the best shirt and pants he owned that weren't his church clothes, and yanked a pair of socks from his drawer. When he shoved them over his feet, his big toe poked through a hole at the top. He'd meant to mend them, but lately he hadn't been in the mood to do anything. Rummaging through the drawer, he finally found a pair that didn't need darning and slipped them on and hurried downstairs.

The living room was already cleaned up, and he heard Lorene humming from the kitchen. When he entered the room, she was washing the dishes. "You don't have to do that."

"Of course, I don't, but I want to." She turned off the tap and faced him, her expression serious. "Let me help you, Jonas. Please."

He wanted to tell her no, but he couldn't. He tried to recall the last time he'd seen his living room so clean and tidy. *When Mary was alive.* Yet he couldn't deny it was nice to see everything so shipshape.

As if she knew he was at a loss, she said, "Why don't you sweep the floor while I finish these up?"

Grateful for something to do, he went to the mudroom and got the broom. By the time the floor was clean, she had done the dishes, cleaned the counter, and was almost finished washing the kitchen window.

"This is a wonderful windowsill for some small plants." She turned and faced him. "I'll bring some the next time I come over."

Next time? "I don't know how to take care of plants. Mary always did it. "

"I can show you."

"That's not necessary—"

"I don't mind." She smiled.

His breath hitched. Her smile was so lovely and warm. And attractive. He cleared his throat. "Lorene, I appreciate what you've done here...especially after what I said earlier today. And a month ago." He ran his hand through his hair. "I'm sorry for being so rude to you."

"Apology accepted."

The warmth from her smile radiated her entire face, causing her eyes to sparkle like clear green glass and reach straight to his heart. His guilt triggered again. "*Danki* for cleaning *mei haus*." He moved away from her, trying to put some distance between her and the rush of feelings coming over him. "But if you don't mind, I'd rather be alone. Please," he added.

She nodded, but didn't look offended like she had the two previous times they'd been together. "If you're sure that's what you want."

"I'm sure." But as she started to leave, he almost called her back. He thought about Mary again, and that halted his words.

"If you need anything," Lorene said, "Just let me know."

"*Danki*." He couldn't help but give her a small smile.

She returned it with a pretty one of her own, turned, and left.

Jonas sat down in his recliner. Despite his jumbled emotions, his loneliness abated slightly. Not much, but he'd take it. *Danki for that too, Lorene.*

CHAPTER THREE

*R*ain, rain, go away." Lorene pressed her forehead against the back kitchen window and watched the battering storm outside. "Come again some other day. . ." She turned around and looked at Celia. "It's a gully washer this morning, isn't it?"

As always, Celia remained silent.

Lorene faced the window again, pressing her top teeth against her bottom lip. If it didn't stop raining soon, she'd have a huge problem on her hands. As it was, her garden was almost completely underwater after two hours of heavy, non-stop rain. That was okay, for now. She had good drainage, and in the past week since she'd gone over to Jonas's, they'd had a dry spell. But so much rain in such a short time was getting ridiculous.

While she preferred to spend time outside, there was always plenty to do indoors. She spent the rest of the day applying wax to the few pieces of furniture she possessed, hand washed the floorboards, cleaned the grout in the tub with a toothbrush. Once finished, she made supper. To her dismay, the rain hadn't subsided. In fact, it was getting stronger, and although it was only four pm, the thick cloud cover made it seem like it was almost dark.

She made the mistake of glancing outside. Instead of her garden plants and lush grass, she saw only water. A knot formed in her stomach. If the rain ceased this minute, she might be able to save some of her heartier vegetables. *Please stop, rain. Please stop.*

A flash of lightning streaked the sky, followed by a sharp crack of thunder that made her jump. The rain increased, slamming against the roof and windows.

Too unnerved to eat, she went to the opposite side of the kitchen—a mere six steps—and peered outside through the window over the sink. It was so dark she could barely see anything. She was about to move away when she saw a small light bouncing up and down the street. The light turned into her driveway and grew bigger and brighter. "What in the world?" she whispered.

Lorene hurried out of the kitchen to the front door and turned the knob. The moment the latch clicked, the door blew open. As she tried to close it, the light moved faster as it became even larger. Who would be crazy enough to go out in this mess? "Hello?" she yelled into the wind. For a moment, she thought it might be Rebecca's husband, Ben, checking on her. But he would have crossed the yard—probably by canoe at this point.

A figure dressed in an oilcloth coat, a rain hat pulled down low, and—were those waders?—made its way up the steps. When the person reached the front porch, the light shined in her eyes. "You okay?" he asked.

"Jonas?" Rain misted on her face even though she was still inside. "Are you *ab im kopp?*"

"Probably," he said, moving closer, water dripping from his hat. "Can I come in?"

She waved him inside, and together they shut the door. Her face and the front of her dress were wet, but that was nothing compared to how soggy he was.

He flipped off his flashlight and looked down at the water puddling around his feet. "Sorry," he said, lifting his gaze, droplets falling from his glasses.

"Don't worry about that. Just get out of those wet things."

"Yes ma'am."

She stilled at the slight teasing tone of his voice. Was he joking with her? Did Jonas even joke? He was busy taking off his jacket and waders, removing his hat last. "What should I do with all this?"

"I'll take them," she said. "Meet me in the kitchen, and I'll make some *kaffee*. You've got some explaining to do." She went to the mudroom in the back of the house and hung up his rain garments. Now she was soaked, so she hurried to her room down the hall, changed into a dry dress, and dashed back to the kitchen. "Now," she said, slightly out of breath from rushing around, "What has gotten into you?"

Jonas was seated at the table, his hands folded on his lap. He'd already wiped the water off the lenses of his glasses and was looking at her, his right eyebrow slightly lifted. "Um..."

She frowned. "What?"

"Your dress is on inside out."

Lorene glanced down. "Oh, *gut* grief. I'll be right back." She stepped out of the kitchen and made sure she was out of his sight line before she yanked off the dress, turned it right side out, shoved it on again, and walked back into the room. "*Kaffee* will be ready in a minute," she said, remembering she'd promised to make him some. "While it's brewing, you can tell me why you're out in the worst storm we've had in years."

"I came to check on you."

She turned, the coffee pot in her hand. "Pardon me?"

"Like you said, this is a bad storm. I wanted to make sure you were okay." He was staring at the table and pressing his thumb against the edge.

Stunned, she couldn't move. He lived a little more than a mile away, and with the water as high as it was, not to mention the brutal wind, the walk couldn't have been easy. "You didn't have to do that," she said softly.

He looked at her. "I know. But I wanted to."

Jonas polished off his second chocolate chip cookie, a delicious ending to the simple and satisfying supper Lorene had made—arugula and cherry tomato salad with homemade vinegar dressing, bread and butter, and cubed cheese and summer sausage from Lewis' Fresh Meats and Deli. The owner, Griffin Lewis, was a former chef and cured the meat himself.

During the meal, she had repeated that he was nuts for coming over here during a huge storm, and maybe he was. Although he knew her neighbors would keep an eye on her, he still didn't like the idea of her riding out the rain and wind alone. Certainly, she was more than capable of handling herself. He just wanted to make sure she was okay.

"Would you like another cookie?" She held up the plate.

"*Nee*, but *danki*. They're *appeditlich*."

Her cheeks turned a light shade of rose as she averted her eyes and set the plate back down on the table. A bright streak of lightning illuminated the kitchen, followed by a sharp crack of thunder. She jumped. "I'll be glad when this is over," she said, her voice barely above a whisper.

"Me too."

"How about we play Dutch Blitz?" Lorene hopped up from her chair.

"*Ya.* That sounds *gut*." Anything to distract her from the storm. He stood and helped her clear the table.

When they were finished setting the dishes on the counter, she said, "I'll be right back with the cards."

He nodded and went to the sink to rinse off their plates. A few minutes later, she returned and sat down at the table. He dried off his hands and joined her.

"It's been years since I've played this game," he said as she dealt out the cards.

She smiled. "I'm sure it will come back to you."

After she gave him a refresher on the rules and they played a hand, she was right. He did remember. He was also more relaxed than he'd been since.... He mentally shook his head. He didn't want to think about that right now. "Why didn't you ever get married?" he blurted, speaking the question as it passed through his mind.

Lorene continued shuffling the cards. "I never met the right man. I didn't want to get married just to be married. I had a happy, satisfying life with *mei* parents." She tapped the end of the stack before peeling off a card. She pushed it toward him, meeting his gaze. "Why do you ask?"

He shrugged and moved the card closer to him. "Do you ever get lonely?"

"Sometimes." She continued to deal the cards. "I wouldn't be honest if I didn't admit that. When I was younger, it used to be difficult at times. Sometimes I felt left out because I was the only single woman among *mei* friends. I also had a tough time after *mei* parents passed away. But I've always had *mei* plants to keep me company. You've already met Celia." She pointed to the shiny leafed plant in the middle of the table.

"They have names?"

"*Nee*, just her." She touched one of Celia's leaves. "She was given to me when *mei mamm* passed away. She's always been special."

He thought about the few flowers and one plant he'd gotten from some of his customers when Mary died. The flowers had soon wilted, and the plant had perished. They were dried out sticks by the time he threw them away. He hadn't thought to take care of them. He'd had enough trouble taking care of himself.

Lightning lit up the sky. A huge cracking sound, followed by a booming crash that shook the house, made them both jolt. "That wasn't just thunder!" Lorene's hand covered her chest. "What happened?"

"I'll find out." He got up from the table and grabbed the flashlight off the counter.

"Oh, *nee*. You're not going out there again," Lorene said. A statement, not a question. *More like an order.* But this time, he didn't mind.

"I'm not that *ab im kopp.* I'm just going to look outside." He walked over to the back door and shined the light through the window. It was difficult to see due to the glare from the light on the glass and the pouring rain, but he glimpsed a fallen tree—right on top of her greenhouse. He winced and turned around. "A tree fell."

Her eyes widened. "Did it hit anything?"

"*Ya.* The greenhouse."

"Oh *nee*." She rushed over to the window, motioning for him to pass his flashlight. He wasn't sure that was a good idea. Hopefully, by morning, the storm would be over, and they could safely assess the damage. But she was so insistent, he handed her the light.

91

KATHLEEN FULLER

"It's ruined," she said, her shoulders slumping. "My plants…my flowers…all gone."

He walked over to her, unsure what to do or say. He lifted his hand, letting it hover over her shoulder for a moment before he finally touched her. "I'm sorry, Lorene."

She didn't shrug off his hand, and the two of them continued to look outside, despite the dim and distorted view. Straightening her shoulders, she looked at him, her face brightening. "It's okay. There's always next year's farmer's market. *Nee* one was hurt, and I have the plans *Daed* made for the greenhouse. It can be rebuilt."

He was surprised she was taking this so well. Impressed, too, now that he knew how much her garden meant to her, both personally and financially.

"We can't do anything about it now," she said with a small smile. "Might as well *geh* back to playing our game."

Jonas's eyes widened. "How do you do that?" he asked.

"Do what?"

"Find the silver lining in everything."

Her smile grew a little wider. "That's how God made me, I guess. I've always been optimistic."

"Don't you ever get sad? Or angry?"

She nodded as another lightning strike, a tiny one this time, flashed outside. "I do. I really had a tough time when *mei* parents died a year apart. I grieved them, but I also had to move on. That's what they would have wanted me to do, and it's what I needed to do."

He had the grieving part down. It was the moving on he couldn't wrap his mind around.

They played cards until the storm was over. After the rain subsided, he followed her to the basement to check for damage. Because her house was on a small incline, an inch or so of water covered the floor. Some houses in the community wouldn't be as fortunate, however. He said a quick, silent prayer that only the basements had flooded, not the houses themselves.

Lorene followed him up the stairs and back into the kitchen. He opened the back door. Unbelievably the sky was now clear, and a full moon had emerged, casting silvery light on the flooded back yard—and the tree on top of the greenhouse.

"It really is gone, isn't it?" she whispered, her tone tinted with sadness.

"*Ya.*" He wished there was something he could say to cheer her up. But he'd never been good at that kind of thing, even with Mary. Without thinking, he found Lorene's hand and gave it a squeeze.

She looked up at him, her bottom lip trembling slightly as she smiled. "*Danki,*" she said, letting go of his hand. "I guess I better fix us some supper."

As she left his side, he glanced at his hand. The skin on his palm tingled

92

from her touch, and his pulse quickened. He closed the door and turned to her. "I, uh, guess I better head back home now that the storm's gone."

"Everything is still flooded, though."

"I've got my waders, remember? They're made for walking in rivers. They can handle the trip home."

"I'll get your things."

He waited for her in the kitchen and stared at the Dutch Blitz pack on the table, suddenly realizing he wasn't eager to leave. But he wasn't going to impose and stay the night, either, not to mention he didn't want anyone to see them and think there was something going on. The chance of somebody else being out and about after such a torrential storm was almost zero, but he didn't want to take the risk. He also didn't know what to do about the surprising emotions that had appeared as he'd held her hand.

When she walked back into the kitchen, she handed him the waders. "They're completely dry," she said.

He put them on, along with the oilcloth coat and hat he'd had since before he'd courted Mary. When he was geared up to go, she walked him to the front door.

"*Danki*, Jonas." She threaded her fingers together in front of her. "I'm glad you came over."

Me too. He hesitated, on the verge of changing his mind and staying a little while longer. Why was he in such a hurry to leave and go back to his empty house?

"Jonas?" she said, lifting a questioning eyebrow.

"Bye, Lorene." He turned and went outside. Leaving was the right decision. He needed to check on his house and property. At least that's what he told himself.

Water covered her yard, driveway, and the road. Walking home would be a literal slog, but not as difficult as it had been during the storm. He gave her a small wave and headed back home, glancing over his shoulder one more time. When he spotted her still on the porch watching him, he couldn't help but smile.

CHAPTER FOUR

*R*eady for me to slice your olive loaf, Jonas?"

Jonas paused in front of the meat counter. Every week since the deli opened, he came here, at first to criticize Griffin, who at the time was not only an outsider in the community but also new to the Amish faith. Jonas was ashamed of his behavior and had apologized. Now Hope and Griffin were married, and Griffin always made sure to stock Jonas' favorite lunch meat— olive loaf. But today he wanted something different, surprising both himself and Hope.

"You want roast beef?" Hope's forehead furrowed. "Did I hear you right?"

"*Ya.* One pound of roast beef. Add a few slices of swiss cheese to that, too."

She nodded as she opened the meat case. Before pulling out the sandwich meat, she glanced at him again over the counter. "Are you okay?"

He was, for the most part. Ever since the storm two weeks ago, his optimism had started to sprout, thanks to Lorene. Trouble was, he hadn't found an opportunity to talk to her. Her garden wasn't the only one the storm destroyed, and she'd been helping others restore their gardens while hers was still a muddy mess. Her neighbor Ben and a friend of his had chopped up the tree that had fallen on her greenhouse, splitting the firewood between Lorene and the two of them. But the greenhouse hadn't been touched. Jonas knew that because he'd stopped by her house three times last week, and four this week, telling himself he was just checking on her. But his excuse didn't explain his deep disappointment when she wasn't there.

"Jonas?"

He blinked, and Hope came into focus. "I'm fine," he said, annoyance lacing his tone. He checked himself. "I want to try something different, that's all."

She gave him a puzzled look but filled his order and handed him the two packages. "Anything else I can get for you

"Nope. That'll do me."

He met her at the cash register. "Where's Griffin?"

Hope tapped the keys on the battery-operated cash register. "He's replacing the floor in the wood smoker. It was ruined by the flood."

"Does he need any help?"

For the second time, she looked at him with surprise. "Um, *nee*. But I'll let him know you offered. *Danki*, Jonas." She handed him his change.

"You're welcome." He put the coins in the small tip basket near the register and walked out the door, positive he'd just surprised Hope for the third time. He was surprising himself, lately.

Instead of going home, he decided to stop by Lorene's again. He had a project to work on in his shop, which had fortunately been spared from the flood because like Lorene's house, it was also on a small hill. But his work could wait.

When he saw her buggy in front of the barn, he smiled, only to wonder if he was doing the right thing. Would she think he was strange coming over and checking on her? It was one thing to keep her company during a storm, but now that the flood waters had receded and danger had passed, he didn't have an excuse. All he knew was that he wanted to see her again. *I miss her.*

Drawing in a deep breath, he walked up the driveway and knocked on the front door. Once. Twice. When she didn't answer, he peeked through the window and saw her on the sofa, sound asleep. She didn't strike him as someone who normally took afternoon naps. Obviously, after working so hard helping others, she needed it.

He went down the steps and started to head to his house, but stopped as a thought occurred. What had he done to help anyone after the storm? Not much, other than offer Griffin assistance. No one had asked for his help either. Not that he blamed them. Who wanted to be around a cranky man? And until recently, he hadn't been too concerned about being alone all the time, blaming his loneliness on missing Mary. But now he was starting to think differently.

He had a prime opportunity to help Lorene, and he wasn't going to walk away from it. He went to her backyard and set the deli package on the patio table. The meat would be okay for an hour or two in the mild spring air. He walked over to the greenhouse and investigated the damage. After he figured out what needed to be done, he set to work.

95

When Lorene opened her eyes, it was nearly dusk outside. Wait, she'd fallen asleep? She sat up, trying to get her bearings. She'd returned home from Juanita Weaver's house earlier today after helping her replant her garden, along with six others she'd worked on. She was worn out. But she hadn't meant to take a nap, only to rest a little before going outside and finally tackling her own garden and figuring out what to do about the greenhouse. She yawned and stood. Thirsty, she went to the kitchen to get a glass of water.

Whack! Whack! Whack!

She stopped and faced the back door. Was someone hammering??

Whack! Whack! Whack!

Lorene opened the door to see Jonas outside, hammering on the frame of her greenhouse. She blinked and looked again, wondering if she was sleep-walking and imagining him there. Sure enough, it was him. She left the house and walked to the greenhouse.

When she reached it, he turned and looked at her. "*Gut* evening." He smiled.

Oh my. Her heart fluttered in her chest. She'd never seen Jonas smile before. Not like this, anyway. It changed his entire face, and when she saw the sparkle in his eyes, she wobbled. *My knees are shaking? Because of Jonas Stoltzfus?* "Wh-what—" she cleared her throat "—are you doing?"

"Nailing together a few boards the tree missed." He held up the hammer. "I hope you don't mind. I found this in the shed."

"*Mei daed's* hammer... I don't mind you using it, I'm just..."

"Surprised?"

"*Ya.* Very surprised.

He walked over to her. "You've been busy helping everyone else. It's time someone helped

you."

The sincere warmth in his words almost brought tears to her eyes. She chalked it up to being so tired from all the physical labor. But there was something else too. Something happening between them she'd never experienced before. She had no idea what it was...but she liked the feeling.

He turned and looked at the greenhouse again. "The damage isn't as bad as it seems. If you want, I can take a look at your *Daed's* plans and get this back up for you in a couple of days."

His timing couldn't be better. She could grow some vegetables in time for the end of summer and have some to sell at the market. It wouldn't be much, but it would be something. She didn't want to take him away from his job, though. "What about your work?"

"It can wait." He faced her again. "Getting this greenhouse up and running is more important."

She could hardly believe what she was hearing. Or that Jonas was the one saying it. She wasn't sure what to say, other than, *"Danki."*

He smiled once more.

She thought she might actually swoon, and she'd never swooned in her life. "I'll, ah, fix us something. To eat. *Ya*, to eat."

"Sounds gut." He went back to work.

The sound of him hammering followed her as she went inside, still floating on the sweet emotions his smile caused inside her. Although she'd been consumed with hard work these past two weeks, he hadn't been far from her mind. Truth be told, she missed him, especially when she was by herself at home. The night of the storm it had been so nice having him there with her. Now he was helping her with her greenhouse. He seemed different, too. Kinder. Less tense. *And his amazing smile...*

She shook her head, but she was still smiling as she started supper. *Lord, you really do work in mysterious ways.*

~

True to his word, Jonas rebuilt the greenhouse in less than a week. While he completed that job, Lorene tackled her garden. Still tired from helping her friends, she worked more slowly than usual, getting rid of the dead plants, tilling the soil again, adding nutrients and compost, dividing the rows, and putting in new veggies and flowers she'd purchased from a nursery two towns away that hadn't been affected by the storm. Picking them up had taken her an entire day since she couldn't drive her buggy to the nursery and had to hire a taxi, but the employees were nice and one of them was a master gardener. They had traded a few gardening tips before she went back to Gatesville.

"Can I help?"

She looked up at Jonas, her knees aching even though she was kneeling on her foam pad. He was a man of few words, and she liked how he always got to the point. She nodded, and he knelt next to her. She handed him a green pepper plant. "That goes there." She pointed to the space next to her.

He took the plant and looked at it. "What do I do?"

She'd forgotten his late wife had always done the gardening, so she explained her method of planting the vegetable. After a few tries, the two of them made short work of the row. When they reached the end, there was one plant left. Lorene reached for it at the same time he did, and their fingers brushed.

"Sorry," she said with a slight chuckle.

He didn't say anything, but his tender look made her forget her sore knees and twinging back. *Oh my.*

He got to his feet and held out his hand. She took it, allowing him to help her up. His glasses had slipped down to the tip of his nose and, without thinking, she gently repositioned them as his gaze held hers.

She needed to move away now. They still had to put the gardening and carpentry tools away as they did every night. She would make supper while he read the paper, and an hour or two after the meal, he would go home...every night.

And every night, she missed him more.

But there was a question that had been in her mind since he'd started working on the greenhouse, and she needed an answer. "Jonas?"

"*Ya?*"

"Why are you helping me?"

He averted his eyes. "Like I said, you needed help."

Disappointment threaded through her, but she decided to press further. "Is that the only reason?"

He paused, still not looking at her. "What other reason would there be?"

His words brought her back to reality. Of course, there wasn't another reason, and her question was a foolish one. "Wow, am I tired," she said, moving away from him and grasping at any excuse to cover for herself. She faked a yawn. "I think I'm ready for bed!"

Jonas gave her a questioning look. "Okay, I'll let you get some rest."

She yawned again, this one more exaggerated than the first. But she couldn't let him leave without thanking him properly. When he started to go, she touched his forearm. "Jonas?"

He looked at her hand for a long moment before finally meeting her gaze. "*Ya?*"

Did his voice sound husky, or was she imagining—more like wishing, actually—it was? Unable to stop herself, she moved closer. "I never would have been able to do this without your help. Well, I could have, but it would have taken me weeks instead of days." Oh great, now she was tearing up. But she couldn't help it. "I'm so grateful for what you've done for me."

His eyes held hers, and the world disappeared. For some reason, words didn't seem enough, and she did something she'd never done to a man other than her father. She hugged Jonas, and to her surprise he hugged her back. For a wiry man, he had strong arms and a solid torso, and she couldn't help but melt against him.

And she did the unthinkable.

She kissed him.

Just a peck on the cheek, and that was all she'd intended. But she couldn't resist kissing his mouth and was stunned when he didn't move away. Was he kissing her back? She had no clue. All she sensed was warmth spreading through her down to the tips of her toes.

He jerked away. And when she saw the shocked look on his face, she knew she'd made a mistake.

"I, uh, better get home." He turned on his heel and rushed off, the same way he'd left the evening he yelled at her without provocation. But today she understood what she'd done. Shame filled her as she trudged back to the house.

"Why did I do that, Celia?" she moaned when she walked into the kitchen. She stared at the plant. *"Why* did I kiss him?" *I'm forty-five years old, but I feel like a confused teenager.* What was she supposed to do now?

CHAPTER FIVE

*J*onas was halfway to his house when he halted on the side of the road. He was running away from Lorene again, this time for good reason. Her hug had stunned him, but that didn't compare to the pleasure he'd experienced in her arms. She was soft and comforting, like a warm blanket on a cold, dark night. Even though he should have let her go, he couldn't. And when she kissed him...the ice around his heart started to melt. There was no way he could resist kissing her back.

Over the past week of them working together, he'd sensed something shifting inside him, and emotions he'd thought had died long ago had come back to life. He couldn't wait to see her each day, to hear the sweet sound of her humming and singing as she toiled in the garden. It made rebuilding the greenhouse not only faster, but pleasant. They had fallen into a comfortable rhythm in the evenings, and it had become harder and harder to go back to home to his empty house. Lorene had brought light and laughter to his life, and until now, he hadn't known how deeply he'd been swimming in darkness. Even better, he hadn't felt a single twinge of guilt for enjoying their time together.

Until the kiss.

He shoved his hands in his pockets and started to walk again, ignoring the loud buzzing of the cicadas and crickets in the fields on both sides of the road. He recognized the growing feelings he had for Lorene. He'd experienced them before, although they were different with Mary. Perhaps because Lorene was so different from his late wife. *I'm different than I was back then, too.*

He'd never thought he would even look at another woman, much less fall for one. Mary was the only one for him, so he thought. But spending time with Lorene made him happy. She was a beautiful woman, both inside and out. And that kiss...*whoa.* She had only given him an innocent peck. He was the one who had turned it into something else...and he couldn't deny he wanted more. When he was finally able to pull away, he saw the bewilderment in her eyes, and he knew he'd crossed a line.

Guilt battled with passion in his heart, and by the time he was at the end of his driveway, he was distraught. He walked to the front porch and sat down on the middle step, unable to go inside. He bowed his head. *What do I do now, Lord? Did I ruin our friendship? Can I even be friends with Lorene, knowing how I feel?* He quietly prayed, waiting for an answer. His own words came back to mind, words he'd spoken to Griffin last year at the community Christmas supper he and Hope had hosted.

Trust me, you don't want to waste your time denying your feelings. I did with Mary for three years. I could have had three years longer with her if I hadn't been so stubborn.

Jonas had been referring to Griffin's feelings for Hope. But now the words applied to himself. He'd missed out on extra time with Mary because he'd been afraid she wouldn't return his love. He'd been young and dumb at the time. Was he going to make the same mistake twice?

His thoughts ground to a chilling halt. What if he revealed his heart to Lorene? Would she reject him? Or what if she didn't, and things between them grew serious...

His breathing almost stopped. He couldn't survive losing someone he loved so dearly. Not again.

The sound of crunching gravel made him lift his head. He didn't have to squint to recognize Lorene walking up his driveway. His heart did a back flip, and his palms grew damp, but he wasn't sure if it from his attraction to her or his fear of the future. She had to be furious with him for running off yet again. *Apology number three, coming right up.* He stood, wiped his hands on his thighs, and thrust them behind his back, determined to focus on his apology and not the terrifying emotions turning in his gut.

She marched toward him, a determined look on her face. Uh oh, he really was in trouble. When she reached him, she put her hands on her hips like she usually did when she was annoyed. "Jonas Stoltzfus," she said, looking him straight in the eye.

He steeled himself for a deserved rebuke for running away from her again. But he couldn't stop gazing at her. Even when she was mad, she was pretty.

She inhaled, dropping her hands to her sides. "I'm sorry."

◁◁

Lorene fought with herself the entire walk to Jonas's. More than once she almost turned around, but she wouldn't sleep a wink tonight if she didn't get things settled between them. She'd kissed him, and she needed to apologize. They were both adults, and there was no need to avoid each other. She'd made a mistake, and she would rectify it.

But as soon as she said the apology, she could sense there was something wrong. She'd expected him to be upset with her, even angry. Instead, his eyes were filled with pain as he looked away from her. "There's *nix* to be sorry about," he mumbled.

"B-but I hugged you. And I kissed you." The words came out in a rush. "And just so you know, I don't *geh* around kissing anyone. In fact, I've never kissed a man before in my life." Maybe she shouldn't have made that particular admission. How awkward. "I mean, I'm not, um, I…" Oh boy. She needed to stop talking.

"It's okay," he said, finally looking at her. His expression was guarded, as if he was hiding something.

"Um, what's okay? The apology? The…" she gulped. "Hug? Kiss?"

He scratched his forehead but didn't respond. Now he was looking pained again as he shifted from one foot to the other.

"Jonas." Uninvited, she sat down beside him on the step. "I really am sorry."

He didn't respond, only scrubbed his hand across his face.

She knew she'd made a mistake, but she hadn't expected the kiss to make him this upset. "I promise I won't do it again," she said. "I was just so thankful for your help."

Turning to her, he said, "And that's why you kissed me?"

Lorene glanced at her lap. Now it was her turn to feel uncomfortable. She valued the truth, and even though it would be embarrassing, she couldn't bring herself to lie to him. "*Nee,*" she whispered. "There's another reason."

"There is?"

This was harder than she thought, and she probably looked foolish to him. Then again, this wasn't the first time she'd been foolish, and probably wouldn't be the last. She lifted her chin and faced him. "I kissed you because I wanted to. I know I shouldn't have, but what's done is done. Time to move on." She crossed her arms over her chest and gave him a curt nod.

Jonas pushed up his glasses. "You're serious, aren't you?"

"Absolutely." She lifted her chin even higher to make her point.

He stared at the ground, threading his fingers through his hair.

Not a good sign. He stayed silent, and she wasn't sure what to do. Get up and leave? Sit here and watch the grass grow? *Why isn't he saying something?* She'd take anything at this point.

Finally, he sat up and blew out a long breath. Looked at her again. "What if I don't want to move on?"

~

Jonas' nerves were twisted in knots, but he couldn't back down. She had been truthful with him, and it was only fair for him to be honest with her, no matter how anxious he was.

"I don't understand," she said, letting her crossed arms drop to her sides.

He started to thrust his hands through his hair again but stopped. Taking a deep breath, he said, "I'm not great with words. All I know is that my life changed the day you brought a meal to me when my ankle was broken."

"It has?"

"*Ya.*" His heart pounded in his chest, but he continued. "For the better."

"Mine too," she said softly.

"I didn't mind the hug or kiss. I kissed you back, *ya?*"

Her face turned redder than he'd ever seen it. "You left so suddenly, I didn't know what to think, other than I'd made a mistake."

He sighed. "I made the mistake. At least I thought I did."

Lorene frowned. "Jonas, you're confusing me."

"Sorry. Like I said, I'm not *gut* at this."

Her expression softened. "Just say what's on your mind."

Those words were the encouragement he needed. "I care about you, Lorene. I didn't think I could ever say those words to another woman after Mary died. But here I am, saying them to you."

Her hand covered her heart. "That's so sweet, Jonas. But…"

Uh oh. He didn't like where this was going. Maybe he should have kept his feelings to himself. "But what?" he managed to say.

"Remember when you asked me why I never got married?" When he nodded, she continued. "I wasn't completely truthful. I'm not like other Amish women. I've always been happy being single, and I'm fine with not having kinner. I've been asked out over the years, but I always refused. I was busy with my gardening, my friends, and my parents. It sounds strange, but I never thought I was missing anything in my life. Until now."

Jonas exhaled, not even realizing he'd been holding his breath.

"But I'm scared," she said, her voice barely audible. "I never expected to feel this way, especially about you."

His brow arched. "What's that supposed to mean?"

"I'm sorry. I'm not trying to insult you—"

"I know," he said, grinning. "I'm just teasing you."

"Well, Jonas Stoltzfus, I didn't know you had it in you." She grinned. "I suspected it, though."

He chuckled. "For what it's worth, I'm scared too." He turned serious. "But I think we can figure things out together, *ya?* I'm willing to try if you are."

"*Ya*," she said, her smile reaching straight to his heart. "I'm definitely willing to try."

EPILOGUE

*N*ovember

Lorene put the last few celery sticks in a mason jar filled with water and set it on a table. There. She'd grown the celery in her greenhouse and had harvested it for tomorrow's ceremony. Rebecca, Hope, and a few of her other friends had recently left after spending the afternoon helping her with the wedding preparations. All she had to do in the morning was put on her navy-blue wedding dress and marry the man she loved.

She slipped on her coat and walked outside. Tables would be set up early in the morning and the ceremony would be held in her backyard. Her garden was empty now, but her greenhouse was filled with seedlings and other plants and flowers again, thanks to Jonas's help. He was developing an excellent green thumb, and together they had built not only a blooming garden, but also a strong relationship. With God's help, they had conquered their fears, together.

"Lorene?"

Hearing his voice, she turned around. He'd cleaned her barn and had settled Nick into his new stall next to her horse, Minnie. Stars sprinkled the night sky as he moved to stand next to her. He smelled like soap and the freshly laundered clothes he'd moved into her bedroom today. His house would be up for sale next week, and tonight would be his last night to stay there.

He put his arm around her waist. "Ready for tomorrow?"

She leaned her head against his shoulder. "*Ya*. More than ready."

"I love you, Lorene." He moved to hold her in his arms. "Did I tell you that today?"

"You did, but you can never say it too much." She kissed the tip of his nose. "I love you too, Jonas. And I'm ready for us to be Gatesville's most unlikely married couple, or so everyone else says."

"*Nix* wrong with that." He kissed her lightly on the mouth, drawing her close. "*Danki* for loving me, *lieb*. You've filled this cranky old man with joy."

"Who are you calling old? And you haven't been cranky since—"

"Since I met you."

She laughed. "There was the time you yelled at me, though."

"I did give you an apology. But if you need another one…" He leaned over and gave her a second sweet kiss. *Oh my.*

She rested her head against his chest, hearing the steady thump of his heartbeat through his sweater. *Bliss.* Love had unexpectedly bloomed between them, and they were ready to start their new life together.

ABOUT THE AUTHOR

USA Today Best-Selling author **Kathleen Fuller** has written over fifty-five books in the Amish and contemporary romance genres. To find out more about her books, visit www.kathleenfuller.com.

FINDING HER AMISH HOME

DEBBY GIUSTI

FINDING HER AMISH HOME
is dedicated to my wonderful readers.
Thank you for your support! You're the reason I write.

CHAPTER ONE

I'm lost!" Melanie Taylor groaned aloud as she steered her Honda to the side of the road and checked her cell phone once again. No bars. No signal. No way to access GPS.

She should have realized cell coverage would be weak at best in the higher elevations of the North Georgia mountains. So much for trying to find her half sister before dark. Reason cautioned her to turn around and head back to Mountain Grove, the small town she had driven through some twenty minutes earlier. A sign on the side of the road had indicated lodging and a diner that would provide for her overnight needs.

Much as she didn't want to change her plans, she had spent twenty-two years without knowing her birth family. She could wait one more night before her patience wore thin. Still, she didn't want anything else to stop her from connecting with the half sister she'd only recently learned existed.

The setting sun hung low in the sky, and a strong blast of wind whipped down the mountain, buffeting her car. Hearing the clip-clop of horses' hooves, she glanced in the rearview mirror and spied a buggy approaching. A man wearing a wide-brimmed black hat tugged on the reins and pulled his mare to a stop next to her car.

She rolled down her window and grimaced at the influx of cold, damp air. Dark clouds overhead warned of an encroaching spring storm, which only complicated her situation. Catching a windblown strand of blond hair, she nodded to the tall man with broad shoulders, whose full lips angled into a troubled frown.

"Something is wrong?" he asked in the irregular—at least to her ears—splay of words typical of the Amish rhythm of speech.

"I'm trying to find Rural Route 95." She held up the address on her cell phone as evidence of her dilemma, then realizing the electronic device might garner his disapproval, she pulled her hand into the car and shrugged. "I think I took a wrong turn when I drove through town."

"This is not something about which to worry." Even with the blustery wind, she heard a warm resonance in his voice that spoke of helpful concern. "Remain on this road for about five miles. Route 95 veers to the left. You'll see a sign for the old quarry."

A rock quarry? "I'm looking for the Schrock family."

His eyes widened ever so slightly. "Tobias Schrock's family?"

"I don't know Tobias. I need to find Fannie Schrock."

"His daughter." The man's face twisted for a moment.

"Is there a problem?" she asked, unsure of how to read his expression.

"Just be careful so you are not caught in the storm." He tipped his head, flicked the reins, and guided his mare forward.

Only five miles to go. Melanie would be at the house soon. Feeling a surge of optimism, she pulled a tube of gloss from her purse, swiped it over her lips, then fluffed her long, blond curls with her fingers. A nervous tingle fluttered through her stomach in anticipation of the family reunion that awaited her. With a toss of her head, she eased her car back onto the mountain road and waved as she passed the buggy. The helpful Amish man returned the gesture, causing her to smile.

She hoped Tobias Schrock would be as accommodating.

The fading rays of the sun cut through the tall pines that flanked the road, and twilight had settled over the mountain by the time Melanie turned onto Route 95. Not long thereafter, she guided her Honda onto the Schrock property, braked to a stop, and stared at the two-story clapboard house. An Amish home, she surmised from the outdoor water pump, clotheslines, and lack of telephone poles and electrical wiring. The small porch was cast in shadow, and a barn with its door gaping open sat at the side of the house. A number of outbuildings were situated nearby.

Chastising herself for imagining the Schrock's lived in a brick ranch with a white picket fence, she climbed from her car and pulled the letter that had precipitated her mountain trip from her purse. Glancing again at the message, she stared at the name the DNA testing company claimed was her biological half sister.

Fannie Schrock.

Pulling in a determined breath, she climbed the rickety porch steps and swallowed with apprehension as the door opened. A large man with a bulbous nose and deep-set eyes lifted his brow in question. He wore a blue shirt and black pants held up by suspenders. His ebony hair was cut below his ears, and a beard outlined his chin and sallow cheeks.

"Good evening, sir. I'm Melanie Taylor." She held out her hand in greeting and waited for the man to accept the handshake, but he remained motionless and stared at her in silence.

Peering around the brooding figure, she spied a woman, probably twenty years her senior, dressed in typical Amish garb and standing near a large wooden table. She was tall and bony, with a pointed nose, pursed lips, and a pensive gaze that made Melanie worry about the next question she posed.

"Are you Fannie Schrock?" Melanie heard the anxiety in her own voice.

The man shifted to obstruct her view into the house. "What do you want?" he demanded.

She offered him a weak smile and cleared her throat. "I'm looking for Fannie Schrock. Does she live here?"

The woman stepped forward and glared at her. "What business do you have with Fannie?"

So, the older woman wasn't Fannie. A rush of relief fluttered over Melanie.

"It involves a DNA test." She clutched the letter in her hand. "Fannie and I were a match."

The woman narrowed her gaze. "This is impossible."

"Actually, I have the information that was sent to me." Melanie held up the letter for the woman to read.

She shook her head. "It is a mistake."

"May I speak to Fannie?" Melanie pressed, suddenly fearful her attempt to find her half sister would go unheeded.

The woman made a shooing motion with her hand. "You've disrupted this home. Leave now and do not return."

She closed the door. The lock clicked into place.

Melanie stood for a long moment, overwhelmed with a sense of loss as her hopes of connecting with her birth family shattered like broken glass.

Why had she even tried to find her biological family? Her adoptive parents claimed she was never satisfied, which wasn't true. She was grateful for having a place to live, for food and shelter, and for the bare essentials they had shared. However, she didn't want things. She wanted love, something the Taylors found impossible to provide.

Hot tears burned her eyes. Why had she thought her life would change for the better because of a DNA test? She didn't deserve to be happy, as her adoptive mother had told her too many times. Through it all, Melanie had believed she would one day find a family who loved her. Now, after her less-than-enthusiastic welcome at the Schrock home, she realized her adoptive mother may have been right.

Melanie returned the letter to her purse and hurried to her car. The wind moaned through the branches of the oak trees and tall pines as she struggled to open the driver's side door and hold it in place lest it catch in the wind.

She glanced up to see the last rays of light line the horizon, and her breath caught. A woman stared down at her from the second-story window. She had an oval face and appeared a bit younger, but it was her expression that caused Melanie's breath to hitch. In spite of the age difference, the woman could be her twin.

～

Melanie guided her car onto Route 95. Mountain Grove was about fifteen miles away. She'd rent a room there and find information tomorrow about the Schrock family and Fannie in particular.

Rain started to fall and hammered the roof of her car. She turned on the wipers and the defroster to enhance visibility. The rain increased in intensity, thunder bellowed, and lightning cut through the night sky.

She veered right at the fork in the road. Her mind was on the Schrocks and, most especially, the woman in the window. Distracted by her thoughts, Melanie failed to notice the pickup truck approaching from the rear until it started to pass her, then swerved into her car as if to run her off the road. She gasped and turned the wheel to keep from colliding with the pickup. Her car careened off the pavement, skidded along the berm, and slammed into a ditch. The airbag exploded. Something hot burned her right arm.

Confused for a long moment, she glanced at the pickup that stopped on the road. A man stepped onto the wet pavement. Unable to see his face between the falling rain and the glare of headlights, she shoved the airbag aside, pried open the door, and climbed from her car.

"You ran me off the road." Frustrated by the accident, she expected an apology at the least.

He raced toward her. Fearful of his haste, she cowered by her car. All too quickly, he grabbed her by the hair and wrenched her head back.

"Let go of me!" she screamed and flailed her arms.

"Strangers aren't welcome in Mountain Grove." His voice, low and menacing, made her heart pound nearly out of her chest.

Struggling to free herself from his hold, she arched her back. He tugged all the harder and wrapped his left hand around her neck. She dug her nails into his flesh.

He growled like a mad dog and threw her into the ditch.

Frigid water soaked her clothing. His boot pressed on her back and shoved her deeper into the rain-filled basin until her mouth and nose were covered by the muddy water.

"Please, God!" an internal voice screamed.

The pressure on her back eased. She lifted her head at the sound of footsteps retreating across the pavement. Stumbling to her feet, she watched as the pickup revved into gear and disappeared from sight.

Gasping for air and shivering with a mix of cold and fear, she climbed back into her car and turned the ignition. The engine failed to engage. She turned the key again and again.

"No!" she cried into the darkness. Something caught her eye, a glimmer of light in the distance.

Needing help, she exited the car and climbed the hill. Her feet were unsteady on the rocky terrain and slid out from under her. She caught herself, pulled herself upright, and continued her climb, following the light that grew brighter.

Her head pounded. Out of breath and holding her aching side, she was relieved when a house came into view. She hurried toward the porch, tripped up the steps, and knocked on the door.

"Help me, please." She glanced over her shoulder into the darkness. "I need help."

The door opened, and a big man stood backlit in the doorway. She heard his exhale of breath as he reached for her.

Her determination waned, and the last of her resolve evaporated as if she had been holding on until she could get to safety. She tried to remain focused and breathed out another plea for help as she collapsed into the man's outstretched arms.

CHAPTER TWO

*J*acob Brubaker wasn't one to call on *Gott*, but seeing the bedraggled woman who had fallen into his arms made him mutter the Lord's name, not in vain, but in a confused prayer.

"Emma, come quickly. A woman is in need."

His sister rushed from the kitchen. A tiny gasp escaped her lips. "*Gott* in heaven, help us to help her."

His sister was far better at articulating her needs to the Almighty.

"Who is she, Jacob?"

He carried the woman to the rocker by the fire. "I saw her on the road. She asked for directions to the Schrock farm. Get a warm cloth to wipe her face."

Jacob lifted the muddy strands of hair from the woman's forehead and rubbed his hand over her pale cheek.

He grabbed a throw from a nearby blanket chest and wrapped it around her slender shoulders. "Ma'am, open your eyes. You are safe, and the fire is hot."

Long lashes fluttered. He cupped her chin and angled it up ever so slightly. "Open your eyes."

She blinked, then jerked with surprise.

"You're safe. My name is Jacob Brubaker. You asked me for directions on the mountain road."

Her blue eyes narrowed. She stared first at him and then at his sister, who returned from the kitchen with a damp cloth and a glass of water.

"I'm Emma Keim, Jacob's sister." She wiped the cloth over the woman's face, then cleaned the mud from her hands and held the glass to the woman's lips. "You are thirsty, *yah?*"

Freeing her hands from under the blanket, the woman took the glass, held it to her lips, and drank deeply.

Emma glanced at Jacob, her gaze pensive.

The woman wiped her mouth and then handed the glass back to Emma. "Thank you."

"You have a name?" Jacob asked.

"Mel . . . Melanie Taylor."

"You are not from here." He stated the obvious.

"I live in Cleveland."

"Ohio?" Emma's eyes widened.

A slight smile toyed at the pretty woman's lips. "Cleveland, Georgia. I was raised in South Georgia, near Fort Rickman."

An Amish community was located not far from the Army post. "You are military?" he asked.

"No, but my father—my adoptive father—worked at the commissary on post."

"But you have come to Mountain Grove to see the Schrocks?" he asked. "Did someone there hurt you?"

"Someone in a pickup ran me off the road." She paused for a moment, as if replaying what had happened. "I turned the wheel to keep from colliding with the truck and ran into the ditch."

She glanced at the burn on her arm. "The airbag exploded."

"I have salve." Emma retrieved the first aid kit. She cleaned the burn, applied ointment, and wrapped it with a bandage, all while the woman continued to explain what had happened.

"The man attacked me and threw me into the ditch. My mouth and nose were underwater. I—"

Emma patted her shoulder. "You are here now."

"My car—"

Jacob nodded. "I'll see to it."

"The keys are in the ignition." She stared at him for a long moment. "I have a small tote in the trunk."

"I will bring it here before I pull the car from the ditch so you can change into dry clothing. After I return with your car, we will eat something *gut* that Emma has prepared."

"But—" The woman flicked her gaze around the main room. "I-I can't intrude."

"Nonsense. You are here and can stay the night. There is a guest room upstairs next to my sister's room." A thought bothered him. "Unless there is someone waiting for you at home. Someone who will worry if you do not return tonight."

She shook her head, then as if realizing her mistake, she caught herself. "I'll call them on my cell."

Perhaps the woman feared revealing that she lived alone. She didn't know Jacob or his sister, and women had to be careful. Her plight tugged at his heart.

He glanced at his sister. "Then it is settled, *yah?*"

"*Yah,*" Emma replied.

Jacob grabbed his coat and hat and headed to the door. In the barn, he retrieved his tools and placed them in the back of his buggy. He would need his mare, Bertha, to pull the car free from the ditch so he could assess the damage. What he had learned working as a mechanic in Knoxville had paid off a number of times. He hoped it would tonight as well.

The rain had stopped, but the night was damp. He found the car and wondered how Melanie had kept from being more seriously injured. Perhaps *Gott* had His protective hand on her shoulder.

The mare pulled the car out of the ditch. Jacob checked the engine, adjusted a loose wire, and was relieved when the motor started. He returned his buggy to the barn, dropped the woman's tote at the house, and then hurried down the hill on foot and drove the car back to his sister's farm.

For the three years he had lived away from the Amish community, Jacob had owned a car like so many other young men he worked with in Knoxville. After his parents and brother-in-law had died in a tragic buggy accident, he had returned to help Emma. Giving up his car had been difficult, although recently he hadn't thought about what he had left in Tennessee. He had thought only of being with his sister and was grateful he could help her.

He had also thought of his future once his sister found someone to love again. Would he embrace the *Englisch* world? Or would he stay in Mountain Grove and return fully to his Amish faith? He had asked *Gott* for direction. So far, the Lord had not provided an answer.

Tonight, the woman dropping into his arms had stirred something deep within him. After giving his heart too freely when he was living *Englisch*, he needed to guard himself lest he get involved with another woman who wasn't Amish.

Someone had run Melanie off the road and had used physical force to frighten her. What was it about the pretty *Englischer* that posed a threat?

He parked her Honda in the barn before he hurried back into the house. "She's in the guest room and will be downstairs soon," Emma said, as if reading his mind.

"Did she provide any more information?"

"Only that the pickup truck came from out of nowhere and surprised her."

His sister pulled another place setting of silverware from the drawer and added it to the table. "She's frightened about what happened."

"Do you blame her?"

"Who would do this, Jacob?"

"With the new housing developments popping up, we have strangers in the area. Their ways are not our ways."

His sister smiled. "Now you are thinking like the Amish."

"Have you forgotten that I am living Amish?"

"While you decide about baptism. You are twenty-four years old. It is time for you to talk to the bishop."

"And what would you have me tell him?"

"That although you lived with the *Englisch* for a few years, you have come back to the Amish faith."

"My mind is not made up yet."

"You want freedom in case something new strikes your fancy." She pursed her lips with mild disapproval, then softened her expression. "You know I appreciate what you've done for me. After Caleb died along with our parents, I did not think I could manage alone."

"The community helped you."

She nodded. "For which I am grateful, but I could not rely on their assistance forever."

"In spite of your pride, Emma, you will find another husband someday."

"*Ack*, another man will not take my Caleb's place."

"A person can find love even after loss, my dear sister." He wagged his finger in a playful gesture.

"Point that finger at yourself, Jacob. I know your heart was broken." She glanced at the pot of stew simmering on the stove and then back at her brother. "What was the woman's name?"

"Sylvia is in the past," he assured her. "Now, I am living in the present."

Footsteps sounded on the stairs. Jacob turned as Melanie stopped on the landing to stare at both of them. "Am I interrupting something?"

"No, please join us." Jacob motioned her forward.

"Dinner will be ready soon," Emma said in welcome. "You are hungry?"

Melanie descended the steps and nodded. "I was excited about my trip and skipped lunch, so your offer for dinner sounds wonderful. Again, I'm grateful for your hospitality."

"It is not a problem." Emma motioned her forward. "Come into the kitchen. I have cooked a pot of stew, and the bread is freshly baked."

"The smells wafted upstairs and made my mouth water."

Emma laughed. "Something tells me you are easy to please."

"Let me help."

"The glasses are by the sink. Fill them with water and place them on the table as I serve the food."

"Your car is in the barn," Jacob informed her. "I can look at the engine in the morning, and there's a mechanic in town who can run a more thorough check."

"I didn't think an Amish man would know about cars."

He was used to the false impressions the *Englisch* had about plain folk. "We Amish know about a lot of things."

Her brow raised, and her eyes widened.

She was slender and about half a foot shorter than his six feet. Her hair fell below her shoulders and was tied with a pink ribbon that matched her rosy cheeks. Even in the dim light from the oil lamps, he could see her flawless skin and blue eyes that held a hint of sadness.

"What about the airbag?" she asked.

"The garage can order a replacement." He glanced at the bandage on her arm. "How is your burn?"

"Much better, thanks to the salve Emma used."

"An aloe-based product," his sister said. "We will apply more in the morning."

"Burns from airbags can be a problem, although the airbag probably kept you from more serious injury."

"For which I'm thankful." She filled the glasses with water and placed them on the table as Emma served the stew.

"Please." Emma pointed to the chair next to Jacob. "We will eat now." After taking her seat, Emma bowed her head.

Melanie hesitated a moment, then as if realizing Emma was giving thanks, their visitor lowered her head. Evidently, prayer was part of her mealtime routine as well.

Jacob glanced down, wishing his heart could be as committed as his sister was to the Lord. Finally, he offered a quick, silent prayer. *Thank you for keeping the woman from more serious harm.*

"This looks delicious," Melanie said after their moment of blessing.

She lifted the fork to her mouth and made a sound of pleasure that brought a curl of warmth to his gut. Not from the food, but from Melanie's obvious pleasure. The newcomer was pretty and nice, but why would she be involved with Fannie Schrock? Tobias had died a few years ago, and Verla Zook had taken over Fannie's care while Verla's brother, Leroy, claimed to manage the property, which under his less than stellar stewardship was falling into disrepair.

The Schrock farm was no place for a sweet woman like Melanie. Unless there was something he wasn't seeing or didn't know about her. Sylvia, the woman he had dated in Knoxville, had seemed sweet and had wormed her way into his heart, only to discard him for someone else.

Women can't be trusted, especially fancy women, his voice of reason warned. Yet sitting next to Melanie made him hush the voice and think only of her blue eyes and blond hair.

CHAPTER THREE

*M*orning came early, as it always did on an Amish farm. Jacob inhaled the crisp air mixed with the scent of hay and thought again of their visitor. No doubt, she would sleep late as was the *Englisch* custom, although he couldn't understand why anyone would want to miss the sunrise, the most beautiful time of the day that reflected all of God's glory. Sylvia hadn't been interested in anything to do with the Lord nor did she ever venture out of her house before noon, no matter how much he tried to convince her that the morning had a special beauty.

He glanced at the upstairs guest room and saw a light flicker in the window. Evidently, Melanie was awake, which surprised him. He hauled feed to the cattle and filled the troughs with water, then washed at the pump and hurried inside. He hung his hat on a wall peg, dropped his coat over another peg, and turned as Melanie hurried downstairs.

Her expression brightened when she saw him.

He stood for a moment, taking in her wholesome beauty. She wore jeans and a sweater and had her hair pulled over her ears, this time tied with a navy ribbon. Her eyes held his gaze until his sister hurried into the room.

"Good morning." Emma smiled. "I hope I didn't wake you with noise from the kitchen."

"Oh, no. I usually get up early." Melanie glanced out the window. "The dawn is always so beautiful."

Jacob's chest tightened at her comment. "Many people do not realize how special the new day is."

124

"The Amish are early risers," Emma added. "It sounds as if you could have come from an Amish background."

The woman's face clouded. "I'm not sure where I came from."

"You have family in South Georgia?" Jacob recalled what she had said the night before.

"I was adopted by a family there, but I'm trying to find my biological family. I—" She glanced down and sighed before she looked at him again. "I did a DNA test to find my family and received a letter saying the company had found a possible half sister. The name they provided was Fannie Schrock."

"You and Fannie are related?" Emma's eyes widened.

"If the test is to be trusted."

"Yet, Fannie is sickly," Emma said. "I do not know how she could have done this test. Surely Verla would not have allowed it. The Amish do not usually do such things."

"Who's Verla?" Melanie asked.

"Verla Zook is the housekeeper who cares for Fannie. She's been with the family since Fannie was born."

"Black hair and a pointed nose?"

"*Yah.*" Emma nodded. "You met her?"

"After I talked to the man who answered the door."

"Probably Verla's brother. Leroy moved in when Tobias's health started to decline. Leroy helps to maintain the small farm, but his demeanor is sharp and leaves a bad taste in my mouth, like the bitterroot we take for fevers and sore throats."

"What about Fannie's father?" Melanie asked.

"Tobias died about five years ago. He had medical problems, although I heard he was showing signs of dementia." Emma poured coffee and handed a mug to Jacob and another to Melanie.

"*Danki.*" Jacob glanced at their guest. "If you and Fannie are related, then was Tobias Schrock your father?"

Melanie's face tightened as if the question troubled her. "I . . . I'm not sure. What do you know about Fannie's mother?"

Emma shrugged. "I know only that her name before marriage was Rebecca Yoder, and she died when Fannie was a baby."

"Our family is from the other side of the mountain," Jacob explained. "Emma and her husband moved here after marriage, and I came to help her after his death."

Melanie's gaze softened. "I'm so sorry for your loss, Emma."

"Death is *Gott's* will that we must accept."

"Yet it is hard." Melanie's voice was filled with concern.

"God provides."

Jacob noticed the cloud of grief that flitted across his sister's face before she hurried to the stove.

"Breakfast is almost ready."

"What may I do to help?" Melanie asked.

"The silverware is in the drawer closest to the sink. While you set the table, I'll fill the plates."

"Jacob, you said there was a mechanic in town. I'll drive there this morning and have him look at my car before I head back to Cleveland."

He was surprised by her comment. "You're leaving?"

"I had hoped to find my sister. Instead, I found people who seem upset to have a stranger at their door."

"The Amish are often reserved around *Englischers*, especially if they don't know them," Emma shared.

"What about talking to the sheriff?" Jacob asked. "He needs to know about the man who accosted you."

"I'm not one to complain to law enforcement, although I would hate for the man to attack someone else driving on the mountain road."

"I have to deliver seed to town. Why don't I meet you at the sheriff's office?" Jacob suggested. "Having someone local with you might be of help."

Her face brightened. "That would be wonderful. Thank you."

"If you have to leave your car overnight at the garage, you could come back here with me," he offered. "That is, if you don't mind traveling in a buggy. It's a bit different from a car, but the sunshine is peeking out from behind the cloud cover, and the weather should be mild today."

"It will be a new experience."

She smiled, and something tugged at his chest. He glanced at his sister, who was staring at him, her brow raised as if she could sense the confusion he felt.

"Just as Jacob mentioned," Emma added as she plated the eggs and bacon, "if your car isn't ready today, you must come back here to stay for another night."

"Are you sure?" Melanie asked.

"Certainly. I would not have made the offer if I did not want you to return to our house. There is a B and B in town, but the rooms are in demand with tourists who love to visit remote mountain spots. It is doubtful there would be a vacancy."

"Walter runs the garage, but he's not known for speed," Jacob admitted. "The repair job might take a few days."

A few days with Melanie underfoot. He didn't know if that would be *gut* or very, very troubling.

◁▷

After dropping her car off at the garage in town, Melanie followed the mechanic's directions to the sheriff's office. She passed the Grove Café and noticed a few folks inside enjoying a late breakfast. Melanie made a note to return for lunch if she needed to stay in town longer than expected.

As much as she appreciated Emma and Jacob's hospitality, she hated to be a nuisance, even if she did enjoy the peace and calm she had found at their house. A home filled with love, she mused. Exactly what she wanted for her own life.

She glanced up at the sound of an approaching buggy. A tall woman, big-boned with a thin nose visible under her black bonnet, guided her mare along the street. As she neared, Melanie recognized the woman she had seen yesterday, Verla Zook.

Another person—considerably smaller in stature—sat huddled next to her, bonnet low, with a cape pulled tight around her shoulders. A light blanket covered her lap. The young woman glanced at Melanie, and her eyes widened. She leaned out of the buggy and waved her hand as if hoping to catch Melanie's attention.

Once again, Melanie was drawn to the younger woman's blond hair and blue eyes as well as the sunken cheeks she had noticed yesterday. "Fannie," she called.

As the buggy passed, Verla glanced at Melanie and grimaced, then she flicked the reins to encourage the mare to increase her pace.

Melanie ran into the street and stared after the women until the buggy disappeared from sight. Her shoulders slumped with disappointment to have once again lost the opportunity to connect with Fannie. Tears of frustration clouded her eyes as she turned back toward the sidewalk.

An engine sounded. She glanced at the oncoming vehicle—a rusty pickup truck covered with mud. Through the dirty windshield, she tried to make out the face of the man behind the wheel. The truck accelerated.

She gasped as the vehicle raced by, sending up a cloud of exhaust. At the intersection, the pickup made a U-turn. The roar of the engine filled her ears. The truck accelerated even faster and headed straight toward her.

Her heart nearly stopped. Paralyzed with fear and unable to move, Melanie cried, "Dear God, help me!"

CHAPTER FOUR

*M*elanie!" Seeing what was about to happen, Jacob leaped from his buggy and shoved her out of the path of the oncoming truck. She tripped over the curb and fell to the pavement, all the while wrestling to free herself from his hold.

"You're okay," he assured her. "It's Jacob."

"But—"

The near crash had shocked her for sure. She blinked as if unable to comprehend what he had said or recognize who was speaking.

"Melanie, you're all right. The pickup's gone." He glanced over his shoulder to ensure the truth of his statement. The truck had raced down the street, turned at the next intersection, and screeched out of sight.

He helped her up and ushered her to the sidewalk.

She brushed herself off, still seemingly dazed. "I . . . I . . . don't know how it happened."

"Were you crossing the street?"

She glanced at the road. "I was on the sidewalk, a buggy went by, and I saw Fannie."

"Fannie Schrock?"

"I presume that's her name—the same young woman I saw in the upstairs window at their farm. Fannie stretched out her hand as if to grab mine. I called to her, but the woman driving the buggy made the horse go faster. Emma said her name was Verla."

"Did Verla see you?"

"She did." Melanie smoothed her hand over her thick hair. "Then she encouraged the horse to go faster as if she wanted to prevent Fannie from talking to me."

"How did the pickup get involved?"

Melanie shrugged. "I'm not sure. I heard an engine and saw the truck approach. He passed by, then turned around at the next block, and raced back."

She looked up at Jacob. "The next thing I knew, you were dragging me over the pavement."

"To keep you from being hit. It looked like you were frozen in place and unable to move. I wanted to get you out of danger, but I didn't mean to hurt you."

He glanced at the deep scrape on her left arm. "The medical clinic isn't far. I can take you there."

"The scrape is minor. Besides, you probably saved me from a more serious injury. I doubt the driver planned to veer off course."

"Did you see him?"

"Through the dirty windshield, but don't ask me to identify him. I saw a bearded face, dark eyes, and a brooding scowl."

"Could you tell if it was the same man or the same pickup that ran you off the road last night?"

"The two trucks looked similar."

Tears filled her eyes, and the confusion he saw in her gaze tugged at his heart.

"I don't understand what's happening, Jacob." Her voice was raw with emotion. "Why would anyone want to hurt me?"

~

Together, Melanie and Jacob crossed the street to the sheriff's office. Once inside, a man in uniform behind the counter motioned them forward.

"I'm Sheriff Hank Sterling. How can I help you?" The sheriff was tall and muscular with graying hair and an intense gaze.

They shook his hand and gave him their names. Melanie quickly explained about being run off the road last night and the near accident today.

"Can you identify the driver?" he asked.

She explained about the glare from the headlights yesterday as well as the mud-splattered windshield that obstructed her view of him today. "Everything happened so quickly."

"Did you see the license plate?" he asked.

"I didn't see much except the hood of the pickup coming straight toward me."

The sheriff scribbled something on a form. "A lot of mountain people drive old clunkers, especially pickups. They ride along dirt roads and rarely wash their vehicles, so finding the driver might be difficult. How can we contact you if we uncover a possible suspect?"

Melanie wrote her cell phone number on the paper the sheriff provided.

"And you're staying at the B and B?" he asked.

She glanced at Jacob. "I . . . I'm staying at Emma Keim's home."

"Near the old quarry?"

Jacob nodded. "My sister's house. That's correct."

The sheriff placed the form in a box on the corner of the counter. "I'll call you if anything comes to light. Stay safe, Ms. Taylor, and let me know when you decide to leave town. Until then, watch your back. Two incidents in as many days doesn't bode well for you. If you think of anyone who might want to do you harm, let me know."

When they stepped outside, Melanie shook her head. "I planned to return to Cleveland today in spite of wanting to connect with Fannie, but someone is out to do me harm, and I need to find out why." She pulled in a deep breath. "The man in the pickup might be trying to run me out of town, yet in reality, he's made me more determined than ever to stay in Mountain Grove."

CHAPTER FIVE

$\mathcal{A}$fter leaving the sheriff's office, Melanie pulled a tissue from her pocket and held it against her arm. Blood stained her shirt where the raw flesh had rubbed against her clothing.

"You need to have a doctor look at your arm," Jacob insisted when he noticed the stains.

Melanie tried to shove off his concern. "It's little more than a scrape."

"A scrape that needs to be cleaned at the least." He motioned her forward. "The clinic isn't far. We'll take my buggy." He helped her up into the seat and slid in next to her.

"I'm okay," she tried to assure him.

"You don't want an infection to set in. Plus, that burn from the airbag could use a little attention as well. Emma's poultice is effective in most cases, but if the doctor examines your scraped arm, he can also check the burn."

"I appreciate your concern, Jacob, although I'm more worried about Fannie. She looked pale and weak when she passed by in the buggy. Do you have any idea about her medical condition?"

"People talk about her being sickly, but I've never heard anyone mention a reason for her condition."

"If it's cancer or kidney disease, sometimes a close relative can help."

"You mean by donating an organ?"

Melanie shrugged. "Or a bone marrow transplant. I don't have any medical background, but I've read articles about how people have saved the lives of their siblings. I'll talk to the doctor."

"If he knows anything."

Melanie raised her brow. "Why wouldn't he know about her condition?"

"Some Amish are wary of doctors. I'm not sure how Verla feels, but she keeps Fannie secluded and out of the public eye. It's rare that they attend Sunday services. Often the excuse is that Fannie is too weak or having a bad day. Plus, I doubt the doctor would reveal a patient's information."

She held up her hand. "I'm not asking him to do anything unethical, but I want him to know I'm in town in case I can help."

"That's very generous, Melanie."

"It's what siblings do, Jacob. They help one another. Just like you help Emma."

The clinic wasn't far. Jacob tethered his mare to the hitching post and helped Melanie down. Together, they entered the small medical clinic. The receptionist was cordial, and Melanie didn't have to wait long before she was escorted into an exam room. A nurse took her vitals and returned with the doctor a few minutes later.

"Looks like you have a nasty scrape that needs debridement," he said after examining her arm. "I'll prescribe an antibiotic to stem any infection."

He checked the burn on her other arm. "You were in an automobile crash?"

"A man ran me off the road. The night was dark, and he started to pass my car and then angled toward me. I had to swerve off the road to keep from crashing."

"Did you notify law enforcement?"

"I just talked to the sheriff." She watched as the doctor applied ointment to the burn and covered it with a fresh bandage.

"The accident happened after I left the Schrock farm last night," she continued. "You probably know Fannie Schrock."

Melanie explained about the DNA testing. "I've heard that her health isn't good and wondered if I could assist her in some way since I'm her half sister."

The doctor paused for a moment and glanced at the nurse. "You'll have to talk to Fannie. She has a caregiver, as I recall, who helps her with her medical needs."

"Verla Zook." Melanie nodded. "But Verla wouldn't let me talk to Fannie. I thought you might know Fannie's diagnosis. If she has a genetic condition, that's something I'd like to know as well."

The doctor nodded. "I understand your concern, Miss Taylor, and your willingness to help Fannie is admirable, but I'm not at liberty to disclose information about my patients. I suggest you contact Fannie or her family."

Melanie's heart sank. Another dead end.

The nurse debrided and bandaged her wound after the doctor left the exam room. "I shouldn't say anything." The nurse lowered her voice. "Verla brings Fannie in on occasion, usually if Fannie is dehydrated or having a rough time. Verla has accepted some basic treatment for Fannie, but she doesn't allow any laboratory tests to be done and certainly nothing that would involve a toxicology screen."

"What are you saying?"

The nurse glanced at the door as if to ensure it was closed before she continued. "The doctor doesn't know what's wrong with Fannie, and it worries him. He's aware of the Amish hesitancy about medical procedures and feels his hands are tied."

"Why would Verla withhold medical care from Fannie?"

The nurse shrugged. "The doctor keeps his thoughts mostly to himself, although he's mentioned his concern a few times when Verla hurried Fannie out of here before he felt she was ready to be dismissed."

"Has he talked to the sheriff?"

"Sheriff Sterling tries not to interfere with the Amish community. He wants to keep the lines of communication open, so he's careful not to overstep his bounds."

"Is ensuring a young woman's health overstepping his bounds?" Melanie's frustration grew. "I'd say it was the right thing to do."

"I hear ya." The nurse sighed. "I've tried to talk to Fannie when she comes in, but getting her away from Verla is a problem. I hope you can help her. Fannie's a sweet person, yet she's overruled by her caregiver. I often wonder if Verla is providing care or doing harm."

∼

Melanie's reticence after they left town worried Jacob. "Does your arm hurt?" he asked, hoping to pull her from her pensive mood.

"It's fine. Thank you, Jacob, for suggesting I visit the clinic and for stopping at the pharmacy so I could pick up the antibiotic. I asked the pharmacist if he knew anything about Fannie's medical condition, but he was as hesitant to share information as the doctor. They're following the HIPAA guidelines, yet it's upsetting."

Melanie shared what the nurse had said. "People are worried about Fannie, but no one is doing anything to help her."

"It seems you arrived at the right time."

She nodded. "I think you're right. Your sister mentioned an old friend who knew Fannie's mother. She might provide more information."

"Wilma Gingerich. She and her husband have a farm not far from here. We could stop by on the way home."

"You wouldn't mind?"

"Of course not. Wilma's a *gut* woman. I'm sure she would enjoy talking to you."

Wilma was hanging wash on the line when they pulled to a stop in front of the farmhouse.

"How nice to see you, Jacob. Did you come to talk to Silas? If so, he's in one of the distant fields. I could ring the bell to fetch him."

"Do not disturb his work. It is you we have come to see." He introduced Melanie who quickly explained about the DNA test and her newfound relationship with Fannie Schrock.

"Jacob's sister said you might have information about Fannie's mother," Melanie said. "I'm wondering if Rebecca could be my mother as well. Plus, I'm worried about Fannie's health and hoped you might shed some light on her condition."

Wilma hung the last shirt on the line and picked up her wash basket. "I know nothing about Fannie's medical condition, but come inside. We can talk there."

They followed her into the neatly furnished home.

She placed the basket by the door and motioned them to the table. "Sit, please, while I pour coffee. Perhaps a piece of cake would be *gut?*"

Melanie nodded. "Thank you. Cake sounds lovely."

Once the mugs of coffee and slices of cake were in front of them, Wilma nodded to Melanie. "The last time I saw Fannie, she appeared quite frail. She has a woman who helps her, but I sometimes wonder if Verla is a bit overzealous in her caregiving."

"I hope to talk to Fannie when Verla is not hovering nearby."

"I am sure Fannie would enjoy seeing you." Wilma took a bite of cake and washed it down with coffee. "So, tell me, Melanie, what do you know about Fannie's mother?"

"Very little except that she died soon after Fannie was born. I'm not even sure if I'm related to her." Melanie explained about being adopted in South Georgia. "I've been on my own for the last three years and finally mustered the courage to take the DNA test."

"Sometimes it is hard to find our true home." Wilma glanced at Jacob. "Yet, you know Jacob and his sister?"

"I stumbled onto them last night." Again, she explained about the accident on the road. "Jacob and Emma invited me to stay."

"They are a family with a big heart." Wilma smiled at Jacob and then turned her focus back to Melanie. "As Emma told you, Rebecca Yoder was a friend of mine. She lived with her father on a small plot of land on the other side of the quarry. Her *datt* was—"

Wilma paused for a moment as if carefully choosing her words. "He was a difficult man, and he demanded so much of Rebecca. She was not allowed to take part in the youth activities—the singings or the games played together like softball and volleyball."

"That sounds like my adoptive father."

Wilma nodded. "It is hard, *yah*. Perhaps that is why Rebecca gave her heart to the *Englischer*."

Melanie leaned closer. "But I thought she was married to Tobias Schrock."

"Tobias was later. Her first love was an *Englischer*. She met him on one of the paths around the quarry where she liked to walk."

"Did they marry?"

Wilma shook her head. "Although I think that was her hope. I saw little of her after he came into her life and presumed she was spending as much time as she could with him. Soon after he left the area, she went to visit a distant relative in South Georgia."

Wilma pursed her lips. "She was gone about six months. I thought I would never see her again, then I bumped into her one day in town."

"When was that?" Melanie's face was pulled tight.

"That's easy to remember. It was right before my Natalie was born. She's twenty-two and was born in August of that year."

"I'm twenty-two, but my birthday is in July."

Jacob heard the confusion in Melanie's voice. He reached for her hand, hoping to provide support.

Wilma's gaze was filled with understanding. "Rebecca never said she was with child, although I could see changes in her slender body. Subtle changes. Most Amish families would encourage marriage, but if the father was outside the faith, this would not be possible. I cannot imagine the ire she faced when her own father found out, especially because of this man being *Englisch*. Rebecca endured a lot and, no doubt, was forced to leave home until the baby was born."

"Until . . ." Melanie's voice was little more than a whisper. "Until *I* was born."

Jacob and Melanie sat for a long moment taking in the information Wilma had just shared.

Finally, Melanie posed another question. "When did she marry Tobias?"

"Hmm." Wilma thought for a moment. "As I recall, Tobias started courting Rebecca soon after she came home. He was older, and some said she was marrying her father, meaning she had gone from the home of one older man to another."

"And Fannie was born later?"

"About a year and a half later. Verla helped with the housework following the baby's birth."

"So my mother knew Verla?" Melanie asked.

Wilma nodded. "Verla and Tobias were childhood friends. A few busy-bodies said she had hoped to marry him, but that may have been idle talk. After Fannie was born, Rebecca lost weight and became extremely weak."

DEBBY GIUSTI

Melanie folded her hands and placed them on the table. "How did she die?"

The Amish woman's face softened. "Walking along the quarry."

Melanie gasped. "She fell?"

Wilma patted her hand. "The truth can be hard to hear."

Tears filled Melanie's eyes. She sat quietly for a long moment, then glanced at Jacob and nodded as if signaling her desire to end their visit. He helped her from the chair and held on to her elbow as they thanked Wilma and walked to the buggy. Melanie's eyes were downcast, and her shoulders slumped ever so slightly as if she was overwhelmed by what she had learned.

"Your mother tried to do what was best for you, Melanie."

"I don't know what to think, Jacob. I did the DNA test to find my biological family, never expecting to learn such a painful story about my mother. I came looking for stability and love, but I'm only finding turmoil and pain. It's not what I expected, and it's not what I wanted."

"But as Wilma said, it is the truth."

She nodded and smiled weakly. "You're right. The past may not be what I wanted to find, but as painful as it is, at least now I know who my mother was and what happened to her."

CHAPTER SIX

*M*elanie's heart ached after talking to Wilma. Jacob was attentive on the ride home, but he didn't try to intrude on her thoughts. She said little at dinner and went to her room early, needing quiet time to ponder what she had learned.

The next morning, she helped Emma with the laundry and was grateful for the Amish dress Emma insisted she wear while her own things were being washed. Slipping into the crisp cotton and learning how to use straight pins to adjust the size brought pleasant thoughts of her mother to mind.

When all the freshly washed clothes were hanging on the line, she breathed in the crisp mountain air, told Emma she would be back in about an hour, and turned toward one of the paths that led up the mountain.

Jacob ran to catch up to her. "Would you like company?"

"If you don't mind, I need some time by myself."

"Of course." He pointed to a path. "The trail on the right is an easier climb and passes through a bit of woods. You'll get to a clearing where you can see the quarry. Just be careful. The paths around the rim are narrow and can be treacherous."

Questions about her mother swirled through her mind as she set out along the path. The forest was cool, and before long, she came to a clearing and was surprised to see thick vines hanging over the rocks at the top of the quarry. The path was narrow as Jacob had said, and she was careful where she stepped. Drawing closer to the edge, she stared at the drop-off, and tears burned her eyes, thinking of her mother's fall.

Walking slowly around the rim, she recognized a farmhouse at the foot of the quarry. The house where Fannie lived. Narrowing her gaze, she saw the young woman sitting in a wheelchair in a patch of sunlight.

Melanie flicked her gaze around the barnyard, searching for Leroy and Verla. Seeing neither of them, she scurried along the path that led down to the farmhouse and waved her hand in greeting as she drew closer.

Fannie glanced up. A look of surprise crossed her face, and she motioned Melanie forward. A quilt covered the younger woman's lap. Seeing it sent a surge of delight through Melanie.

Fannie smiled, and her face, although pale, lit up. Melanie dropped to her knees next to the wheelchair, took Fannie's outstretched hand, and blinked back tears of joy.

"You got the results from the DNA testing?"

"I had it sent to my friend Eli Lehman's address," Fannie said. "He secreted the letter to me. You're Melanie?"

She nodded. "Rebecca was our mother."

"But she died soon after I was born, so I never knew her." Fannie glanced back at her house. "Verla takes care of me. I overheard her talking to her brother, Leroy, about my mother giving a child up for adoption before she married my father. I told Eli that I wanted to find my sister, and he paid for the test."

She glanced at Melanie's dress. "You were driving a car when you stopped here the other night, so I didn't think you were Amish."

"You're right, Fannie. I'm not Amish, but I'm staying with Emma Keim and her brother, Jacob, and the dress belongs to Emma."

Fannie leaned closer and lowered her voice. "I don't believe our mother took her own life."

Melanie gasped. "Is that what people say?"

"It's what Verla says, but I know in my heart that a loving mother would never leave her newborn child."

A heaviness settled over Melanie. "Yet she left me in South Georgia."

"She had to because of her *datt*. He was hard on her. My own *datt* said my grandfather was a bad man. My father courted and married Rebecca to get her away from her father."

"What else did your father say?"

Fannie smiled. "He said she was beautiful and kind and loving, and he would do anything for her. That's why he had Verla help with the housework after I was born, but our mother never regained her strength."

Melanie tightened her hold on Fannie's hand. "Tell me about your condition. What's your diagnosis?"

At mention of her medical condition, Fannie's face dropped. "Verla says it's genetic and passed on from my mother, but she never allows the doctors to test me, so I'm not sure what's wrong. All I know is that I've gotten worse recently."

"I want to help you, Fannie."

"You must be careful. Verla has been agitated recently. Something suspicious is going on, but I haven't determined what it is."

"Your father died a few years ago?"

"*Yah*, and before his condition grew bad, he and Verla visited Mr. Davis, a lawyer in town, and made her my guardian. She controls everything as long as I'm sick. The strange thing is that my father never trusted lawyers or anything to do with the *Englisch*."

"He was trying to take care of you," Melanie said with assurance.

"Maybe, but I wish he would have found someone other than Verla. She can be so hateful."

"I'll talk to the lawyer. Maybe I can care for you since we're related."

"Oh, Melanie, that would be *wunderbar*." Fannie glanced at the house again. "You must go before Verla sees you."

Melanie didn't want to leave. She ran her hand over the quilt, recognizing the tiny stitches and the intricate pattern. "Where did you get this pretty lap blanket?"

Fannie's face brightened. "My *mamm* made it for me before she gave birth."

The door to the house opened. "What are you doing here?"

"It's Verla!" Fannie's eyes widened. "You must leave."

"Leroy!" Verla screamed for her brother.

Melanie squeezed her sister's hand, then raced toward the path, and scurried up the side of the quarry. Glancing back, she saw Verla wheel Fannie into the house. The younger woman's hand hung over the side of the wheelchair and fluttered as if Fannie was waving goodbye.

"Protect her, Lord," Melanie prayed. "And let me find a way to help my sister."

~

As time passed, Jacob became worried about Melanie and hurried along the path looking for her. His stomach was in knots thinking of what could have happened. At the top of the trail, he stepped into the clearing and let out a sigh of relief when he spotted her coming toward him.

Noticing the tears on her cheeks as she neared, he took her hand. "Something happened."

"Fannie was sitting outside in her wheelchair, so I was able to talk to her. She told me more about my mother, and I'm sure the results of the DNA test are accurate." Then she explained how Eli had paid for the test and received the results for Fannie.

"Eli is a fine person. He helps me with the harvest and some of the farm-work at times."

She also explained about Verla taking over guardianship of Fannie when Tobias died. "Fannie's condition is growing worse, but Verla won't allow her to get medical testing. I fear she wants her to remain infirm."

Melanie's tears nearly broke Jacob's heart. He squeezed her hand and pulled her close. She stepped into his embrace, and he could smell the lavender in her hair and a hint of citrus. Her body was soft and warm, and her nearness took his breath away. He closed his eyes and rubbed his hand over her back to soothe her upset, which made him want to hold on to her all the more.

"Shh, Melanie. I'll help you uncover what's happening to Fannie. You're not alone. I'm right here with you."

She drew back, her eyes filled with tears. "Thank you, Jacob."

"Family is so important. I realized that when I left home and lived in Knoxville. I tried to pretend that I was happy, but my spirit was low. After Emma's husband died, I came home to help her. I also came home because I needed to be with family."

"You're a *gut* brother as you and Emma would say."

He smiled. "And you'll be a wonderful sister to Fannie. She has no one else."

"Now that I'm convinced Rebecca Yoder was my mother, I long to learn more about my biological father. Surely someone will know about the *Englis-cher* who stole my mother's heart."

"We'll keep asking questions about him. Hopefully, someone will have answers."

"Could we go to town and talk to Mr. Davis, the lawyer? If I'm Fannie's half sister, then I could take over her care, and she would no longer need Verla."

"But you'll need to prove you're related."

"Wouldn't the DNA testing be enough proof?"

"We'll have to find out."

Jacob wanted to help Melanie. If she could care for Fannie, she would stay in the area, so he could get to know her better. If not, she would leave Mountain Grove, which wasn't what he wanted.

~

Melanie wiped the last of the tears from her eyes and offered Jacob a weak smile. "I appreciate your help so much, Jacob."

"Let's go back to the farm," he suggested.

She glanced at Fannie's home, hoping to spot her half sister one more time, but the yard and outbuildings stood silent.

Jacob squeezed her hand, and she turned to him. "For some reason, I want to stay here a little longer. Maybe it's knowing my mother walked these paths."

His gaze was filled with understanding. "After you went to bed last night, Emma told me the house your mother lived in on the other side of the mountain was struck by lightning a few years ago and burned."

He pointed to a path. "That's probably the way she came to the quarry."

"I wish I had known her."

Jacob wrapped his arm around her, and she leaned into him and stared at the path, trying to envision her mother. "Maybe she looked like Fannie," Melanie mused. "She's very pretty."

"And maybe," Jacob said with a smile, "she looked like you, Melanie. You're beautiful."

Her cheeks flushed, and although she appreciated the compliment, she wondered if he was just being nice because Jacob was so very nice. She glanced at him again. He was also handsome and hardworking and considerate of others.

He gazed into her eyes, and her knees went weak. He leaned closer. Her heart lurched in her chest, and her neck grew warm. She stared at his parted lips as he bent down to—

"Hello there!"

A voice startled both of them. She stepped back and blinked at a wizened old man wearing khaki cargo pants and a navy hoodie on the path ahead.

"How many years has it been?" He raised his brow. "I didn't think I'd ever see you again."

Melanie threw Jacob a questioning glance and then turned her attention to the older man hurrying toward them.

"Remember me? Bubba Owens? I talked to your fiancé about the Indian artifacts he uncovered."

She was clueless about what the man was referencing. "I'm sorry, sir. You must have the wrong person."

He stopped three feet from them and narrowed his gaze. "Well, if that don't take the cake. You could be her twin."

"Twin? You must mean Fannie Schrock?"

He shook his head. "I'm talking about a woman named Rebecca. She used to wander these trails along with her fiancé."

Melanie's heart skipped a beat. "Rebecca Yoder? She was my mother."

He gave her a definitive nod. "That's where the resemblance comes from.

You've got her pretty eyes and oval face and sweet smile." He glanced at Jacob. "So, is this your husband?"

Melanie's cheeks warmed. "Jacob is a friend."

The two men shook hands. "Good to meet you. Any chance you know about Native American Indians?"

"Ah, no, sir." Jacob looked at Melanie, then back at Bubba. "You're an Indian buff?"

"Self-taught. I explore these caves."

Melanie peered at the stone quarry. "I don't see any caves."

"It's the kudzu."

She glanced again at the overhanging vines that trailed over the top of the ledge and covered much of the upper levels of the quarry.

"The caves are hidden behind the kudzu," he said, no doubt seeing her confusion. "They're easier to spot in winter when the vines go dormant. Still hate that Georgia brought the pesky plant into the state. Grows a foot a day. Ends up covering everything."

Bubba dug in his pocket. "Here you go." He placed an Indian arrowhead in her hand. "Take that home. A souvenir. Your dad had lots of them."

"My dad?"

He shrugged. "I heard he left to finish another quarter of college, but he planned to return. When I didn't see him again, I thought he and Rebecca had settled somewhere else."

The arrowhead was smooth, and Melanie held it tightly in her hand. "Do you have any more information about Rebecca or her fiancé?"

"Wish I did." He tugged on his beard. "Are you interested in Indians?"

"I'd like to know more about them."

"Check at the library. Ask for Alice Meyers. She's the town historian. She'll know about the Indian culture around here."

"And my father?"

"Chances are she'll know something about him as well."

Melanie felt a surge of excitement. At last, someone might have information about her father. "Thank you, Bubba."

"Good seeing you folks. Have a nice day now."

"What an interesting man," Jacob said as Bubba disappeared along one of the paths. "I suggest we head to the library and talk to Ms. Meyers. Hopefully, she'll provide more information."

Melanie's spirits lifted. She took Jacob's hand, and they hurried back to the house. Finding Fannie had been a surprise. Learning more about her mother and perhaps the man who could be her father was an added blessing.

"I never thought God would be interested in my life, Jacob, but I'm beginning to think He guided me to take that DNA test and is helping me discover my past."

Coming to Mountain Grove had been a good decision despite the man who wanted her to leave town. Did he have secrets he wanted to keep buried? Melanie needed to uncover the truth about her past. Only then would she know the truth about her mother and father.

CHAPTER SEVEN

*A*fter lunch, Jacob hitched his mare to the buggy, and he and Melanie rode to town. She had changed back into her *fancy* clothes, and although she looked lovely, he had enjoyed seeing her in the pretty blue dress that matched her eyes. For a few moments, as they stood on the edge of the quarry, he had imagined Melanie being Amish, and his heart had warmed to her even more.

The clip-clop of the mare's hooves on the pavement set a soothing cadence to their trip. Melanie sat quietly and seemed lost in her own world. No doubt, she was thinking of her parents and all she had learned in the last two days. More than anything, he hoped the town historian would provide additional information.

The outskirts of Mountain Grove came into view. "The lawyer's office is on this side of town. Let's stop and see when Mr. Davis can talk to you. If he's busy now, we could come back after our visit to the library."

Melanie nodded. "That sounds like a good idea. If you'll drop me at the curb, I could run in and check with his receptionist."

But a sign on the door read *Out to Lunch, Back at Two.* Melanie peered through the window, then glanced at her watch as she returned to the buggy. "The office is closed for lunch, but they'll open again at two o'clock, which is thirty minutes from now."

Jacob could see her disappointment. "Hopefully, you'll find more information at the library."

The library sat near the post office and the mayor's office. He tied Bertha to the hitching post and helped Melanie down from the buggy. He kept his hand on her waist and looked down at her sweet face, knowing she was anxious.

"Take a deep breath and try not to be nervous," he told her. "If Alice doesn't know anything, maybe she can lead you to someone else who remembers your father."

Melanie looked up and nodded. "I'm not good at praying, Jacob, but I'd like to let God know that I need His help. Could you say a few words?"

Jacob grimaced and then hung his head. He had left the Amish faith when he had worked in Knoxville. Coming home, he had embraced the Amish life but not the faith. "I'm not sure *Gott* is interested in what I have to say."

"That's how I feel. Maybe if we join together, He'll hear our prayer." Melanie held out her hands.

He wrapped his around hers, and they both bowed their heads.

"Dear *Gott*, Melanie longs for information about her birth family. She also wants to help Fannie. Could you lead her through this process to learn the truth?"

She glanced up and smiled. "Amen."

He pointed her toward the door of the library. "Ready?"

"I am. Let's find Ms. Meyers."

They didn't have far to look. Alice Meyers was at the information desk. "How may I help you?" she asked with a sweet Southern drawl.

Alice was tall and slim with curly brown hair and expressive eyes that stared at them over the top of her reading glasses. Melanie introduced herself and mentioned meeting Bubba Owens at the quarry.

"He talked about an Amish woman named Rebecca Yoder, who lived near the quarry, and a college student interested in Native American tribes. The *Englisch* student came to Mountain Grove twenty-some years ago. Evidently, he and Bubba had a lot in common."

The historian *tsked*. "Twenty years is a long time to remember library patrons, but let me check our files."

Alice typed something into a nearby computer, scrolled through a list of names, and then shook her head. "I don't have a Rebecca Yoder listed, but the system went digital a few years ago. If she didn't renew her library membership, her name would have been dropped from our records."

Jacob could see the disappointment wash over Melanie's face.

"Bubba talked about caves and Indian artifacts," Melanie added. "Does that bring anything or anyone to mind?"

Alice raised a finger to her lips and looked over her glasses. "I remember a young man who wanted information about local caves."

"You do?" Melanie's eyes widened. "Do you remember his name?"

The historian thought for a moment and then shook her head. "All I can recall is that he was enthusiastic about Indian lore and attended college in Atlanta."

Melanie's earlier excitement deflated. "If you think of anything else, could you contact me? I'm staying at Emma Keim's farm near the quarry. You can reach me on my cell phone." She provided the number.

Jacob followed Melanie outside. "I'm sure Alice isn't the only person who knows something about the college student. We'll keep asking questions until someone else remembers him."

"So where do I start?"

"Let's go back to the lawyer's office. He should be back from lunch by now."

George Davis stood and shook their hands when the receptionist escorted them into the lawyer's office. He was middle-aged with a round face and pleasant smile and motioned them to the two chairs positioned across from his desk.

"Please, sit down so we can discuss your situation. You told my receptionist you're related to Fannie Schrock."

Melanie pulled out the paperwork from her DNA test. "You can see that the DNA results show us as probable half sisters."

"And Fannie submitted her own sample?" the lawyer asked.

Melanie explained about Eli's help and Fannie's desire to find the other child Verla had talked about.

He handed the DNA report back to Melanie. "So why did you come to see me?"

"I learned that Tobias Schrock, Fannie's father, gave guardianship of his daughter to Verla Zook before his death."

The lawyer steepled his fingers and nodded. "That's correct."

"Yet she seems to be keeping Fannie from the medical care she needs. Verla takes her to the clinic for little more than triage and refuses any significant testing. The clinic's doctor doesn't even know what's wrong with Fannie, yet her health is in decline."

"I wasn't aware of the situation, but I don't know how I can help."

"You could dissolve Verla's guardianship so I could take care of her."

"Under normal circumstances, once Fannie turned eighteen, she no longer needed a guardian, but her failing health may be an issue. Either way, she has to file a petition to terminate the guardianship. I'd be happy to talk to her if she can come to my office. Or I could visit her if that would better accommodate her needs."

"I fear either way Verla will fight to maintain her position." Melanie scooted closer. "Tell me one thing. If something happens to Fannie and if there is no other next-of-kin, who gets the Schrock property should Fannie die?"

"I would be speaking hypothetically, of course, since I'm not at liberty to discuss the Schrock case." He pulled on his jaw. "The father in the hypothetical case could have named the guardian as the benefactor of his inheritance if his only child died."

Melanie looked at Jacob. They both realized the significance of what the lawyer had shared, especially if Verla wanted the Schrock property.

"The Schrock farm is small," Jacob mentioned. "Is there any reason to think it could be a sought-after piece of real estate?"

The lawyer chuckled. "You might want to check with a real estate broker for a current assessment of the property." He paused for a minute. "As you probably are aware, one of the first gold rushes in the US was in Dahlonega, Georgia, located here in the North Georgia mountains. I know nothing about the quarry now, but some years ago, there was speculation about a possible gold vein running through the unmined area."

"Is that why the quarry stopped production?"

"Actually, it was unprofitable to get the stone down the mountain. The town's elevation and distance from a major city complicated the shipments. The owner of the quarry decided to call it quits. Tobias worked at the quarry and bought the land for a few pennies on the dollar. A good move, especially when speculation surfaced soon thereafter about a possible gold vein. Of course, nothing panned out." He smiled. "No pun intended."

"So, the land lost value."

"Soon after Tobias set up his daughter's guardianship, as I recall, but there's something else to take into consideration."

"What's that?" Melanie asked.

"Speaking hypothetically again, the guardian receives financial resources from the state of Georgia."

"Verla gets paid by the state to care for Fannie?"

The lawyer shrugged.

Melanie nodded. "I understand. You can't reveal anything about the Schrock case." She glanced at Jacob and then stood. "Thank you for talking to us, Mr. Davis."

"My pleasure. Remember, I'd be happy to help Fannie if she wants to terminate the guardianship."

"I have one more question," Melanie added. "Do you remember a college student who explored the quarry about twenty years ago?"

The lawyer shook his head. "Sorry, that was before my time. My wife and I moved here twelve years ago."

Melanie nodded. "I just thought I'd ask."

After leaving the law office, Jacob helped her into the buggy. "So if Verla knew about the possible gold mine, she may have encouraged Tobias to make her Fannie's guardian."

"I wonder how Tobias died."

"Maybe he had the same disease as Fannie."

"What about my mother? Did she accidentally slip off the path, or did something else happen?" Melanie sighed. "I never thought trying to find my birth family would turn into a mystery, but it certainly seems that way."

Jacob pointed to the garage ahead. "Let's check on your car."

The mechanic was pleased to see them. "Perfect timing." Walter smiled at Melanie. "Your car's ready to go."

Jacob hated to hear the mechanic's good news. While her Honda was being worked on, Melanie had been forced to stay in Mountain Grove. Now that she had her vehicle back, she could come and go as she pleased.

What really troubled Jacob was that she would return home to Cleveland, Georgia. He had only known her for a short time, but Melanie was special. She was caring and compassionate. He didn't see her as a *fancy* person, he saw her as a woman trying to find her way, and when they had prayed together, he had felt closer to *Gott* than he had in years. If only something would happen to encourage Melanie to stay in Mountain Grove.

CHAPTER EIGHT

*A*fter paying the mechanic, Melanie climbed into her Honda. So much had happened since the night she had arrived in Mountain Grove. She had found her half sister and information about her mother and hoped to eventually learn more about her father.

She waved as she passed Jacob in his buggy. As glad as she was that her car was fixed, she would rather have been sitting next to him in the buggy on this pretty day.

Melanie rolled down her window to enjoy the fresh spring air and stared at the surrounding fields and gentle hills. Mountain Grove was breathtakingly beautiful. She felt a sense of homecoming and contentment here. It was as if she had found her roots.

She sighed at the futility of that thought when she didn't belong here. The man who had run her off the road the first night had told her as much, yet she hadn't been deterred by his attack, and she wouldn't let his words upset her now.

Seeing the various Amish farms tucked into the hillside lifted her spirits and made her wonder what life must be like for Amish women. Emma was busy but also content and faithful to *Gott* and to the Amish way. The simplicity of Amish life attracted Melanie. Her adoptive parents had been focused on earning money so they could buy the latest cell phones or computers or televisions. They worked hard but for the wrong reason, at least in Melanie's mind. Plus, they never stopped to enjoy life or to thank God for their blessings.

Melanie had seen the world through a different lens since she came to Mountain Grove. She saw beyond the daily chores to the beauty of a routine and life geared toward family. Given the opportunity, Melanie would enjoy delving more deeply into the Amish lifestyle, but she didn't want to overstay her welcome.

She needed to ensure Fannie was out from under Verla's control before she left Mountain Grove. She would explain the process to terminate Verla's guardianship and would give Fannie her phone number and address so the two sisters could stay connected. Much as Melanie didn't want to say good-bye, she knew Fannie would have to make up her own mind about any relationship they might have in the future.

Emma was weeding her garden and waved when Melanie turned into the drive. "Let me help you," she said after she parked her car near the barn.

"I'm already done," Emma assured her. "The afternoon is beautiful. Go for a walk and enjoy the fresh air."

"I'll do exactly that, but if you don't mind, I'd like to change into the blue dress you let me borrow."

"Of course. It is hanging on a wall peg in my room."

"*Danki.*" Melanie hesitated for a moment before adding, "It may sound foolish, but when I wore the dress, I felt a connection with my mother."

"I understand how you feel. After my husband died, I could not part with his things. In some way, it made me feel he was still with me." Emma smiled ruefully. "Eventually, I was able to pack the items up and give them to a family in need, although I kept his hat. It hangs in my bedroom. Silly, some would say, but it brings me comfort."

"I'm sorry, Emma."

"*Yah*, it is hard at times, but we do not understand *Gott's* ways."

"Have you thought of marrying again?"

Emma shrugged. "For so long, I was not interested, although at the last barn raising, I talked to a nice man. His wife died about a year ago. He had a warm smile and a twinkle in his eye that made me think of what could be."

Melanie was touched that Emma had confided in her. "Have you told Jacob?"

"*Ack*, no. My brother would insist I go to town more often."

"The man you met works in town?"

"No, but his farm is on the way. Sometimes I see him in his fields. I know it sounds strange, but he always looks up and waves when I pass in the buggy."

"Perhaps he senses your presence."

Emma's cheeks warmed, and she giggled.

Melanie had to laugh too. "You must write me and let me know about this man. What's his name?"

"Zachariah Hartsfelder." Emma caught her arm. "But what is this about writing letters? You are not leaving?"

"Soon, Emma. You and Jacob have been so gracious to let me stay here."

"We have enjoyed your company. It is a joy to have you with us. I will miss you, and—"

Melanie waited, hoping Emma would say something about her brother.

"Jacob will miss you too. He had a girlfriend in Knoxville, but she was not meant for him. She was—" Emma hesitated. "She was an *Englischer* and not interested in giving up her *fancy* life."

"That is a problem, for sure." Melanie wanted to share her own attraction to the Amish life, but she knew Jacob wouldn't be interested in another *fancy* woman after he had returned to his Amish faith.

"I'll change into the dress and then take that walk you suggested."

Just as before, the dress made Melanie feel close to her mother. She smoothed her hands over the cotton skirt and swept her hair into a bun, taking care that it covered her ears. If the Amish allowed mirrors, she would have enjoyed seeing herself. Instead, she stood in front of the window and could tell by her reflection in the glass that the dress fit perfectly.

Once she was satisfied with her appearance, Melanie pulled the small baby quilt from her tote—the blanket she'd been wrapped in when she was adopted and the only item she had from her birth mother. The pattern was identical to the quilt Fannie's mother had made for her. Melanie had recognized the same intricate details and the tiny stitches on Fannie's blanket that made each quilt a work of love. Before leaving Mountain Grove, Melanie wanted Fannie to examine them side by side so she, too, would know for certain that they were sisters who shared the same mother.

After hurrying downstairs with the quilt over her arm, Melanie waved goodbye to Emma and headed for the path she had taken earlier that led to the top of the quarry. The breeze picked up a bit, and a few clouds darkened the distant sky. Surely, the sun would continue to shine for the next hour or so. She breathed deeply, inhaling the crisp scent of new grass and spring leaves. A few trees were flowering, adding to the freshness that filled the air.

The wind grew stronger at the top of the quarry. Melanie shivered as she stared down into the steep pit. She didn't want to think about her mother slipping to her death, but it was a reality she couldn't ignore. Again, she longed to learn what had caused her mother to stumble and fall that day and why her father had not returned to the area. He was an *Englischer*, like Melanie, but perhaps he didn't want to live Amish.

Tomorrow, she would stop at the library and talk to the historian again in hopes she might have remembered something more.

Glancing at the Schrock home, she saw Verla on the front porch. The tall, slender woman wrung her hands and paced back and forth.

Melanie's heart quickened. Hopefully, nothing was wrong with Fannie. If only she could run to the house and check on her sister, but she knew the strict guardian would try to keep Fannie secluded.

"Are you Melanie?"

Hearing her name, she turned to find a young man climbing the path.

"I'm Eli Lehman," he said.

"You're Fannie's friend. Is something wrong?"

"She asked that I deliver this to you." He shoved a note into Melanie's hand. She unfolded the lined paper and read the neat script.

I have become much weaker, Fannie had written, *and asked Verla to take me to the clinic, but she refused. She's nervous, and I heard her talking to Leroy about visitors. Help me, Melanie. I know we're kin, and I can trust you.*

Melanie's heart nearly stopped. "Jacob is coming back from town, Eli, and should have arrived by now. Take this note to him. I'll stay here and keep watch."

"Be careful around Verla. She's not to be trusted."

"Hurry, Eli." She placed the paper in his outstretched hand. "Tell Jacob to bring help."

Eli needed little encouragement. He started running along the path and soon disappeared from sight.

Melanie edged closer to the quarry and peered down at the small farmhouse. A late-model sedan turned into the drive and pulled to a stop. An older couple, well dressed and meticulously groomed, stepped from the car. Verla hurried to greet them, then returned to the house and wheeled Fannie onto the porch.

Even from this distance, Melanie could see that her half sister's health had declined. Fannie's shoulders were stooped, and her head listed to one side. She raised her arm and had trouble holding it out to shake their hands. The woman leaned down and hugged Fannie.

As she did, her sister's gaze flicked to the top of the ridge. Fannie's eyes widened. Verla must have noticed Fannie's surprise because she too looked at the top of the quarry where Melanie stood.

The older couple seemed oblivious to the distraction and kept talking to Fannie. Verla left them for a moment and hurried to the barn. Melanie's gut tightened, and she had an uncomfortable feeling that the overly protective guardian was up to no good.

In a matter of minutes, Verla hurried back to the porch, shook hands with the visitors, and wheeled Fannie inside. The older couple looked at each other as if confused by Verla's actions. They stared at the closed door for a long moment, then shrugged and walked slowly toward their car.

Discouraged that she wouldn't be able to see Fannie, Melanie's heart sank, and tears burned her eyes as she retraced her steps along the path. Dark clouds rolled overhead, and a stiff breeze made her skirt billow in the chilly air.

She shook her head with regret and walked around a particularly hazardous section of the path that angled near the drop-off. A noise sounded behind her.

Glancing back, she saw a huge presence. A hand wrapped around her waist, and another covered her mouth, muffling her attempt to scream. Verla's brother, Leroy—the same man, she now realized, who had attacked her the first night—dragged her toward the edge. She kicked and flailed her arms, trying to free herself, but his hold only tightened.

The door to the house opened. Fannie wheeled herself onto the porch and looked at the rim where Melanie struggled against Leroy's control.

Fannie screamed.

The older couple turned at the sound of her cry. She fisted her hands in the air and attempted to stand. Verla rushed outside to calm her. The older coupled seemed even more confused by Fannie's outburst.

"You've messed up everything," the man growled into Melanie's ear.

She continued to struggle against his hold and bit his hand that covered her mouth. He slapped the side of her head. Her knees went weak. The baby blanket slipped from her arm and dropped to the ground.

"Get up and walk," he demanded.

Unable to retrieve the quilt, she stumbled forward, pushed along by his weight. Where was he taking her?

Melanie flicked her gaze over the rocks, trying to see some way to free herself. Glancing back, she saw the couple drive out of sight as Verla wheeled Fannie inside.

The man shoved Melanie toward a thick stand of kudzu vines. Something moved to her left. She twisted her head and caught sight of the back of a stooped, older man wearing a fleece hoodie.

Bubba.

If only she could get his attention, but he was running away from her along the path, seemingly oblivious to her plight.

Leroy shoved aside the veil of kudzu. Her heart nearly stopped, seeing the small cave. He pushed her head down so she could fit through the opening and followed her into the cool interior. She blinked, trying to adjust her eyes to the darkness, and noticed the primitive drawings on the walls. Instinctively, she knew this was one of the caves her father had explored.

Leroy would kill her and leave her in the cave. Jacob would wonder what had happened to her, but no one would ever find her body.

CHAPTER NINE

*E*li came running down the mountain path as Jacob turned the mare into the barnyard and jumped from the buggy. "Is there a problem, Eli?"

"Fannie sent this note to Melanie. I met her along the mountain path. She said you needed to see it."

He unfolded the paper and read the script. "Melanie went to the Schrock farm to help Fannie?"

Eli nodded. "She was on the path when I left her and was waiting for Fannie to appear. Melanie's worried about her and so am I."

"Take my buggy to town and notify the sheriff."

"He's never been interested in Fannie's well-being before."

"Give him the note. Tell him what you know. You've got to convince him that Fannie needs help."

Emma came out of the house. "What's wrong, Jacob?"

"I need to find Melanie."

Jacob raced along the path; his feet couldn't move fast enough. His heart pounded hard from exertion but even more from fear of what he would find at the quarry. If the man who had attacked Melanie the first night was hanging about the Schrock farm, he would pose a danger to Melanie as well.

Jacob broke through the thick forest and stepped into the clearing. For as far as he could see, the area was still with no one visible at the Schrock farmhouse or beyond. He couldn't even be certain that Verla and Fannie were inside. Could Melanie have gone there, and if so, was she finally able to talk to Fannie, or was Verla still keeping her from her sister?

He glanced around, unsure of what to do, and then he hung his head. "*Gott*, forgive my past. I haven't been faithful, but I need You in my life, and I need You to help me find Melanie."

He was startled when he opened his eyes. Bubba stood not more than ten feet away. The older man put his finger to his lips, an indication for Jacob to be silent. Then he pointed to an overhang of kudzu and motioned for Jacob to follow him, but they didn't go toward the kudzu. They hurried around to the rear of the outcrop of granite to where Bubba pulled aside a less dense cluster of hanging vines. Again, he put his finger to his lips and motioned Jacob forward.

Grateful for the man's guidance, Jacob entered the dark and dank cave. Bubba followed him and signed for him to keep moving. They turned a corner in the cave, and sounds came from the interior.

Jacob's heart lurched hearing Melanie's voice.

"You'll never get away with this," she said, her tone tight with fear.

"Of course, I will. You were inquiring about Rebecca and came to see where your mother died. Like her, you slipped and fell to your death."

"Jacob will know the truth."

"The sheriff won't believe him."

"What about Fannie?" Melanie demanded. "Verla's not giving her the medical care she needs."

"What makes you think you know everything?"

"Because I can tell she's sick, yet Verla hasn't let the doctor run any tests on Fannie. How can he help her if he doesn't know what's wrong with her?"

"Verla will get medical help for Fannie soon enough."

"Does it involve the older couple?"

He laughed. "They're pushovers."

"What do you mean?"

"They wanted to find their granddaughter so badly that they believed everything Verla told them."

Jacob looked at Bubba. The old man shook his head in frustration. Then he signaled for Jacob to go one way, and he would go the other along two adjoining paths.

"Enough talking," the man demanded. "Say your prayers, girlie. You don't have long to live."

A scuffle sounded. Melanie screamed.

Jacob envisioned the man trying to overpower her. He didn't wait for Bubba. He ran straight toward the entrance of the cave. Melanie was sitting on the ground with her arms bound behind her back. Leroy had his hands around her neck. Jacob slammed into him and sent him flying.

Bubba hurried to untie Melanie. Leroy climbed out of the cave. Jacob ran after him and grabbed his shoulder. Leroy turned too quickly, and a portion of the path crumbled under him. He started to fall. Jacob latched onto his arm and called for Bubba. Between them, they pulled Leroy to safety and tied him with the extra rope they found nearby.

Once Leroy was secured, Jacob raced into the cave and fell to his knees beside Melanie. She was rubbing her wrists and gasping for air.

"Oh, Jacob, you saved me." She wrapped her arms around his neck and hugged him tight.

"I thought he was going to kill you."

She nodded. "If you hadn't arrived in time, he would have. He and Verla cooked up some type of plan to claim Fannie was related to an unsuspecting older couple."

A siren sounded in the distance.

"Eli went to town to get the sheriff," Jacob told her as he helped Melanie to her feet. "Can you make it down the mountain?"

"Of course. I need to make sure Fannie is okay."

At the edge of the quarry, they saw the sheriff rap on Verla's door. He went inside when she answered his knock. Bubba hurried ahead to ensure the sheriff learned the truth about what had happened. By the time Jacob and Melanie reached the farmhouse, Verla was in handcuffs and being taken to the sheriff's squad car.

"You did this," she screamed at them. "You ruined all my plans."

Melanie and Jacob ignored the angry woman and hurried inside.

Fannie was sitting by the woodstove, her face drawn. "Oh, Melanie, Verla didn't tell me what she planned to do. She just said I needed to remain quiet. Once I realized she was passing me off as you, I tried to fight back."

"Verla can't hurt you anymore."

The sheriff opened the front door and peered inside. "I called an ambulance to take Fannie to the clinic. As weak as she looks, I want the doctor to check her over."

"And run tests to determine what's causing her illness," Melanie added.

The sheriff had something in his hand. "One of my deputies found this near the rim of the quarry." He held up a baby quilt.

"Thank him for me." Melanie took the quilt and showed it to Fannie.

"It's identical to mine." Her eyes filled with tears.

Melanie nodded. "Our mother made a quilt for each of her daughters." The two sisters embraced and then talked about their plans for the future as they waited for the ambulance.

When the EMTs arrived, Melanie looked relieved. Jacob knew she didn't want to be separated from Fannie again, but her sister needed medical help.

Once the ambulance left the Schrock farm, Melanie turned to Jacob. "Will you take me to town? I want to talk to the older couple before they leave Mountain Grove."

"Do you know who they are?" he asked.

Melanie nodded. "I think they're my grandparents."

CHAPTER TEN

*M*elanie was overcome with anxiety when Jacob brought his mare to a stop at the B and B next to the same car she had seen at the Schrock farm. He helped her down from the buggy, and together they hurried inside the quaint inn. A tall, gray-haired man with an overnight bag at his feet and a slender woman of comparable age, carrying a pricey leather tote, stood by the reception desk in the parlor.

"I'm sorry you decided to leave early, Mr. and Mrs. Westerbrook," the woman behind the desk said.

"There was an unfortunate mix-up," the man explained. "Sometimes when you want something so badly, you make a mistake. We're sad about what happened but glad we didn't give our hearts and our support to a phony."

Unwilling to have anyone disparage her half sister, Melanie blurted out, "Fannie wasn't involved with Verla's scheme."

They turned, surprise written on their faces.

The receptionist, no doubt sensing the tension, rubbed her hands together. "If you don't mind, I'll excuse myself," she said, "and give you folks some privacy."

Melanie nodded and waited until the woman had left the room. "My name is Melanie Taylor, and this is Jacob Brubaker."

She moved closer to the couple who continued to stare at her. "Twenty-two years ago, I was given up for adoption and have always wanted to find my birth family." She told them about the DNA test and her attempt to meet Fannie. "Verla stood in my way, but she couldn't stop me from learning that

158

Fannie and I had the same mother but different fathers. Your son wasn't Fannie's father. He was mine."

Mr. Westerbrook's eyes widened. "I hardly think we're ready to believe you, Miss Taylor."

"It's Melanie," she reminded him. Then glancing around the B and B's parlor, she added, "Where's your son, Mr. and Mrs. Westerbrook? Why isn't he here with you?"

Tears glistened in Mrs. Westerbrook's eyes. She took hold of her husband's arm as if needing support and pulled in a deep breath before she started to explain. "Our son spent the summer before his senior year of college in Mountain Grove doing research on one of Georgia's early Indian tribes. While here, he fell in love with an Amish girl and planned to marry her over the following Christmas break."

The older woman splayed her hands. "Knowing he had a bright future ahead, we opposed the marriage and pulled strings to get him into a prestigious indigenous study program that was starting immediately in South America. He didn't have an opportunity to tell her about his change of plans in person and instead wrote to her, explaining that he would be gone for an extended number of months."

Mr. Westerbrook patted his wife's hand as she pulled in another breath. "I'm not proud of our actions, but we kept that letter and then kept the letters she mailed to him."

"What happened when his program was over?" Melanie asked.

The older woman shook her head with regret. "Our son became ill halfway through the program and died of encephalitis. It took years for us to come to grips with losing our only child. Eventually, we realized we needed God in our lives. Earlier this year, we opened the woman's letters and learned she had been pregnant with his child, which our son never knew. We hired a private investigator only to learn that she too had died. The PI put us in contact with Verla, who led us to believe that Fannie was our granddaughter."

Melanie thought of the pain her mother had endured thinking the man she loved had abandoned her.

"We were so desperate to connect with our deceased son's child that we didn't request any DNA testing," Mr. Westerbrook added. "Although we probably would have done so later. Verla wrote us and said Fannie needed medical care and that money was tight. We came prepared to help her financially. Our desire for a granddaughter clouded our better judgment."

"Fannie didn't try to scam you," Melanie assured them. "It was Verla's ploy to get your money."

Mrs. Westerbrook glanced at her husband and then at Melanie. "I hope you understand our hesitancy to accept you into our lives, dear, after everything that's happened. Perhaps we can have a paternity test run at a later date?"

Melanie didn't want to be tested. She had found Fannie, and that's all that mattered. With a heavy heart, she turned to the door just as it opened, and the historian ran inside.

"I saw Jacob's buggy and hoped you were here. I found what I was looking for." Alice Meyers placed a typed booklet in Melanie's hand. "Norman Westerbrook. That was the young man's name. He wrote this while he was in Mountain Grove and gave me a copy. I'm sorry I couldn't locate it yesterday when you came to the library."

Melanie's heart nearly stopped as she rubbed her finger over the cover.

The historian continued. "The pamphlet includes information about what he found at the quarry and in the surrounding area. He had hoped to obtain permission from the Department of Natural Resources to open a small museum in Mountain Grove with Indian artifacts. He mentioned giving tours of the area. It would have been a wonderful addition to our town."

Melanie barely heard Alice. Her focus was on the yellowed pages as she skimmed the pamphlet, knowing later she would read the text word for word. Turning to the last page, she gasped, seeing the photograph of a handsome young man. His name was written in script below the photo. Norman Westerbrook.

Staring at the photo, she saw something that made tears fill her eyes and confirmed Norman truly was her father.

The older couple moved closer. "Did our son write that pamphlet?" Mrs. Westerbrook asked.

"My father did," Melanie said with authority. She held up the page bearing his photo. "Is this your son?"

They both nodded, tears filling their eyes as well.

Melanie pointed to the picture. "The top of your son's left ear is folded over."

"Why, yes, dear. It's called cryptotia. It's a genetic condition where the upper cartilage of the ear is partially buried beneath the skin. We always told him it was a mark of a genius."

"My adoptive mother had less pleasant words to call it." Melanie pushed her hair away from her left ear, exposing her own folded ear that was identical to her father's.

"Oh my goodness!" Mrs. Westerbrook stood for a long moment, then she stepped forward, wrapped her arms around Melanie, and pulled her close. "You truly are Norman's child."

～

Melanie couldn't stop talking about finding her grandparents when Jacob took her back to his sister's house later that day. Happy though he was about her good fortune, he knew she would be leaving Mountain Grove soon. Emma was eager to hear everything that had happened when they arrived home. A few times, she glanced at Jacob, and he knew she was aware of his own heartache.

"The sheriff found us before we left town," Melanie shared. "Leroy confessed to shoving my mother over the edge of the quarry to her death. Verla had him convinced the quarry was loaded with gold and assured him the land would be theirs if they bided their time. She had hoped to marry Tobias, but when my mother came back from South Georgia, he courted her, much to Verla's upset. She plotted to poison my mother and spread rumors that she was suffering from postpartum depression. After her death, Verla again hoped to marry Tobias, but when he failed to show interest in her, she added drugs to his food and convinced him to make her Fannie's guardian as his health declined."

"And Fannie??" Emma asked.

"In a similar way, Verla doctored Fannie's food to cause the diverse and sporadic symptoms. Toxicology testing will reveal some of the medications Verla used to sicken Fannie."

"That's why Verla never wanted the doctor to run tests on Fannie," Jacob added.

"How is she now?" Emma asked.

"She's staying at the clinic for a few days, but the doctor said he's optimistic about her making a full recovery."

"And your grandparents?" Emma asked.

Melanie's smiled. "They were as happy to find me as I was to find them."

Emma's eyes were somber when she glanced at Jacob. "I'm so glad for you, Melanie."

Jacob turned to the door and grabbed his hat. "The chores will not get done by themselves."

Melanie followed him outside. "Jacob!"

He ignored her and headed to the barn.

She grabbed his arm. "What's wrong?"

He pulled free. "Nothing's wrong, Melanie, although I know you'll leave Mountain Grove and move closer to your father's family."

"But Fannie lives here."

"Will she stay in Mountain Grove?"

"If Eli makes his feelings known, I'm sure she will. Plus, it's taken me a long time to find my half sister. I'm not going to leave her now."

"I'm happy for you." Although he knew his expression showed anything but happiness.

She shook her head with frustration. "If it wasn't for you, Jacob, I never would have found any of my family. You were with me the entire time. You encouraged me, and I learned so much about real family life by the way you helped Emma and the faith you shared."

Jacob offered her a weak smile. "I left everything when I moved to Knoxville, but helping you, Melanie, allowed me to come closer to *Gott* and to realize how important my faith and the Amish way of life are. I'm the one who needs to thank you."

"You don't realize how special you are, Jacob. I . . . I've never been in love, but since I've come here, something has taken over my heart. I . . ." She looked up at him, her eyes wide, causing his heart to hitch.

She stepped closer. "Since I've been here, I've learned what real love is, the caring and understanding that you showed me. Your gentle acceptance of what I needed to do, your willingness to help, and the way you make me feel special when we're together."

He couldn't take his eyes off her.

"I don't want to leave Mountain Grove," she continued. "I don't want to leave Fannie, but most especially, I don't want to leave you."

"Oh, Melanie!" His heart soared. He pulled her into his arms, feeling her soft curves, inhaling her delightful scent, and losing himself in her gaze. "I've loved you since the moment I first saw you when you asked for directions. Something snapped in my heart, and I couldn't keep you out of my thoughts. When you appeared at my door later that same night, I couldn't believe it was you again. Since then, I've been falling more and more in love with you."

"Are you sure, Jacob?"

He nodded. "Cross my heart."

Jacob pulled her closer and lowered his lips to hers. He never wanted to let her go, and from her response, he knew Melanie felt the same.

CHAPTER ELEVEN

wo months later, Melanie walked arm in arm with Fannie as they left the Schrock house, where Melanie had been staying, and climbed into Fannie's buggy. On the way to Emma's house, Melanie confided in her sister.

"Emma invited Eli and Zachariah Hartsfelder to dinner. She's excited for you now that you and Eli are courting, and she thinks Zachariah will ask to court her soon."

"I'm so happy for Emma." Fannie smiled. "I never thought I'd survive long enough to marry Eli. My improved health is something for which I thank *Gott* daily. With you helping me, Melanie, I've gained my strength again."

Melanie squeezed her sister's hand. "So many *gut* things have happened since I came to Mountain Grove. The bishop said I'm learning about the Amish faith quickly, and he's pleased with the way I'm picking up the Pennsylvania Dutch dialect. He says I may be able to come into the faith through baptism sooner than he had first thought."

"I'm sure Jacob is happy about that."

They turned onto Emma's drive and parked the buggy near the barn. Jacob ran from the house and helped Fannie down. She hurried to meet Eli on the porch. As the sweet couple scurried inside, Jacob wrapped his arms around Melanie and lowered her from the buggy.

"The bishop told me you are his star student." His eyes twinkled as he pulled her to the side of the barn and out of view from the house.

"Did he tell you that baptism might be earlier than expected?" she asked.

163

Jacob nodded. "He did. I'm preparing as well and will only be a little ahead of you. It might be premature, but—"

The seriousness of his gaze had Melanie concerned. "Is something wrong?"

"I hope you don't think so."

She couldn't follow his logic and took a step back. He looked so worried, which made her even more unsettled.

"The day you found your grandparents, I told you that I've loved you since the first moment I saw you. Now that we're both preparing for baptism, I have something to ask you."

"What is it, Jacob?"

He reached for her hands and held them tight. "Will you marry me, Melanie?"

Her heart skipped a beat, and tears of joy stung her eyes. "Oh, Jacob! I love you more than anything, and being your wife would make me the happiest woman in the world."

He pulled her closer and lowered his lips to hers. She sighed with contentment as they kissed for a very long time. All her dreams had come true. She had connected with her loving grandparents, who would be joining them later today. She had a strong bond with her delightful half sister Fannie, a close relationship with Emma, and a new faith. Plus, the Amish community had reached out to her with a warm welcome.

As they walked toward Emma's house to join the others, Melanie snuggled closer to Jacob. She had found her Amish home, but the best part was finding an amazing man who made her a better person. God had led her to Mountain Grove to uncover the truth about her past, and in so doing, she had learned the value of a life based on faith and family.

Her future with Jacob would be filled with an abundance of blessings. Melanie had found her happily ever after and knew without a shadow of a doubt that Jacob would love her and cherish her all the days of her life.

ABOUT THE AUTHOR

If you enjoyed this story, I hope you'll consider other books by Debby Giusti.

SMUGGLERS IN AMISH COUNTRY is available now.

Watch for IN THE SNIPER'S CROSSHAIRS, an October 2022 release:

Amish widower Matthias Overholt saved Lily Hudson's life once and opened his home and his heart to the pretty Englischer, *but as the killer closes in, Matthias fears he might not be able to save her again.*

Order Debby's books on Amazon at:
https://www.amazon.com/Debby-Giusti/e/B001IXU4FO

Debby loves to hear from her readers.
Connect with Debby in the following ways:

Website: www.DebbyGiusti.com
Email: Debby@DebbyGiusti.com
Blog: www.seekerville.blogspot.com
Facebook: https://www.facebook.com/debby.giusti.9

A MATCH FOR THE TEACHER

PATRICIA DAVIDS

CHAPTER ONE

*T*he moment Mathias Troyer dreaded was here. The van his brother-in-law hired to carry the family fifty miles from Mount Iron to Badger Creek, Ohio, turned off the highway onto a farm lane. Ahead stood the large house where his friend William was preparing to get married. She would be here, too. The woman Mathias couldn't forget. The bride's sister Karen Troyer.

The last time they were together, he'd made a dreadful mistake and humiliated her. It hadn't been entirely his fault. His cousin Ogden deserved part of the blame, but according to Ogden's letters, Karen had forgiven him. He said she was in love with him now, but her feelings toward Mathias were a different matter. Did she still harbor a grudge after six long months? It wasn't the way Amish people acted. Forgiveness was everything.

His sister Rachel nudged him. "I imagine you're eager to see the sister of the bride again."

Terrified was more like it. Ogden's last letter said Karen had agreed to speak with Mathias. Could he mend things with her? The thought of facing her left a knot in his stomach.

His sister's stepdaughter, eight-year-old Becky, turned around to stare at him. "Why are you eager to see the bride's sister?"

"Because he is sweet on her," Rachel answered. "Ever since they met last fall at your father's and my wedding."

Rachel had found unexpected happiness late in life with Thomas, a widower with two children. Mathias envied her. He'd let his chance at happiness and a family slip away.

Becky grinned. "Is she pretty?"

"Girls are nothing but trouble," Samuel mumbled. At ten, his major interest was baseball.

Becky crossed her arms on the seat back. Her bright blue eyes sparkled with curiosity. "Are you going to court her?"

"I'm here to see my friend get married, not to court anyone."

Becky giggled. "If you like her, you should court her and marry her."

"Leave Mathias alone." Thomas gave his daughter a stern look. She turned around in her seat.

Samuel frowned. "If you marry, will you have to stop teaching school?"

Mathias shook his head. Samuel sighed with relief. "*Goot*, because you're the best teacher ever at Mount Iron."

It was unusual to find a man teaching in any Amish community. Although Mathias had been reluctant to take the position at first, he enjoyed it. His relationship with his scholars was the most rewarding thing in his life. Still, he prayed marriage and a family were part of *Gott's* plan for him. He wanted a love like the one Rachel and Thomas had. Like the one Ogden said he shared with Karen. The only woman Mathias ever cared about.

The van came to a stop. Rachel began gathering the children's jackets and small suitcases. "Come along, *kinder*. Your father and I are *newehockers*, and we are late.

"What's a *newehocker*?" Samuel asked.

"We are the couple's side-sitters. Your *daed* will be at his brother William's side. I will sit with my friend Lisa during the wedding and at the dinner after. It's a fine honor."

"Sounds boring to me." Samuel lunged out the van door when the driver opened it. Thomas got out and went to take care of the luggage.

Becky came back to Mathias and laid a hand on his arm. "You should get married. Before *Daed* married Rachel, he was sad all the time, but now he's always smiling. He says it's because he has the love of a *goot* wife." She hurried away without waiting for him to reply.

Rachel chuckled. "Out of the mouth of babes. She's right."

He rolled his eyes. "Don't start."

"There was something between you and Karen. I saw it."

"She has chosen Ogden. I hope to make amends for both their sakes." Mathias got out of the van last. He looked toward the upstairs windows of the house and rubbed his damp palms on his pant legs. Was she watching him? Dread and anticipation made his heart race. "What should I say to her?"

Things started off so well between them. He couldn't explain the thrill the first time Karen smiled at him. They'd talked for hours after Rachel's wedding, long into the night. He found excuses to visit her daily at her cousin's home, where she was staying. He'd been certain she felt something for him, too. Then things fell apart.

Rachel gave an encouraging smile. "I'm sure your little mix-up has been forgotten."

Sighing heavily, he looked away from the house. "What woman would forget a fellow left her to walk home four miles. Alone. At night. In the pouring rain. On their first date."

~

Early morning light poured through the second-story bedroom's tall corner window overlooking the flower garden below. It promised to be a beautiful day for a wedding. Karen Yoder smiled at her little sister. Despite the happy occasion, Karen knew a bittersweet moment.

Lisa had met William at their friend Rachel's wedding six months ago. Karen met someone who made her heart sing at the wedding, too. Mathias Troyer. Now Lisa was happily getting married while Karen struggled to forget Mathias.

Nee, I'm over him.

Karen shook off his troublesome memory. Today was Lisa's special day. The wedding party had gathered before dawn that morning at the groom's home. Lisa sat in front of a small mirror in the bedroom belonging to William's sister Pamela, one of the bride's attendants. Lisa appeared breathtakingly happy in the royal blue dress and bright new *kapp* she had made for this day.

Rachel rushed into the room. "I'm sorry I'm late."

Lisa got up and hugged her. "I'm just glad you made it."

The groom's mother, Sally Burkholder, came in and clapped her hands to get everyone's attention. "I need Lisa and the *newehockers* to go down to the buggies now."

Lisa and William decided to marry at the home of Lisa's aunt and uncle, who lived five miles away. They owned a barn large enough to accommodate the hundreds of guests expected to attend the unusual April wedding. Lisa's parents were busy preparing the feast that would take place at their home after the wedding. As was the custom, they wouldn't attend the actual ceremony.

Lisa turned to Karen. "How do I look?"

Her dress emphasized the blue of her sparkling eyes and the rosy color of her cheeks. She couldn't stop smiling. Karen hid the stab of envy that struck her heart and hugged her sister. "Like a happy, blessed bride."

Pamela took Lisa by the shoulders and turned her toward the door. "Don't keep my brother waiting."

Lisa giggled. "Okay, I'm ready."

The bride and her attendants headed out with William's mother. Karen planned to drive herself in her pony cart. She needed to hurry home after the wedding to help her parents before the guests arrived. After taking a quick glance around to make sure nothing important had been left behind, she followed the chattering group. In the hall, she stopped short. Ogden Martin stood just outside William's room.

She'd met Ogden at Rachel's wedding, too. He started making a nuisance of himself as soon as he moved to Karen's community a few weeks later. She declined his many requests to walk out together. Undeterred, he began proposing and refused to take no for an answer.

He came by her home in the evenings, even after she refused to see him, and followed her everywhere. Two weeks ago, he'd confronted her at the restaurant where she worked as a waitress and made a scene. The manager fired her. She'd been too ashamed to tell her parents why. Finally, she confided in her sister. Lisa insisted Karen go to the bishop of their congregation.

Ogden claimed Karen led him on, encouraged his attention, but Bishop Fisher believed her side of the story. He instructed Ogden to leave her alone or be chastised in front of the whole church. She thought that would put an end to Ogden's harassing behavior.

Karen glared at Ogden now. "What are you doing?"

"William forgot his tie. Mathias is downstairs. I wonder what fine joke he has planned for today?" Ogden opened the door and stepped inside the room.

Filled with dread at the thought of facing Mathias, Karen braced herself to see him. She went out to where the wedding party was getting settled into two buggies. William stood with his back to her, greeting someone. When he stepped aside, she saw Mathias.

Her heart thumped wildly, betraying her claim to be over him, as the memory of those first sweet days came flooding to mind.

The moment their eyes had met, a wonderful feeling uncurled inside her. It only grew as they spent time together. When he invited her to attend a barn party, she'd been delighted. Her schoolgirl-like crush ended that night after Mathias abandoned her to walk home alone.

Embarrassed and frightened, she waited for an explanation the next day. Ogden came to tell her it had been a jest that Mathias planned. With her humiliation complete, she returned to Badger Creek, where William and Lisa soon became engaged while Karen worked doggedly to forget Mathias Troyer. He'd never even apologized for the cruel joke he'd played on her.

She forgave him as her faith required, but she prayed he would stay away today. Now he stood in front of her.

Tall and slender, handsome as ever in his black *mutza* suit and vest, with his black hat pushed back on his curly brown hair, the sight of him still had a

172

powerful effect on her emotions. How often in those early days did she dream of running her fingers through those same curls? His chestnut brown eyes and thick dark eyelashes did funny things to her insides. She thought she was prepared to face him, but she wasn't.

A new worry crept into her mind. Did he have a prank planned for today? Nothing could go wrong on her baby sister's special day. Karen wouldn't stand for it.

"It could've been your wedding today, too, if you'd only said yes," Ogden whispered in her ear.

Clenching her fists, Karen refused to look at him. "Go away. The bishop has forbidden you to annoy me."

"I'm not afraid of old Bishop Fisher. In fact, I'm no longer a member of this congregation anymore. You'll like the church I've joined. Bishop Hochstetler and I have already discussed having our banns read."

"I will not marry you. Not now. Not ever," she whispered harshly, trying not to draw attention to them.

He gripped her arm so hard it hurt. She jerked away and scowled at him. He appeared contrite and patted her shoulder. "I'm sorry. Oh, look what I've done. I didn't realize I had axle grease on my hand. I hope you can get that out."

Karen stared at the oily black smear across the sleeve of her new dress and another on her shoulder. "You did that on purpose!"

"If you would marry me, such things wouldn't happen to you. I'd take care of you." He smiled and walked away. She fumed as he stopped to speak with his cousin Mathias. Two birds of a feather.

Tears stung her eyes as she stared at the lovely blue dress she had sewn for her sister's wedding. Although not part of the wedding party, Karen would oversee the bride's table at the meal after the ceremony. She wasn't going to accept gifts for the couple looking like she had greased a wheel and wiped her hands on her clothes. Maybe she could change into one of Pamela's dresses and explain later.

Karen hurried into the house and up to the bedroom. Pulling off her ruined garment, she stared at the stains. She should get them out before they set, but she didn't have time. Ogden would not make her late to her sister's special day. She found a maroon dress and just finished pinning the front closed when she heard a knock. Someone from the wedding party must be looking for her.

"I'm coming."

The door opened before she reached it. Mathias stepped inside the room. He held his hat in his hands and wore a contrite expression as he stared at the floor.

She gaped at him in shock. "What are you doing here?"

CHAPTER TWO

$\mathcal{M}$athias gathered his courage and looked up. Karen stood before him, every bit as beautiful as he remembered. Her dark auburn hair, bright green eyes, and the freckles she professed to hate made his chest tight with joy, but the scowl on her face reminded him what he needed to do.

"I'm here to apologize, Karen. Thank you for agreeing to hear me out in private this way. I am sincerely sorry about what happened last fall."

"I did NOT agree to see you."

He blinked hard. "But Ogden said—"

"Ogden sent you up here?" Karen's eyes flashed with anger.

He nodded slowly. This wasn't going well.

"Ogden said he explained what happened the night I left the party. I'm truly sorry for the terrible misunderstanding. Ogden hopes that you and I can make peace. He cares for you deeply and wants me to be friends with his future wife."

"I will not be mocked by the pair of you again."

Mathias took a step back. "I don't understand."

She pointed to the door. "Leave. Now."

"Please, explain what I've done."

"Leave!"

It was his worst nightmare. She wouldn't listen to him. He gathered his tattered pride, walked to the door, and grasped the doorknob. It came off in his hand. He stared at it blankly for a second. He tried to fit the brass knob back on the spindle, but the spindle and opposite knob fell out the other side with a resounding clunk.

"I told you to leave." Her voice, cold as the winter wind, sent a chill up his spine.

"Ah, I can't." He turned around and held out the knob. "It came off."

"A doorknob doesn't just come off."

He stared at it in his hand. "This one did. The screw must have worked loose."

"Well, put it back on and get out."

He stepped aside so she could see for herself. "The knob and spindle dropped out the other side. There's no way to open the latch."

"You did this on purpose. You and your conniving cousin." She pushed past him and began beating on the door. "Let us out!"

"I saw the last buggy drive away. Ogden is waiting for me beside the barn. I don't think he can hear you from here."

"We can't be locked in." She spun around and ran to the window. Throwing up the sash, she began yelling for help. There was no reply.

Mathias frowned. Ogden should be answering her cries. Surely, he could hear her now.

～

Karen turned to glare at Mathias as she advanced on him. "Ogden put you up to this, didn't he? He wants me to miss Lisa's wedding."

Mathias faced her with a dazed expression. "Why would he play such a trick? He loves you."

"He doesn't know the meaning of the word. Don't just stand there. Do something!"

He turned around to examine the door. "The hinges are on the outside. We can't pull the pins and remove the whole door. Someone will return to look for you when you don't arrive."

"They may not miss me until the ceremony is over. I'm not part of the wedding party. What is wrong with that man and you?" This couldn't be happening.

"This is not Ogden's doing. I'm sure of that," Mathias said.

"Then this is your idea."

"*Nee.*"

He appeared innocent and confused.

"I imagine Ogden needed someone to keep me occupied while he rigged a way to lock me in. Who better than his faithful, unquestioning lapdog of a cousin?"

Mathias turned beet red. "I'm here to apologize for my behavior last fall. Now maybe you will listen to my explanation."

She turned her back to him and walked to the window. The bedroom was on the second floor. It looked like a twenty-foot drop to the flower garden below. The beautifully blooming daisies wouldn't provide much of a cushion if she jumped.

"Please, Karen?"

The sincerity in his voice made her give in. "Okay, explain."

"A young boy brought a message that my sister needed me urgently. Ogden offered to explain and bring you home. When I got to my sister's, I learned she didn't send for me, so I waited for Ogden to bring you back. When you didn't come for hours, I assumed you wanted to stay at the party with him. I didn't learn you had walked home until the next day when Thomas came to my place demanding an explanation. By then you had left."

She crossed her arms tightly over her chest. "Ogden told me you had a quick errand you needed to run. He offered to take me home, but I didn't feel comfortable going with him and said no. He assured me you would be back soon, and he left. So did everyone else while I waited. You never came. Then I walked. The next morning, Ogden stopped by and told me you had planned to play a little joke on me."

"I don't know why he would tell you such a thing. It wasn't true. I'm sorry, Karen. What else can I say?"

She spun to face him with her hands on her hips. "Say you can get us out of here."

"I don't believe Ogden has done this." Mathias's gaze swept around the room. "What is the point of locking you in? Us in?"

"To prove he has control over my life whenever he decides to use it. He is obsessed with me."

"He loves you, that's true. I wish I could show you the letters he has written about you."

"The feeling is not returned."

Mathias frowned. "You don't mean that. You make him so happy."

She held up one hand. "Don't tell me what I mean. You have no idea what he has put me through. Stop before I say something I'll regret."

He tossed his hat on the bed and sighed. "I'm not sure what to think. He should have heard you calling if he is waiting for me by the barn."

Mathias turned to the door, took two steps back, and threw his shoulder against the panel. It didn't budge. He stepped back three more paces and tried again with the same result. He rubbed his arm. "This isn't going to work."

Discouraged, Karen leaned out the window and looked along the side of the house. The window of the next room sat only a few feet away. She straddled the windowsill and reached as far as she could. Her fingers just brushed the other window jamb.

"What are you doing?" he asked.

"If I can reach the window of the next room, I might be able to climb through it." She slipped, shrieked, and toppled forward.

~

Mathias caught Karen by the waist and pulled her back into the room. "Now is not the time to do something foolish. You could break a leg or much worse if you fall."

She sank to the floor as he stood over her. Her face had gone pale, her hands were trembling. "*Danki.*"

"The thing to do is stay calm and wait until someone returns looking for us."

She drew a deep, shaky breath. "I will not miss the wedding. What we need is a rope to climb down."

She had determination and more spunk than sense. He patted his pockets. "I must've left my lariat in my other pants."

"Very funny. We can make a rope out of the bed sheets."

There were two twin beds in the room. Karen stood, pulled off the quilts, and tossed them aside before stripping the sheets. Knotting two together, she yanked on them. The knot slipped. She tied it again, and this time it held. Adding a third and fourth sheet left her makeshift rope only about fifteen feet long. She went to the window and dangled it outside. He moved beside her to look out. It didn't reach the ground.

He eyed it dubiously. "I'm not sure it will take your weight, but I'm certain it won't take mine."

She pulled the sheets in. "Only one of us has to get out. I can open the door once I'm back in the house."

He nodded. "True."

"Now we need something to secure it."

Two beds with delicately turned spindles in the Jenny Lind style and a small dresser were the only furniture in the room. He grabbed the footboard of one bed and pulled. An ominous crack told him it wouldn't be strong enough. "I reckon I'm going to have to be your anchor."

Her eyes widened. "You think I'm going to climb out the window with only you holding me up?"

"Hey, I'm content to wait."

She gave a low growl of frustration. "I am not. Can you hold me, or will you drop me?"

"I'd like to promise I can lower you to the ground safely, but as this is my first escape from a second-story bedroom window with bedsheets, I have no idea if I'm strong enough. I'm a teacher, not a lumberjack. If you're looking for muscles, look elsewhere."

She glared at him. "I wish I could."

He tossed his hands in the air. "Problem solved. We wait."

"It's not solved." She tossed the end of the sheet to him and sat on the window ledge. "Tell me when you're ready."

He'd get better results arguing with a post. Grasping the fabric, he sat on the floor and braced his feet on the wall below the window. "I'm ready, but please change your mind."

"Don't drop me," she snapped.

"Don't tempt me," he shot back.

They glared at each other for a long moment. He closed his eyes and gave in. How could he still find her so attractive when she clearly loathed him? "Okay. I'm ready."

"*Goot.*" She maneuvered her legs out the window, turned onto her stomach, and clutched the sheet.

"Wait," he said.

"For what?"

"Do you accept my apology for last fall? Am I forgiven?"

"Are you seriously asking me that now?"

"I am. In case the worst happens."

"I forgave you ages ago." She slipped backward, and the sheet nearly jerked out of his hands.

Mathias gritted his teeth as he slowly lowered her. The third knot went past his hands and over the window ledge. She had to be getting close. He heard a ripping sound and toppled backward with only a foot of fabric still in his grip. The sheet had torn in two. Tossing the rag aside, he lunged to his knees to look out the window. She sat on the ground among the bright yellow daisies. "Are you hurt?"

She tipped her head back to glare at him. "You dropped me."

"*Nee.* The sheet tore. Go around and let me out."

"I don't see why I should." She got to her feet and stomped off.

"You've got petals sticking to your—skirt," he shouted, but she had already disappeared around the corner of the house.

Mathias turned and sat with his back against the wall, prepared to wait until the three-hour wedding service ended, but two troubling questions kept running through his mind. Where was Ogden? And why had he lied about Karen's feelings?

CHAPTER THREE

*K*aren went round to the front of the house. Her pony and cart were still waiting by the barn. She didn't see Ogden anywhere. Going inside, she hurried up the stairs. She might have threatened to leave Mathias locked in, but she couldn't do it.

The doorknob with the spindle attached lay on the floor by the door. Had the screw simply worked loose as Mathias suggested? It did happen in older homes. She searched for the screw but couldn't find it.

Was it in Mathias's pocket along with a screwdriver? He'd had time enough to loosen the screw.

No, this had taken some planning and timing. Ogden was responsible, she knew it. Mathias only arrived a few minutes before Ogden soiled her dress. He couldn't have known she'd gone to the room alone unless Ogden told him.

Inserting the spindle, she turned the knob and opened the door. Mathias sat beneath the window looking forlorn.

She gestured to him. "Come on. We need to get going."

He scrambled to his feet and grabbed his hat. "How far to where the ceremony is being held?"

"Five miles."

He hurried down the stairs. "Is there another buggy or a wagon we can take?"

"My mare is still hitched to my cart by the barn."

Taffy stood dozing in the shade but perked up when Mathias unsnapped her lead from the fence. He got in the cart and helped Karen in, then handed her the lines. "You know where we are going. I don't."

At least he was showing some common sense by not insisting that he drive. Had he been telling the truth when he denied helping Ogden? If only she could be sure. Her faith required her to trust every man at face value, but Ogden's actions proved some men were untrustworthy. She urged Taffy down the lane and out onto the highway. They rode in silence for almost a mile.

Mathias cleared his throat. "I'm sorry about this."

She cast him a sharp sidelong glance. "Did you have any part in planning this stunt?"

He clapped a hand to his chest. "*Nee*, I did not. I know you hold a poor opinion of me, but I am not a liar."

She wanted to believe him. Could a man sound as contrite as Mathias and still be lying? She glanced at him. He looked more confused than devious. "Ogden duped us both."

"You're wrong about him. I've known Ogden since we were children. He's more like a brother to me than a cousin. What would he gain by this? He loves you."

"If you must defend him, I'd rather not hear it."

"I'm puzzled, that's all. When did this start?" Mathias sounded as if he genuinely didn't know.

"As soon as Ogden moved here from Mount Iron, he began asking me out."

"What went wrong?"

She glared at him. "Nothing went wrong. I didn't want to go out with him, but he wouldn't stop coming around."

"Are you sure you didn't give him false hope?"

Her mouth dropped open. "You mean did I lead him on? That's what Ogden told the bishop when I complained."

Mathias's expression softened. "I'm simply trying to understand."

"I did nothing to encourage Ogden. I politely said we weren't suited. He became angry, waylaid me on the way to work, and on the way home. He constantly accused me of breaking his heart, and then things got worse."

"How so?"

"He started asking my friends to convince me of my mistake. He told me I would be sorry if I didn't keep seeing him. I still refused. One day he ran out in front of my buggy and spooked my horse into bolting. I've never been so frightened. Then he came to my work and got me fired. That's when I went to our bishop. He believed me. He spoke to Ogden and told him the church didn't look kindly on such behavior. If Ogden didn't stop bothering me, steps would be taken."

"The bishop actually threatened to shun him?"

"You're taking his side, aren't you? Of course, you are. You're his faithful cousin."

"I'm his faithful, unquestioning lapdog of a cousin."

Karen glared at him. "I see there's nothing wrong with your memory."

"*Nee*, but I'm truly upset Ogden used me, no matter what transpired between you."

"I just told you what transpired," she snapped.

"Every coin has two sides."

"Would you do me the greatest of favors?"

He frowned. "If I can."

"Don't speak to me until we reach my *onkel*'s home. Better yet never speak to me again." She slapped the lines against Taffy's rump, as eager to part company with Mathias as she was to reach the wedding.

Mathias hung on tight as Karen took the corner into a farm lane too fast. She didn't slow down until they reached a large white farmhouse surrounded by dozens of buggies. He heard singing from inside the large barn. The service had started.

He took the lines from her hands. "If I can do anything to make up for my part in this, I will. Go. I'll take care of the horse."

She didn't bother responding. Jumping from the cart, she hurried inside. Mathias got down and patted the winded mare's neck. Over her back, he saw Ogden step out of the shadows.

He sauntered up with a friendly grin. "I see you made it."

Stunned, Mathias gaped at him. "What did you hope to accomplish with this prank?"

"Are you upset over a little joke? Karen is always so serious. Pretty funny, don't you think? How did you escape?"

"She risked life and limb to climb out the window on a rope made of sheets."

"Resourceful. Your idea?"

"It doesn't matter. Karen never should have been put in that position."

"When did you become so stodgy? You used to be up for a good jest any time."

Mathias couldn't believe what he was hearing. Ogden didn't seem to understand the seriousness of what he had done. "When we were kids maybe, but that kind of behavior belongs in the past. Karen would have been heart-broken if she had missed seeing her sister get married."

"It could have been her wedding day, too. I told her that. She keeps denying that she is going to be my wife."

Mathias shook his head. "Cousin, this isn't the way to win a woman's heart."

"I tried all the usual ways, but she refuses to accept I'm going to be her husband. She's stubborn, but I'll convince her."

Mathias pulled off his hat and raked his fingers through his hair. "You are badly mistaken. Surely you would rather have a wife who loves you."

"She will come to love me."

"Ogden, I care for you as a brother. I'm telling you this for your own good. Karen will not marry you. The harder you try to force her into a relationship, the more she will hate you."

Ogden suddenly frowned. "You want her for yourself, don't you? I saw the way you looked at her just now. She's not for you. She's mine. What *Gott* has joined together, no man may put asunder."

"If you persist, you could be shunned."

"If I must leave the Amish, then I will. She's worth it."

His cousin's casual assertion shocked Mathias. "Leaving the church isn't something to be talked about lightly. You made a vow before *Gott* on the day you were baptized."

"You don't understand what it is to be in love."

Ogden walked away, leaving Mathias shaking his head in disbelief. He glanced toward the hay barn where the singing had stopped. Poor Karen. There had to be some way he could help her and bring Ogden to his senses.

~

Many of the four hundred guests were still eating, but the wedding party had retired to an upstairs bedroom. The wedding couple were meant to be resting before the evening meal and the visiting that would last late into the evening. Sitting with her mother, Mrs. Burkholder, the newlyweds, and the attendants, Karen relayed the story of her morning's misadventure.

"I can't believe Ogden would do such a thing," Thomas declared.

Karen gritted her teeth. "He deliberately tried to keep me from attending the wedding. William, did you send Ogden to your room to fetch your tie?"

William touched the black bow tie he wore for his wedding day but would never wear again. "I had it on when he arrived."

"I saw him go into your room when we were leaving. He said you'd forgotten your tie. He had enough time to loosen a screw then or when Mathias was talking to me."

"You must tell the bishop," Pamela said. "He will deal with Ogden."

Karen shook her head. "Ogden told me he has joined Bishop Hostetler's church. Bishop Fisher can't do anything to him now."

"Then you should go to Bishop Hostetler. Tell him what Ogden is doing," Lisa said firmly.

Karen sighed. "And then what? Ogden can join another congregation. I can't live this way, always looking over my shoulder, wondering what he will do next."

"Perhaps you should consider his offer," Mrs. Burkholder said.

Cries of outrage filled the room as Karen's sister and friends voice their disagreement.

Karen's mother held up her hand for silence. "That is not the answer, but I may have one."

Karen turned to her. "Please tell me."

"Your father has been planning to start his own bakery for some time."

Karen looked around. "We know that. How does that help?"

Thomas leaned forward. "I talked to your father about a place in Mount Iron that might suit his needs. It's an existing bakery that will require very little renovation to get up and running. Your father is returning with us to check it out when we leave tomorrow. If he likes what he sees, he'll start searching for a house to buy."

"You should go with him, Karen," her mother said. "When Ogden comes to see you, I'll tell him you have taken a trip to visit a friend. It won't be a lie."

Karen sank back into her chair. "We might move to Mount Iron. The village where Mathias lives?"

"I don't believe Mathias had any part in what happened," William said.

"Nor do I," Thomas added.

Rachel looked around the room. "I've known him since birth. He and Ogden were close when they were young. The boys were pranksters in school, but Mathias wouldn't help Ogden do something this shoddy."

"Can you assure me that none of you will tell Ogden where I've gone?" Karen asked.

Mrs. Burkholder frowned. "Running away is not the answer. Our faith says we must not resist evil."

Lisa gave her new mother-in-law an understanding look. "Ogden isn't evil, Sally. He's simply confused. Time apart will give them both a chance to reexamine their feelings."

Karen didn't need to reexamine anything, but she wanted Mrs. Burkholder on her side.

Mrs. Burkholder thought it over, then nodded. "That is true. A little distance may not be a bad idea."

The couples all exchanged looks, then Rachel nodded. "You have our word. Ogden's parents have moved to a settlement in Florida. Mathias is the only person in Mount Iron who keeps in touch with him."

Karen chewed on the corner of her lip as she thought about what to say next. Her mind whirled. Ogden's outrageous behavior was driving her out of her home, but what choice did she have? He'd never leave her in peace if she remained. It was so unfair.

Taking a deep breath, she forged ahead. "Can you assure me that Mathias won't tell Ogden?"

Rachel gazed at Karen earnestly. "I would like to tell you my brother won't say anything, but you must ask for his promise yourself."

CHAPTER FOUR

*A*s a friend of the groom, Mathias expected to help however he could at the wedding. So, he stood at a large suds-filled metal tub on a folding table set up in the backyard behind Karen's home and washed dishes.

Thomas carried out a tray of dirty plates and set them beside the others waiting for Mathias to finish washing. He then picked up a tray of clean dishes and went back inside. With hundreds of people to feed, the flow of dishes seemed never ending, but Mathias didn't care. The mindless task required little thought.

A breeze stirred the bright green leaves and delicate white flowers of the apple trees around Mathias on a beautiful spring afternoon. The smell of freshly mown grass and the fragrant scent of blossoms from the orchard filled the air making it a perfect day for a wedding.

Laughter and cheerful chatter filled the air. Becky and Samuel had found other children to play with. They were engaged in a game of hide and seek. Becky stood counting with her eyes closed as she leaned against a nearby tree. Everyone seemed to be enjoying themselves. Everyone but him.

His attempt to patch things up with Karen had only made it worse. She'd probably never speak to him again. The thought pressed his spirits into the dirt. Karen might not speak to him, but he wanted to help her. There must be some way to make Ogden realize what a mistake he was making.

A woman delivered a load of plates to the table beside him. He didn't look up. "*Danki.*"

"I want to talk to you."

His head snapped up, and the wet dish he held slipped from his fingers to clatter against the metal tub. "Karen."

She looked around. "Have you seen Ogden?"

"Not since we arrived. I tried talking to him. He's determined to marry you."

"Then he's doomed to disappointment."

"He's so mixed up. He says you'll come to love him in time."

She kept looking in all directions. "Right after pigs learn to fly."

"I wish I could make him believe that." Mathias sighed heavily.

Karen pinned her gaze on him. "You said you'd do anything to make up for your part in his schemes. Did you mean it?"

"I did." Drying his hands on the apron tied around his waist, he waited for her to give him a task, any task, that he would gladly perform.

"Then this is your chance. I'm leaving Badger Creek."

Stunned, Mathias quickly recovered. "How can I help?"

She gazed at him intently. "By not telling Ogden."

Mathias frowned. "Karen, he loves you. Moving away without telling him would be cruel."

"It's the only way."

He saw her mind was made up. "Why tell me? Why not keep your move a secret?"

"Because my father hopes to start a bakery in Mount Iron."

His heart dropped, then started beating wildly. Did this mean she'd be living in his community? If so, he'd see her often. How long could he conceal his true feelings with her nearby?

Her eyes narrowed. "I'm not sure I can trust you, Mathias."

His spirits plummeted lower. "You're concerned that I'll tell Ogden."

"Will you betray me?"

"*Nee*, I will not."

"Can you promise me you'll never reveal my whereabouts to him?"

Mathias considered her request. "I can't lie to him if he asks me directly."

Karen blew out a huff in disgust. "I knew I couldn't trust you."

She turned away, but he caught her arm. "Wait."

The glare she leveled at his hand made him let go instantly. "Sorry. I won't betray your confidence. Not ever. If he asks specifically where you are—I'll tell him the truth. That I promised not to reveal your whereabouts and I must keep my word."

Karen stared at him for a long moment. "Can you do that?"

"You trusted me when you crawled out that window."

Her eyes flashed. "And you dropped me."

"The sheet ripped. You can't blame me for that."

"Maybe not," she admitted without sounding as if she meant it.

186

"I won't tell Ogden where you are. I promise, but may I tell him you are safe and well?"

"Not even that."

He held up both hands. "All right."

"I wish I knew if I could believe you."

He crossed his arms over his chest. "Karen, if you didn't have some faith in me, you wouldn't be sharing this information."

"Your sister, Thomas, and William have great faith in you. Don't let them down."

She walked away. Mathias stared at the suds in his tub. If she moved to Mount Iron, they would belong to the same church group, attend the same prayer services, frolics, and picnics. Would she ever come to see him in a better light? From her expression and tone, he doubted it.

She sounded dead set against marrying Ogden. Mathias had spent the last months reading Ogden's accounts of their romance with a heart full of pain, but if she didn't want Ogden, she was free to walk out with anyone.

Mathias sighed. It wouldn't be with him. How could he approach the woman he knew his cousin loved so desperately? It would be a betrayal Mathias couldn't live with.

"Nice gal." Thomas deposited more plates on the table beside Mathias.

"Yeah." Mathias nodded in agreement.

"She and her father will travel to Mount Iron with us tomorrow."

"I heard. If Ogden sees her and her father leave with us, he'll know where she is going."

"She needs a disguise," a low voice whispered from beneath the table. Mathias stepped back and saw Samuel hiding there.

"How long have you been eavesdropping?" Mathias demanded.

"Shh, I'm hiding from Becky."

Thomas leaned down and grinned at his son. "Eavesdropping is wrong, but that is a *goot* idea. I'll tell Rachel."

Samuel saw his chance and made a break for the tree, touching it before Becky caught him.

Thomas patted Mathias on the shoulder. "I thought Karen had a thing for you when she visited us last fall."

Mathias plunged his hands into the water. "Did you notice any pigs flying by?"

Thomas chuckled. "*Nee*, why?"

"Because that's about the time Karen Yoder will have a thing for me." Mathias took the tray of dirty dishes and plunked them in the water.

∾

Karen changed into her mother's oldest work dress when it was time to leave. Lisa and Rachel had chosen a moment when several groups of wedding guests were leaving. Two hired vans sat in front of the house waiting for passengers. Lisa draped their grandmother's shawl around Karen's shoulders. No one had seen Ogden that morning, but if he was lurking nearby watching for Karen, Lisa hoped changing outfits would confuse him.

Rachel handed Karen a bundle of blankets that looked as if she was carrying a baby, secured a large bonnet on Karen's head to help hide her distinctive hair and stepped outside. Karen followed with her head down, hoping the oversized traveling bonnet would shield her face.

"Don't look for him," Lisa whispered in her ear.

Resisting the urge, Karen concentrated on kissing each of her family members goodbye. Tears sprang to her eyes as she kissed her sister.

"Have a *goot* trip, cousin," Lisa said loudly.

Karen kept her head down and stepped into the back of the vehicle waiting to take them to Mount Iron. Her father sat up front with the driver. Rachel and Thomas occupied the middle seat with Samuel. Becky sat in the back with Mathias. He stared out the window, ignoring Karen.

Becky patted the spot beside her. "Sit with me. I had a *goot* time at the wedding, didn't you? I made three new friends. We're going to write to each other."

"That's *wunderbar*." Karen smiled at the child but didn't look at Mathias. She'd trusted him with her plan, but she wasn't comfortable around him.

"Everyone ready?" the driver asked.

"I am," Becky shouted. "I can't wait to tell my friend Mary Sue about my trip."

Becky kept up a near constant flow of chatter for the next five minutes. When she fell silent, Karen looked to see if she had fallen asleep. The child was frowning.

"What's wrong?" Karen asked.

"Everyone getting married seems really happy."

"That's natural," Rachel said. "Folks are happy when they fall in love and happier still when they decide to spend their lives together."

Becky turned to Mathias. "Why aren't you getting married?"

Samuel scoffed. "Not everyone wants to get hitched."

"He hasn't found the right woman," Rachel said, a hint of humor in her voice.

Becky tipped her head to the side. "Who is the right woman?"

"The one who falls in love with him," Thomas said. "Like your stepmother fell in love with me."

Becky turned to Karen. "How does he find the right one?"

Samuel chuckled. "He needs a matchmaker."

"I do not," Mathias snapped, clearly annoyed.

Becky turned in her seat to gaze at him. "What's a matchmaker?"

Karen glanced at Mathias's beet-red face and smothered a laugh.

She couldn't help enjoying his discomfort. "A matchmaker is someone who finds the right people to go together. Is there anyone in Mount Iron that Mathias likes, Becky?"

"He likes all his students, and we like him."

"I meant is there a special woman he walks out with?"

Mathias glared at Karen. "There isn't. Now please change the subject."

Becky leaned toward Karen. "He isn't happy," she whispered.

Karen chuckled. "He doesn't seem to be."

Sighing heavily, Becky nodded. "He needs a wife for sure."

"That's what I think, too." Rachel smiled sweetly at him.

Mathias crossed his arms over his chest. "I don't need a wife."

His tense tone said the teasing had gone on long enough.

Becky touched Karen's arm. "Do you think you could help me find him a wife?"

She looked at the child in shock. "Me? *Nee.*"

"She's the last person who should be a matchmaker," Mathias said.

Karen glared at him. "And why is that?"

"Because...what do you know about romance, anyway? You're still single."

She pressed her lips closed on her retort.

"See? He's not a happy person," Becky whispered.

The child patted his arm. "I'm going to be a matchmaker and find you a wife, Mathias." She grinned at Karen. "Would you like to marry him?"

"Maybe."

He looked her way in surprise.

"If he was the last man on earth."

Mathias's eyes filled with pain before he looked away. Karen wished she had bitten her tongue. When had she become so cruel?

189

CHAPTER FIVE

$\mathcal{O}$n his own again for breakfast.

Mathias searched his near empty kitchen and found a box of cereal at the back of the cupboard. He poured a bowl and sat at the table to eat it. The whole-wheat flakes were stale.

Since his sister's marriage to Thomas, Mathias had gotten in the habit of walking across the road to their place for breakfast. He was always welcomed warmly. Rachel was an excellent cook. Becky and Samuel would usually say or do something that made him smile. It had been a good way to start his day. But with Karen and her father staying there since the wedding last week, his presence would be unwelcome. To Karen anyway.

After dumping his cereal in the trash, he went out to care for his animals, then walked toward the schoolhouse. When he rounded the bend in the road, he saw Karen and her father standing in front of the building that until a few months ago had been the village's only bakery.

Henry Yoder saw him first. "Mathias, come and give us your opinion."

Karen glanced his way and then looked down.

Would she ever be glad to see him? He longed to see the light of welcome in her eyes. A foolish wish.

He stopped beside her father. "My opinion on what?"

"The real estate agent will be here shortly to show us the inside. Do you think this place could be profitable? Having only counter service will keep costs down. I won't need waitstaff."

Mathias shrugged. "I'm not sure I'm the right person to ask. Karen, what do you think?"

She looked up in surprise. "You want my opinion?"

"You worked for a restaurant, right?" he asked.

She nodded. "I did."

Her expression brightened as she studied the building. "I think adding a few tables inside and serving coffee would encourage people to linger and perhaps purchase something to take home. Especially the *Englisch* customers. Local teenagers might like a place to hang out so maybe a few tables outside as well."

Her father glanced around. "Maybe. Mathias, do you know why the business closed?"

"The *Englisch* owner's wife died. His heart wasn't in it anymore."

Henry nodded. "A man must put both his head and his heart into his work." He walked off to look at the back of the building.

Mathias smiled tentatively at Karen. "Your ideas are good ones."

She crossed her arms and shifted her weight from one foot to the other. "That doesn't mean my *daed* will act on them."

"Maybe not at first, but I think he will eventually see the wisdom in your words. I could remind him that a few tables inside would be nice once he is ready to open if you think it will help."

She looked surprised. "*Danki*. I want this to be a success for him. It has been his dream for a long time."

"And are your dreams still the same?" he asked softly.

Karen's gaze flew to Mathias's face. Did he truly care about her hopes for the future? She shrugged. "Mine are the same as every other Amish girl, I guess."

"I recall you said a husband to love you and as many children around your table as *Gott* would give you."

"That's right." She had told him that months ago, and yet he remembered. "What do you want, Mathias?"

"To keep teaching. *Goot* friends to share my joys and sorrows. Faith to sustain me in troubled times. A chance to make life better for others. To aid our brothers and sisters when they are in need."

Karen tipped her head slightly as she gazed at him. "Is that what you truly want?"

He glanced at her and then stared at the ground. "I must sound foolish."

"Why?"

"Because I'm a farmer who isn't asking *Gott* for rain, which we need, or for a bountiful harvest."

"I don't think you sound foolish at all."

He seemed embarrassed. "Foolish is a teacher who is late for school. I hope both you and your father find what you are looking for here." He tipped his hat and walked on but stopped a few feet away to look back. "If you or your father need a friend, I'm right down the road."

Karen watched him leave, overcome by a sense of having lost something important. Not once in all the times Ogden had spoken to her had he asked for her opinion or about her dreams for the future. He'd never revealed his own hopes beyond his obsession to have her for his wife.

Months ago, she and Mathias had shared a similar conversation when they were getting to know each other after his sister's wedding. If things had turned out differently, they might still be friends. Was it too late? What if she accepted the friendship he offered?

Ogden had managed to come between them back then. Would Mathias's friendship with Ogden allow him to come between them again?

~

During the next several days, Karen's attitude toward Mathias softened. His family, especially the children, adored him. He wasn't intrusive but greeted her kindly when they saw each other. Members of the community spoke well of him. Karen started to believe she had been wrong to be so critical.

The annual school picnic in Mount Iron took place on Saturday. According to Rachel, parents, grandparents, and family would attend. They'd visit the schoolhouse to view the artwork and projects the scholars had completed during the year. The children would enjoy games and good food supplied by everyone.

Karen helped Rachel prepare potato salad, fried chicken, and chocolate brownies. Samuel looked forward eagerly to the father-son softball game that would take place later in the day. Becky wanted to show Karen the pictures she had drawn of her friend Mary Sue's kitten.

Thomas and Karen's father went on ahead to set up lawn chairs. Rachel managed to herd the children out the door with two quilts over her arm. Karen followed with an overloaded picnic basket. She knew Mathias lived across the road, but she didn't expect him to be waiting for them just outside.

"Let me get that." He took the heavy basket from her hands and grunted. "What did you pack in this thing, Rachel?"

"All of the foods that you enjoy plus enough for the Zook children." Rachel looked at Karen. "Their mother has been poorly. I said I would supply a meal for them today. Thank you for letting me know the children were in need, Mathias. I'll speak to the bishop's wife about seeing that more meals are taken to the house."

Mathias chuckled. "She's feeding us and seven Zooks. No wonder this weighs a ton."

Karen glanced at him curiously. "How did you know the children were in need?"

"The last two days they've brought only an apple apiece to school for lunch. I went out to the house last night and found Mrs. Zook in bed with a sprained back. Mr. Zook had his hands full running his dairy alone and trying to take care of her. I said I would see that the children enjoyed a good picnic lunch today. Rachel will make sure the leftovers go home with them."

Karen regarded him with new eyes. There was more to Mathias than she had given him credit for. He wasn't like Ogden. "That was thoughtful of you."

"It's part of my job. Teachers are often the first to notice when something is wrong at home. Children may be ashamed to ask for help. If they aren't forthcoming, a visit is in order."

"The bishop trusts Mathias to let him know if it's something serious," Rachel said.

Samuel hopped alongside Mathias. "I sure hope we get on the same team."

"I hope so, too, but you'll play your best even if it's against me, right?"

"Right. Hey, I see Johnny." Samuel waved and took off.

"I thought it's a father-son game," Karen said.

"It is, but the Weaver twins lost their father a few years ago, so I fill in when I'm needed. Rachel, let me get this basket over to the tables, then I'll find us a place to sit."

"Thomas and Henry have taken care it," she said. "We're in the shade by the ballfield."

"I'll help you unload this." Karen took hold of the basket handle. Her fingers brushed against his sending a jolt of awareness up her arm.

Their eyes met. His pupils widened. Heat rushed to her cheeks, but she couldn't look away. A thrill sent her heart fluttering in her chest.

Becky squirmed in between them. "Mathias can Mary Sue and I have a brownie?"

He blinked twice, then looked down. "Sure. Help yourself. Karen, can you get this? I see Mrs. Weaver going into the school, and I must speak to her."

"Of course," Karen said, glad of a chance to compose herself.

He rushed off, but at the door to the school, he paused and looked back at her. A wry smile curved his lips, and her foolish heart skipped a beat.

"Don't do it, Karen. Don't fall for him again," she whispered.

"Talking to yourself?" Rachel began unpacking the hamper.

Karen blew out a deep breath. "Trying to talk some sense into myself."

"Is it working?" Rachel's voice shimmered with humor.

Karen shook her head. "It is not."

~

Mathias hummed a happy tune as he walked home from school on the following Monday afternoon. He slowed as he neared the bakery hoping to see Karen, but he didn't see her or Henry at the building. She might be at Rachel's house. He picked up his pace, eager to see her again.

He wasn't sure how Karen felt about him yet, but he'd seen something in her eyes at the picnic that encouraged him to hope they could spend more time together. The long afternoon spent lounging on a quilt with her and his family, watching the children compete in games, and enjoying her company made it feel like their months apart hadn't happened.

He would ask her to go for a buggy ride this evening. It seemed like a reasonable next step. He wanted to hold her hand, put his arm around her shoulders, and draw her close for their first kiss. His feelings for her grew stronger by the day.

When he reached his house, he noticed her sweeping Rachel's front porch. She smiled when she caught sight of him. He waved and she waved back. He stopped at his mailbox to gather his courage before going to speak to her. Opening it, he pulled out several letters and the newspaper.

"Rachel wondered if you might like to come to supper tonight."

Startled at hearing her voice so near, he spun around with a foolish grin on his face and dropped his letters.

They bent to retrieve them together. His fingers closed over hers as they grasped the same envelope. She didn't pull away. Mathias rose slowly, keeping hold of her delicate hand. His heart hammered so hard she must hear it. She kept her eyes down, but her cheeks were flushed.

She drew her hand away still clutching his letter. "About supper?"

"I reckon I have to eat." He closed his eyes. What a dumb thing to say. "I meant I'd be delighted."

When he looked at her again, her face had gone pale. She stared at his letter with wide eyes. He glanced down and immediately recognized the handwriting. A chill crawled up his spine. It was from Ogden.

"You wrote to him?" Her voice shook with disbelief.

"I didn't. This is the first I've heard from him. You can read it if you want."

"Take it." She thrust it at him. "Does he know I'm here?"

Mathias ripped open the letter and started reading. His heart sank.

"What does he say?" Karen demanded.

"That you have vanished. He is worried sick for fear something terrible has happened." Mathias saw the anguish in his cousin's shaky handwriting and pleas for any information about Karen. His heart ached for what Ogden must be going through. If Karen disappeared without a trace, Mathias knew he would be inconsolable.

She took a step back. "You want to tell him. I can see it in your eyes."

"This plan is cruel."

"I should have known you were the last man on earth who would help me. What was I thinking?" She spun around.

He dropped the letter and reached for her. "Karen, wait."

She didn't look back as she ran into Rachel's home and slammed the door.

～

"The last man on earth," Mathias muttered as he scrubbed the blackboard at the front of the schoolroom. "When I'm the last man on earth who owns flying pigs, she might trust me."

It had been two weeks since the arrival of Ogden's letter. Mathias had answered it with his usual descriptions of his student's antics and nothing more. He didn't mention Karen. It had been a hard letter to write.

Henry Yoder bought the building and began setting up his bakery. Mathias saw Karen scrubbing windows, mowing the lawn, and painting furniture. The community had pitched in to help, but Mathias stayed away. He passed the store on his way to school each morning and again each evening. He'd seen Karen every day, but he hadn't spoken to her.

"Why should I waste my breath? She doesn't want to talk to me."

"Did you say something, Teacher Mathias?"

He turned around to see Mary Sue taking her seat in the second row of desks.

He smiled at the shy child. "You caught me talking to myself."

"You sound sad."

"Do I?" Perceptive child. "I need someone to ring the bell for class to start this morning. Would you like to do that for me?"

"Sure." She rewarded him with a big smile.

It might boost Mary Sue's confidence to be assigned a grown-up task.

"Should I ring the bell now?"

He glanced at the clock. "Go ring it loud."

Mary Sue jumped out of her seat and hurried to the door. It took her several pulls on the rope before the bell began peeling. The outside door opened, and the students started filing in.

Becky stopped beside Mary Sue. "Did teacher let you ring the bell?"

"Uh huh." Mary Sue gave one more tug, then headed to her seat, still grinning.

At least he'd made one person happy today. Mathias stepped to the board and wrote out the arithmetic assignments for all the classes.

Later, when the children filed out for recess, he sat on the steps of the school, determined not to look toward the bakery. Instead, he gazed down the hill at the river a hundred yards away across the road. The water looked deceptively calm here above the rapids a quarter mile downstream, but the undercurrents were as treacherous as Karen believed him to be. Why couldn't he stop thinking about her?

Becky came over and sat beside him. "I miss seeing you at breakfast."

"Your *mamm* has enough people to feed. She doesn't need another one."

Despite his resolve, he glanced down the road and saw Karen lifting some packages from the buggy. She didn't look in his direction. Seeing her daily and knowing he had no hope tortured him. Why couldn't he forget her and go on with his life? Why did the pain in his heart deepen every day?

"You should come to breakfast. Karen makes the best cinnamon rolls. Even better than *Mamm's*."

He glanced at his niece. "Has she asked about me?"

Becky shook her head. Mathias chided himself for having even a tiny bit of hope.

"Samuel misses you, too," Becky said.

Mathias wasn't in the mood for small talk. "You both see me every day at school. How can you miss me? Run along and play with your friends."

How much more he could take?

CHAPTER SIX

*B*ecky and Mary Sue walked home together after school on Friday. Samuel followed them, tossing a soft ball into the air and catching it.

Mary Sue glanced at Becky. "Teacher is sad."

Becky nodded. "I've noticed that, too."

"He didn't even want to play catch with me this week." Samuel missed his ball and had to run pick it up. "Could he be sick or something?"

"My big brother Johnny acted like that once. My *mamm* said he was heartsick."

Samuel stopped walking. "Johnny has something wrong with his heart? He seemed fine when we played catch last night."

Mary Sue scowled at Samuel. "*Daed* got upset with Johnny for losing his new ball in the river. *Mamm* says you have to stay away from there."

Samuel rolled his eyes. "I'm to blame. I overthrew him and the ball rolled downhill and into the water. It was gone before we even got to the bank. Tell me what's wrong with your brother."

"He liked some girl, but he thought she didn't like him. He's fine now because he found out she really does like him."

Samuel nodded wisely. "Girls are trouble."

"We need to find out who Mathias likes," Becky said.

Mary Sue frowned at her. "And then what?"

"We ask her if she likes him, too." Becky pointed at her brother. "Samuel, you ask him."

"I'm not going to ask him what girl he likes," Samuel said in disgust.

Mary Sue stopped and turned to Becky. "Your *mamm* is his sister. She should ask him."

Becky grinned at her. "You're pretty smart, Mary Sue."

"I am?" Mary Sue looked surprise, then smiled. "Yeah, I am."

~

Karen was helping Rachel prepare supper when Becky and her friend Mary Sue came in and sat at the table. Becky folded her arms on the tabletop. "*Mamm*, I need your help."

"With homework?"

Becky shook her head. "Mathias is sick."

"What?" Karen and Rachel exclaimed at the same time.

Becky nodded toward her friend. "Mary Sue thinks it's his heart."

Rachel crossed the room to sit beside Becky. "There is nothing wrong with Mathias's heart. The man is as healthy as a horse."

"Mary Sue's brother had the same thing. Her *mamm* said he was heartsick over a girl."

Mary Sue nodded. "That's right."

"Ah," Rachel said. "I understand."

Karen turned away and pressed her hand to her chest. The thought of Mathias being seriously ill had shocked her. She struggled to compose herself.

"Mary Sue, why do you think Mathias is heartsick?" Rachel asked gently.

"He doesn't pay attention to us like he did before. He always looks sad."

"He doesn't come over for breakfast anymore," Becky added.

When Karen had her emotions under control, she turned around and saw Rachel glance at her, then back at Becky. "He's just being considerate."

Becky frowned and leaned closer to her mother. "Samuel says he doesn't play catch with him anymore. Not once this week."

"Those do sound like serious symptoms of heartache." Rachel turned to Karen. "What is your opinion?"

Karen snorted. "I'm the last person you should ask about romance."

"Ah," Rachel said. "That comment still rankles, doesn't it? I believe our faith requires us to forgive those who injure us even if it's not a physical injury."

Karen had forgiven Mathias a long time ago, but her doubts wouldn't let her trust him.

"*Mamm*, Mary Sue and I want you to ask Mathias the name of the girl he likes, then we can find out if she likes him too," Becky said. "If she does, and they get married, he'll be happy again."

Rachel grinned at Karen. "The children seem to have it all figured out."

Karen frowned at her. "You aren't suggesting you believe this nonsense about Mathias being heartsick?"

"I know my brother pretty well, and Becky is right. He's been moping around enough that even the children at school have noticed. I see him watching you."

"He hasn't been."

"You know that because you are watching him?" Rachel's coy tone said she already knew the answer.

From the bakery window, Karen could see the schoolyard and often noticed Mathias sitting on the steps when the children were outside. She saw him looking in her direction couldn't read his expression from so far away.

She tried for an offhand tone. "He passes by the bakery morning and evening. He hasn't stopped in once."

"Because he knows he won't be welcome. You made that plain."

"Karen, why don't you like Mathias?" Becky asked.

"Oh, she likes him, Becky," Rachel assured her. "And he likes her."

Karen had forgotten the children were listening. "It's more than a matter of liking someone. A woman shouldn't waste her time with a fellow who isn't marriage material."

Becky's eyes widened. "I never thought of that. What kind of man should you marry?"

Rachel quickly wiped a grin off her face. "*Ja*, Karen, give us your list of qualities a man should have." She swept her arm to include Rachel and Mary Sue. "Educate these young ones."

How embarrassing. Put on the spot by her friend and a pair of second graders.

Karen took a deep breath. "A good man should be kind and generous. He should be brave and faithful to *Gott*."

"And handsome," Mary Sue stated.

Karen shook her head. "Looks are not important. A hard-working man is an attractive man. He should like children, too."

"Mathias likes children," Rachel said.

"That is only one quality. A man should have all of them before you consider spending the rest of your life with him. Most importantly, he should value you as an equal partner."

Becky turned to Mary Sue. "That's a long list."

Mary Sue shrugged. "Not so bad if you subtract handsome."

"Let's go talk to *Daed*. He is out in the barn." Becky got down from the table.

"Wait!" Rachel held out her hand to stop them. "What do you intend to ask your father?"

"He's been married twice. He must know how to find a wife. Samuel is asking him how he knew you were the right one."

Rachel waited until the girls were out of the room before she started giggling. "What I wouldn't give to hear that conversation."

She turned to Karen. "Your advice is wise. I hope Becky takes it to heart when she's older."

"I wish it was as easy as I made it sound."

"It is up to *Gott* to fashion our helpmate. Your job is to be open to His will."

"You found the perfect man with Thomas."

"Do you think it was easy to step into the shadow of the woman he loved and lost? And then say, of course I will raise her children as my own? I had many doubts. I prayed about it, and so should you. No man is perfect. No woman is either. We must accept and acknowledge our own flaws before we can accept the flaws of others."

Karen turned back to stir the gravy. She did have flaws. Somehow, she had enticed Ogden into his disturbing behavior. Would Mathias act the same if she gave him the chance? She wanted to trust him.

"It's a big day for you and your father tomorrow," Rachel said. "The grand opening of Yoder's Fine Baked Goods. I can't believe how quickly the two of you have turned that place around."

"We couldn't have done it without the community's help, especially Thomas. Father is so excited. This has been his dream for all the years he worked in another man's bakery. I hope my skills are up to the task of working beside him."

"I'm sure they are. I have tasted your cinnamon rolls and your scrumptious doughnuts. Once word gets out, you'll be busy for sure."

"As long as word doesn't get to Ogden." Had Mathias answered Ogden's letter? Had he betrayed her? She tried to quell her irrational fear. Mathias wouldn't do that. If he had, Ogden would be here by now.

"You won't be able to keep your move a secret for long. When your mother and little brothers arrive here, Ogden is bound to figure it out."

"I'm hoping it'll be long enough by then for him to lose interest in me. I pray that I'm out of sight, out of mind."

Please, Gott, *answer my prayers. Make Ogden stay away.*

CHAPTER SEVEN

On Saturday morning, Mathias walked toward the bakery where the grand opening was underway. If he could just talk to Karen, he'd be able to reassure her and maybe share something of his feelings for her. He cared for her deeply and desperately wanted to put things right between them. Seeing her day after day and not speaking had worn him to the bone. Things had to change. Either there was some hope for him or there wasn't.

Three cars and four buggies occupied the parking lot already, including a police cruiser. Karen stood at the front door with a tray of cupcakes in her hand. "Free samples. Today only," she called out to the people walking toward her.

Mathias knew the moment she caught sight of him. Her smile disappeared, and her expression turned to stone. His heart sank. He walked up and gazed at the variety of cupcakes on her platter. "It looks as if things are going well."

Her smile returned, but it didn't reach her eyes. "Free samples, today only."

He picked one with coconut icing. "Did you make this one?"

"I won't answer that until after you taste it."

He frowned. "Why not?"

"If I tell you my father made it, you'll say it's delicious. If I tell you I'm the one who made it, you'll say it tastes like sawdust."

Any hope of a reconciliation died in his heart. "I'm sorry you have such a low opinion of me."

He put the cupcake back and walked away knowing he couldn't bear to see her every day anymore. It hurt too much. He couldn't stay in Mount Iron.

Knowing what he had to do, he walked past the school and down the road a half-mile to the farm of Benjamin Lehman, the president of the school board.

~

Samuel, Becky, and Mary Sue were enjoying their third cupcake of the afternoon behind the school when a sound inside the building caught their attention. Samuel licked the frosting from his fingers. "No one is supposed to be in there. It's Saturday."

The girls followed him around the corner. One of the windows went up. "This should make it less stuffy. Thank you all for coming on such short notice."

"It's only Mathias," Becky said.

"Why have you called us all together?" the bishop asked.

"To tell you that I am leaving Mount Iron at the end of this school year. I wanted to give the school board enough warning to find a replacement."

The children looked at each other in shock. Becky took off running with Samuel and Mary Sue close behind her. She burst into the schoolroom and faced the bishop and three couples. Ignoring them, she ran up to Mathias and threw her arms around his waist. "You can't leave. You just can't."

~

After the prayer service on Sunday, Becky, Mary Sue, and Samuel sat on the tailgate of a wagon parked among the black buggies beside the barn. They hadn't joined the other children playing tag.

"We have to do something. Mathias can't leave." Becky stared at her brother and her friend, knowing one of them would have a solution.

Mary Sue grabbed Becky's arm. "I have an idea. We can help teacher do all the things on Karen's list. Then she'll know he is husband material, and she can tell him that she likes him, and maybe he'll stay."

"What list?" Samuel asked.

Becky thought about Mary Sue's suggestion. "Karen said a fellow must be kind, generous, brave, hard-working, and like children before she'll consider marrying him. Getting married makes people happy."

"Mathias is all those things already," Samuel said.

"But Karen doesn't know that," Mary Sue insisted. "We need to show her."

"How?" Becky asked.

"I don't know," Mary Sue snapped. "I can't think of everything."

Samuel nodded slowly. "What would a generous man do who likes children?"

"Do you remember when Mathias bought treats for all of us at school?" Becky asked. "That was generous."

Mary Sue looked discouraged. "That was for Christmas."

Samuel turned to the girls. "It would be even more generous if he did it for no reason. Becky, you should ask. He'll do anything for you. I'll offer to take the money over to the bakery and tell Karen we need them delivered. When she comes over, she'll see how generous and kind he is and that he likes us."

Becky nodded. "Okay. I'll do it."

Mary Sue clapped her hands. "Yay! We can mark kind and generous off the list."

On Monday morning, Mathias walked toward the school as usual, but when he got to the bakery, he stopped. There were three cars in the parking lot. The success of this business meant a lot to Karen and her father. Even if she didn't speak to him, they deserved his support. Besides, he wanted to see her.

Two police cruisers pulled in and parked. A pair of strapping young men in uniform got out of each one.

They nodded to Mathias as they walked past him to go inside. "I'm telling you, Jake, this place is even better than Mott's before it closed," the shorter one said.

"You kidding me, Dave?"

"Nope. I stopped in Saturday when they opened. You ain't never had a scone as good as their apple-pie-flavored one, unless it's the apricot."

"I thought you were a donut man, Dave," one of the others said.

"I like donuts, but a man should experience new things." The door closed behind them cutting off the rest of their good-natured conversation.

"Apricot scones. That does sound *goot.*" Mathias opened the door and stepped inside. Karen stood behind the counter wearing a large white apron over her green dress. Her eyes widened at the sight of him.

If only she would look kindly upon him instead of scared or disgusted. She raised her chin. "I'll be right with you."

She turned her attention to the officers, who paid and took their scones and coffee to the table in the corner.

Mathias stepped up to the counter. "I hear your apricot scones are *goot.* I'll try one."

She kept her face politely blank. "Would you like coffee with that?"

"I would."

"To go?" she asked hopefully.

Mathias was tired of running from her scorn. "I believe I'll have it here." He gave her the brightest smile he could muster. "I see your father took your advice about tables and chairs."

The tight line of lips softened. "He did."

"Wise choice. It looks nice in here. Is he going to put tables outside, too?"

"Maybe." She handed him a scone on a paper plate and a foam cup of coffee.

"I wish you every success, Karen. I didn't tell Ogden you were here."

"*Danki.*"

If she was relieved, he couldn't tell. He took his breakfast to the table by the door and sat where he could watch her. She ignored him for the most part, though she occasionally glanced his way. Each time he noticed, he raised his coffee cup in acknowledgement. When she finally flounced into the kitchen, he regretted his actions. He just wanted her to smile at him. If she did, he could hold on to hope, because he was falling in love with her.

Was it possible to love someone who didn't love him in return? Perhaps he and Ogden were more alike than he thought. Except Mathias knew he couldn't make Karen love him.

At school, he tried to keep the day as ordinary as ever. Most of the children knew he was leaving. The rest would learn it soon enough from their peers. He could hear the whispering going on, but he didn't curb it.

He wrote out the arithmetic assignments on the board, then lifted the heavy German Bible and selected a passage to read aloud as he always did. "Second Corinthians 13:11," he announced.

"Finally, brethren, farewell. Be perfect, be of good comfort, be of one mind, live in peace; and the *Gott* of love and peace shall be with you."

Mary Sue started sniffling. He put the Bible back on his desk. "I know you have heard I am leaving. It is true, but your schooling must continue. Ready?"

The children rose in unison and recited "The Lord's Prayer" with him. When they finished, they filed to the front of the room and lined up by grades. Mathias picked up the *Unpartheyisches Gesang-Buch*, their German songbook. He chose three hymns the children knew well since they sang daily at school. Their sweet voices raised in song made his throat tighten with emotion. He would miss this.

A little before lunch, Becky raised her hand. He called on her. She left her desk and came to stand by him.

"I was wondering if we could have a special treat today."

"A treat. Why?" Certainly an unusual request.

"Because you're going away, and we're all sad about that."

He arched one eyebrow. "And a special treat will make you feel better?"

"Maybe a little." Her lower lip quivered as tears filled her eyes.

Guilt made him want to comfort her. "I reckon a treat won't hurt."

Samuel got up and came to stand behind Becky. "I can go to the bakery and get cupcakes for everyone if you give me the money."

Something about this wasn't right. Samuel never volunteered for anything. Mathias gave the two children a stern look. "What's going on?"

"We don't want you to leave," Mary Sue said from the second-grade row. The other children repeated her sentiment until everyone was begging him to stay.

He held up his hand for silence. "I appreciate that you don't want me to leave. I'm sorry, but I must go."

He pulled out his wallet. "Okay, Samuel, you can order cupcakes for everyone and bring them here."

The children broke into cheers. "For after lunch," Mathias said to quiet them. "Now, get back to your studies."

Karen came through the door from the kitchen just as Samuel walked in. She looked at him in surprise. "Aren't you supposed to be in school?"

"Mathias sent me. He wants to order cupcakes for all of us at school. There are twenty-three kids and the teacher." Samuel passed the money to her.

She raised one eyebrow. "Mathias is ordering two dozen cupcakes?"

Samuel nodded. "He's a kind and generous man."

"I see. What flavor would you like?"

Samuel looked flustered. "Gee, I don't know."

"What if I make them one third chocolate, one third vanilla and one third strawberry?"

The boy smiled and licked his lips. "Sounds *wunderbar*. Can you bring them over at one o'clock? I have to get back to class." He turned and bolted out the door.

"We don't do deliveries," she called out, but he didn't stop.

"Who wants a delivery?" her father asked from the kitchen.

"The school."

He pushed open the swinging doors. "That'll be fine. You can do it this once, but make sure Mathias knows we won't make a habit of it."

"Can't you take the order over?" she asked. Facing Mathias again was not what she wanted to do.

Her father shook his head. "I have a meeting with my suppliers. They'll be here at twelve-thirty. It won't take you long to go down there, will it?"

"It certainly won't." She would not spend one more minute in Mathias's company than necessary.

At five to one, Karen boxed up the requested cupcakes and walked to the school. The children were out on their lunch break, but instead of the usual games of catch or swinging, the *kinder* huddled in small groups.

Mathias came to the doorway. "The treats are here, children."

Instead of mobbing her, they all ran to Mathias to hug him. He looked stunned by the sudden onslaught of attention.

Mary Sue started crying and held up her arms. He lifted her to settle her on his hip and mop her tears. "Okay, that's enough. What's the matter?"

Becky raced to Karen's side. "Mathias is sure kind to children, isn't he? He's generous, too. Did you notice that?"

Mathias waded through the adoring school children toward her. "Thank you for delivering these. Sorry for the trouble. I thought Samuel would bring them back with him."

"It's no trouble." She leaned down to peer at Mary Sue's face. "What are you crying about?"

"Teacher's going away, and it breaks my heart."

"And mine," another child added.

"I feel the same." One of the older girls sniffled into her handkerchief.

Becky gazed at her with sorrow-filled eyes. "Won't you miss him, too?".

Karen looked across the sea of sad children and then focused on Mathias. Mary Sue had her arms around his neck and her cheek against his chest. Karen suddenly wished she could do the same thing because she felt like crying, and she wasn't even sure why.

She cleared her throat. "I heard you were leaving."

"It's for the best."

Mary Sue sniffled. "*Nee*, it isn't. We'll miss you."

"Because he's kind and generous," Becky said.

"And he likes children," Mary Sue added.

"It's clear that he does." Karen gazed into Mathias's eyes, stunned see them fill with gratitude.

"*Danki.*"

"*Du bischt wilkumm.*" She spun on her heels and hurried toward the shop before she threw her arms around him and begged him to stay, too.

The next day and the day after that, Mathias stopped in the bakery on his way to school. Each time, he tried a different scone. Karen remained coolly polite, but her gaze softened. He took a sour cream raisin scone to his table with a cup of coffee on Thursday morning. She served all the customers, then vanished back into the kitchen.

When she came out again, he strolled to the counter. "Those sour cream raisin scones are *wunderbar*. Please tell your *daed* how much I enjoyed them."

She almost smiled. "It's my recipe. Today is the first day we've had them for sale."

"I'll spread the word about how *goot* they are." He settled his hat on his head and left.

On his way out the door, Mathias ran into the same police officers with two more men in uniform again. He nodded to them. "I can highly recommend the sour cream raisin scones if you like raisins."

"I do," one of them said. "Thanks, buddy."

"Glad to help."

As they went in, Mathias heard the one called Dave say, "I told you these Amish are friendly folks."

~

At the end of school Thursday, Samuel pulled Becky and Mary Sue to the side of the building. "Our cupcake plan worked great. Now I've got a way to show Karen how brave Mathias is, but one of you will have to be brave, too."

Mary Sue stood tall. "I can be brave if it means teacher Mathias will stay here."

"What do you have in mind?" Becky asked.

"You know that old tree that hangs out over the river? The one where some kids had a rope swing over the water until the community made them take it down."

Mary Sue and Becky looked at each other in confusion. Becky stared at Samuel. "They took it down because someone drowned playing there."

"That doesn't matter. We aren't swinging on a rope. Mary Sue, I want you to climb out a little way on that branch and start shouting for help. Say you were trying to get your kitten down. I'll run get Mathias, and he will climb up and rescue you."

Skeptical, Becky shook her head. "Mary Sue doesn't climb trees. It's a bad idea."

Samuel shrugged. "Okay, but the end of school is only two weeks away. What do you suggest?"

CHAPTER EIGHT

$\mathcal{K}$aren stayed in the living room with Rachel after her father and Thomas had gone to bed. She stared at her mending as she tried to decide what to do.

"Do you want to talk about it?" Rachel asked.

Karen looked up. "About what?"

Rachel smiled softly. "About why you have been staring at the hole in your father's sock for the last ten minutes without setting a single stitch."

Karen put her mending aside. "I fear I have been mistaken about Mathias."

"How so?"

"The catastrophe on our first date, getting locked in the room with him and almost missing my sister's wedding, I thought he and Ogden must be in it together. I didn't believe I could trust Mathias. I made no secret of that. But he hasn't told Ogden where I am. I've seen how he is with the children, how much he cares about their welfare. I may have been unduly harsh."

"I'm glad you can admit that. I know he likes you a lot."

"Maybe once, but not anymore. It's all my fault, and I don't know how to undo that." Humiliated by her actions, she burst into tears.

Rachel came over, sat beside Karen, and put her arm around her. "All you have to do is talk to him. Tell him how you feel."

Karen sniffled. "Just bare my heart and be prepared to be rejected or laughed at?"

"I thought you said you were wrong about Mathias."

"But what if I'm not?"

"The only way to find out is to sit down and talk to him in private. Just the two of you. If he is over you, which I don't believe he is, then you will be certain."

Karen heard a sound at the door to the hallway. Becky stood there. "Mathias is kind and generous and he likes kids. Isn't that enough?"

Karen dried her eyes on her father's unmended sock. "I know how much you like him."

"You like him, too," Becky said.

"You don't understand. Liking someone isn't enough." Karen turned away to hide her tears.

Becky sighed. "Can I have a drink of water, *Mamm?*"

"Of course, *liebchen.* Go help yourself."

Rachel turned to Karen. "My brother is leaving this town, the job, and the children he loves. Don't let him make a mistake he'll regret for a lifetime. Please, talk to him."

"I'm so ashamed and afraid."

"Of what?"

Karen turned her face away. "I must have done something to make Ogden treat me the way he did. What if that was my fault? Now Mathias is leaving, and so many people will be unhappy all because of me."

Rachel took Karen by the shoulders. "They are grown men. Responsible for their own actions. None of this is your fault."

Karen fell into her friend's arms and wept.

Becky stopped at Samuel's room on her way back to bed and went in.

He sat up rubbing his eyes. "What?"

Feeling the weight of the world on her shoulders, she settled on the foot of his bed. Would they ever convince Karen that Mathias was a worthy man?

"Do you have a reason for keeping me up, Becky?"

"We have to go ahead with your plan tomorrow morning."

Samuel grinned. "Okay. I told you it was a *goot* idea."

It wasn't, but she was desperate.

~

Mathias made his regular stop at the bakery with hope in his heart. Karen had spoken to him kindly the day before. Maybe things between them would get better if he just gave it more time. The bell over the door chimed merrily when he walked through the door. The place was busy. He didn't see a single empty table.

He peeked around a broad-shouldered police officer and saw Karen behind the counter. His good mood evaporated. She looked pale and exhausted.

Her eyes were puffy and red with dark circles under them. Even the officer noticed. "Is something wrong, miss?"

She shook her head. He got his donut and joined his friends at their usual table.

Mathias stepped up to the counter. She kept her eyes down. He swallowed hard. "Is it me? Do you want me to leave? I don't want to upset you."

She sniffled. "We need to talk—"

The door burst open, and Samuel came running in. "Mathias, come quick. Mary Sue's stuck in a tree over the river. I'm scared she'll fall." Samuel ran out the door with Mathias close behind him. The boy led the way to the river-bank. An old tree leaned precariously over the water. Mary Sue straddled a large limb over the water. She held a kitten clutched to her chest.

"I'm scared, teacher. Help me." Her eyes were enormous and frightened.

"Stay still, Mary Sue." Mathias tried to speak calmly. "I'm coming to get you."

"We'll take over," one of the police officers said. They had followed along with Karen, her father, and the other customers.

Mathias looked at the bigger man. "That branch may not hold your weight. I'm smaller, plus she trusts me. I'll go. Maybe you could get downstream and be ready to grab her if she falls in."

The officer turned around. "Zane, have everyone spread out along the riverbank with whatever long poles or branches they can find. Ted, notify Water Rescue. Get the buoy and rope gear from the trunk and be prepared to make the best throw of your life. Dave, get an ambulance on its way here." The offices nodded and took off at a run.

Mathias turned to Samuel. "Go get Mary Sue's parents."

His eyes widened. "But she'll get in trouble."

Mathias put his hand on the boy's shoulder. "That doesn't matter. Go."

Samuel took off. Mathias shed his coat and vest, dropping them in the grass along with his hat. Someone grabbed his arm.

Turning he saw Karen's eyes were as wide and frightened as Mary Sue's. "Be careful."

"I will. Head down river. Get long branches, something she can grab hold of if she goes in the water."

The officer at Mathias's side gave a quick shake of his head. "That's not going to happen. You've got this. I'll come up behind you as far as is safe. That way you can hand her to me."

Mathias started praying as he climbed. He prayed to accept *Gott*'s will and to find strength in *Gott*'s love to save this child.

It was easy enough until he reached the branch she had gone out on. It was a dead limb with peeling bark. He had no idea if it would take his weight.

"Mary Sue, can you come this way?"

"I don't think so. Sassy is scared." She held tight to the kitten.

"Because she knows you are. Let go of her. She'll come to me. Remember when you brought her to show and tell? She hopped right up on my desk to say hello."

"I remember."

"*Goot.* Put her down and let her come this way."

"Okay." Mary Sue's tiny voice shook. Mathias wasn't sure how long she could keep her balance on the limb she straddled. Her hands trembled as she placed her kitten on the branch.

"Here, kitty, kitty." Mathias tried to coax the kitten closer. Sassy crept along the limb with her belly against the wood. The rumble of Ironstone rapids less than a quarter of a mile away remained a terrifying reminder that a fall from here wouldn't leave the kitten or the child much chance to be rescued.

Finally, the kitten inched close enough that he could grab her.

"Give her to me," the officer said.

Mathias handed her down. "I'm afraid I don't know your name."

"Officer Jacobs. You can call me Jake. And you are?" The man took the kitten and handed her to someone below.

"Mathias Troyer. I'm her teacher."

Mathias then focused on Mary Sue, smiling to reassure her. "Okay. I need you to creep toward me as carefully as Sassy did." An ominous creak followed his words. "Come to me now, Mary Sue."

"I'm scared. Really scared. I'm not making it up."

"I'm scared too, but I won't let anything happen to you. *Gott* loves you, and He wants you to be safe, too." He leaned out as far as he dared and stretched out his hand. If he could just get hold of her. The limb creaked loudly.

"Easy, Troyer." Jake whispered. "That limb won't hold. Back up. We don't need two people in the water."

Mary Sue was making slow progress when Mathias heard a commotion below.

"Mary Sue, what are you doing up there?" her mother shrieked.

"I'm sorry, *Mamm.*" Mary Sue wailed and started to slide sideways. In a second, she'd fall.

Mathias stretched his full length along the limb. She toppled over. He lunged and grabbed her ankle, holding on as best he could.

"Swing her to me," Jake shouted.

Mary Sue and her mother were both screaming. Mathias had no choice. He couldn't hang on to her and get back himself. He swung the child backward in an arch and felt the man he couldn't see grab her.

"I've got you, Mary Sue! You're safe."

A cheer went up from those watching. Mathias breathed a prayer of thanks for her safe rescue as he sat up. The limb snapped, plummeting him into the rushing river below.

CHAPTER NINE

*K*aren screamed when Mathias disappeared under the water. This couldn't be happening. She ran along the bank with a stout branch in her hand. Where was he? Why wasn't he coming up? It couldn't end like this.

Please Gott save him.

His head broke the surface five feet from her. He gasped for air and flailed. She stepped into the water to extend her branch. "Mathias, grab it."

Catching the thin leafy end, he hung on as the current pushed him toward the shore. His hold on the branch slipped. He grabbed for a better one. His head was barely above the water as the current threatened to drag her in, too. Was the limb strong enough to hold him? Was she?

Gott give me strength.

"Karen." He coughed and gasped. "I love you."

The branch broke just below her hands. The current swept him downstream, past the trees that blocked her view. She screamed as he vanished from sight.

Frantic, she ran toward the next open stretch of riverbank. Rounding a thick shrub, she saw a police officer throw a red flotation bag attached to a rope. It splashed down beside Mathias. He grabbed the rope. The police officer and three of the neighbors began hauling him to shore. She pressed her hands to her heart as she prayed they could get him to safety.

Thomas on his buggy horse came splashing chest deep through the water toward Mathias from downriver. If Mathias lost his grip on the rope, there was still a chance Thomas could catch him before the rapids.

Another police officer waded in to help Mathias ashore. He stumbled and fell in a fit of coughing. She raced to him, falling to her knees at his side. He looked at her in dazed disbelief. "You let go."

"*Nee*, the branch broke."

Another coughing fit overtook him. A police officer took her by the shoulder, helped her stand, and moved her aside. "The ambulance is on its way. Please stay back."

Karen retreated. Her father along with Rachel, Samuel, and Becky ran to her. The children were sobbing. Thomas rode out of the water, got off his horse beside his wife, and hugged her close.

Rachel pressed a hand to her chest. "Karen, is he alright?"

Karen shook her head. "I don't know. He managed to get hold of a branch I had. He said he loved me, then the branch snapped at my hands. Just now, he said I let go of him. How could he think I would leave him to drown?"

"It all happened so fast," her father said. "He'll understand you were trying to save him."

"I didn't mean for this to happen," Samuel sobbed.

Thomas knelt and took both children in his arms. "Of course, you didn't. You were only trying to help Mary Sue."

An ambulance and a red truck with Water Rescue on the side in bold white letters stopped on the road above. One of the police officers conferred with the drivers and led them down to the riverbank. Karen and the others waited for word as the ambulance crew worked beside Mathias. She shivered when they put an oxygen mask on his face, covered him with blankets, and slipped him onto a white plastic board. A police officer came over to speak to them.

"I'm Officer Jacobs. Mr. Troyer swallowed a lot of river water. The paramedics think some entered his lungs. They're going to transport him to the hospital. They'll likely keep him for observation. Is his wife here?"

Rachel stepped forward. "He's not married. I'm his sister."

"You're welcome to come with him. He told me he never learned to swim. He is one brave man. God was watching over all of us today."

"Amen." Rachel turned to her husband. "Take the children to the house. I'm going to the hospital."

Karen stepped to Rachel's side. "May I come, too?"

Officer Jacobs shook his head sadly. "Sorry. Only one."

～

Mathias lay in the back of the ambulance with an oxygen mask over his face and a searing pain in his chest that had nothing to do with his dunking. Why had he said anything to Karen?

Rachel rode on the seat beside the paramedic making notes about Mathias's heart rate and breathing. She laid her hand on Mathias's arm. "Karen wanted to come. She didn't let go of you. The branch in her hand broke."

Could he believe that? He didn't see or hear the branch snap, but maybe he'd been too worried about dying. "You didn't see her face. She was shocked. I never should have said anything. Now she'll think I'm just like Ogden, only using sympathy to gain her affections."

"Is that what your faith tells you? To assume what others think? To put your doubts in their minds?"

He coughed twice more. "*Nee.*"

"Because?"

"Only *Gott* knows the hearts of men."

"I'm glad you remember that much from our parent's teachings. If you want to know what Karen is thinking, you must ask her. Don't be a fool and throw away your chance at love. *Gott* spared you today for a purpose."

"I'm afraid," Mathias admitted.

"Of what, dear brother?"

"That she'll never love me the way I love her. That I'll end up like Ogden, obsessed with being near her."

"You are not like Ogden. He would never willingly move away to spare her feelings. You care more about her than you let on. That needs to change."

"I told her I loved her. What more can I say?"

"Have that conversation when you aren't about to be swept away to your death. Something tells me it will go better."

Panic as the current pulled him under, his desperate need for air, it all swept over him again, tightening his chest. Gasping, he started coughing.

The paramedic laid a hand on Mathias's arm. "Take slow deep breaths. I've heard the Amish take care of each other. I sure saw it in action today. Where did everybody come from? I thought you folks didn't use phones."

Mathias drew in slow breaths. The panic receded. He was alive. *Gott* in His infinite mercy had spared him.

He managed a smile for his worried sister. "Reckon the Lord just used Yoder's Fine Baked Goods to bring everyone to the right place instead of telephones."

~

Becky slipped into her brother's room that night and pulled a chair to his bedside. She drew her knees up to her chin. "Told you it was a bad idea."

"I never thought someone would get hurt. I'm going to tell *Mamm* and *Daed* what we did in the morning. I can't sleep for thinking about it."

"We should 'fess up to Mary Sue's parents, too."

"Do you think she told on us?" he asked fearfully.

215

Becky shook her head. "If she had, her folks would be over here talking to ours."

Samuel lay back with his arms behind his head. "Yeah, you're right."

"Did you hear the police officer tell Karen that Mathias was brave?"

"I also heard Karen say Mathias told her he loved her. Then she left him in the river to drown."

Becky scowled at her brother. "She didn't do that on purpose."

Samuel rolled his eyes. "Mathias thought so. And she didn't say she loved him back. He's going to leave now for sure."

Sighing, Becky stared at the ceiling. "They need to talk to one another."

"I doubt that will happen unless they get locked in a room together."

Becky sat up. "Samuel, I have an idea."

"Don't tell me. We're in enough trouble already."

It just might work. "We can't confess to our folks until Monday evening."

Samuel eyed her suspiciously. "Why Monday?"

"Because we need to tell Mathias first. After school."

Samuel rolled to his side and pulled the quilt over his shoulder. "I'm not going to get much sleep this weekend, am I?"

~

Karen waited anxiously to hear about Mathias. Rachel returned home Saturday morning to report he had been released from the hospital with no lasting harm. He didn't seek Karen out. Rachel assured her Mathias didn't believe she had deliberately left him to drown, but Karen needed to hear it from his own lips.

Knowing how close she had come to losing him made her realize how much she loved him. Did he truly love her?

She didn't see him on Sunday. He didn't come visit his sister as Karen thought he might.

Sunday night she paced in her room. What if he didn't come into the shop tomorrow morning? What if he decided he didn't love her?

Dropping onto the side of her bed, she faced an unbearable thought. "What if he never wants to see me again?"

Tears filled her eyes. She fell back, turned on her side, and buried her face in her pillow. When her tears finally dried up, she spent a long night of painful reflection on her treatment of Mathias. She had to make things right between them. If he cared enough to listen.

~

Each time the shop bell rang that morning, her heart jumped into her throat, but he didn't show up. The police officers stopped in to inquire about him and Mary Sue. They introduced themselves as Jake, Ted, Dave, and Zane. Her father happily gave them the information they wanted and told them their breakfast was on the house for a week.

The shop quickly filled with customers who had read about the rescue in the newspapers and wanted more details. Her father's retellings forced Karen to relive those horrible moments again and again.

The next time the bell jangled, she looked up hoping it was Mathias. Ogden stood poised in the doorway.

She stared in shock, barely recognizing him. He wore blue jeans and a bright flowered shirt. *Englisch* clothing. He glanced around the shop. "Nice."

When he spotted her, Karen wanted to sink through the floor.

He strolled to the counter. "Did you think you could hide from me?"

CHAPTER TEN

aren raised her chin, even though her heart hammering with fear. "I'm not hiding. I'm working with my father. Can I get you something?"

"You know what I want, but I will take some coffee. I left the church for you."

"You'll be shunned. Then we can never be together." She filled a cup with shaking hands and set it on the counter.

He grabbed her arm and squeezed. "This was a poor attempt to avoid me. I'm furious with you." His soft voice sent shivers down her spine.

"Let go, Ogden. You're hurting me."

The customers turned in their direction, including the officers. Karen didn't want a scene in her father's new business, or for her father to come out of the kitchen and confront Ogden.

"This is a nice place." Ogden looked around, then focused on her. "It would be a shame if something happened to it. Are you ready to admit we belong together?"

The bell over the door jangled, but she didn't take her eyes off Ogden. She needed time to think. In her heart, she knew he could hurt more than her father's business.

Forcing a smile, she lowered her eyes. "Let's meet and discuss this after we close this evening. You and I have a lot of catching up to do. We can't do it with all these people around."

"Ogden, what are you doing?" Mathias demanded.

Karen looked up. Her heart surged at the sight of his face. Ogden turned to glare at him. "Can't you see? I'm talking to my intended."

Mathias took a step closer. His eyes drilled into Ogden. "Karen isn't going to marry you. You can't force her. Leave her alone."

"She wants to walk out with me after work. Tell him, Karen." Ogden's voice held a threat she couldn't ignore.

"We're going out later," she whispered.

Ogden grabbed her arm again. "Louder Karen. I don't think the hero I read about in the newspaper heard you."

She couldn't speak for the fear clogging her throat.

Mathias knew he had to do something, but his faith didn't permit him to interfere. All he could do was try to reason with Ogden. He laid a hand on his cousin's shoulder. "Please, Ogden. Let her be."

Ogden laughed without turning around. "I didn't come all this way for you to get between me and what's mine."

Mathias felt hands moving him aside as Jake stepped behind Ogden. "Let the lady go."

Ogden spun around and threw the cup of hot coffee at Jake's face. A second later, he was on the floor with two police officers holding him down.

"You just assaulted an officer of the law, buddy. In front of witnesses." Ted cuffed Ogden's hands behind his back.

"Please don't hurt him," Karen pleaded.

"The Amish won't testify against me," Ogden screamed.

Karen's father came rushing out of the kitchen. "What's going on. Is that Ogden?"

"These peaceful folks may not testify, but we have no religious restrictions against throwing a man like you in jail." Zane and Dave pulled Ogden on his feet.

"You have the right to remain silent," Officer Dave began as they led Ogden out the door.

Karen's father grasped her hand. "Are you okay?"

Karen nodded, even as she wavered on shaky legs. Mathias longed to gather her close.

Her father handed Jake a towel. "I'm so sorry."

Jake mopped his face. "Your scones are worth the pain. I take it you know him?"

Mathias saw neither Karen nor her father were going to answer. The Amish didn't involve outsiders in their difficulties except in the most extreme cases. He stepped forward. This much he could do for her.

"Ogden Troyer is my cousin. He plagued Karen with unwanted attention in Badger Creek. It got so bad she moved here in secret. I'm ashamed of his behavior, but we will not press charges."

Jake nodded. "You don't need to do that. We don't take kindly to stalkers or people who assault officers. He'll be locked up for a few months, but not forever. Ma'am, you need to file a restraining order. I'll be happy to hand it to him when he gets out. We'll make sure you and your father aren't bothered again. I've got to get going, but we'll see you tomorrow. Officer Dave is addicted to your baked goods. You know what they say about cops and donuts."

Karen shook her head. "*Nee*, what do they say?"

His eyebrows shot up. "In the movies? Cops are always in donut shops when the crime goes down."

She shrugged. "I've never seen a movie."

"Gotta love the Amish." Jake's bemused expression puzzled Mathias as he walked out.

Karen took a deep breath. "I couldn't speak up. This is all my fault."

"None of it is your fault," her father said. "If you are okay, I've got filling on the stove. I don't want it to burn."

"I'm fine, *Daed*," she assured him.

He nodded and went back into the kitchen.

"Your father is right. It's not your fault," Mathias said. "Look, I've got to get to school."

Karen rubbed her arm. "We must pray for him."

Mathias nodded, but he had to ask before he left. "Did you mean it when you said you'd walk out with him?"

She bent to wipe the spill off the floor. Her hands shook. "I did."

Mathias wasn't sure what to make of that information, but maybe now wasn't the best time to have a conversation. Or confess his love again. He needed to think things over before he said more. Karen had been through enough.

Karen stood up and clutched the coffee-stained towel, ready to explain, but Mathias was already out the door. He hadn't given her a chance to tell her side of the story. Why not? He didn't think she agreed because she wanted to be with Ogden, did he?

Somehow, she made it through the rest of the day, but all she could think of was explaining to Mathias and assuring him she had no interest in seeing Ogden again. Ever.

When a handful of students came in for an afternoon treat, she knew school was out. One of them was Becky. "Hi, Karen. Teacher said he needs to speak with you over at the school."

Karen tipped her head slightly. "Now? We don't close until five."

"He said it was important."

"Okay. *Daed*, I'm going over to the school for a few minutes." Knowing Mathias wanted to see her raised her spirits. Now she could explain everything.

Karen walked out the door with the child. "Becky, how is Mary Sue?"

"She's okay. Is it true that Mathias said he loved you?"

Glancing down at the curious child, Karen sighed. "That is between me and him. Sometimes people say things in the heat of the moment they don't really mean."

"I think he means it." Becky skipped ahead to the school door, holding it open.

Karen stepped inside. Mathias sat at his desk reading a sheet of paper. He wrote something on it, laid it aside, and picked up another page.

Karen's heart overflowed with happiness at the sight of his dear face. Did he really love her? Was that what he wanted to tell her? Why wasn't she brave enough to ask? Or tell him how she felt. Maybe she was.

She gathered her courage. "I hope I'm not interrupting."

His shocked expression surprised her. "Karen, what are you doing here?"

"Ah, Becky came to the shop and said you wanted to see me."

"I didn't send her."

Embarrassed and confused, Karen took a step back. "I can come back later. Or not at all, if that is your wish." She turned and grasped the doorknob. It wouldn't turn.

"*Nee*, wait." He rushed toward her.

"The door is locked." She looked at him for an explanation.

"What? It might be stuck, but it isn't locked. I have the key in my desk." He tried the doorknob, then pushed against the door with his shoulder once. He pushed again, grunting with effort.

The familiarity of their predicament made her smile. "See? Locked."

"This is ridiculous. Who would lock us in? I'll get the key." He went to the front and riffled through his desk. "It's missing."

Gott and most likely Becky had given her this opportunity. Karen wasn't going to waste it. She walked to his desk and sat on the corner. "I reckon someone thinks we need to talk."

He cleared his throat. "It appears so. What would you like to say?"

"Did you mean it when you said you loved me?" The words came out in a rush. She couldn't believe she was being so bold.

He glanced away. "I did, but I know you don't feel the same. You don't have to worry that I'll burden you with unwanted attentions."

His admission gave her the courage she needed. She prayed she would get this right. "What makes you think your attentions are unwanted?"

A faint frown appeared on his face. "Aren't they? You've made no secret of that before."

"I'm very sorry for the way I treated you, Mathias. Can you forgive me?"

Raking a hand through his unruly curls, he took a few steps away. Had she misjudged him again?

"I've spent the whole day wondering if you wanted Ogden after all."

Her mouth dropped open. How could he assume that?

A tiny voice in her head reminded her she hadn't given him the chance to know her heart. "Mathias, I wanted to keep Ogden from making a scene in my father's business or worse. I was stalling for time. *Daed* has everything riding on our success."

Mathias blew out a deep breath of relief. "You mean you don't want to marry Ogden?"

Karen walked over to him and put her arms around his neck. "I'm rather hoping I can marry you."

Mathias's heart nearly exploded with joy. He threw back his head and laughed with relief. Then he picked her up and whirled her around, happier than he'd ever been in his life.

Setting her feet on the ground, he bent to rest his forehead against hers, almost afraid this happiness wasn't real. "Did you just propose to me, Karen Yoder?"

"I only made a suggestion, Teacher Mathias."

Slipping his arms around her, he drew her close. No dream could feel this good. Nothing had ever felt as right as holding her this way. "I'll take it under advisement."

He bent to kiss her sweet lips. The world melted away until they were the only two people in *Gott's* great universe.

She broke off the kiss before he was ready to let her go and cupped his face with her soft hands that smelled of cinnamon, baked apples, and fresh bread. "I love you, Mathias. I'm sorry it took me so long to realize it."

"All that has gone before means nothing compared to the joy in my heart now. Only one thing could make me happier. Will you marry me, Karen?"

A radiant smile curved her lips and sparkled in her eyes. "*Ja*, I will."

"Are you sure this is what you want? You've had a difficult day, months really, with Ogden's pursuit. I don't want you to feel pressured into anything. I can wait for an answer. Truly. If you decide you don't want me, I'll go away and never bother you."

She wrapped her finger around his suspenders and pulled him close. "Stop talking and kiss me again."

"If you insist." He smiled, then proceeded to show her how much he loved her with a long, tender kiss.

Sighing at last, she rested her head against his shoulder. "Does this mean you aren't leaving Mount Iron?"

"I've found an amazing reason to stay. *Gott* is great," Mathias whispered in her ear. "He has formed for me the perfect soulmate."

She chuckled softly. "I'm not perfect, but who am I to argue with His wisdom. So, how are we going to get out of here?"

"I'll slip out the window."

"Don't you need some sheets?"

He chuckled. "It's not that high. I can jump."

She traced his lips with her finger. "A sprained ankle would be such a hindrance to our wedding. We could just ring the bell until someone comes to see what's wrong."

He nodded. "We can do that."

"Later?"

"Definitely later."

Mathias pulled her close and kissed her as if he would never let her go.

~

Outside under the window, Becky hugged Mary Sue and Samuel with happiness. "We did it," she whispered.

Becky flopped down in the soft green grass to gaze at the puffy white clouds drifting across the blue sky. Sighing in contentment, she pulled the key to the school door from her apron pocket. "This matchmaker business isn't all that hard. I enjoyed it."

Samuel and Mary Sue plopped down on each side of her. He took the key from her hand. "We need to confess what we did to Mathias and our folks."

Her brother sure knew how to ruin the moment. Becky snatched the key from him and locked her fingers around the cool metal. "We will. Later."

ABOUT THE AUTHOR

Patricia Davids is an internationally published, award-winning, USA Today bestselling author of over 40 inspirational and Amish romance novels. Born and raised in central Kansas, Patricia combines her faith, Midwest values and quirky humor into emotionally rich stories that deal with contemporary subjects. She has sold over 3,000,000 books world-wide since her first novel appeared in stores in 2006. Visit her at www.patriciadavids.com.

If you enjoyed this story, you'll also like *The Inn at Harts Haven*, as a desperate young woman attempts to hide in plain sight among the Amish of a small Kansas community:

https://www.amazon.com/dp/B09HKT6MFB

IVY'S NEW BEGINNING

JENNIFER BECKSTRAND

CHAPTER ONE

*T*he Eicher's home was Ivy's favorite place to attend church services. So many bushes and trees surrounded the house that nobody noticed when you fled to the barn to cry your eyes out.

It wasn't that Ivy needed to have a *gute* cry every time she attended *gmay*, but for sure and certain, she was glad the Eicher's barn was hidden from view of the house today. The women were enjoying their turn at fellowship supper with homemade bread and three kinds of church spread, blissfully unaware that Ivy had slipped away. With tears streaming down her face, she marched into the barn, planted herself on a convenient hay bale, and tried very hard not to feel sorry for herself. She tried even harder not to let her heart turn to stone, even though she had been tempted to do just that for the last three years. If she stopped caring, she'd lose her humanity, her compassion, and her connection to the very people who'd made her cry in the first place.

As a teenager, Ivy had been hurt and dismissed so often, she had talked herself out of caring, and her well-rehearsed indifference had cost her everything. *Mamm* and *Dat* were gone, her *bruderen* wanted nothing to do with her, and she had wandered almost beyond her ability to return. Her sister, Esther, was the only person in the world who cared if Ivy lived or died, and sometimes Ivy doubted even Esther's love. Ivy had treated Esther very badly in the past. If Ivy were Esther, she wouldn't be able to stand Ivy. Ivy had done her best to repent and make amends, but her efforts never felt like enough. Esther had put up with a lot from Ivy, not to mention Esther's husband, Levi, and Esther's *dochter* Winnie, who used to be Ivy's *dochter* but was being raised by Esther because Ivy had been a horrible mother.

It was a jumbled, tangled mess of Ivy's doing, and now her nose was stuffy, her ears plugged, and the hem of her apron a soggy mess.

The barn had to be at least ten degrees cooler than the outdoors, and in early March, it wasn't exactly warm outside. Ivy wrapped her arms around herself and tried to borrow some warmth from the hay bale. It was like trying to get water from a stone. Hay bales weren't exactly the ideal sitting spot. You inevitably got poked in the *hinnerdale* and scratched on the ankles. She should have fled to Eicher's pasture, where at least she could have found a convenient horse to sit on.

Ivy didn't even need to work at feeling sorry for herself. She had a lot of reasons, and she'd brought every bad thing upon herself.

Even though it hurt to care so much, she let the ache overtake her, like a wave at the lake she couldn't outswim. Esther had said—and she'd been right —that it was better to feel bad feelings than to keep them bottled up. Nothing *gute* came of trying to suppress your honest, deep emotions, except maybe clear sinuses and less laundry.

The barn was suddenly flooded with light as someone opened the door on the other side of the stalls. "This is the perfect spot. Nobody will even know we're gone."

Ivy had no intention of letting anybody see her in such a condition. She leaped to her feet and retreated to an empty stall. Lord willing, whoever wanted a tour of the barn wouldn't stay long.

"I don't know, Menno. Maybe we should get back. My *dat* will want to go soon. He'll be looking for me."

"*Nae*, he won't. He'll just think you walked home. It's only a mile to your house from here."

Ivy peeked through the space between the wall and the stall door. Rebecca Neuenschwander stood with her back against a post while Menno Troyer loomed over her, one hand propped on the post above her head and the other hand stuffed in his pocket. Rebecca was fourteen, maybe fifteen years old. Menno was a couple of years older, and several inches taller.

Rebecca frowned, catching her bottom lip between her teeth. "I don't know. It all seems so sudden."

"Come on, Rebecca. We've loved each other since the eighth grade."

Considering that Rebecca was fresh out of eighth grade, that didn't sound like an incredibly long time or an incredibly enduring relationship.

Menno reached out and caressed Rebecca's neck with his stubby fingers. "Do you love me or don't you?"

"I...I love you," Rebecca stuttered.

"It doesn't seem like you do. When people are in love, they do things for each other. Can't you do this one thing for me? I love you, Rebecca. I *need* you." He said "need" with such longing in his voice, he sounded like he was passing a kidney stone.

Ivy's eyebrows traveled up her forehead. Seventeen-year-old boys were predictably unoriginal and outrageously manipulative—not all of them, of course, but Ivy had seen enough in her thirty years to know what manipulation looked like. Teenage girls yearned for acceptance and belonging. Ivy heard that same line a dozen times when she was Rebecca's age. It made her angry at her younger self for falling for such nonsense and angry at Menno for spouting it.

Rebecca squared her shoulders, trying to act more sure of herself, but it was definitely an act. Even in the dim light of the barn, Ivy could see the uncertainty in Rebecca's eyes, her instinctive hesitation.

Good for you, Ivy thought.

Rebecca traced a line on the floor with her foot. "The bishop said we shouldn't even kiss until after marriage."

"He says that, but it's not a commandment, and nobody waits until they get married to kiss." He moved back to his original argument, probably as a distraction. "Don't you love me?"

"I love you more than ice cream and candy canes," Rebecca said.

"Then what are you waiting for? Christmas?" Menno pulled Rebecca into his arms and kissed her with all the eagerness of a seventeen-year-old boy. "If you love me, show me." He skipped his lips down Rebecca's neck.

Ivy bit down on her tongue hard. Menno needed a *gute* spanking and a very cold shower. She huffed out a breath. If she could save even one girl from making the mistakes Ivy had made, it would be worth sticking her neck out. She wasn't about to let Menno trick Rebecca like boys had tricked her. She wiped the moisture from her cheeks and stepped out of the stall. "It wonders me if Rebecca brushed sugar on her neck this morning. It must taste wonderful *gute*."

Menno widened his eyes and took a giant step away from Rebecca. "I didn't know anybody was in here."

Ivy folded her arms and cocked her eyebrow. "Obviously."

Rebecca turned a bright shade of red, which soon gave way to a sickly green color. "Um. Hi. We're...we thought no one was in here." She glared at Menno as if all the problems in the world were his fault.

Ivy tilted her head to one side. "Menno, I think I hear your *mamm* calling. Maybe you should go and see what she wants."

Menno, looking younger and more vulnerable than his seventeen years, didn't need another word of encouragement. He bolted out of the barn faster than a bullet shot from a rifle. Rebecca's eyes flashed with surprise, probably at the very idea that Menno would leave her behind like that. "Um, well, nice to see you, Ivy. I have to go. My *dat* will wonder what happened to me."

"Yes, he will." Ivy put a little scold into her tone. She stopped herself before launching into a lecture about the risks of loving seventeen-year-old boys and being alone in barns with them. Rebecca didn't need a lecture. She needed empathy and some gentle advice. Ivy wasn't the best person to give anyone advice, because she'd messed up her life something wonderful, but she was here, and Rebecca was here, and Ivy was the only one who had witnessed the whole thing.

And maybe she wouldn't be all bad at helping Rebecca understand boys and kissing and puppy love. Ivy had been in the exact same spot fifteen years ago. But Ivy couldn't just charge in like a pair of using horses as she sometimes did. She used to be a teenage girl. They were high-strung and easily offended. This was going to be a little tricky. She smiled wryly. "Of course I won't tell your *dat*. Nobody likes a tattletale."

Rebecca eyed Ivy suspiciously. "That's what I keep telling Ruth Ann. She won't keep her mouth shut. Nobody tells her their secrets anymore."

Ivy glanced toward the barn door where Menno had just exited. "It looks like you and Menno really like each other."

Rebecca's frown reached all the way to her toes. "Please don't tell my *dat*. It was just a kiss. Boys and girls kiss all the time."

Ivy didn't want Rebecca to get defensive. Defensive teenagers rarely listened to reason. Ivy knew that from personal experience. But neither was she willing to let Rebecca wheedle her way out of acknowledging the truth. Ivy had never been the subtle, beat-around-the-bush type. "He was practically chewing on your neck."

Alarm flashed in Rebecca's blue eyes. "He was not." She pulled the neckline of her dress away from her throat and stuck out her neck for Ivy to look at. "See. No chewing."

Ivy bit her lip to keep from laughing. Rebecca was technically right. No teeth marks. "He didn't just want a few kisses, though, did he?"

Rebecca lowered her eyes *and* backed into the post. "Please don't tell my *dat*."

"I won't tell your *dat*."

Rebecca studied Ivy's face. Ivy saw the moment when Rebecca decided to believe her. "Okay. *Denki*. He wouldn't understand." She let out a long sigh of relief. "I guess I should go. I don't want Dat to leave without me."

"Five minutes ago, you had plenty of time," Ivy said. "We need to have a talk."

Rebecca narrowed her eyes. "About what?"

"*Cum*," Ivy said, motioning to the uncomfortable hay bale. "Let's sit."

Rebecca didn't look at all eager to have a talk, but she was also in a tight spot. She knew Ivy knew what she and Menno had been up to. "*Ach, vell*, I really can't stay long."

"Your *dat* will just think you walked home. It's only a mile." Ivy wasn't above using Menno's argument to get Rebecca to stay, and if it was a little reminder to Rebecca that Ivy had overheard the whole conversation, all the better. She strolled to the hay bale, sat down, and patted the spot next to her. "Menno is wonderful handsome."

Rebecca smiled weakly and sidled next to Ivy on the hay bale. "*Jah*. All the girls think so."

"You're eager for him to like you, aren't you? Eager to please him?"

"When you're in love, you do things for each other, things that make the other person happy."

Ivy nodded slowly, trying to be tactful and empathetic when she really wanted to shake some sense into the lovesick teenage girl. Ivy truly didn't have the patience for this kind of conversation. She should give up before she even started.

She pressed her lips into a hard line and drew her brows together. Fifteen-year-old Ivy would at least want thirty-year-old Ivy to try to save Rebecca from a lifetime of regret. "So when you're in love, you do things to make the other person happy? Like make him a cake? Or let him kiss you?"

Rebecca's gaze didn't leave Ivy's face. It was obvious she suspected Ivy was trying to back her into a corner when all Ivy wanted to do was throw eggs at Menno's house. "For sure and certain, I would make him a cake. He likes cake. Chocolate especially."

"What if he asked you to cut off your foot to show him you loved him? Would you do it?"

Rebecca paused for barely a second. "Menno would never ask me to cut off my foot."

"Why not?"

"Because he loves me."

Ivy nodded eagerly. Rebecca was backing herself into that corner. "So you're saying that because Menno loves you, he wouldn't ask you to do something harmful or something that would hurt you, like cutting off your foot or robbing a bank?"

Rebecca folded her arms and pursed her lips stubbornly. "I'm not going to say what you want me to say. There's nothing wrong with kissing the boy I love and doing...you know, other things."

Ivy growled to herself. Rebecca was smart. She wouldn't let herself be backed into a corner that easily. But Ivy still had a few tricks up her sleeve. "If there's nothing wrong with *other things*, why don't you want your *dat* to know?"

Rebecca looked away. "He wouldn't understand."

"What wouldn't he understand?"

"How much I love Menno." She turned her body completely away from Ivy, as if she was embarrassed, as if she knew deep in her heart she was wrong.

Ivy knew all too well how easy it was to let the hunger for acceptance get in the way of seeing things clearly. She took a deep breath and tried to remember how she'd felt as a teenager. Beneath her confident, flirtatious exterior, she'd been a scared, insecure girl who had just wanted to be loved. She'd confused attention with affection, and that had gotten her into all sorts of trouble. Her heart swelled to the size of Colorado, and she hooked her elbow around Rebecca's arm. "Your *dat* was once a teenage boy. Don't you think he remembers what it feels like to be in love, even a little?"

Rebecca shook her head. "He won't talk about Mamm or dating or what a boy wants in a girl."

"I'm sure he knows about all those things. You should ask him." That was probably a bad piece of advice. She couldn't imagine Isaac Neuenschwander would want wayward Ivy Zook poking her nose into his personal business. But if he couldn't talk to his own daughter about love and *other things*, then he deserved to be irritated. "Your *dat* was in love once."

Rebecca snorted with unhappy laughter. "I don't think so. He doesn't understand me anymore. Menno understands me. Menno loves me."

Ivy frowned. If Rebecca wanted to be persistently stubborn, then Ivy would be persistently blunt. Menno was *not* going to get what he wanted, not if Ivy had anything to say about it. "Rebecca, I'm going to be honest with you because you're smart enough to handle the truth. Your *dat* might not remember what it's like to be fifteen, but I do. I was lonely and insecure. I wanted boys to love me, so I did things I will always regret. I jumped the fence and got pregnant."

"I'm not going to jump the fence," Rebecca said, a distinctly defensive tone to her voice.

"Maybe not, but that doesn't mean you won't have regrets. I just pray your regrets aren't anywhere near as heavy as mine. When you choose to harm yourself in hopes of making someone love you, you will always regret it."

"Do you regret having a baby?"

"I can't imagine the world without Winnie in it, but I caused a lot of pain to a lot of people, including myself. My *mamm* and *dat* both died, and I made Esther's life miserable. When I made the choice to do *other things* with boys, I made the choice to hurt people."

The corner of Rebecca's mouth twitched upward. "Ruth Ann calls it The *Unmentionable*."

Ivy sighed. "Do you understand what The Unmentionable is?"

Rebecca fingered the edge of her apron as her face turned bright red. "Sort of. Ruth Ann explained it. Sort of."

Ivy suddenly felt very protective of little Rebecca Neuenschwander. She slid her arm around Rebecca's shoulder. "I saw your face when Menno started chewing on your neck."

"He wasn't chewing."

Ivy laughed halfheartedly. "Okay. Not chewing. I saw the look in your eyes. You don't really want to do those *other things* that Menno wants you to do, do you?

Rebecca seemed to wilt like a daisy. "I want him to love me."

"And you're afraid if you don't do The Unmentionable, he won't love you anymore?"

Rebecca shrugged, as if defeated by her uncertainty. "I don't know."

"Shouldn't Menno love you for your smile and your smarts? Shouldn't he love you because of who you are instead of what you can do for him?"

"I supposed he should…I mean…I think…I'm sure he does."

That wasn't a completely honest answer, but at least Rebecca was thinking on it. Ivy wouldn't hurt her for the world. "Menno is a *gute* boy. I'm sure he loves you for all those things." She wasn't sure, but what would it hurt to give Menno the benefit of the doubt? Well…it might hurt a lot, but Rebecca needed to think that Ivy trusted her judgment.

Rebecca nodded. "He does. He loves me so much."

"*Gute,*" Ivy said. "We all want to be loved and accepted. We all want to belong. You're smart enough to see that doing The Unmentionable before marriage is unwise and unsafe. It will only hurt you in the end."

Rebecca seemed to gain confidence. "I suppose you're right."

"You'd drink a cup of water from the well, but you wouldn't drink a cup of water from the toilet, even if you were terribly thirsty. Both cups are full of water, but not anywhere near the same. The Unmentionable is actually a wonderful thing if it's done at the right time."

Rebecca winced. "I really don't want to hear."

Ivy giggled. "Ignorance is not bliss, *heartzley*. When a boy asks you to marry him, he is telling you that he is willing to commit to you and only you, to love you for your whole self. Besides, you deserve better than a few stolen kisses in a barn. It stinks in here."

"*Jah*, it does. I didn't even think of that. How does Menno expect love to bloom with the smell of manure in the air?"

Ivy laughed. "Boys can be *dumm*. I know from personal, painful experience."

Rebecca lost her smile. "Some of the *fraaen* talk about you."

"I know."

"Is that why you were crying?"

Ivy folded her arms. "What makes you think I was crying?"

Rebecca's expression was sympathetic. "Your eyes were red, and you were hiding in the barn. I know the signs."

Ivy waved away Rebecca's concern. "Willa Troyer called me a disgrace and a wanton woman. Dinah Eicher agreed with her. They were stirring church spread and didn't even know I'd heard them. Everybody has mostly stopped rebuking me to my face. That's something to be glad about."

It was Rebecca's turn to sympathize. "They shouldn't talk about you like that. My *dat* says everyone has boards in their own eyes. They shouldn't be looking at other people's splinters."

Ivy laughed. "Are you talking about the mote and the beam?"

"*Jah.* Why do we criticize other people for their sins when we all have our own sins to worry about?"

"Well, the board in my eye is pretty big."

"But don't you believe in repentance?" Rebecca asked.

"Of course I do." It was why Ivy kept trying with her Amish community. This was where she belonged, and she shouldn't judge people just because they sinned differently than she did. But their jabs and criticisms still hurt.

Rebecca tilted her head to one side, as if trying to figure Ivy out. "You should get married."

Ivy laughed out loud. "Married? Who would marry me?"

Rebecca huffed out a breath. "You're wonderful pretty. And you're nice. I didn't know you were so nice. They say rude things about you. I just thought you'd be kind of snotty." Rebecca's eyes went wide, and she clapped her hands over her mouth. "I shouldn't have said that. Here I talk about other people being rude, and I'm the one who's being rude."

Ivy laughed again to hide the inevitable pain, like a sliver of glass lodged against her heart. "Snotty? You think I'm snotty?"

"*Nae.* I don't really know you." Rebecca grinned. "You're nice. Really nice."

Ivy felt a cozy fire kindle in her chest. "*Denki.* I don't know that anyone has ever called me nice before."

"Well, they should." Rebecca stood and brushed the hay off her dress. "I really need to go. My *dat* will be worried, and you don't want to see him when he gets worried. His eyebrows get low over his eyes, and all these wrinkles come out on his face. And he starts grinding his teeth. It's embarrassing."

Ivy couldn't imagine Isaac Neuenschwander sporting wrinkles. Even though he had a fifteen-year-old daughter, he was still relatively young, no older than thirty-six or thirty-seven. And quite good looking—though Ivy made a point to ignore the unmarried Amish men. She'd tried to get Levi Kiem to fall in love with her and had made a complete fool of herself. *Gute* Amish men wanted nothing to do with her. There was only so much rejection she could take, and ignoring them seemed the best way to avoid their censure.

Ivy leaned back on her hay bale and smiled. "We don't want that happening. Your *dat* might break a tooth."

"For sure and certain." Rebecca turned toward the door, then turned back, looking hopeful and unsure of herself at the same time. "Do you think we could talk again? I mean just woman to woman?"

Ivy was stunned. Rebecca actually thought that Ivy had something to offer her? "I...for sure and certain, but I'm afraid you might be disappointed. I don't know all that much about anything. I used to smoke and drink, I couldn't care for my baby, I dated loser boyfriend after loser boyfriend. I'm not someone a girl like you should want to hang out with. In case you haven't noticed, I've completely failed at life."

Rebecca shook her head. "My *dat* says you're not a failure unless you give up. Besides, I can't talk to anyone else. Ruth Ann can't keep a secret, and Lily Burkholder just goes on and on and won't let anyone else get a word in edge-wise. I used to try to talk to my *dat* about boys, but that's when he started grinding his teeth and frowning."

Ivy laughed. "It sounds like your *dat* is definitely going to break a tooth."

"For sure and certain."

"You're welcome to come to my house anytime you want. I make jewelry to sell on the Internet, so I'm home all day. I'll show you all my fancy beads, and you can help me string them, if you like. It's easy, and we can visit while we string."

Rebecca nodded eagerly. "I'd like that. *Denki.*" She flicked a piece of hay from her dress. "Now I'd really better go."

"*Jah,*" Ivy said. "If only to save your *dat*'s teeth."

Rebecca giggled, then her expression turned thoughtful. "You said I deserve better."

"You do."

"Well, I think you deserve better too."

CHAPTER TWO

*I*saac pressed his fingers to his forehead and massaged the spot right between his eyebrows where he'd had a dull ache for months—ever since Rebecca had turned fifteen and had started looking and acting like a young woman instead of a girl. He was in no way cut out to be the *fater* of a teenage girl. Life used to be so easy. He used to be happy-go-lucky and care-free, but then Rebecca grew up almost overnight, and he had turned into a raging, hand-wringing, pacing-the-floor-in-the-middle-of-the-night parent.

He searched Eicher's house one more time and then all around their yard but couldn't see Rebecca anywhere. No doubt she was off with her friends, giggling and talking about boys and planning to get into all sorts of trouble. Or worse, she wasn't just planning on getting into trouble. Maybe she was already immersed in it. Perhaps she was playing poker in Eicher's cellar, or some pimply young man was kissing her in the back of his buggy. The thought made Isaac's heart plummet to the ground. He passed Ruth Ann Byler, who was one of Rebecca's best friends. "Ruth Ann, have you seen Rebecca?"

Ruth Ann looked almost guilty. "Can't you find her?"

"*Nae*, and it's time to go home." Isaac scanned the yard. No sign of Rebecca. Menno Coblenz came out from behind some bushes. Isaac furrowed his brow. Boys should not be lurking behind bushes. It made *faters* suspicious. Isaac couldn't approve of Menno. He was much older and seemed to be overly interested in Rebecca. Isaac gave Menno a curt, stay-away-from-my-daughter wave. "Menno, have you seen Rebecca?"

"Lately?" Menno said, not even pausing in his march toward the house.

Okay. He'd get no help from Menno.

Ruth Ann pasted a smile on her face as her gaze followed Menno across the grass. "Have you looked in the barn?"

The barn? Why would Rebecca be in the barn?

Unless she was involved in some mischief.

Isaac strode toward the barn, not bothering to hide how much of a hurry he was in. Who cared if anyone thought he was overreacting?

He wasn't ten feet from the door when it swung outward and Rebecca emerged. Her *kapp* was completely straight, and she didn't look particularly disheveled. Maybe she hadn't been kissing anybody. But she could have been playing poker.

"Where have you been?" he asked, with more anger in his voice than he wanted. He couldn't help himself. He worried about Rebecca constantly.

Of course she got defensive, glaring at him as if he'd accused her of breaking one of the Ten Commandments. "Can't you see, *Dat*? The barn." She held out her hand, palm up, and motioned to the barn, as if she were educating someone who'd never seen one before.

Isaac swallowed his anger but couldn't keep the accusation out of his voice. "What were you doing in the barn? Fellowship supper is over. It's time to go home."

Rebecca huffed out a breath. "You and Freeman Sensenig were talking about fishing. I figured I'd have at least an hour to wait."

"You used to like to talk about fishing," Isaac mumbled. Just one more thing he and Rebecca didn't have in common anymore.

Rebecca rolled her eyes. "Oh, *Dat*. I still like to talk about fishing, but you and Freeman go on and on and on. It's kind of rude for you to make me wait like that." She headed toward the house. "Come on, then. I've been waiting and waiting. I'm *froh* you're finally ready to go."

She was right. He shouldn't be mad at Rebecca when he had been the one at fault. He followed after her. Wait a minute! Isaac pulled up short and growled under his breath. He'd almost fallen for that trick. "Hold on a minute, *maedel*."

Rebecca sort of slowed down, but she didn't turn around, and she didn't stop walking away from him. "Let's go, *Dat*. You've kept me waiting long enough."

He hated having to be firm with Rebecca, but he wasn't going to just let it go. Why had she been in the barn, and why had she avoided his question? Just what or *who* was in that barn she didn't want him to see?

Before he could throw the door open and storm into the barn, it slowly creaked outward. Ivy Zook walked out, looking suspiciously innocent and unnervingly pretty. Ivy had been a member of their Colorado district for two or three years, but everybody avoided her. She'd jumped the fence, used drugs, gotten pregnant, and left her baby with her *schwester*, Esther, to raise. She'd even tried to trick Levi Kiem into marrying her by pretending to be interested in getting baptized. And even though she'd been baptized three years ago, nobody trusted her as far as they could throw her.

Isaac was momentarily distracted by Ivy's uncommonly blue eyes, a deeper blue than usual because it was obvious she'd been crying. He tamped down his sympathy and remembered Ivy's untrustworthy reputation. "What were you doing in there?"

Ivy raised an eyebrow and folded her arms. "Nice to see you too, Isaac."

Isaac wasn't about to let her get away with avoiding his questions like Rebecca had. "Were you playing cards?"

Ivy glanced behind her as if to check that Isaac was talking to her. She squinted in his direction. "Um, playing cards? *Nae.*"

"Then what were you doing in there with my daughter?"

Ivy tilted her head to look past Isaac. Rebecca was just disappearing behind the bushes. "Really, Isaac. There is no need to get testy."

Isaac took a deep breath. Ivy was wrong—he had every reason to get testy —but he shouldn't forget his manners. Jesus said to treat everyone with kindness. "Why were you and Rebecca in the barn?"

Ivy's eyes flashed with defiance and amusement. Did she think Isaac's distress was funny? "We were having a really nice conversation about teeth and toilets and robbing banks."

Isaac's agitation shot into the sky. "You robbed a bank?"

Ivy laughed. She was enjoying torturing him. "Of course not. I stole some money from an ATM once, but a bank will get you real prison time."

"That doesn't make me feel better."

Ivy sighed and grinned at him. It was a sweet, sympathetic look that completely disarmed him. "Let me put your mind to rest. Rebecca is not going to rob a bank. She's too smart for that."

"She's fifteen. Easily persuaded." He gave Ivy a pointed look.

Ivy looked thoughtful for a second. "She's a smart girl. She'll figure it out."

"Figure what out?"

"Life. Aren't all teenagers just trying to figure out where they fit into the world?" Ivy flashed a dazzling smile. "She adores you, you know."

Isaac was rendered momentarily speechless. Ivy seemed so sure and so impressed. "She used to."

"*Ach,* she still does. But you've really got to stop clenching your jaw. She's worried about your teeth."

"I don't clench my jaw."

"*Jah,* you do. I personally saw it not thirty seconds ago."

Growling softly, Isaac scrubbed his hand down the side of his face and relaxed his jaw. Once again, he had been thrown off track. "I would be very grateful if you would keep your distance from my daughter. She is easily swayed by other people, and you aren't the best influence."

Pain flashed in Ivy's eyes. Isaac was sorry to hurt her feelings, but he didn't regret saying it. His daughter was his most important concern. Ivy seemed to recover quickly from his remark. She smiled, though the smile didn't quite reach her eyes. "Still think I'm going to rob that bank?"

"You'll forgive me if I'm suspicious," Isaac said, not feeling a bit contrite. "Neither you nor Rebecca will tell me what you were doing in the barn, so I have to assume the worst."

There was that look of amused defiance again. "Why do you have to assume the worst? Why can't you assume the best?"

"Because I'm the *fater* of a teenage girl."

"That's not a reason. That's a flimsy excuse."

He didn't mean to raise his voice, but Ivy was being stubborn. "It's an excellent reason. I do nothing but worry about her."

She looked genuinely sorry for him. "*Ach*, Isaac. You can't add one cubit to your stature by worrying about it."

Isaac's jaw nearly dropped to the ground.

Ivy pressed her lips together, obviously trying to stifle a smile. "You're astonished I can paraphrase a scripture, aren't you?"

Isaac pretended to not know what she was talking about, but she was exactly right. He never would have guessed that Ivy could quote a scripture or that she could come up with a very *gute* one. "I know that worry does me no good. But it makes me feel better."

Her intense gaze knocked him off balance. "Does it?"

"Of course."

"Worry doesn't make anyone feel better. When you feel helpless, I guess worrying makes you feel like you're doing something useful, even if all you're doing is giving yourself an ulcer."

"Well then, give me one less thing to worry about, and stay away from my *dochter*. Will you do that, for the sake of my stomach?"

Ivy turned her face from him. "I'm afraid I can't help you. I'm not responsible for your stomach problems."

Irritation flared inside his chest. "I'd hoped you'd be more cooperative."

"*Ach*, Isaac, I don't know how you could have expected cooperation from a wayward, sinful woman who seeks to lead astray your *dochter* and all the other youth of the district." Her tone dripped with honey and vinegar, as if she were mocking him.

He frowned. "I never said that."

"Of course you did, but you're in *gute* company, so I don't expect you to feel bad about it." She suddenly looked very sad, as if she were carrying the weight of the world on her shoulders—or maybe just the weight of her own sins. "If I were in your shoes, I'd want my *dochter* to stay away from me too. But it wonders me if you could show a little Christian charity for someone who will never be free of her past or the scrutiny of her neighbors." Obviously done with the conversation, she headed toward the house, roughly following the route Rebecca had taken. "*Gotte* be with you, Isaac. I hope you can resolve your stomach problems and get your teeth fixed." She turned and was gone in a flash of purple and white.

A second too late he realized he'd been outwitted again. Rebecca had managed to avoid his questions, and Ivy had distracted him with her blue eyes and that comment about his teeth.

What was wrong with his teeth?

CHAPTER THREE

Cathy Larsen squinted into her phone. "I'm still not very good at this."

Ivy leaned in to look at the screen. "A little to the right. We want the turquoise stone to be in the center of the photo."

The phone jiggled when Cathy shook her head. "All the blogs say the photos need to be a little off center. They're more visually appealing that way."

Ivy wasn't so sure, but Cathy had been so kind to come and help her out that she didn't want to argue. Cathy's jewelry pictures had turned out well enough in the past.

Cathy snapped a few pictures of Ivy's latest creation. "I'd buy this one for myself, but I don't wear any jewelry except my arthritis magnet bracelets. I'm telling you, you're missing out on a money-making opportunity. Arthritis bracelets are the jewelry of the future."

"They're not very pretty."

"They could be. You're the artistic genius. Figure out a way to make them pretty and charge outrageous money for them. People will pay."

Ivy smiled to herself. Cathy seldom had a nice thing to say about anyone, and even more rare was a compliment for Ivy. Still, she didn't deserve the praise. Stringing beads together wasn't exactly hard.

Cathy came every Friday to photograph the jewelry that Ivy sold in her Etsy shop online. Cathy's grandson Dewey, a sixteen-year-old computer genius, uploaded the pictures to Ivy's Etsy shop and handled all the online sales. Ivy was making over a thousand dollars a month selling her handmade jewelry online. The bishop had approved it, and Ivy was able to support herself with her work. Esther had bought Ivy a little two-bedroom house with the money *Dat* had left to them, so she had no rent, and her expenses were minimal. She spent next to no money on clothes—a nice perk of being Amish —plus there was no electricity bill, no makeup expenses, no car insurance, no car, and no cigarette tax. Ivy had quit smoking five years ago, and it had been one of the hardest things she'd ever done, but her life had gotten a lot less expensive after that.

She'd started the Etsy shop three years ago and was selling every piece of jewelry she made. Dewey said she could make even more money if she were faster at crafting necklaces and earrings. It was wonderful nice that people liked her jewelry. No one who visited her Etsy shop knew anything about her past or what a terrible person she had been. It was very nice just to be the woman who made stylish jewelry that Englischers liked to wear.

Ivy set the little turquoise earrings inside the circle of the necklace. "Will you take a couple of pictures of both of them? I think I'll sell them as a set."

"Do you have some raspberries or a sprig of parsley you could put with them?" Cathy asked. "Those food pictures look so nice with a sprig of parsley."

Ivy grinned. Cathy always wanted to be helpful. "I'm afraid I don't."

Cathy frowned. "I'm bringing parsley next time."

"Wait," said Ivy. She grabbed the scissors from the drawer, ran outside to the blooming forsythia bush in her backyard, and cut off three stalks laden with bright yellow blossoms. She ran back into the house to show Cathy. "We can use these in the photos."

Cathy nodded. "A spring theme. I like it." She patted Ivy on the cheek. "I used to think you were dopey."

Ivy slumped her shoulders. "I *am* dopey."

"You gave Esther the run-around, and nobody liked you, but you were never dopey. Just misguided and selfish. And vain."

Ivy swallowed hard. "I know."

Cathy scowled at her. "I don't mean *now*. You don't have a very good supply of garden herbs, but you've turned into quite a nice young lady. I'd set you up with one of my grandsons, but Dewey's the oldest. He's just a little out of your age range."

Warmth spread through Ivy's chest. It was the nicest thing Cathy had ever said to her.

Cathy finished snapping the pictures. "Okay, I think that's all." She held out her phone. "Will you show me how to send these pictures to Dewey?"

Ivy had shown Cathy how to send her pictures to Dewey every week for the past three years, but she didn't mind at all. Cathy was kind enough to come over and take pictures even though she was almost ninety and had trouble holding her phone steady. It was the least Ivy could do.

"Is that little girl still coming over to help you?" Cathy asked.

Ivy curled her lips. Rebecca wasn't little, a fact that Menno Coblenz was all too aware of. Rebecca had come over four times in the last two weeks. While they worked on jewelry, Rebecca talked about all the things teenage Amish girls talk about, and Ivy tried to slip a little advice into every conversation—but not too much. She didn't want to be insufferable. Rebecca came in the afternoons because her *dat* was always working the fields, and she didn't want him to find out. Ivy was definitely tempting Isaac's wrath, but Rebecca needed someone to talk to. Ivy knew how it felt to feel so alone.

"She's actually a big help. I probably need to start paying her."

"Don't do that. Then they get expectations, like paid time off and health benefits."

Ivy laughed. Cathy was an adorable pessimist.

They both jumped when Rebecca burst through the back door. "Ivy," she said breathlessly, "my life is over!" She stumbled into Ivy's arms and sobbed.

Cathy grimaced and shoved her phone in her purse. "I'm sorry I have to leave," she said over the din of Rebecca's crying, "but I have no compassion, and teenagers make me grumpy." She shrugged on her jacket. "Good luck." She closed the door quietly behind her, as if she didn't want anyone to know she was leaving.

Ivy awkwardly patted Rebecca on the back. She could relate to Cathy. Neither of them was cut out for this compassion stuff. "It's okay, Rebecca. It's going to be okay. No matter what happened, your life isn't over." She nudged Rebecca away from her so she could look into her eyes. "Should I make you some chamomile tea? That always makes me feel better."

Rebecca nodded. "I'd like that, but nothing will make me feel better. My life is over."

Ivy pulled a chair out from under the table and invited Rebecca to sit. Then she grabbed the tea kettle from the stove and filled it with water. "Tell me what happened."

Rebecca held a white handkerchief, and she strangled it with both hands. "It's Menno. He did something terrible."

Ivy's heart sank like a stone in the lake. She turned her back and fiddled with the knobs on the stove so Rebecca wouldn't see the distress on her face. "What did he do?" If Menno had talked Rebecca into doing The Unmentionable, Ivy would not only egg his house, but his barn, his buggy, and his cow. *Ach, vell*, maybe not the cow. The poor cow had no control over Menno's behavior.

Rebecca sniffled into her handkerchief. "Last night he took me to a real nice dinner at Dairy Queen. He paid for a large fry *and* a Blizzard." She blew her nose. "I should have been suspicious."

"How could you have known?" Ivy said, slamming the tea kettle down on the burner.

Rebecca seemed to take heart from Ivy's indignation. "How *could* I have known?" She dabbed at her eyes. "After dinner, he parked the buggy at Chapman Park and wanted to do The Unmentionable right there in the parking lot." Rebecca pressed her hand to her heart. "In. The. Parking. Lot. Can you believe it?"

Actually, Ivy could believe it, but Rebecca was looking for shock. "How terrible!"

"I remembered what you told me. I said, 'Menno, you can forget it. I'm not going to cut off my hand for you. And I won't rob a bank or do *other things* until after we're married. So you can just stop asking.'"

"What did he say?"

"At first he was just irritated. He tried to talk me into taking my shoes and stockings off." She rolled her eyes. "As if I couldn't see right through that plan. Then he got mad and said I didn't love him, and I said if he really loved me, he'd wait until we were married. He got even madder. Do you know what he said? He said, 'I bought you a nice dinner at Dairy Queen. You love Dairy Queen.'" Rebecca looked guiltily at Ivy. "I do love Dairy Queen."

"That doesn't matter, Rebecca."

Rebecca sighed. "I know, but I felt kind of bad for a few seconds. But then he asked to take my stockings off again, and I said, 'Do you think you can buy my virtue for a Salted Caramel Blizzard?'"

Ivy let out the breath she'd been holding. "*Nae*, he can't." They met eyes and laughed. "*Ach*, Rebecca. I've never been prouder of anyone in my whole life." She pulled out a chair, sat next to Rebecca, and put her arm around her shoulders. "You did the right thing, *heartzley*, no matter how mad he was."

She sank in her chair. "I think I did the right thing. I don't know."

"Of course you did the right thing."

"That's not the worst of it. This morning *Dat* and I went to the dented supermarket for groceries, and Menno was there with Lily Burkholder. *Lily Burkholder*, my used-to-be second best friend. He was holding her hand in broad daylight. I pretended not to see him, but when my *dat* was looking at hats, Menno came looking for me, dragging Lily with him." She pitched her voice higher. "'I hope you're not sad, Rebecca, but Lily and I are dating now.' I guess I looked pretty shocked. He said, 'You're wonderful selfish, and I need a girlfriend who shows more gratitude.'" Rebecca burst into tears again. "He broke up with me because I'm not grateful enough. *Ach*, Ivy, what can I do? I love him so much."

Ivy gathered Rebecca into her arms again. "I'm so sorry, Rebecca, but a boy who would break up over The Unmentionable isn't worthy of you. Can you see that?" *Dear Heavenly Father, help her see the truth.*

"I thought I was doing the right thing, but I love him, and it hurts really bad."

"I know it hurts now, but you deserve better." She gave Rebecca's shoulder an extra squeeze. "Do you believe it?"

Rebecca nodded, her face still buried in Ivy's shoulder. "I suppose."

"Believe it, because it's true." Ivy handed Rebecca a napkin from the holder in the middle of the table. Rebecca's handkerchief was quite soggy.

"Please don't tell my *dat*."

"You should tell him. He'd be very proud of you."

"*Nae*. He'd just grind his teeth and send me to my room."

A large silhouette suddenly loomed in the frosted back door window. Whoever that silhouette belonged to banged on the door. Ivy furrowed her brow and glanced at Rebecca. "Who is that?" Ivy stood, opened the door, and caught her breath.

Isaac Neuenschwander stood on her back porch, his expression as dark as a thundercloud. "Where is my *dochter*?"

Ivy had just about had enough of Isaac Neuenschwander. He was blunt and rude and didn't care about anyone's feelings but his own. But he was also a *fater*, and no *fater* wanted his *dochter* spending time with Ivy Zook. She tried to act as if daggers weren't shooting out of Isaac's eyes, as if he'd just come for a social call. "No need to panic, Isaac. She's here, safe and sound." She opened the door farther so Isaac could see Rebecca sitting at the table. Rebecca smiled sheepishly and gave her *dat* a little wave.

Ivy could tell that Isaac was trying to rein in his temper, even if he wasn't doing a very *gute* job of it. "I've been worried sick because I couldn't find you when I came in from the field. I finally got Ruth Ann to tell me where you were and what you'd been doing here. For the last two weeks." Every word was punctuated with anger. "Didn't I tell you to stay away from Ivy Zook?"

"*Jah, Dat.*"

"Is that all you have to say?"

Rebecca lifted her chin. "You only told me to stay away from Ivy because you think she's a bad person, but she's not a bad person. Ivy's nice, and she talks to me, unlike *some* people."

Isaac drew his brows together. "I talk to you all the time."

Ach, Ivy would rather be anywhere but stuck between Rebecca and her *fater*. She should never have let Rebecca come over to her house, even though she had truly been trying to save her from Menno Coblenz. But nobody liked Ivy. Certainly, nobody trusted her. She had been a fool to think she could help Rebecca. Nobody wanted her help, and neither Isaac nor Rebecca had asked for it. "Please, Rebecca," she said. "Maybe you should just go home with your *dat*, and we can talk about this later."

The teapot whistled, and Ivy's nerves were pulled so tightly, she jumped at the sound. She quickly lifted the teapot from the burner and turned off the stove. It was a pretty *gute* guess she wouldn't be making Rebecca any tea.

Momentarily distracted, Isaac reached out and brushed a tear from Rebecca's face. It was a surprisingly gentle gesture from a very angry *fater*. "You've been crying. What's wrong?"

"Nothing's wrong. I haven't done nothing wrong."

He scrubbed his hand down the side of his face and heaved a sigh. "You're right, Rebecca. You haven't done anything wrong." He turned on Ivy. "The wrongdoing is yours. I told you to stay away from my *dochter*, and you encouraged her to disobey me. The two of you are keeping secrets from me, making plans behind my back. She's only a child, and you've corrupted her."

"She has not, *Dat*."

Isaac's eyes looked like they would pop out of his head at any moment. Now Rebecca would worry about his teeth and his eyesight. "She convinced you to break one of the Ten Commandments. Honor thy *fater* and thy *mater*. That's corruption if I ever heard it."

"It was my choice to disobey you, *Dat*. Ivy told me I should talk to you. She never encouraged me to go against you."

Isaac hesitated for less than a second. "She shouldn't have let you in the house."

Ivy appreciated how loyal Isaac was to Rebecca, wanting to give her the benefit of the doubt. It was a very attractive quality in a man, even if turning his anger away from Rebecca meant turning it on Ivy. She was also impressed that Rebecca felt comfortable arguing with her *dat*, even defying him in a way. Most Amish girls wouldn't dare stand up to their *faters*. She looked at Isaac with new respect. It was clear he wasn't a tyrant in his own home.

"Don't you believe I should make my own choices?" Rebecca wasn't backing down. Ivy found her resolve both admirable and exasperating. "Don't you believe the Scripture that says, 'I was a stranger, and you took me in'? *Dat*, I was a stranger to Ivy, and if she hadn't helped me, I'd probably have done something very bad, like rob a bank or *other things*."

"That's just silly," Isaac said. "You're my *dochter*. It's my job to help you. Ivy *is* a stranger. She knows nothing about you or our family and cares even less."

Ivy couldn't remain silent with that aspersion hanging over her head. "That's not fair, Isaac. I care very deeply, and I know a fair sight more than you do about teenage girls."

Isaac glared at her. "You'll never know my *dochter* better than I do." He marched out the still-open door. "*Cum*, Rebecca. You are not allowed to come here ever again. Do you understand?" He took off his hat and waved it in Ivy's direction. "I will speak to the bishop about this. You should be shunned for coming between a *fater* and his *dochter*."

The thought of shunning didn't upset Ivy in the least. Shunning was so rare here as to make it almost nonexistent. Ivy had done nothing worse than offend Rebecca's *dat*, and she had tried to get out of the way. Such a small transgression wouldn't even warrant a visit from the *Aumah Deanuh*, the head deacon, or a kneeling confession on Sunday. They had let her get baptized, and she done much, much worse in her day. She sighed, tired of the conversation and tired of Isaac Neuenschwander. "Most of the members already shun me. I don't see that as a great punishment."

Rebecca hadn't made a move to follow her *dat*. "You can't have her shunned, *Dat*," she moaned, as the tears started up again.

Isaac again proved himself to be a *gute* man when he marched back into the kitchen, nudged Rebecca to her feet, and hugged her tightly, whispering words of comfort even though he was as mad as a hornet.

It was all so confusing. And endearing. And Ivy wanted to go take a long nap.

He pulled a sparkling white handkerchief from his pocket. Apparently, Isaac was *gute* at laundry. He handed it to Rebecca. "*Cum.* Let's go home and make cookies. I'll even let you lick the spoon."

Rebecca sighed as if her *dat* had said something funny. "*Dat*, I'm not six years old. I don't need to lick the spoon."

"But you like to lick the spoon."

Rebecca pressed the handkerchief to her nose. "I hate to keep secrets from you, *Dat*. Ivy told me to talk to you, but I just can't. You don't understand. You don't care anymore."

Isaac was clearly taken aback. "Of course I care."

"Why do you get mad when I ask questions?"

"I do not." Isaac cleared his throat. "I'm sorry. I didn't know I was doing that. Can you give me an example?"

"I asked you what puberty was, and you snapped at me."

A flush traveled up Isaac's neck, but to his credit, he didn't turn tail and run out the door. "I'm sorry. I shouldn't have done that. Does the secret you're keeping have something to do with...puberty?" He nearly choked on the word. Ivy did her best not to show her amusement at Isaac's discomfort.

Rebecca lifted her head and looked her *dat* in the eye. "Promise you won't get mad?"

Isaac furrowed his brow and glanced at Ivy. Ivy nodded slightly. "I will do my best not to get mad. Or snap at you."

Rebecca pressed her lips together. "Ivy, could I have that chamomile tea now?"

Ivy nodded and slid the teapot onto the stove once more.

"Let's sit down," Rebecca said. Her *dat* obediently sat, a silent acknowledgement that Rebecca was now in charge of the conversation. Ivy had been sure she couldn't be any more astonished or impressed than she already was. She'd certainly gotten a wrong first impression of Isaac.

Ivy sat across from Rebecca. At her small table, that put her next to Isaac.

Isaac gave Ivy a doubtful half smile, which was more friendliness than he'd shown in the three years since her baptism. The small gesture sent a zing of electricity right to her heart. She couldn't blame him or anyone else for being less than friendly. She wasn't someone that people in the district wanted to get to know.

Rebecca's courage seemed to falter. "*Dat*, don't be mad."

"I'll do my best," Isaac said. There was an edge of irritation to his voice. Even understanding and sensitive *dats* had their limits.

"I was in the Eicher's barn with Menno that day when you were looking for me."

Isaac didn't change his expression, but his right eye twitched ever so slightly. "Menno Coblenz?"

Rebecca nodded. "I love him, *Dat*."

More eye twitching from Isaac, now accompanied by some jaw grinding as well.

Rebecca didn't seem to notice her *dat*'s distress, thank *Derr Herr*. She was upset enough as it was. "Do you know what The Unmentionable is, *Dat*?"

Isaac's eye stopped twitching, probably because he had narrowed both of them to slits. He rested his elbows on the table and laced his fingers together. "Do you?"

"Ruth Ann told me because you didn't want to talk about it."

Isaac sucked in a breath, as if he were about to yell. He leaned back and slowly let it out. "So what happened?"

By this time, Rebecca's face was glowing bright red, but Ivy admired her bravery. She kept going. "Menno wanted to do The Unmentionable right there in the barn after fellowship supper."

Isaac's knuckles turned white. "I see."

"I wasn't so sure, but then Ivy was hiding in the barn, and she told Menno to go away. Then she told me that if Menno really loved me, he would wait until after we got married."

Isaac's gaze flicked in Ivy's direction. The look was brief but teeming with emotion. Ivy forgot how to breathe.

"I mean, I wouldn't cut off my foot for Menno or rob a bank. He took me to Dairy Queen too, but I told him we should wait. Then this morning I saw him at the dented grocery store holding Lily Burkholder's hand. He didn't even love me enough to wait a whole week to find a new girlfriend." Rebecca scrunched the handkerchief in her fist. "I came over here, and Ivy told me I'd done the right thing, even though I love Menno better than my own soul."

Isaac grabbed Rebecca's hand. "You did do the right thing. I'm proud of you."

Rebecca studied her *dat*'s face and must have been comforted by what she saw there. Her relief came out as a giggle. "It's a sin to be proud."

"Not if it's a *fater* being proud of his *dochter.*"

"Aren't you proud of Ivy too, *Dat?*"

Isaac turned and gave Ivy a brilliant smile. Ivy had never in her entire life been smiled at like that. Her heart raced, and her palms got sweaty. "I'm wonderful proud," he said.

"She's smart, and she used to be a teenager, and the way she explains things makes sense."

The teakettle whistled again, and in relief, Ivy jumped up to make the tea. Surely, she was blushing from head to toe. It was Isaac's fault for looking at her like that. His gaze made it hard to stay mad at him. Besides, she had no right to be angry. She didn't deserve any better than Isaac's disdain. She had indeed invited Rebecca into her house against her *fater*'s wishes. She had done many things that would make her unworthy for the rest of her life.

Ivy poured a cup of chamomile tea for each of them, and they sat at the table talking about unimportant things, which felt *gute* after such an intense conversation. Rebecca told her *dat* about Ivy's jewelry business, and Isaac gave them an update on how planting season was coming.

After twenty minutes or so, Isaac thanked Ivy for the tea, Rebecca gave her a hug, and *fater* and *dochter* strolled out to the buggy laughing and talking as if there had never been a fight. A twinge of regret caught Ivy by the throat. Oh, how she envied Rebecca and Isaac. Ivy had destroyed every loving relationship she'd ever had, and now she was reaping the lonely consequences.

She tried not to dwell on that as she closed the door and cleared away the tea. Things had turned out well, though she didn't expect to see Rebecca at her door ever again. Isaac had been very understanding, but he was still a protective *fater*.

And Ivy was still Ivy.

CHAPTER FOUR

*T*he next morning Ivy went out to her garden to see if anything could be done about it. Several small patches of snow still dotted the ground. In other places the mud was deep and thick. Ivy had never had a green thumb, but a few years ago, she had found that she enjoyed working the soil and watching things grow. This year she was going to plant a whole row of peas and maybe try a few raspberry bushes. The peas could go in next week if the soil was ready.

How would potatoes do next to the tomatoes?

She turned and looked back toward the house. Her small lawn was covered in a sea of purple crocuses, and the cheery yellow daffodil heads were just starting to emerge. She had planted more than a hundred daffodil bulbs last fall. They were going to be stunning. She regretted not having any tulips in her yard, but the deer ate them as fast as they popped out of the ground. It was useless to plant them.

Buds were showing on her cherry tree, the lone tree in her yard. In another couple of weeks, the tree would explode with blossoms. Ivy loved to sit in the yard when the cherry tree was in full bloom. The smell was intoxicating, and the low hum of thousands of honeybees was soothing music to her ears.

A glorious, unruly forsythia bush grew against the house and spread its branches eight feet in every direction. Ivy had never had the heart to trim it after it dropped its blossoms, so it threatened to take over one whole corner of the yard. The bush itself wasn't very attractive, but *ach*, it was a sight to see in the spring!

She slid on her gloves and tapped her hoe on the hard-packed earth. The soil was dense but wouldn't be too hard to work if she put some elbow grease into it. She bent over the break up a dirt clod, stood up straight, and nearly fainted when she saw a dark figure out of the corner of her eye. He was leaning against the trunk of the cherry tree with his arms folded, staring in her direction. She gasped and raised her hoe like a sword until she realized the dark figure was Isaac Neuenschwander.

Ivy closed her eyes and huffed out a breath. "You scared me."

His brow furrowed in a look of confused concerned. "Why aren't you married?"

Irritation overtook her. *Why aren't you married?* He'd startled her half out of her wits to ask *that*? She glared at him. "Why aren't you handsome?" It was the first thing that had come into her head, even though it couldn't have been further from the truth. Isaac was intolerably handsome.

He winced, then bloomed into a smile. "I'm afraid that's not my fault. I was born with this face." He gazed at Ivy until the silence between them got awkward. Why was he here?

Ivy propped her hoe on the dirt. "Don't you have a field to plant?"

"Finished yesterday."

"And you're here because…?"

He shrugged, that grin still firmly in place. "I'm curious, and I just had to come over and ask. Why aren't you married?"

Ivy gripped the hoe and tapped it against a rock. "It's not a very nice question for someone my age."

He raised his eyebrows. "Isn't it? You can't be more than twenty-five, twenty-six."

She snorted. "Flattery will get you nowhere. I'm thirty."

"I'm puzzled. You're quite possibly the prettiest girl in Colorado, you're smart, you stick your nose where it shouldn't go, and you protect teenage girls from inappropriate boys."

"Believe me, that's not normal behavior for me. I usually try to stay out of everybody's way."

He lost his smile, pushed away from the tree trunk, and came to her, grabbing hold of the hoe just inches from where her fingers were wrapped around it. "Ivy, please forgive me for being so rude to you. It was unfair of me to make assumptions about you. You didn't have to do what you did for Rebecca. Do you know I grateful I am?"

He was much closer than he needed to be, and Ivy found his closeness unnerving and extremely pleasant. She drew in a breath and savored his manly smell before taking a step back and gathering her wits and her common sense. "No one should have to learn things the hard way when an easier way will do. I just wanted Rebecca to know there was an easier way."

"I'm frustrated that I didn't see this coming. I'm a terrible *fater*."

"Not terrible at all. It must be hard to raise a teenage daughter by yourself."

He nodded. "It didn't used to be hard. Believe it or not, I have always loved being Rebecca's *fater*, even when she was a *buplie* who ate every three hours and needed a diaper change even more often than that. Even when Magdalena left us."

Ivy frowned. Magdalena was Isaac's first wife. She'd left when Rebecca was a *buplie* and died a year later in a car accident. Isaac's heart must have broken twice.

"I loved rocking Rebecca to sleep," Isaac said, "feeding her baby food, soothing her when she cried, and singing her lullabies from the *Ausbund*."

Ivy grinned. "There are no lullabies in the *Ausbund*."

"They were the only songs I knew." He expelled a deep breath. "Rebecca and I have had so many adventures together. As a little girl, she rode the horse while I plowed. She started helping with the dishes at age four and learned how to read English at age five. She would sit on my lap and read *The Budget* newspaper with me, asking me to say the words that were too big for her to understand. I taught her to fish and make Yankee Bean soup, and we sat on the porch in the evenings making up stories and laughing at silly jokes."

"She truly does adore you."

Isaac smiled as if he didn't agree but didn't want to argue. "Things are different now. Rebecca is becoming a woman, and I'm terrified. We have always been able to talk about anything, but teenage girls are different. She started getting irritated when I asked the most harmless questions, like why she suddenly wanted to do her own laundry and why she spent so much time in the bathroom."

"Oh, dear. I see where you went astray."

Isaac chuckled. "*Jah*. I think you do. I'm sorry to admit I clammed up when she asked why hair was growing in her armpits, and she told you my reaction when she asked me what puberty meant. I think I might have had a stroke. I borrowed a book from the library and gave it to her to read for herself."

"You didn't!"

"I'm afraid I did. The first time I noticed the boys were noticing Rebecca, I just about choked on my own tongue. I understand why men joke about buying shotguns to scare the boys away from their *dochters*. And is it wrong that I want to take a cattle prod to Menno Coblenz?"

Ivy laughed. "I wanted to throw eggs at his house."

It didn't seem that Isaac could smile about Menno yet. Maybe he'd never be able to. "I'm wonderful glad you were hiding in the barn that day. I'm sorry I accused you of not caring." He narrowed his eyes and searched her face. "But you hide it well. You've hidden it well for years." He took a step forward. Ivy took another step back. They both still had hold of the handle of the hoe, and they were slowly walking a circle around the hoe. "Why are you hiding, Ivy?" He stepped toward her.

She stepped backward and tried to laugh, but years of pain were hard to laugh off. "I'm not hiding anything."

"*Jah*, you are." He leaned closer, and Ivy found it impossible to pull back. "There's an amazing, compassionate, *wunderbarr* woman in there, and all you show the world is someone who doesn't care, doesn't want any friends, and wants to be left alone."

Ach. Gotte surely must be laughing at her. Ivy let go of the hoe, pressed her palms to Isaac's chest, and shoved him away from her. He didn't go very far. He was rock solid, and she was only 5'4". He gripped the hoe handle as surprise popped all over his face.

"Do you know how I long for friends in the *gmayna*? Do you know how many times I've reached out my hand only to have it slapped away? Do you know how many quilting bees or canning frolics I've been invited to? Except for Esther's, none, Isaac. None. Not that I blame anybody. Who wants to be friends with someone like me?"

"I do," he said quietly.

"Do you? Because until I helped Rebecca, you wanted nothing to do with me."

"Because you were hiding, Ivy. How can anybody be your friend when you separate yourself from everybody?"

Ivy growled like a bear. "I have *never* done that. You know about my past. I haven't tried to hide the fact that my *schwester* is raising my *dochter* and that I once treated Esther very badly. You know about the smoking and the drinking and the fool I made of myself over Levi Kiem. It's the problem with everybody in the district. You think you know me, but because I did something nice that you didn't expect me to do, you accuse me of hiding." Ivy suddenly ran out of energy and indignation. It was useless to try to set Isaac straight. He would never see her as anything but a broken woman—pitiful and needy. And why should he? That was who she was.

All she truly wanted was for him to leave her alone.

She took off her garden gloves and tapped them against her leg. "It's not that I've been hiding," she said weakly. "It's that you haven't been looking. None of you has ever cared to look."

Isaac's eyes flashed with pain as if she'd slapped him. "You're right." He looked at her as if he were seeing her for the first time. "I'm ashamed to say that I've been blind. We've all been blind."

Ivy didn't know that she'd ever been able to convince someone so easily. And Isaac was convinced. Regret traveled across his face.

"I'm sorry for how we've treated you, how *I've* treated you. That stops today. You deserve better."

Maybe she did deserve better. Maybe she didn't. But now both people in the Neuenschwander household had told her the same thing. "It doesn't matter," she finally said, because in the end, it really didn't. As soon as Isaac Neuenschwander walked out of her yard, his life and her life would go back to exactly the way it had been. Rebecca would quit coming over, and the members of the *gmayna* would continue to ignore her.

"There aren't enough words to tell you how sorry I am. I am not the worst offender, but I should have stood up for you. You were a stranger, and I should have taken you in."

Isaac looked truly miserable, but Ivy couldn't dwell on his pain. She had enough of her own to bear. She snatched the hoe from him and backed away. "I'm *froh* you and Rebecca worked it out, and I'm *froh* you're talking to each other again." She turned her back on him and strode to the spot where she wanted to plant peas. "Do me one favor and keep her away from Menno. Will you do that for me?"

Before she could draw another breath, Isaac was at her side, his eyes alight with an intense emotion Ivy couldn't read. He nudged the hoe from her fingers and threw it to the dirt. "I want to kiss you so bad, I can't breathe."

Ivy's pulse stopped, and she couldn't swallow. For some strange, crazy, inexplicable reason, she wanted to kiss him too. Badly. Wildly. So much that she couldn't breathe either. She bit down on her tongue and backed away, hoping against hope he couldn't hear her heart hammering against her ribcage. "That's a little dramatic, isn't it? As far as I can tell, you're still breathing."

"Barely," he whispered, making her heart do seven somersaults and a cartwheel. "Could I...could I kiss you?" He leaned closer. "Please."

She probably should have picked up the hoe and banged him in the shin with it, but her wits were hanging from a thin string. "The bishop says no kissing until marriage," she mumbled.

She wasn't sure how he'd done it without her noticing, but he was suddenly right next to her again. She held her breath as he gently cupped her face in his hands and kissed her like she'd never been kissed before—and she had been kissed by a lot of guys. At least a dozen. Probably two dozen.

She sighed inwardly. She had no will to resist. Might as well enjoy it. She could muster regret later. She snaked her arms around his neck and pulled him closer. He was so warm, and his short beard was pleasantly rough against her face. She kissed him until she was breathless and giddy and too dizzy to stand on her own.

He pulled away and propped his forehead against hers, a brilliant smile on those perfect lips. "Let's get married."

"What?" she said, accidentally knocking her forehead against his in surprised shock. She winced, drew back, and pressed her fingers to her forehead. "Ouch."

He rubbed his forehead while grimacing in pain. "Sorry. That wasn't the most ideal way to propose to you."

"There is no ideal way to propose to me, Isaac. We barely know each other."

"We've kissed. We should get married."

She raised an eyebrow as she peered at him. "What *have* you been teaching Rebecca?"

"I just mean that if you love someone enough to kiss them, you love them enough to get married. So let's get married."

Ivy eyed him as if he'd grown an extra foot. "Yesterday we were screaming at each other."

"We were not screaming at each other."

"Yesterday you thought I was corrupting your daughter. You can't just forget all that and ask me to marry you. I'm not going to say yes just because you're a *gute* kisser."

He grinned. "You think I'm a *gute* kisser?"

"That's beside the point."

"Not to me. You just made my day."

She rolled her eyes and tried to ignore the way her insides twisted around themselves when he looked at her. "You seem to have forgotten that I am Ivy Zook."

"I don't care who you *were*, Ivy. I care about who you *are*."

"Yesterday you cared very much about who I was," she said.

He had the audacity to chuckle. "You shouldn't care about who I was, only about who I am now."

She folded her arms and glared at him. "You've changed that much in the last twenty-four hours?"

He paused, but she couldn't hope he was coming to his senses. "Actually, I have changed." He reached out and caressed an errant strand of hair away from her face. "I watched how you interacted with Rebecca. You cared only about her, not about calling her to repentance or dismissing her teenage concerns. You really listened. Because you were sympathetic, she trusted you. And because she trusted you, she followed your advice. I don't think I could have managed that if I'd tried."

"That's no reason to propose to me."

Isaac shook his head in disagreement. "It's the best reason to propose to you. I looked at you, really looked at you, for the first time yesterday. I saw a kind, loving, beautiful woman. I saw someone who is patient, humble, and unafraid to do what's right. You could have sneaked out of that barn and pretended not to see a girl in trouble." He shuddered. "You could have broken

Rebecca's trust and reported the whole thing to me. I certainly didn't praise you for keeping that secret. But you also didn't make excuses. You suffered my wrath for a girl you barely know."

"You were kind of rude," Ivy said.

"I was very rude, and I'm ashamed to admit I wouldn't have been rude to anyone else in the district. I was small-minded and short-sighted."

"It's true that you don't have much to say for yourself. And that brings me to another question. Why aren't you married?" She wasn't for a minute considering his proposal, but she was curious why a handsome, sensitive man who was also a *gute* kisser wasn't married yet. Magdalena had been gone for almost fourteen years.

He drew his head back and grinned. "Why aren't you ugly? It would be so much easier to resist you."

She twisted her lips wryly. "Afraid to answer the hard questions?"

He folded his arms and trained his eyes on the pasture behind Ivy's yard. "It hurt too much to think about marrying again."

Ivy immediately regretted asking the question. "I'm sorry."

"Magdalena was very unhappy. She left when Rebecca was only three months old. She wrote me a note. I know I'm not perfect, but it was quite unkind, telling me all the ways I had failed her as a husband. A few months later I received the divorce papers in the mail. She got her revenge for whatever she'd thought I'd done wrong. I couldn't marry again if I wanted to stay in the church. She'd sentenced me to a life of loneliness. After all that pain, I didn't want to marry again, but I set out to prove Magdalena wrong by being the best *fater* I knew how. Magdalena died while driving drunk when Rebecca was nearly two. Because I was officially a widower, the church would have allowed me to marry again, but I didn't have the heart for it." He looked at her and seemed to glow from the inside. "Until yesterday. What do you say, Ivy? Will you marry me?"

If he'd quit looking at her that way, she'd be able to think a lot more clearly. It was impossible to say yes, but it surprised her at how unhappy she was to disappoint him. "This is way too fast."

A slow smile crept onto his lips. "That's not a no."

"We barely know each other," she pointed out.

"I know as much as I need to know." She stood her ground, and he sighed. "All right. You're taking a bigger risk, so I can't blame you for wanting more time. I'm willing to postpone the wedding until September."

She cocked an eyebrow. "How generous."

He leaned in and placed a swift kiss on her mouth. She didn't know whether to roll her eyes or swoon. "I'm going to be honest," he said. "I wasn't planning on getting engaged when I got here."

"You're not engaged," she said.

He pulled a watch from his pocket and glanced at it. "I have to go, but could I come and sit tonight?"

"Sit?"

"The rules for courting at our age aren't anywhere near as strict as for *die youngie*. Could I come every day? We could sit on your back porch and watch spring come on."

She couldn't believe she was actually letting him drag her into "courtship." But she couldn't resist Isaac's warm smile, and maybe she wanted to see where this nonsense would take her. Over a cliff probably. "The cherry tree will soon smell heavenly."

It was unbelievable how a word from her could make Isaac so deliriously happy. "*Ach*, Ivy, thank you." He walked across the lawn toward the side of the house. "I'll see you tonight. You won't regret this."

She already did.

But not much.

CHAPTER FIVE

*I*vy was *gute* at stringing beads to make beautiful necklaces. She was *gute* at shaping wire and glass to make stylish earrings. She had an eye for fashionable jewelry, even if she didn't wear it herself. But she couldn't quilt to save her life. Her stitches were too far apart, and sometimes she missed catching the bottom fabric with her needle. Maybe she never got invited to quilting frolics because she couldn't quilt, not because people didn't like her.

"I'm really not *gute* at this," she said to no one in particular as she sat poking her needle haphazardly into the quilt laid out on frames in Edna Bontrager's front yard.

"*Ach*, I'm sure you're too modest," Edna said, threading her needle for the third time. "Let me see." She put on her reading glasses and leaned over to look at Ivy's row of stitches. "*Ach...ach, vell*, I like that you're trying so hard."

Ivy smiled wryly. "Quilting is not one of my talents."

Edna patted Ivy's hand. "The gifts that *Gotte* gives."

"It doesn't matter," said Ivy's *schwester*, Esther. "Quilting is only half the fun of a quilting frolic." Esther gave Ivy a small smile. Esther was probably the best quiltmaker in the state, and Esther thought Ivy's quilting was atrocious. Esther made and sold quilts in a small shop right in her house, and she was very particular about who she let work on her quilts. Ivy wasn't allowed to so much as touch Esther's sewing box.

This was the fourth quilting frolic Ivy had been invited to in as many weeks, and she had to agree with Esther about that. The best part of a frolic was the company. Quilting didn't take a lot of concentration, so the *fraaen* laughed and talked and told funny stories about their families while they quilted. Ivy loved closing her eyes and listening to the happy voices that filled the air. Sometimes she even joined in when there was the least danger of her being noticed. She didn't want to do or say anything that would ruin the newfound goodwill that the women of the *gmayna* seemed to feel toward her.

Many of the women had gone out of their way to be extra kind to Ivy, and Ivy felt as if she were blooming like her cherry tree in early spring. Lord willing, their kindness would lead to deeper friendships and genuine fellowship.

Ivy had seen Isaac nearly every day for two months. Every day he asked her to marry him, and every day she had told him *"nae"* or "not today" or "I don't know." But she was coming to a crossroads, because it was getting harder to deny her feelings. She cared for him deeply. She didn't think she was in love yet, but she couldn't be sure. She really didn't know what it felt like to be in love. He was so annoyingly earnest, so charming, so kind and eager. The very first Sunday after he'd proposed to her, he'd come into the kitchen where the women were preparing fellowship supper, pointed at Ivy, and said, "That's the woman I'm going to marry."

Ivy's face had never felt so warm, and some of the women gasped or giggled. Sarah Hoover, who had been standing next to Ivy slicing bread, nudged Ivy with her elbow and grinned like a mischievous cat. *"Ach,"* she had said, "men can be so infuriating sometimes. We women certainly have to put up with a lot, don't we?"

Ivy had smiled because Isaac was most definitely infuriating, and it was the first time Sarah had said more than three words to her.

For the last two months, everywhere Isaac went, he announced he was going to marry Ivy. He apparently couldn't temper his excitement, even though Ivy hadn't so much as hinted that she was thinking about thinking about his proposal. She wanted to smack him and kiss him at the same time. He'd drafted Rebecca into his plan, and Rebecca was almost as eager for a wedding as Isaac was.

Isaac's adoration had given Ivy newfound popularity. If Isaac, a respected member of the *gmayna*, saw something *gute* in Ivy, then maybe she wasn't so bad. Esther had tried to pull Ivy into frolics and parties for years, but no one had trusted Esther's judgment because Esther was Ivy's *schwester*. Still, Ivy appreciated Esther for trying. But real progress had only come when Isaac had first declared his love. And declared it again. And again.

The early May day was chilly but clear, and after being cooped indoors all winter, the ladies didn't mind bundling up in sweaters and coats if it meant they could be outside to quilt. Ivy pretended to take a stitch, but it was all for show. The quilt would be better off without her help. "Edna, how is your bunion?" she asked. Edna had been limping around for three weeks, and it appeared she would need to have surgery.

261

"Ach, it aches something wonderful." Edna pointed her needle in Ivy's direction. "Don't get old. It's not for the faint of heart."

Ivy giggled. "I don't think I have a choice."

Linda Kiem sat across the quilt from Ivy. Linda was Esther's sister-in-law, married to Levi's *bruder.* "Ivy, what kind of fertilizer do you use in your garden? Esther says you grow the best vegetables."

After a discussion on fertilizer and gardens, Gloria wanted Ivy's opinion on pruning cherry trees, and how was her jewelry business going?

Ivy's heart warmed. This was trivial, insignificant chatter, but their genuine interest in her life made Ivy feel as if she was part of something bigger, a large and tight circle of women who cared about each other and created a space of belonging for her.

Sarah had a home business cutting leather for fancy Western boots made in Texas. "Ivy, you've got to come over sometime and see my workshop. Esther says you have a talent for organizing, and my husband cannot keep that place clean to save his life."

Esther smiled at Ivy. "You should see the place where Ivy makes her necklaces. There are hundreds of different kinds and sizes of beads and wire and clips and clasps. She's got them all organized into boxes."

"It really would be impossible to do any work if I didn't have my beads carefully organized." Ivy smiled to herself. For some reason, Isaac had taken an interest in Ivy's bead business. *Ach, vell,* she knew the reason, and it made her happy. And a little worried. He brought her fancy beads he found at swap meets and interesting rocks he came across in his fields. Ivy didn't really have use for the rocks, but it was sweet of him to think of her.

Ivy looked around the circle of women surrounding the quilt frames. Winter had given way to spring, her jewelry business was doing better than expected, and a *gute,* kind man wanted to marry her. He even had a daughter who Ivy adored and who seemed to adore Ivy. Ivy was happier than she'd ever been.

But she had never felt so uneasy.

Did she love Isaac? Love was a foreign feeling because she'd never really been in love before, not with any of her live-in boyfriends, not even with Winnie's father. The thought of loving Isaac scared her. What if Isaac realized she wasn't *gute* enough for him? How could she agree to marry him when he deserved better than a woman with a sullied past, a woman who had intentionally rebelled against her community's most deeply held beliefs? He deserved better, even if he was too blind to see it. What if she lost her head and went back to her old ways and broke Isaac's heart? She wouldn't be able to bear it, but she didn't trust herself to stay out of trouble.

Linda grinned and leaned forward, as if to get closer to Ivy, though she was on the other side of the quilt. "What I really want to know is how you got

Isaac to fall in love with you. Every single girl in the district has been trying to do that for years."

Edna nodded, a twinkle in her eye. "My daughter tried everything she knew to catch Isaac's attention. That was ten years ago. Now she's married and has four *kinner*."

Willa Troyer had been sitting silently, seemingly engrossed in her quilting. If it were possible to sulk and quilt at the same time, Willa was doing it. Willa had never married, and she was in her late thirties, close to Isaac's age. "Maybe Ivy tricked Isaac into falling in love with her like she tried to trick Levi."

Linda scolded Willa with her eyes. "That's silly, Willa. And unkind."

Willa seemed to wither under Linda's stare. "I'm just saying what everybody is thinking."

Ivy's face burned. *Was* that what everybody thought? Of course it was. No *gute*, solid Amish man would knowingly get involved with a woman like Ivy unless she had tricked him. All she could think to do was what she'd been doing for the last three years, even though an apology never seemed to help. "I'm...I'm sorry about what happened with Levi." She pressed her lips together, resisting the urge to explain herself. Nobody wanted to hear her excuses. When Ivy had first come to Byler, she had been desperate for love but also for stability and security. She had seen Levi as someone who could give her both, a *gute* man who would treat her kindly and never leave her destitute to fend for herself. Her desire to win Levi's heart had been born of desperation. Willa hadn't seen the days Ivy had spent trying to make amends to Esther. Willa certainly hadn't seen the nights Ivy had watered her pillow or the hours she'd spent pouring over the Bible, trying to find comfort in its pages. Ivy wasn't proud of how she'd treated Levi or Esther, but *Gotte* had forgiven her, and Willa had no right to ask for more remorse. She dipped her head as if concentrating on her stitches. "I'm not like that anymore."

Esther smiled and patted Ivy's leg. "Of course you're not."

Ivy's heart warmed at her *schwester*'s touch. Esther would always watch out for Ivy.

Linda glanced at Willa and also gave Ivy a smile. "It's not what everybody is thinking, Willa. I for one would prefer you don't put words in my mouth. My Ben was once very much like Ivy. People can change. In fact, that's the *gute* news of the gospel. What are we doing here if we don't believe that?"

Others around the quilt murmured their agreement, and Edna deftly moved the conversation to the minister's sermon in *gmay* last Sunday.

Willa didn't look convinced or contrite, but she fell silent and concentrated more intently on her quilting. Ivy felt sorry for her. It was painful when others disapproved of you. Very painful indeed.

Willa stood and ambled to the small table on Edna's lawn where Edna had set a pitcher of water and some plastic cups. She poured herself some water and took a sip. Ivy jumped to her feet, trying to act uninterested in anything but getting herself a drink. She sidled close to Willa while pouring herself some water. "Willa," she said softly. "I'm sorry if I've done anything to offend you. I want us to be friends."

The lines around Willa's eyes deepened. "I'm not interested in being friends with you."

Ivy shouldn't have been surprised, but she was a little hurt. "*Ach*, okay." They stood in awkward silence for a few seconds while they both finished their water. Ivy set her cup on the table. "I suppose I should get back to the quilt."

"The only reason everybody is being nice to you is because of Isaac. Isaac is handsome and kind and godly. We all love him like a *bruder*." Willa turned so her back was to the women sitting at the quilt. "We all want Isaac to be happy. When Magdalena left him, the light went out of his eyes. I'd hate to see that happen again because of you. I don't care what anybody thinks; I know you tricked him into proposing to you."

"It's not like that."

"You're being especially coy about it, but I can smell your real purpose from a mile away. You want to snatch him up before he realizes what a huge mistake he's made. And he *will* realize it's all a mistake and see you for who you truly are. I only pray he sees it before you marry. You're not worthy of him, and you know it. We all know it. Only Isaac seems blind."

Ivy wouldn't give Willa the satisfaction of thinking she'd distressed Ivy in any way, even though Willa was right. Ivy wasn't worthy of Isaac, and she never would be. She put an extra lilt to her voice so Willa wouldn't suspect she'd hit a sore spot in Ivy's heart. "*Ach, vell*, love is blind, so they say."

"Isaac is smart. He will come to see you for who you really are. Lord willing, it will be before he shackles himself to you for life. I pity how miserable he would be."

Ivy took a deep breath, unsure if she appreciated Willa's unrestrained honesty or resented it. It had certainly achieved its purpose. Ivy was riddled with doubt. There wasn't much left to say to Willa so Ivy trudged back to her seat at the quilt she couldn't help with.

Esther looked up from her stitches when Ivy sat down. "Everything okay?"

Ivy nodded, too full of confusion to say a word.

Ivy's heart nearly leaped out of her chest when Isaac's buggy pulled in front of Edna's house.

Gloria scrunched her lips together. "Here comes Loverboy now. If he doesn't temper his enthusiasm, he's going to make himself completely unbearable to be around."

Isaac jumped out of his buggy and came straight for Ivy with a brilliant smile on his face.

"*Hallo*, Isaac," Edna called, her eyes twinkling in delight.

Esther winked at Ivy. "*Ach*, Isaac, how often must you make a pest of yourself? This is a women's gathering. No men allowed. What do you want?"

Isaac's grin was so wide, his lips were in danger of flying off his face. He pointed to Ivy. "I'm going to marry her someday soon. Just thought you all should know."

Edna leaned in and whispered, "The real question is, are *you* going to marry *him*?" Her expression made Ivy giggle.

Gloria groaned. "*Ach*, Isaac, we've heard it before. Is that all you can talk about?"

"*Jah*. It's all I can talk about, concentrate on, and dream of. I'm just waiting for Ivy to come around to my way of thinking."

Ivy stabbed her needle into the quilt. "You are the most exasperating, impossible, persistent man." Her giggling made her words seem less like a scold and more like a compliment. She couldn't help it. He was so aggravatingly charming.

He chuckled, and his tender look took her breath away. "Those are my best qualities."

"For sure and certain," Esther said.

Isaac looked around at the group of women. "I hate to take away your best quilter, but I need to show Ivy something."

Ivy snorted. "I'm sure they'd be very grateful if you took me away so they can quickly unpick my stitches."

Esther's jaw dropped in mock disbelief. "Ivy, what makes you think we would do such a thing?"

Linda smiled wryly. "Maybe because that's what we did the last time." Everyone but Willa laughed at Linda's uncensored honesty. Even Ivy.

Ivy stood up and sighed in resignation. "Next time I promise I won't do anything but thread other women's needles and keep the water dispenser filled with ice. And I could make a batch of Scotcheroos."

Edna's expression froze in place. "*Ach, vell*, maybe just the needles and the ice."

"She's getting better at Scotcheroos," Esther said, unable to contain her laughter.

Edna shook her head. "I nearly broke a tooth last time."

"I could bring Oreos," Ivy said, not the least bit offended about her Scotcheroos. The last batch she made had been so hard and dry, eating them was like chewing on sandpaper.

"I like Oreos," Sarah chimed in.

Linda giggled. "Me too."

Isaac reached out to take Ivy's hand, then seemed to remember everyone was watching and promptly pulled back. Still, he stayed in Ivy's orbit until she climbed in the buggy and shut the door.

Isaac got in the other side, picked up the reins, and grinned at her. "Do you find me annoying?"

"Very."

She wasn't about to tell him how she really felt about him.

CHAPTER SIX

*I*saac chuckled as he pulled away from Edna's house. "If you find me annoying, that means you're at least thinking about me."

Ivy rolled her eyes. "All the time."

Isaac's heart did a cartwheel. "You think about me all the time?"

"*Ach, vell*, mostly trying to figure out how not to be home when you come around."

He pretended to be deeply wounded. "I think about *you* all the time too. My horse has started to notice. He tries to plow in a crooked line just to see if I'm paying attention. Most of the time I'm not."

Ivy giggled. "Potatoes will still grow in a crooked row."

"That is the most profound thing I've ever heard anyone say. You should put that in a book."

Ivy peered out the windshield, and her lips curled upward. "What was it you needed to show me?"

He winked at her. "I mostly wanted an excuse to be with you."

"Isaac Neuenschwander! Did you bear false witness to the quilting group?"

He opened his eyes wide as if the very thought was horrifying. "Of course not. I do have something I want to show you. We'll be there in ten minutes."

"I guess it doesn't matter. They didn't want me to be there anyway."

Isaac didn't like that Ivy was always so quick to put herself down. "Of course they wanted you to come. They invited you, didn't they?"

"I'm a terrible quilter."

He nudged her arm with his elbow. "You see! For sure and certain if you could quilt, they would have invited you for the quilting. But since you can't quilt, they invited you because they like you and want to be your friend."

Ivy shook her head and looked him square in the eye. "Willa says they invited me because they like *you*, not me."

Isaac wanted to scoff at that, but until recently, the *fraaen* of the *gmayna* had been less than welcoming. "I don't care," he finally said. All he cared about was convincing Ivy to love him.

"I care. I want friends."

"You're making more friends every day. I'm *froh* they invite you to quilting frolics. Once they get to know you, you'll have more friends than you know what to do with."

She shrugged. "That's optimistic, but it's nice of you to say." She huffed out a breath. "Willa thinks I tricked you into asking me to marry you."

"As I remember it, you refused my marriage proposal. A woman who wanted to trick me into marriage wouldn't have said *nae*."

She gave him a weak smile. "And don't you forget it."

"If anything, I'm trying to trick *you* into marrying *me*."

Her smile grew stronger. "And don't you forget it."

Isaac laughed. "Just so long as you don't realize you're being tricked."

She slumped her shoulders. "Willa isn't the only one who thinks I'm trying to trick you into marriage."

Isaac knew that for sure and certain—just this morning Freeman Sensenig had warned him to be careful. *She tried to fool Levi Kiem, Isaac. Best tread carefully.* "Willa's just jealous. She proposed to me three years ago."

Ivy's mouth fell open. "She proposed to you?"

"*Jah.* She said, 'Isaac, we're both old and in need of a spouse. Why don't we just get married for companionship?' It was a sensible plan, but I couldn't bring myself to marry a woman I don't love. And I'm not old. I'm only thirty-seven, not one gray hair on my head or in my beard. Don't listen to Willa."

"Like as not, Willa's wildly jealous. But I don't like anyone believing that I'm trying to reel you in like a fish on a hook."

Isaac gave her a wide grin. "*Ach*, Ivy, that's just what I am, a fish on your hook. I'm completely helpless when it comes to you."

She cuffed him on the shoulder. "Don't tease."

"I'm not teasing. I'm telling the honest truth."

She locked her gaze to his face. "Then I'm going to be perfectly honest with you. I'm not worth all this fuss. I've done a lot of bad things. I'm sure Willa has never touched a cigarette or a beer can. She's probably never said a bad word in her life."

"But she was unkind to you. I'd rather marry a smoker than a hypocrite."

A laugh exploded from Ivy's lips. "You wouldn't. Kissing a smoker is like licking a fireplace."

His lips curled upward. "I've never tried that before."

Her smile faltered. "What I'm saying is that maybe you should forget me and find someone more worthy."

Isaac didn't like that suggestion at all. Was she trying to let him down gently? Was she not interested in him? Did she find his persistence annoying? His heart sank. He loved her enough to seek for her true feelings. He furrowed his brow and studied her face. She looked very unhappy. "Is that really what you want me to do? Forget you and look elsewhere?"

"*Nae,*" she whispered. "I don't want that, but maybe it would be better for you—"

He thought he might burst with relief. "It wouldn't be better for me. I love you, Ivy. I want to marry you."

"And I'm trying to be unselfish, for once in my life."

He grunted his disapproval. "What's unselfish about breaking my heart?"

"If you asked a hundred people in the *gmayna* if you should marry me, ninety of them would say *nae.*"

Isaac liked that Ivy was willing to have honest conversations, even if they were hard and uncomfortable for her. Especially for her. He winked and squared his shoulders. "Who wants to hear ninety *dumm* opinions? I don't care what they think. I love you."

Her smile was tentative and heartbreaking. "The truth is—and I hate to bring this up—I don't understand why you love me. It's all so sudden. I'm afraid you'll stop loving me when you know me better."

Isaac took the drastic step of pulling to the side of the road and dropping the reins. He took both of Ivy's hands in his. They were as cold as ice. "I'm trying to be patient, Ivy, but you've got to stop putting yourself down. You got baptized three years ago and left the world behind. If anyone doubts your sincerity after three years, then they don't deserve to be called a Christian, and if they don't believe that Jesus paid for your sins and washed you clean, then they don't understand the *gute* news of the gospel." He squeezed her hands. "Do *you* understand the *gute* news of the gospel?"

She seemed to stiffen her spine. "I understand the gospel well enough, but you don't buy a lame horse unless you can't afford anything else."

"You are not a lame horse, Ivy. You're the woman I didn't even know I needed." He grinned. "Besides, potatoes will still grow in a crooked row."

He could tell she was trying not to smile. "I have no idea what that means."

The laughter tripped out of his mouth. "It's your motto, not mine."

Her eyes sparkled in annoyed amusement. "I didn't mean anything profound. I was just giving you encouragement."

"It means that things don't have to be perfect to be *wunderbarr*. Rows don't have to be straight to yield *gute* potatoes. You don't have to be like Willa for me to love you. In truth, if you were like Willa, I wouldn't love you. I love you for who you are. Who cares what you've done?"

She arched an eyebrow in his direction. "Okay, then, why do you love me? Two months ago you were very suspicious."

"I've already apologized for that, and I hope you know how bad I feel."

She nodded. "I do. But now you're avoiding the question."

He wanted to pull her close and kiss that troubled look off her face. "You'll probably think I'm strange, but I fell in love with you ten minutes after I walked into your house that first time. We were sitting at your kitchen table with Rebecca, and I could tell she trusted your opinion, even though I couldn't understand it. Then she told me how you were hiding in the barn when she and Menno went in there—how you stopped her from making a huge mistake. You assured her that if Menno really loved her, he'd be willing to wait. For some reason, Rebecca believed you. I don't think she would have believed me. You gave her the advice that every *fater* wants his *dochter* to hear. You wanted to protect her, and she was willing to listen to you. That says more about your character than anything I might have heard about you. I wanted to kiss you so badly, I had to get out of your kitchen before I did."

Ivy's eyes widened in surprise. "I had no idea."

"I'm *froh*. I would have made a fool of myself, and you never would have said yes to my proposal."

"I still haven't said yes to your proposal."

He winced. "Don't remind me." He raised her hand to his lips and kissed her knuckles one by one. "You're pretty, but that's not why I love you. You make beautiful jewelry and keep a fine garden, but that's not why I love you either. You have been through a thousand hard things, but you have survived them all, learned from them, and come out a stronger and more angelic person because of them."

"I wouldn't go so far as to call me angelic."

He chuckled. "There are different kinds of angels. The archangel, ministering angels, the Angel of Death."

She snorted with laughter. "I suppose the Angel of Death could be more my personality type."

"That's not what I meant," he protested through his laughter. "The blessed apostle Peter cut off someone's ear. Matthew was a tax collector. The apostles sometimes bickered among themselves. But Jesus still loved them and called them to do his work. Your past doesn't matter anymore. I love you because you did a wonderful *gute* thing for my *dochter*. And that wonderful *gute* thing revealed your true character. I love you because you're kind and unselfish and quarrelsome."

"But what if you change your mind?"

"I won't change my mind. There's nothing you can do that would make me change my mind." He put his arm around her. "Will you marry me?" He lowered his head close to hers.

Her lips twitched. "I don't know."

He pulled back and huffed out a breath. "Am I being too persistent?"

She scrunched her lips together. "I don't know."

Isaac frowned to himself. Was he too pushy? In his eagerness, was he doing exactly the opposite of what he wanted to do? He didn't want to put any pressure on her. It was just so hard to temper his passionate enthusiasm. He took a deep breath, let go of her hands, and jiggled the reins. It took a minute for the horse to move because he'd found a nice patch of grass to nibble on. "That's okay. I just like being with you."

"And I like being with you," she said, a doubtful look in her eye.

He was definitely putting too much pressure on her. Did she feel she had to be perfect? He guided the horse down a dirt lane and stopped in front of Randall Ellis's house. Randall was an *Englisch* friend of Isaac's.

"Where are we?" Ivy asked.

"You'll see."

Isaac unhitched Beauty and led him to the pasture next to Randall's front gate. The horse immediately began grazing. Isaac took Ivy's hand, and they walked up Randall's sidewalk together. "Randall has a rock tumbler. I thought you might be interested in some of his rocks."

"What is a rock tumbler?"

"You'll see."

Randall was a tall, portly man of about fifty years old. He answered the door and took them to his workshop where he had three rock tumblers going at once. They made an incredible din. Randall showed Ivy how he chose rocks, big and small, and tumbled them until they shined like polished metal. Ivy got very excited about the prospect of using tumbled rocks in her jewelry. Randall had hundreds of already-tumbled rocks he said he'd sell to Ivy for a dollar apiece. They made arrangements to meet again and sort through Randall's rocks.

Randall pointed to Isaac. "He brings me interesting rocks from his fields, and I tumble them. It can take up to two months, but some take less time."

"I'll keep looking for *gute* rocks," Isaac said, nodding to Ivy. "For your jewelry."

While Randall told them how he tumbled rocks, Ivy lost that worried look, and seemed happier than Isaac had seen her all day. After spending over an hour at Randall's house, Isaac hitched up the horse, and they got back in the buggy.

"That was *wunderbarr*," Ivy said breathlessly.

"I knew you'd like it."

Worry lines appeared around her eyes. "You're too *gute* to me, Isaac. I don't deserve you."

He clenched his teeth. "You deserve every *gute* thing, Ivy."

"You're grinding your teeth, Isaac."

"Yes, I am."

"I really like you, Isaac, and the more time I spend with you, the more worried I get that you'll decide you don't like me. Then I act like someone I'm not in hopes of not losing you. I don't feel like I can be myself because if you truly saw the real me, you wouldn't want to marry me anymore, and so then I start trying to be someone I'm not because I don't want to lose you."

Isaac cocked an eyebrow. "I have no idea what you just said."

She blew air from between her lips in frustration. "I'm maybe, sort of, probably falling in love with you, but I'm terrified you'll leave me."

He couldn't help but smile, even if she was upset. "You're maybe, sort of, probably falling in love with me?"

"Maybe."

"You can be sure of my love, Ivy." The muscles of his jaw jumped up and down. "I can see that I'm putting too much pressure on you. You've had too many bad experiences not to be wary."

She frowned. "It feels easier to just be lonely and single than to risk my heart like that."

Isaac wanted to stomp his foot and tell her she was worrying for nothing. He wanted to kiss her and tell her all would be well. But he realized that would also be putting pressure on Ivy, pressure that she didn't need and that would only confuse her further. For sure and certain, he was going to stop putting pressure on her, maybe back off a little and give her some space, maybe cool his jets—as Rebecca said. Then he would try to make Ivy see that the other women would be her friends even if she didn't have Isaac in her life. He would find a way to make Ivy feel sure of his love.

He needed to go home and make plans. He couldn't think straight with Ivy sitting next to him. "Would it make you feel better if you told me all the bad things you've ever done in your life? That way, you get it all out there, and then you won't have to worry about me deciding I don't love you anymore. I'll know everything."

"And then you will have all the information, and I won't feel like I'm tricking you."

Isaac resisted the urge to growl. "I'm tricking *you*, remember?"

"I suppose." Her expression grew serious, her eyes fearful, her spine stiff. "*Jah.* I want to tell you everything, then you can decide."

Isaac pulled over to the side of the road, and Ivy began to talk.

CHAPTER SEVEN

*I*vy hissed as she skewered her finger on a piece of wire. She was trying to figure out the best way to secure a shiny coral-colored pebble onto a necklace. Wire kept the pebble in place, but it also covered much of the beautiful rock. But it had to be secure. She wouldn't sell a necklace that would fall apart the first time it was worn. If she couldn't figure out how to secure rocks to necklaces, she wouldn't be able to use any of Randall's rocks. And she really wanted to use his rocks. They were stunning.

"Are you okay?" Rebecca asked.

Ivy looked up and did her best to smile, even though she didn't feel much cheer today. "I'm okay. These rocks are tricky."

"But so pretty," Rebecca said.

Rebecca came three days a week to help make jewelry, and Ivy paid her a little bit of money for each piece she made. Rebecca was very creative and came up with some *wunderbarr* bead combinations that Ivy wouldn't have thought of.

Ivy found that she truly enjoyed Rebecca's company. Rebecca was smart and thoughtful, but she was also young and vulnerable and desperately needed another woman's attention. Rebecca trusted Ivy, and Ivy suspected Rebecca told her things that she didn't even tell her best friend Ruth Ann or, for sure and certain, her *dat*. Rebecca needed someone who would listen without judging—someone who knew what it was like to be a teenage girl and didn't get embarrassed by the personal stuff. Ivy didn't get embarrassed by much, not after all she'd been through.

"I have something to tell you," Rebecca said. "But please don't tell my *dat*."

Ivy stifled a groan. She hated keeping secrets from Isaac, but maybe it didn't matter now. She hadn't seen him for a week. "I won't tell him, but you know it's best if you tell him everything."

Rebecca nodded. "I know, and I will. It's not a bad secret. It's a *gute* secret about Menno that will make *Dat* wonderful happy."

Ivy couldn't believe that any news of Menno would make Isaac happy. "I'm *froh* to hear it."

The words seemed to explode from Rebecca's lips. "Menno still loves me. He wants to be my boyfriend again."

Ivy did her very, very best to act as if this news was the best she'd ever heard. "*Ach*, that's nice, Rebecca."

Rebecca saw right through Ivy's fake enthusiasm. "You don't have to worry, Ivy. Menno agreed we will only kiss once every week and not even talk about The Unmentionable until we get married. He doesn't care how long he has to wait. He loves me, and that's all that matters. He only held Lily's hand to make me jealous. *Ach*, Ivy, I love him so much."

While Ivy longed to point out that Menno had dropped Rebecca like a hot potato two months ago and he'd selfishly toyed with Lily's emotions as well, she would have to tread carefully. Rebecca was in love, and if Ivy offended her, she'd lose any influence she had. "I'm happy for you, Rebecca. How sensible of you to set some rules with each other. Menno will turn out to be a fine young man after all." She wasn't convinced, but she would try to be happy for Rebecca's sake.

At least one of them was happily in love.

Ivy couldn't pretend she wasn't deeply worried. She hadn't seen Isaac for a week, not since the day she'd told him about everything—all her mistakes, her bad decisions, her long string of unworthy boyfriends, and the selfishness that had destroyed her family.

At the time he hadn't seemed concerned, except for the distress he said he felt for all the pain she had gone through—even if it was pain of her own making. When he'd dropped her off at her house, he'd hugged her and told her that her past didn't matter to him. She'd watched his buggy drive away, hopeful that maybe he still wanted to marry her. But now she wasn't so sure.

It was clear he was at least still thinking about her. He left a small bag of beads and rocks in her mailbox every morning, even though he never knocked on her door or came to look at her garden. But maybe he was trying to let her down gently. Maybe the rocks and beads were meant to soften the blow of separating from her. Had he decided that her sins were just too much to shoulder? She had expected as much, but that didn't make his rejection any less painful.

Rebecca might have some helpful information if Ivy could wheedle it out of her. "You will tell your *dat* about Menno, won't you?"

"*Jah*. Of course." Rebecca grinned. "But maybe I'll wait until after he's eaten a *gute* dinner. He's always in a better mood when he's full."

Ivy nibbled on her fingernail. "How...how is your *dat*? I haven't seen him for a while."

"*Ach*, he's fine, I guess. After he met you, he stopped pacing around the house at all hours of the night, and he stopped grinding his teeth." She rolled her eyes. "It was really nice not to have to hear *that* every day. But he was up pacing again the last two nights. He's worried about something. Do you think he suspects I'm back together with Menno?"

"I don't think so," Ivy murmured, her heart aching. More likely he was worried about how to break the news to Ivy that he wasn't interested anymore.

Rebecca jumped as if she'd been poked with a pin. "*Ach, du lieva.*" She pulled a folded piece of paper from her apron pocket. "I almost forgot to give you this. It's from my *dat*."

Ivy's hand shook slightly as she reached out to take the paper. Was this the I-don't-want-to-marry-you note she'd been expecting? She'd rather not read it in front of Rebecca for fear she'd disintegrate into a puddle of tears. Unfortunately, her curiosity got the better of her. She unfolded the note, trying to act as if she didn't really care what Rebecca's *dat* had to say.

Dear Ivy,

After we talked on Tuesday, I was ashamed of myself for putting so much pressure on you to marry me. It struck me that maybe you don't want to marry me, but you don't know how to tell me. If that is the case, please just tell me, and we can both move on with our lives. I am going to quit smothering you, and I'm going to stop asking you to marry me. I want you to discover that the fraaen *in the* gmayna *want to be your friends—not because of me—but because of you. Even if we don't get married, the* fraaen *will still like you. They just needed some time to get to know you.*

Sincerely,

Isaac

Ivy took a deep shuddering breath. He was trying to let her down easily, making it sound like breaking up was her idea and not his. It was the nicest way a guy had ever broken up with her, but that was small comfort when Isaac was truly the only man she'd ever loved.

"Are you okay?" Rebecca was studying her face, her brows drawn together in concern. "What did he say? Was it rude?"

"*Nae*, it wasn't rude," Ivy choked out.

Rebecca didn't look convinced. "You know how clumsy he is with words. Remember how I thought he didn't care about me anymore? Sometimes he just doesn't know what to say."

Rebecca was too young to understand Ivy's heartache, but there was no one else to confide in. "I don't think he wants to marry me anymore," she said, her voice cracking into a thousand pieces. She cleared her throat. She would not cry in front of Isaac's *dochter*.

"You're wrong, Ivy. Whatever he said, I'll make him come right over and apologize. He loves you. It's all he talks about." Rebecca eyed Ivy closely. "Do you love him? *Dat* might be afraid you don't love him. Maybe that's why he's been pacing the floor. It's okay if you don't love him—you can't make yourself love someone who you don't want to love. That's what Ruth Ann says."

"Like as not, he's trying to figure out a way to break the news to me gently." She reached out and patted Rebecca's hand. "I've made too many mistakes to overlook. Don't you make the same mistakes."

"*Ach*, Ivy, didn't I tell you that you deserve better? Why are you so down about yourself?" She huffed out a breath. "Honestly, it's getting old. Do you love my *dat* or not?"

"I don't know," Ivy said, even though it was a bald-faced lie. She loved Isaac terribly, but she didn't want to upset Rebecca, and she most certainly didn't want to make Isaac feel bad. After everything she'd told him, he was doing a logical, sensible thing. At least he would have no regrets. Ivy had several regrets, but telling Isaac her whole story wasn't one of them. At least he would never be able to say she'd tricked him into marriage. Ivy reached out and laid her hand on Rebecca's arm. "I have a favor for you. Don't tell your *dat* any of this. He has enough to worry about."

A smile played at Rebecca's lips. "I won't tell him, but you know it's best if you tell him everything," she said, throwing Ivy's own words back at her.

Ivy smiled in spite of herself. "Do as I say, not as I do."

Rebecca laughed. "It's easier to give advice than to take it."

"So true."

Rebecca glanced at the clock on the wall. "*Ach*, Ivy. I'm sorry, but I have to go. Menno is taking me out to supper at Mesa View Restaurant. He's even hired a driver to get us there. Isn't that romantic?"

Ivy's stomach flipped over. Mesa View Restaurant was the fanciest and most expensive place to eat in Monte Vista. The last time Menno had paid for Rebecca's food, he'd expected something much more valuable in return. Ivy didn't like it. Not one little bit. "I've heard it's wonderful expensive. Why...is he taking you there?"

"He says he wants to apologize for how he hurt my feelings."

"That's nice of him," Ivy said, this time not even trying to hide the suspicion in her tone.

Rebecca frowned. "You don't have to worry. Menno and I are going to get married. He's already asked, and I've already said yes. Menno has agreed to my rules. If that doesn't prove his love for me, I don't know what does."

"I suppose you're right," Ivy said, but then she couldn't help but add,

"Please be careful, Rebecca. I feel very protective of you. You're like a little *schwester* to me."

Rebecca laughed, the relief evident in her voice. "Of course I'm right. And you're too old to be my *schwester*. You're more like a *mater*."

Ivy gave Rebecca an indignant huff. "I'm not *that* old." She pointed to her *kapp*. "You won't find one gray hair on this scalp and no wrinkles either."

Rebecca scrunched her lips together. "Does anyone have wrinkles on their scalp?"

They both laughed. Rebecca gathered up her jewelry supplies and put them away before giving Ivy a hug and blowing out the door like a fresh spring breeze. She was buoyantly happy, and even though Ivy was worried about her, she couldn't begrudge her a little joy.

Ivy sat back down to work on her necklace, but keeping her hands busy did nothing to stop her thoughts from going right back to Isaac Neuenschwander. *Ach*, maybe she wished she'd never met him. Then again, the memories of their time together would always be precious to her.

Someone knocked on the back door, and Ivy rose from her chair to answer it. Esther, Linda Kiem, Edna Bontrager, Sarah Hoover, and Gloria Nelson came in on the breeze that had blown Rebecca away.

With an oven mitt on each hand, Sarah carried a casserole dish covered with tinfoil. "We just heard," Sarah said, "and we brought food." Ivy didn't know what was in the dish, but it smelled heavenly.

Gloria rifled through the drawers until she found Ivy's only trivet. "We're indignant for you—that's all we can say. Indignant." She set the trivet on the table, and Sarah set her dish on top of it.

Ivy wasn't sure if she wanted to know why they were indignant, because she suspected it had something to do with Isaac.

And she was right. "I thought better of Isaac," Linda said, shaking her head. "I really did." She pulled out a chair next to Ivy and sat down, curling her fingers around Ivy's wrist. "But don't give up on men in general. Most of them are smarter than a bag of potatoes."

"We all married men who are smarter than a bag of potatoes." Edna sat on the other side of Ivy.

Linda shook her head. "But I sometimes wondered about Ben. I truly did."

The other women gathered around the small table and sat. Esther brought in two chairs from the other room so she and Linda would have a place to sit too.

Ivy's heart lodged in her throat. "What...what happened?"

Edna drew her brows together in puzzlement. "You don't know? Isaac told Freeman Sensenig that—how did he say it?—that your marriage plans are on hold."

Linda nodded. "That's how he said it. Then he said that no one should be planning on a wedding between you and him."

"Of course, Freeman wouldn't be able to keep a secret if he had a box for it," Edna said. "Freeman told Ben, and Ben told Linda, and Linda notified the rest of us."

Esther pressed her lips together, concern saturating her features. "Has he changed his mind? Or have you? Because if you've changed your mind, we won't feel indignant anymore."

Ivy could barely squeeze the words out of her throat. "He...he's changed his mind."

Gasps and exclamations from the rest of the group.

"It's shameful." Gloria pressed her hand to her heart. "That's what it is. Shameful."

Everyone else nodded their agreement.

The fire in Gloria's eyes warmed Ivy's aching heart. "After all that big talk!"

"He said he was going to marry you. He spread that news around like manure," Sarah said.

Gloria nodded. "That's what it was—manure. Are you embarrassed? I'd be embarrassed." Gloria never minced words, even if they were hurtful. Ivy's face warmed, and her heart turn to ice.

Edna cleared her throat and gave Gloria a pointed look. "She hasn't done anything to be embarrassed about, Gloria."

Gloria frowned. "I'd still be embarrassed. But there's no need to be embarrassed. This is all Isaac's doing."

Ivy slumped and did her best not to burst into tears. "It wasn't all Isaac's doing. It wasn't *any* of Isaac's doing. He was just being sensible and careful. Who would want to marry someone like me?"

The other women at the table made sounds of protest. "That's nonsense," Gloria said.

"You all know what I've done, who I am. None of you wanted to be my friend either." Ivy glanced at her *schwester*. "Except Esther, and she had to be nice because I'm family."

Esther squared her shoulders. "That's how it was at first, but you've changed, Ivy. Now things between us are more like they were when we were growing up. I couldn't have a better friend."

"We haven't been kind," Gloria said, "and we're all ashamed of ourselves, aren't we?"

Everyone nodded, and Ivy felt a thaw in her chest. "Willa said you were only being nice because of Isaac."

Gloria blew a puff of air from between her lips. "*Ach*, Willa is jealous." Her cheeks turned bright pink, and she wrung her hands. "I suppose your relationship with Isaac was why I first decided to invite you to a quilting frolic. I admit I've been a poor Christian. Can you forgive me? I know you better now, and I want your friendship even if Isaac jumps in the lake."

"Me too," said Sarah.

Edna's eyes were full of emotion. "We want your friendship, and we're sorry."

Ivy heart all but burst out of her chest. "*Denki*," she said breathlessly. "That means the world to me."

"Well, it's long overdue." Gloria huffed and stood as if all the emotion at the table was too much for her. She pulled six forks out of the silverware drawer and set one in front of each of them. Then she peeled the tinfoil off the casserole dish. Steam rose from the bright orange cheese melted over an abundance of sliced potatoes. "We came over to comfort you with a pan of Edna's funeral potatoes. They're delicious and symbolic at the same time."

"What does symbolic mean?" Sarah asked.

"It means Isaac is dead to us." Gloria stuck her fork right in the middle of the pan, scooped out a healthy helping of cheese and potatoes, and pulled until the strand of cheese trailing behind it snapped. "Dig in before it gets cold," she said.

Ivy giggled at the audacity of eating food straight out of the pan. Everyone grabbed a fork and scooped up a morsel. Ivy blew on her potato before taking a bite. It was everything Gloria had said. Cheesy, potato-y, creamy goodness with just a hint of garlic and onion. They ate to their hearts' content while they laughed and talked about men, quilting, necklaces, and spring cleaning. They commiserated with Ivy, talked about giving Isaac the cold shoulder, and imagined ways to make Isaac regret his decision.

They treated Ivy like a true friend.

And when all the potatoes had been eaten, Ivy wasn't so sad anymore.

CHAPTER EIGHT

*I*vy peeked into the mailbox. A single stone sat in its depths with an envelope propped next to it. Ivy couldn't understand it. Isaac had told Freeman, and Freeman had told everyone else that the wedding was off. Why was Isaac still leaving rocks in her mailbox?

All it did was prolong the pain. With a heavy heart, Ivy took the stone and the envelope out of the mailbox. It had been nearly two weeks since Ivy had seen Isaac. Last week was Off-Sunday so she would probably see him at *gmay* tomorrow. Her heart skipped a beat. Did she want to see him at *gmay*?

She opened the envelope and read the card stuffed inside. "Hope you are well."

Hope you are well?

Why had he even bothered to write a card? What did he care if she was well? What did she care that he hoped she was well? She wanted to throw the pretty pink stone at the back of his head. Maybe she could bean him at *gmay*. It would be impossible to do it without getting caught, but it might be worth a kneeling confession just to see the look on his face.

She looked up at the sky and growled loudly, even as a tear ran down her cheek. She wanted to be ferociously mad at him. Anger hurt less than heartbreak. But she couldn't muster any anger, only the profound disappointment of dashed hopes.

She rolled the stone around in her palm. It was light pink with veins of lighter pink running just below the surface. Rose quartz. It would look beautiful fashioned into a pendant. Isaac had a *gute* eye for value. At least she could benefit in some way from his strange breakup gifts.

Ivy looked up to see two Amish girls jogging toward her. They most definitely weren't out for some exercise because they both ran like the wind was chasing them and they both wore flip-flops. When they got closer, Ivy recognized Rebecca's best friend Ruth Ann and Lily, Rebecca's former rival for Menno's love.

"Ivy," Ruth Ann called, waving frantically just in case Ivy hadn't already seen her.

Both girls finally made it to Ivy, panting as if they were taking their last breaths. Ivy slipped the stone and Isaac's annoying note into her pocket. "Are you girls okay?"

Lily pressed her fingers into the space just below her ribcage and glared at Ruth Ann. "I told you we should have taken the buggy."

Ruth Ann doubled over and sucked air into her lungs. "My *bruder* needed it, and I couldn't tell *Mamm* the reason I wanted to take it."

Ivy furrowed her brow. "Is everything okay? Do you want to come in for a drink?"

Ruth Ann panted while shaking her head. "Don't tell Rebecca's *dat*, okay?"

Ivy wasn't in the mood to agree to keep one more secret from Isaac. She folded her arms. "What's wrong?"

"Rebecca's going to Durango."

Ivy narrowed her eyes. "What do you mean Rebecca's going to Durango? Who's taking her?" Ivy knew the answer before she even finished her question.

Lily caught her breath. "She told Ruth Ann not an hour ago."

Ruth Ann nodded. "Not an hour ago."

"She said Menno knows a man in Durango who can perform a wedding for them," Lily said.

Ivy gasped. That was a trick she hadn't expected from Menno.

Lily leaned against Ivy's sturdy mailbox. "Ruth Ann was suspicious, so she came to me." Lily glanced at Ruth Ann. "I'm glad you did."

"Me too," Ruth Ann said. "I thought Lily and Menno were still a couple, and something sounded fishy to me."

More fishy than Menno taking Rebecca to Durango? Ivy thought her skin might peel off her face.

"Weeks ago, Menno tried to talk me into doing The Unmentionable." Lily paused. "Do you know what The Unmentionable is, Ivy?"

Ivy's stomach clenched. "I have a pretty *gute* idea." And she had a pretty *gute* idea what she was going to do to Menno when she caught up with him.

"But he'd just broken things off with Rebecca, and I was suspicious. I told him I wasn't going to rush into anything. Lots of *die youngie* rush into things, but my *mamm* would have made me clean toilets every day for a year if I rushed into things." Lily was still breathing heavily, but it was obvious she was as mad as a hornet. "He took me to Dairy Queen four times and even tried to take off my stockings once. Can you believe it? Take off my stockings!"

"I believe it," Ivy said.

"I finally told him I wasn't ever going to do The Unmentionable." Lily hissed like a snake. "He wasn't happy about it but told me it was okay, that he wanted to marry me, and he would wait. But now I find out he's been secretly seeing Rebecca for almost three weeks, and he's taken her to Durango." She narrowed her eyes. "I'm through with Menno Coblenz. He's a liar and a cheat. Besides that, he's too short, and he has a weird mole on his chin."

Thank *Derr Herr* for weird moles.

Ruth Ann wrung her hands together. "Rebecca didn't want me to tell anyone she was leaving. She wanted it to be a surprise when she came back married, but I don't think Menno really loves Rebecca. He just wants her to rush into things because he couldn't get Lily to do it."

Ivy's pulse raced with urgency, and she grabbed both of Ruth Ann's hands. "You say she's gone to Durango. Did Menno hire a driver?"

"She said they were taking the bus." Ruth Ann started to cry. "What if the bus has already left?"

"We're going to find out."

Ivy didn't have a buggy, but she did have a cell phone—with permission from the bishop as long as she only used it for emergencies. This was definitely an emergency. "Come with me," she said. She led the girls into the house, grabbed her cell phone from the drawer, and called her least favorite driver. "Hello, Cathy?"

Cathy Larsen was the fastest driver Ivy had ever seen, except for maybe Ivy's last boyfriend who had regularly gone thirty miles per hour over the speed limit. Ivy always felt like she was taking her life in her hands when Cathy drove her anywhere. But today, Ivy was grateful for Cathy's bad driving. They didn't have a moment to lose if they were going to catch that bus.

"Turn right at the next stop sign." Ivy was practically yelling so Cathy could hear her over the screeching engine.

Cathy didn't come anywhere close to stopping as she turned right and headed down the gravel road. "Let this be a lesson to you young ladies." Cathy glanced in her rearview mirror at Lily and Ruth Ann, who were slouched in the back like two frightened kittens in an animal control van. "No good comes of keeping secrets. And no good comes of stealing other girls' boyfriends."

"I didn't steal him," Lily protested. "He broke up with Rebecca first."

"Well, then let this be a lesson never to be someone's rebound girlfriend."

Ivy grabbed onto the handle at the top of the door as Cathy rolled along at breakneck speed.

"I don't think we're going to make it," Ruth Ann said, which was never a *gute* thing to say to Cathy. She always tried to prove people wrong.

Just as expected, Cathy pressed on the gas.

"If we get in an accident, we won't get there at all," Ivy cautioned.

Cathy glanced at Ivy. "We could call the bus station and tell them to hold the bus because we've got a woman in labor."

Ivy made a face. "They wouldn't hold the bus for that."

"We could tell them that someone on the bus is using weed and needs to be arrested."

"What's weed?" Ruth Ann asked.

Cathy cast a warning look over her shoulder. "You don't need to know."

Ivy held her breath as Cathy took a turn too fast, and the tires spit gravel into the air. "Weed is legal in Colorado, Cathy."

The car slowed briefly. "It is? What is this world coming to? First they get rid of Hostess Twinkies and now this."

"I think Twinkies are back," Ivy said.

Cathy tapped on the steering wheel. "That's the first good news I've heard all day."

Ivy pointed a quarter mile down the road. "It's this farm coming up on the left."

Instead of slowing down, Cathy drove like a mad woman and slammed on her brakes in front of Isaac's house. "Go get him quick. Time's a wastin'."

Ivy jumped out of the car, grateful to be on solid ground. She burst into Isaac's house, not even stopping to knock. She called his name as she ran through his house, but he wasn't there. Lord willing, he was in the fields, or she'd have to go to Monte Vista without him. Ivy had said three prayers in the last twenty minutes, but she said another one just in case.

Dear Heavenly Father, help me find Isaac. Now.

Hopefully *Gotte* wouldn't think she was trying to boss him around, but some prayers just had to be that urgent. She flew out the back door and slammed it behind her, her eyes scanning the fields as she ran. She nearly fainted with relief when she caught sight of Isaac behind a plow. She ran into the field and was quite surprised when he practically exploded into a brilliant smile. Her heart ached just seeing that smile, but her own pain meant nothing right now.

"You're here," he said. There was such happiness in his voice that Ivy was struck momentarily speechless. "I've missed you."

"Have you?" she said, more out of sheer surprise than anything else. She shook her head and collected her wits. "It doesn't matter."

"Of course it matters. I want—"

"Rebecca's in trouble."

He stopped short. "What happened? Where is she?"

283

Ivy started to unhitch Isaac's horse. "You've got to come with me now. Menno is taking her to Durango."

"What about Menno?"

She unbuckled the harness. "I'll tell you everything in the car, and whatever you do, don't get mad at Lily or Ruth Ann. They're mortified. If you're going to be cross, it's best to say nothing to them."

He grabbed his horse's bit and led him toward the barn. "Cross? When have I ever been cross?"

She followed him. "I can give you a list later."

Ivy helped Isaac water and stable the horse, then they both jumped into Cathy's car. Ruth Ann was too distressed to say a word, so Ivy sat in the back with the girls and told Isaac everything while Cathy drove as if the police were chasing her. By the time Ivy was done with her story, Isaac was grinding his teeth so loudly that Ivy could hear it from the back seat.

Cathy glanced at Isaac right before she took a sharp turn. "You're going to crack all the teeth in your head if you keep doing that."

Isaac pressed his fingers to his forehead. "Can you drive faster?"

No! Ivy wanted to yell, but Cathy kept her speed constant.

She pointed about a mile down the road. "There's a patrol car just behind that gas station. If I get another ticket, I'll lose my license, and then where would all you Amish people be? Up the river without a K car."

Cathy slowed considerably as they drove into town. The traffic lights wouldn't let anyone pick up much speed. Cathy pulled in front of the bus station. "Go," she said. "I'll find a parking spot and meet you in there."

Isaac, Ivy, Lily, and Ruth Ann jumped out of the car. Isaac was way ahead of everybody and reached the doors first. Ivy and the girls ran in behind him. He found someone in uniform and asked about the bus to Durango. The attendant pointed to some doors opposite the entrance. "It was supposed to leave four minutes ago," she said. "But you might be able to catch it."

Isaac and Ivy bolted out the back door just as the bus pulled away from the terminal. Ivy gasped. Isaac yelled at the top of his lungs and chased the bus for nearly a hundred yards, but it didn't stop. He stood at the end of the street, head hung down, shoulders slumped. Ivy sat down on the steps, propped her elbows on her knees, and buried her face in her hands.

"Ivy? What are you doing here?"

Ivy looked up. Like a vision, Rebecca was standing in front of her, a travel bag in her hand, a curious and stunned look on her face. Squealing at the top of their lungs, Lily and Ruth Ann ran down the stairs and nearly knocked Rebecca over in their eagerness to hug her.

Rebecca's eyes were as wide as saucers, and she and the other two girls started talking all at once. "What are you doing here?"

"Did you miss the bus?"

"Where's Menno?"

"I'm sorry, Rebecca. I had to tell. I hope you're not mad."

Isaac finally turned around, saw his *dochter,* and ran straight for her. Ivy stood and held up her hand as if stopping traffic, giving Isaac a look of warning. He frowned at her, clenched his teeth, then took a deep breath.

"What happened?" Ruth Ann said. "Why aren't you on that bus?"

"I got off," Rebecca said.

Lily was panting so hard she could barely get her words out. "My heart stopped when I saw that bus leave."

The girls seemed to sense Isaac's eyes on Rebecca. Ruth Ann and Lily both took a step away to make room for Isaac. Rebecca's tears always softened her *fater* up, but instead of crying, she stood up straighter and met his gaze. "I'm sorry, *Dat,*" she said.

"Sorry isn't enough this time."

"I'm sorry I frightened you. It was wrong of me. But I'm still here, and if Ruth Ann hadn't told—" She gave Ruth Ann the stink eye. "If Ruth Ann hadn't told, you would never have known I thought of leaving."

"Do you think that makes me feel better?" Isaac's jaw tightened. He truly was going to lose his teeth someday.

Ivy couldn't have been more impressed with Rebecca. She wasn't moaning and sniffling like a little girl. She was standing up and taking responsibility. Did Isaac even recognize the transformation?

Ruth Ann decided to be brave too. "I'm *froh* I told Ivy and your *dat,* Rebecca. Menno wasn't being honest with you. He and Lily were still a couple."

Rebecca frowned. "I thought so. Menno called me Lily twice on the bus."

Lily giggled, despite herself.

Ruth Ann's eyes nearly popped out of her head. "He did?"

A ghost of a smile formed on Rebecca's lips. "He didn't even realize he'd done it." Suddenly, Rebecca seemed to burst. She sighed and threw her arms around Ruth Ann. "I'm *froh* you told. You're a true friend, even if you can't keep a secret." Lily moved in for a three-way hug, and the girls giggled and gushed as if they were long-lost *schwesteren.*

Isaac cleared his throat—loudly—and the gushing stopped. He looked like he wanted to tear the branches off the nearest tree. "So, *dochter,* do you think this is all fun and games?"

Ivy hated to get between *fater* and *dochter,* but she needed to step in before Isaac said something he'd regret. And he would say something he regretted. Ivy could see it on the tip of his tongue. "Why don't you tell us what happened, Rebecca?"

Cathy Larsen came out the door and hobbled down the stairs. "So, you found her." She narrowed her eyes in Rebecca's direction. "I hope you're planning on paying for a new set of tires on my K car. I left about an inch of rubber on the road."

Rebecca looked less confident with Cathy than even with her *dat*. "You shouldn't have gone to all this fuss. As you can see, I'm fine."

"That doesn't make anything right." Isaac was nearly snarling. It wasn't his best look, but he was still wonderful handsome. Ivy felt the loss of his affection like a shard of glass in her throat. "We didn't know you were fine, and you just as easily could still be on that bus."

"You're right, *Dat*. It's not right to blame anyone but myself."

Isaac nodded curtly, but he was plainly pleased that Rebecca wasn't trying to skirt the blame.

"Can you tell us what happened?" Ivy asked again.

Rebecca glanced at her *fater*, then Ivy, then Ruth Ann. Her hands shook as if she'd just had a terrible fright. She took a deep breath. And then another one. Her bottom lip quivered. She pulled a tissue from her apron pocket and pressed it to her lips. Ivy thought for sure and certain she would start to cry, but she seemed to regain her composure by sheer force of will. Maybe she wanted to prove to her *dat* that she wasn't a little girl anymore. "I thought Menno loved me."

"I'm sure he did," Ivy said weakly, trying to make Rebecca feel better. But maybe she didn't need to console Rebecca with empty assurances. She was acting very grown up about the whole thing.

Rebecca snorted. "Maybe. But for sure and certain he loves himself more."

Lily nodded enthusiastically. "He does."

"He kept telling me he was willing to wait until we got married, but then he came up with this silly plan to go to Durango and have a wedding without the blessing of the bishop. I thought it would be okay because he loved me enough to want to marry me. We got here early and found seats on the bus." She looked at Isaac. "While we sat there, I remembered what Ivy had told me about her family. About how she'll regret hurting them every day for the rest of her life. I don't want regrets like that."

Ivy pressed her lips together. Someone had learned from her mistakes. Maybe her life hadn't been completely wasted.

Rebecca looked at her *dat* with tenderness in her eyes. "I thought about how badly it would hurt you not to be there to see me get married. You taught me how to use a spoon, *Dat*. I couldn't get married without you."

Isaac's expression relaxed for the first time since he'd heard the news about Rebecca. "I also taught you how to drive a team and walk and talk and whistle."

Rebecca giggled. "Okay, okay, *Dat*. You taught me everything I know."

Ivy smiled to herself. Except maybe all that stuff about puberty.

"Then Menno called me *Lily* twice, and he kept trying to put his hands where they didn't belong. That's when I knew it wasn't about love for him."

Lily folded her arms. "He asked me to go to Durango with him four weeks ago."

Rebecca's mouth fell open. "He didn't!"

"He did. And he asked me to marry him too."

Rebecca shook her head in disbelief. "I'm *froh* I got off that bus."

"Me too," said Isaac.

"After he called me *Lily* the second time and I had to push his hands away for about the thirtieth time, I decided I wasn't ready to get married and that I wanted my family there when I did." She sidled closer to Isaac, and he put his arm around her. "I couldn't disappoint you, *Dat*, no matter how much I love Menno, which I don't anymore because he's a big *dummkoff*."

"So you got off the bus," Lily said.

Rebecca nodded. "I knew Menno would try to talk me out of it, so I told him I was going to try to sleep the whole trip and encouraged him to do the same because he would need his energy for our wedding. He got up wonderful early this morning to get ready for our trip, so I knew he was tired. It was a matter of three or four minutes of stillness, and he fell asleep." Rebecca giggled at the memory. "Just before the bus left, I quietly slipped out of my seat and left Menno sleeping peacefully. He'll probably wake up halfway to Durango and wonder what happened to me."

"And be so disappointed," Isaac said, as if he were in a much better mood than he had been just moments before.

Lily offered her hand to Rebecca. "I think we should promise each other that we'll never fall in love with the same boy again."

Rebecca took her hand. "We also have to promise to watch out for each other so that if a boy tries to date both of us, we'll know."

Cathy's lips curled slightly, which was as close to a smile as she ever got. "I think we've all learned some valuable lessons. All the Amish girls should be warned about this Menno character, and don't fall asleep on the bus or you could end up taking a lonely trip to Durango."

"I am definitely going to warn Menno's *fater*," Isaac said. "Menno needs to learn to control his hormones."

"*Dat!*" Rebecca squeaked. "Don't say that word out loud right in front of my friends!"

Ivy laughed. For someone who'd come a long way in a few short days, Rebecca still had some growing up to do. And thank *Derr Herr* she could still be a girl for a while.

"Come on," Cathy said, taking Rebecca's arm. "I'm parked at a frozen yogurt place right around the corner. Let's go get a treat to celebrate Menno's trip to Durango. I'm paying." She led Rebecca on a slow march up the steps and into the bus terminal with Lily and Ruth Ann close behind.

Isaac gave Ivy a sideways glance. "I'm very fond of frozen yogurt."

Her mouth went dry. Who cared about frozen yogurt at a time like this? "Are you?" was all she could think to say.

He cupped his hand around her arm. "I was too frantic to thank you earlier but *denki*. *Denki* for being a friend to my *dochter*. Your advice saved her from a great deal of regret. And probably saved me from a stroke."

"And a few cracked teeth." She couldn't look him in the eye for fear of what she'd see there. He was grateful, but that didn't mean he'd changed his mind about marrying her.

"*Ach*, Ivy, you're bleeding!" He took her hand and lifted it closer to his face.

Ivy studied the blood pooling around and under her pinky fingernail. "*Ach, du lieva.* Ruth Ann slammed the car door before my hand was clear of it. It caught my finger, but I was too anxious to even notice the pain. I yanked it out before Cathy drove away."

Isaac pulled a gleaming white handkerchief from his pocket and handed it to Ivy. "I'm so sorry. It must sting something wonderful."

Ivy nodded. "It does now." She gingerly wrapped her finger in Isaac's handkerchief, sorry to create more laundry for him.

"I guess you won't be able to quilt with *die fraaen* for a few weeks." He pumped his eyebrows up and down. "They'll be disappointed, won't they?"

Ivy thought of the pleasant stomachache she'd gotten eating a whole pan of funeral potatoes with Linda and Sarah and the others. Even if Isaac didn't love her anymore, she had friends who believed in her. "I suppose they will be disappointed."

"Of course they will." Isaac looked more than pleased with himself. "I told you so. I told you they like you, and not because of me. You wouldn't believe me, but now you see I'm right." He grinned. "You might as well go ahead and admit that I'm always right. It will save so much time later."

She couldn't interpret the dancing light in his eyes. An anvil sat on her chest even as butterflies took flight in her stomach. She couldn't understand Isaac. She would probably never understand him, and she couldn't take the suspense any longer. "If you don't want to marry me, just come right out and say it. I'm tired of all this beating around the bush to spare my feelings. The rocks in my mailbox are beautiful, but they won't soften the blow of rejection."

He looked at her as if she'd swallowed one of those rocks he'd given her. "What do you mean if I don't want to marry you anymore? I want to marry you more than ever."

She opened her mouth, promptly closed it, and then opened it again. She probably looked like a fish gasping for air. "You...what are you talking about?"

He stared at her in puzzlement. "In case you haven't noticed, I love you, Ivy."

A ribbon of hope threaded its way down her spine even as her confusion deepened. "But you told Freeman the wedding was off."

"I wanted to prove that *die fraaen* would still want your friendship even if you and I weren't a couple. I told you I was going to do that."

"*Nae*, you didn't."

"*Jah*, I did. Don't you remember? I said I was going to quit being pushy and try to make the others think the wedding was off."

Ivy frowned, annoyed at him for putting her through weeks of heartache and ecstatic that he still wanted to marry her. "You did not. You said that once they got to know me, *die fraaen* wouldn't care if we were a couple. You never said you were going to trick them into believing the wedding was off. They brought me potatoes and everything."

Isaac huffed out a breath. "For someone so smart, you sure are thick sometimes."

"Me? You're the one who didn't tell me your plan. What was I supposed to believe?"

"I'm sure I told you the plan." Isaac scratched his head and furrowed his brow. "Maybe I had that conversation in my head."

"I'm sure you did," Ivy said. "Then you stayed away for three weeks."

He suddenly looked very weary. "The longest and most miserable three weeks of my life. I didn't want to pressure you, especially when I wasn't sure you wanted to marry me. You did say I'm ugly."

"I did not. I asked you why you weren't handsome."

He winced. "I remember. The best and worst day of my life."

She made a face. "I was just lashing out because you were so rude. You asked me why I wasn't married."

"I'm still puzzled about that," he said. "But, Lord willing, you will be married to me very soon."

She wasn't going to let him sidetrack her. "You told Freeman the wedding was off, and you wrote me that note saying it was okay if I didn't want to marry you. I thought for sure and certain you had changed your mind and were trying to let me down gently."

He wrapped his fingers around her upper arms. "I love you to my very bones, Ivy, but you think so little of yourself that you found it easy to believe I didn't want to marry you. I should have guessed what you would think. I thought you were uncomfortable because I was being too pushy."

"I was uncomfortable because I don't I deserve you."

He ground his teeth together so hard, Ivy could hear the sound from where she stood. He pulled her to him, and his lips were mere inches from hers. "For someone so smart, you're kind of thick." And then he kissed her, right there at the bus terminal in broad daylight without regard for the bishop, the rules, or the people who might be watching. Brilliant, blinding fireworks exploded in her head as Isaac snaked his arms around her waist and drew her in so tightly, she could feel the soft thud of his heart against her palms. She, in turn, wrapped her arms around his neck and tugged him downward. This was where she wanted to stay for the rest of her life.

He pulled away, and she clung to him as if she'd drown if she let go. "Do you still think I'm a *gute* kisser?" he asked.

"The best," she whispered breathlessly.

He chuckled. "If you marry me, I'll try to live up to my reputation every day."

CHAPTER NINE

*T*he wedding took place just two weeks later in June, when the early summer roses were blooming in Ivy's garden. She sat next to Isaac at the *eck*, holding hands with him under the table, smiling so wide her face hurt. She couldn't help it. She had never been so perfectly happy in her life. Isaac had orbited around her all day like she was the Earth to his moon. She had the love of a *gute*, kind man, the comfort of friends, and the security of a solid, sturdy home. She would never want for another thing in her entire life.

Ivy watched as her *newehockers*, Lily, Ruth Ann, and Rebecca, went around to each table and passed out chocolate bars, each wrapped with a paper that said, "Ivy and Isaac. The happy couple." Cathy's grandson Dewey had printed out the papers, and Rebecca and Ruth Ann had wrapped them around the candy bars and secured them with a dot of glue. Esther had wanted to pass out pens with the happy couple's names on them, but there hadn't been time to order them. Ivy didn't mind. Chocolate said "love" better than a pen did.

Ivy and Isaac had married under the cherry tree in Ivy's backyard. As was customary, the entire *gmayna* had been invited, along with a few other neighbors and *Englisch* friends, like Cathy Larsen, who was everybody's favorite and most-feared *Englischer*. Menno Coblenz had, thankfully, not shown up. His absence probably had something to do with the fact that Isaac had paid Menno a visit and told him he couldn't come.

Ivy smiled at the beautiful place settings and cake centerpieces. She had rented pink and green dishes because they reminded her of spring, which reminded her of hope and joy and new beginnings. Each table was set with a cake topped with pink and yellow frosting flowers. Sarah had baked every one. She wasn't just *gute* with funeral potatoes.

And funeral potatoes were *not* on the menu.

Ivy's friends had spent the better part of two weeks scrambling to get ready for the wedding, preparing food and making cakes, renting tents and tables. Esther wouldn't hear of a small, simple wedding. "You only get married once, Ivy," she said. "It's got to be as big as any other Amish wedding. We've got to invite the entire *gmayna*, of course." Gary was the only *bruder* of Ivy's who had come to the wedding. The other three said they didn't want to leave their farms, but they didn't really like Ivy and certainly hadn't forgotten how she'd hurt the family. None of the three *bruderen* had been especially close to Esther or Ivy, and Ivy truly didn't care that they had chosen to miss the most important day of her life. There was only so much indignation and self-right-eousness Ivy would have been able to abide.

Isaac tilted his head toward her. Ivy wanted to smooth her hand down the fine hairs on the back of his neck. "I want to kiss you so badly right now," he said.

Ivy beamed at her husband. "I want you to kiss me even more badly than you want to kiss me."

Isaac motioned toward Rebecca. "If I didn't know better, I'd say Rebecca is even happier than I am, except no one could be happier than me."

"I am," Ivy teased. "You made me fall in love with you, and then you dropped me like a hot potato. The happiness I feel is doubly *gute* after being so sad."

Isaac opened his mouth wide in mock indignation. "I did not drop you. I never would have done that. I love you like a popsicle loves the freezer." He squeezed her hand tightly. "Can I give you your wedding present now?"

"A present? You didn't need to get me a present. You are the best present I could ever ask for."

He slid his hand into his pocket and pulled out a stunning pink oval stone with veins of white running through it, polished to a brilliant shine. "I found this rock in my fields on the day I first kissed you. It didn't look like anything special, but it felt like a special day, a day of new possibilities, so I kept it. I asked Randall to tumble and polish it for me. He got wonderful excited. It's called rhodochrosite. He said it's a rare find." Isaac slipped the rock into Ivy's hand. "A rare find, Ivy. Just like you."

He looked at her with so much love in his eyes, Ivy thought her heart might burst with joy. She curled her fingers around the rock, feeling its cool, polished surface against her skin.

As if he couldn't resist any longer, Isaac reached out and smoothed his knuckles down her cheek. "*Behold, I have refined thee. I have chosen thee in the furnace of affliction*," he whispered. "All the things you've been through have tumbled and bumped and polished you. I'm sorry for the pain. I'm sorry for your regret and your broken heart. But the polishing has left you a million times more beautiful than this rock. And I'm the one who gets to spend the rest of my days discovering that beauty."

Ivy sighed, pressed her fingers to her lips, and touched the tips of her fingers to Isaac's palm. He trembled at her touch. She would thank *Derr Herr* every day for the gift of Isaac Neuenschwander. The gift of *Gotte*'s love.

The gift of a new beginning.

A new hope.

Spring.

ABOUT THE AUTHOR

Jennifer Beckstrand is the USA Today Bestselling author of *The Matchmakers of Huckleberry Hill* series, *The Honeybee Sisters* series, *The Petersheim Brothers* series, and *The Amish Quiltmaker* series for Kensington Books. Two of Jennifer's books were nominated for the RWA RITA® Award, and she is a #1 Amazon bestselling author. ***His Amish Sweetheart***, the delightfully romantic third book in the Petersheim Brothers series, releases June 28, 2022. Connect with Jennifer at jenniferbeckstrand.com.

THE CEDAR BOX

MOLLY JEBBER

CHAPTER ONE

M *t. Hope, Ohio, 1916*
       Aunt Lydia opened Madeline's bedroom door. "Good morning. Time to scoot out of bed and head to the store. I've cooked scrambled eggs and fried bacon for your breakfast before you go." Her aunt crossed her arms against her chest and waited.

"Good morning." Madeline stretched and yawned. She ran out of things to do at the store during the day, so being there two hours early wasn't necessary. But she didn't want to argue. "Aunt Lydia, I'll wash my face, change clothes, and pin my hair in a bun, and then I'll be ready."

"Very well. Don't be long." Aunt Lydia rolled her eyes and shut the door.

Madeline missed her family and friends from Berlin, Ohio. She'd been with her aunt, who was like a stranger, for three days. Her aunt had never married or had *kinner*. She hoped Aunt Lydia would show a softer side in the weeks to *kumme*. Madeline was homesick already.

Ten minutes later, Madeline entered the kitchen. "Aunt Lydia, please sit. Please don't hobble on your broken leg using those makeshift crutches. You worry me. I don't want you to fall again." She wanted Aunt Lydia's leg to mend as soon as possible.

"*Danki* for taking over my general store. I can manage around here, but getting in a buggy every day to go to work would be too much. I'm glad we'll have a chance to get better acquainted. You were six and eight the two times your family visited. It's hard to believe you're twenty. We're all busy these days, and it's difficult to take the time to travel to visit family."

The short, plump widow with dark brown eyes was more negative than positive when talking about some of the Amish in Mt. Hope. *Mamm* said Aunt Lydia gossiped too much, and they'd kept their distance. Madeline could understand why. She felt sorry for her aunt. It must be lonely not to have a husband or *kinner*. She pulled out a chair. "Let me serve you."

"I will, but you don't have much time." Aunt Lydia eased into the chair and leaned her crutches against the wall next to her.

"I'll hurry." Madeline poured her a cup of coffee and set her breakfast in front of her. She served herself a plate of food and a glass of water. "Your friends have brought supper the last three evenings. It's so thoughtful of them."

"We Amish take care of one another." Lydia said matter-of-factly and sipped her coffee.

"Leave the dishes in the sink. I can wash and dry them when I return home." Madeline finished her breakfast, carried her dirty plate to the sink, and bid her aunt farewell.

She grabbed her light shawl, harnessed her horse to the buggy, and drove to the livery. The third day of April was here, and the warm sun on her cheeks and comfortable coolness made for a beautiful day. Madeline smiled. She left the buggy with the liveryman and strolled to the store. She turned the sign, threw her quilted bag under the counter in a cabinet, and hung her shawl on the sturdy metal hook behind her.

An attractive tall man with light blue eyes and wavy, sandy-blond hair entered. "Greetings." He removed his straw hat. "I'm Adam Coblenz. I don't believe we've met."

"I'm Madeline Yoder. I came to manage my aunt's store while she recovers from a broken leg. Are you shopping for anything in particular?" She couldn't stop staring at him. Those big blue eyes of his alone were enough to make her heart flutter.

"To be honest, I noticed you in the window. I wanted to meet you. I hope I'm not being too forward."

Madeline blushed. She wasn't offended. She was over the moon happy. "Not at all. I'm glad you came in." She hadn't found the right man for her in Berlin. There was Micah Beachy, but he hadn't asked to court her. They'd talked and played horseshoes at social events a few times. She'd been to his *haus* for supper, and he'd been to hers. She considered him a friend and nothing more.

Adam walked to a shelf along the wall. "I'll take the cedar box." He grabbed it and held it to his nose. "I love the aroma of cedar." He carried it to her and paid for his purchase.

"You made a good choice." She beamed. She didn't want him to leave. He had such a pleasing voice she could listen to him all day.

"May I take you to dinner tomorrow? Your sign says you close from noon to one."

She was thrilled. Since she'd started running the store, she'd closed it from noon to one to enjoy a peanut butter sandwich made from the peanut butter and bread she kept in a bag under the counter. She'd brought the food the first day she worked at the shop and left them there. "*Danki*. I'd love to." She bit her bottom lip. She shouldn't have been so eager. He might think she wasn't a proper Amish woman. She couldn't help herself. She didn't think any of the men in Berlin were near as attractive as Adam.

"I'll be here tomorrow at noon sharp." He tipped his hat, smiled, opened the door, and stepped aside for an older woman to enter. "Let me hold the door for you, Mrs. Hershberger." He waited until she was in the store and then left.

Mrs. Hershberger scowled and approached Madeline. "The nerve of him."

"What did he do?" Madeline widened her eyes.

Mrs. Hershberger waved a dismissive hand. "Never mind. He's not worth discussing. You must be Madeline. I checked on your aunt before I came here. She's mastered those crutches better than I could. I dropped off a chicken casserole, so you or she wouldn't have to cook. Are you taking good care of her?"

"I'm doing my best." Madeline was thankful for the casserole. "That's very thoughtful of you to think of us. *Danki*."

Mrs. Hershberger was direct and a bit harsh. She had her nose in the air. "Don't get used to it. I won't be dropping off food every day." She pointed to the shelf in back of the counter. "I'd like a tub of lard."

Madeline lifted the lard tub and brought it back to the counter. This woman reminded her of her aunt. It wasn't a surprise they'd be friends. Madeline put the lard in a bag and accepted the coins for payment. She opened her mouth to ask again what Mrs. Hershberger meant by her comment about Adam, but she closed it. She didn't know the woman, and it might be nothing. Berlin had their share of gossips, and she was sure the same was true about Mt. Hope. "Is there anything else I can get for you?"

"No." Mrs. Hershberger held her lard. "I don't have time to chat. I promised to bake a sugar cream pie for my husband."

"Have a good rest of your day," Madeline said.

She waited on customers until five and then drove to her aunt's haus. "I'm home."

"Was the store busy today? Rose Hershberger said she would stop at the store. Did she? She left us a delicious casserole. She's fixed it before for a ladies' social we had last month, and I had told her how much I liked it. She's a dear friend."

"I wouldn't say busy, but we had several customers. She did, and I thanked her for providing supper." Madeline didn't know her aunt well enough to say anything about Adam. Since Mrs. Hershberger wasn't fond of him, she was afraid her aunt would agree with her friend.

***

Madeline dusted the shelves at the store on Tuesday morning. The shop was lined with shelves on the three walls, displaying games, toys, Amish dolls, canned vegetables and fruits, and gifts for adults. In addition to basic necessities, the store had quite the assortment of offerings. She watched the clock until noon. She hadn't had many customers, and she had run out of things to do.

Adam opened the door and held the small cedar box he'd purchased. "Ready?"

Her heart soared. "Yes." She grabbed her quilted bag and hurried out. Would he return the box? She would wait for him to tell her why he had it.

He walked alongside her to the sandwich and ice cream shop close by. They sat at a round white table with chairs. A red and white checkered tablecloth covered the tabletop and matching napkins were at each place setting. She liked the décor. And she liked Adam. "*Danki* for bringing me here. It's pretty and quaint."

"I'm glad you're here with me." His eyes gazed into hers. "I want to know everything about you."

Before she could answer, a woman approached them. "Adam, who is your guest?"

"Lois, meet Madeline Yoder. She's taking over her aunt Lydia's store until her leg heals. Madeline, this is Lois Miller. She and her husband, David, are my best friends. They own this ice cream café and store."

"I love the way you've arranged your shop, and ice cream is one of my favorite desserts." Madeline grinned.

"*Danki.*" Lois put her slender hand on Madeline's shoulder. "You'll have to *kumme* to visit us at our home while you're in town. Where are you from?"

"Berlin, Ohio." Madeline smiled. "You're so sweet. I appreciate the invitation."

In addition to her lovely smile and friendly demeanor, Lois was pretty, with a slender frame and big green eyes. "What would you like to order? I recommend our ham salad."

"Sounds delicious, and I'd like some iced tea. *Danki.*"

"I'll take the same," Adam said. He waited for Lois to leave. "Tell me about you."

She shrugged. "There's not much to tell. I live with my parents. We work on the farm, and I bake bread and desserts on the side for extra money. We visited Aunt Lydia when I was young, but I don't remember too much about her. We're getting better acquainted."

Lois returned and set iced teas on the table. They thanked her.

Adam raised his brows. "Do you have a beau in Mt. Hope?"

"No. I'm not being courted by anyone." She chuckled. "If I was, I wouldn't have accepted your invitation to dinner."

Adam blew out a breath. "You're right. I didn't mean to insult you."

"You didn't offend me. I wanted you to ask me to dinner."

Adam's frown turned to a grin. "What else do you like to do in your spare time for fun?"

"In the winter, when my friends and I have more time, we play board games. In the summer, I like to enjoy long walks, canoeing, and fishing. What about you?"

Adam traced the rim of his glass. "I like spending time with my son. His name is Timmy. He's five and a lot of fun. My *fraa*, Lisa, passed away two years ago. I found her in the kitchen on the floor one afternoon. The doctor guessed her heart gave out, but he didn't know for sure what caused her death. I own the third farm to the right of your Aunt Lydia's."

She pressed her hand to her heart. "I'm sorry about your *fraa*. How tragic. You're blessed to have a son. I love *kinner*. Timmy sounds delightful."

"He can be a handful, but he's sweet-natured, and he's brought such joy to my life." His eyes sad, Adam stared at his folded hands on the table. "My *fraa* was a wonderful woman. I'll never forget her, but time has helped us heal. But enough sad talk." Adam sat back in his chair and pushed his iced tea to the side to make room for his plate.

Lois served them dinner. "Enjoy."

They both nodded.

Madeline picked up her spoon. "Do your parents live here? Any siblings?" None of what he told her so far would give her any reason to avoid him.

"No siblings, and my parents died last year within six months of each other. *Mamm* died from influenza, and *Daed* passed away from a broken heart. The doctor wasn't sure of the cause of his death, but he was never the same after *Mamm* was no longer with us. He died in his sleep."

Her heart ached for him. "You have had your share of loss." Madeline was glad he had Lois and David. He must be lonely without his *fraa* and parents. She couldn't imagine being in his position.

"I'd like to take you for a buggy ride. I'll give you the grand tour of Mt. Hope. It should take all of ten minutes." Adam chortled. "We can go to the edge of the woods by the pond and have our dinner." She glanced at the clock. "It sounds lovely. I would like to stay and enjoy your company, but I should return to work. It's almost one."

"Time went fast." He paid the check, and they said goodbye to Lois. He walked her to the front door of the store. "I'll be here at noon again tomorrow."

"*Danki* for dinner. I'll look forward to seeing you." Madeline smiled.

"You're *wilkom*. And tomorrow can't *kumme* fast enough." Adam waited for her to unlock the door, and then he opened it.

She went inside, and he closed the door behind her. After he left, she twirled in a circle. She was giddy, and she really liked him a lot. How could she be so taken with this man? They'd just met. She didn't care. She was glad he didn't ask to meet her after work, so she didn't have to introduce him to Aunt Lydia. She wasn't ready to risk Aunt Lydia having a negative attitude about him, like Mrs. Hershberger. She held her breath for a moment and hoped none of her aunt's friends would notice them. It was worth the risk to keep him a secret from her aunt for a little while longer.

~

Madeline waited on two customers Wednesday morning, and then she restocked the shelves with supplies she'd received right after her arrival. She glanced at the clock and counted the minutes until she'd meet Adam again.

He stepped into the shop, and he had a package in his hand. "I brought you a gift."

"*Danki*." He was thoughtful. She didn't care what the present was, she'd love it because it was from him. She untied the twine and peeled back the brown paper. "This is the cedar box you bought from the shop when we first met. I love it." She set the box on the counter.

"I have a purpose for the box." He opened the lid and unwrapped the oatmeal cookie he'd put inside. "A snack for you to enjoy this afternoon."

"It's perfect." His kindhearted gesture made him all the more attractive.

"I'm taking the box with me, and I'll return it when you least expect it with a surprise inside."

"I love the idea." Madeline couldn't believe how hard he was working to show his interest in her. She cared about him, but reality started to set in. Would she leave her family and friends behind and grow roots here with him if their friendship blossomed into a courtship?

"I also brought sandwiches and lemonade. The weather is cool, but the sunshine makes for a pleasant day. I have a light blanket in the buggy for you if you need it."

Madeline went outside with him and stepped into the buggy. She had left her shawl in the store, and she was glad he had a blanket. She pulled the cotton blanket over her legs. "I haven't explored Mt. Hope, so I'll enjoy you taking me to a new spot."

He drove outside of town, and they parked the buggy overlooking a large pond. He pulled a patchwork quilt from behind their bench seat and spread it on the ground. He set the basket he'd brought with their dinner next to Madeline. Then he passed her a sandwich and kept one for himself. He opened the jars of lemonade and gave her one. "It's pretty with the trees, and the pond is a nice quiet place to talk and enjoy our dinner away from the automobiles and hustle and bustle of town. I'm baffled and relieved you don't have a beau in Berlin. Has any man there ever caught your attention?"

She shook her head. "Micah Beachy is the closest I've *kumme* to having a suitor, but we're just friends. Have you shown interest in any other woman after your *fraa* died?" Micah didn't make her heart want to jump out of her chest with joy. Nor did he occupy her thoughts most of the day. But Adam did both.

"No. After Lisa's death, I needed time to mourn. And Timothy keeps me busy."

"You brighten when you mention Timmy." She suspected Adam was a good *daed* to the little boy. She hoped to meet him. She would like to have as many *kinner* as God would give her after she found the right man to marry.

"He asks lots of questions. He doesn't know a stranger, and he behaves most of the time. Lois has asked me to bring you to her and David's *haus* for a visit. Would you like to go there this evening? You could meet Timmy."

"Are you sure you want me to meet your son? My time in Mt. Hope is temporary. I don't want to mislead you or Timmy." She was torn. She didn't want to leave Adam. But she had a life in Berlin. She didn't understand how a courtship would work for them.

He frowned. "I was hoping I'd given you a reason to stay. Madeline, I would like to court you, and let's see if our friendship blossoms into wanting a future together."

"I'm interested in you, too." She fumbled with her hands. "I'd like to court you, but it means leaving my life and the ones I love behind. I'm not happy living with my aunt. I'm not sure she would even be in favor of me living with her if I stayed after she's healed." Madeline couldn't imagine not having him in her life or staying here. It was complicated.

"I sprung a courtship on you too soon. You need time to ponder this decision. I'm a patient man. I pray you'll stay and give us a chance." He held her hand for a moment and gazed at her. "I wish we had all day together, but I should take you back to the shop. It's almost time for you to reopen it."

She nodded. "Please don't misunderstand. I care about you very much. I wish we lived in the same town."

Adam's face grew serious. "I have something to share with you. I was going to wait, but I want you to hear this from me. I need to tell you more about Lisa and me. I met Lisa when I left Mt. Hope to experience the outside world. Her *daed* was a banker in Akron, Ohio. She didn't have siblings, and she had no interest in becoming Amish."

Madeline was shocked. "What did your family say?" She could never leave Amish life. Would he leave again? She had a lot to consider before she'd agree to court him. Her heart told her to trust him. But her mind warned her to be cautious.

"They were upset." He sighed. "I was in love with Lisa. She was smart, pretty, and outspoken. We attended church, which was much different from our Sunday service. We sang hymns accompanied by piano music. The reverend's messages were much the same as our bishop's."

"Did you live with her parents, or did you have a *haus*?" Madeline's chest tightened. She was disappointed.

"I bought a farm near her parents with her *daed*'s help. I've since paid him back. He hired me to work in his bank, and I made enough income to hire a property manager for the farm," he said.

"Did you have any regrets?" She wasn't sure what to make of his story.

"I didn't regret marrying Lisa, and Timmy is truly a gift from God. But I missed the Amish life. It's easy to get caught up in the things of the world and always wanting the next best thing."

Madeline raised her brows. "What brought you back to Mt. Hope?"

"Lisa's parents were all consuming. When Lisa passed, I sold the farm and quit my job at the bank. Through prayer and reading Scriptures, I believed God wanted me to return to the Amish life and put Him first. I also wanted to raise Timmy as Amish, where God is the main focus. I didn't want him to long for modern conveniences and all the outside world has to offer."

"Do you take Timmy to visit them?" Madeline wondered how he'd have the time.

Adam shook his head. "No. It's difficult to travel when I have a farm to manage. They write letters to him, and I help him write back."

Madeline and Adam quickly finished their dinner. "Time to get you back to work." They put the blanket and basket back into the buggy and headed to town. He pulled the mare in front of the shop.

Madeline glanced at the shop's front door. A customer stood outside waiting for her to reopen. "I'd like nothing more than to continue this conversation, but I must go." She didn't want to leave. She had more questions.

"I'll be back at dinnertime tomorrow." Adam brushed her hand with his. "You can ask me anything." He passed her the cedar box. "Please take this. There's something inside for you."

She accepted the box and stepped out of the buggy. "*Danki*. You're spoiling me, but I have no complaints." She waved to him, and then she unlocked and opened the door for the woman. "I'm sorry to keep you waiting."

The gray-haired woman grunted and entered the store. "I'm Laverne Keim. You can call me Laverne. You're Madeline, right?"

"Yes." Madeline said.

"Lydia said you'd be here working for her. Take my advice. You shouldn't be anywhere near Adam Coblenz. Your aunt would have a fit if she knew. You must not have told her. Like I said, Adam is the last man you should consider for a suitor." She pointed her cane at Madeline.

Madeline gasped. "He's been nothing but a gentleman." This woman should mind her own business.

Laverne harrumphed. "Suit yourself."

Madeline forced a smile. "How can I help you?"

The woman walked over to the shelf with toys and puzzles. She directed her cane to the shelf. "I want to buy two puzzles for the little boy who lives next to me."

Madeline pulled two puzzles off a shelf. "How old is he? This one has pieces shaped like fruit, and the other has more difficult pieces. They are for *kinner* between two to four."

"I'll take the puzzle with the fruit pieces." She removed a coin purse and paid Madeline for the puzzle. "*Danki* for your assistance."

Madeline was on borrowed time. Any day now, a friend of her aunt's was bound to tell her Madeline was talking to Adam. Maybe she should go ahead and break the news to her aunt soon.

Two Englischers walked into the shop. The tall lady with her hair pinned in a fancy hairdo scanned the shelves. "Diane, do you see any toys Henry might like?"

"Your grandson would love this little train, Clara." The shorter woman lifted a small train.

"He would love it. I'll buy it." Clara dropped the newspaper she had tucked under her arm, and she bent to pick it up. "There's President Wilson's picture in the paper again. Each time I read anything about President Wilson, I'm upset. I'll be glad when he's not the president anymore. He's an embarrassment. Don't you agree, Diane?"

"Yes. He raises my dander, too. I don't agree with a thing the man says." Diane ran to the window. "Clara, hurry. A handsome man parked a Chevrolet Baby Grand automobile outside the ice cream shop. It's grand for sure."

Madeline shouldn't care about such things, but she went to the window. The car was painted white, and the interior was red leather. It was a spectacular automobile. She returned to the checkout counter.

The women approached her, paid for their purchases, and went on their way.

Madeline's throat constricted. Adam may have driven an automobile. He'd used modern conveniences and probably had become knowledgeable about

President Wilson and the government. Had he left all interest in such things behind?

She sold more toys, and for the rest of the day, business was slow. She opened the cedar box and removed the note inside. She read it and held it to her chest. He asked her to not let his past alter her decision about considering him. She wanted to trust him, but a part of her was fearful of his prior life and the changes she'd have to make. She locked the door, drove home, and went inside the *haus*. "Aunt Lydia, is everything all right?" Her aunt's lips were in a grim line, and she had her arms crossed against her chest.

"Laverne visited me and said you were with Adam Coblenz in his buggy. He's trouble, and I don't approve of you spending time with him. How long have you been talking to him? Why haven't you said anything to me about this? I don't appreciate you going behind my back."

"I'm sorry. I wanted to form my own opinion of Adam. He asked me to dinner a couple of times, and I've gotten acquainted with him. I like him, and he likes me. He told me about his past. I was shocked but happy he's returned to the Amish life." She prayed she could help her aunt understand he wasn't a bad man.

Aunt Lydia narrowed her eyes. "I understand you're no longer a child, and you are old enough to make your own decisions. But while you live under my roof, he's not *wilkom* here. I can say without reservation, your parents would agree with me, given his past."

"I don't want to upset you. Have you spoken with Adam since he's been back? I believe God forgives us when we recognize our wrongs and ask forgiveness. Adam's sincere in raising his son, Timmy, Amish. Please don't misjudge him." Madeline wasn't ready to let Adam go. She had reservations about him, but she didn't want her aunt or family to make this decision for her.

"Did he tell you he left Sadie Bontrager to pursue what the outside world had to offer? She waited for him to return, and he sent her a letter saying he had proposed to another woman. He shattered Sadie's heart."

Madeline's cheeks warmed. He should've told her about Sadie. "I apologize, Aunt Lydia. I should've told you Adam and I were talking. I disagree he's trouble. He shouldn't be punished forever for his past." She had to defend him. She was falling in love with him. She didn't want Aunt Lydia to assume he was unsuitable for her. Her aunt was being unfair. Madeline hoped he had a reasonable explanation about Sadie.

Aunt Lydia scoffed. "I can't stop you from talking with him in town, but be careful. You may have to choose between your family and him."

～

On Thursday in the early evening, Adam drove to Lois and David's place to pick up Timmy. He went inside.

Timmy ran into his arms waving a paper. *"Daed*, look at my picture."

He looked closer at the drawing. "Is this us wading in the pond? And is the woman in the clouds *Mamm?"*

"Yes. My clouds are Heaven. She's living there now."

"I like it." Adam hugged him. "You are five, but you look eight in this picture."

"Lois said I could draw anything I wanted, so I made me older." Timmy giggled, as they entered the *haus.*

Adam ruffled Timmy's hair and set him on his feet.

Lois grinned. "David went to the neighbor's *haus* to borrow a saw blade. He should be back soon." She patted Timmy's back. "I'm happy to let Martha take care of the shop anytime you need me to watch Timmy. I love spending time with him. I don't want to let Timmy go each time you *kumme* to get him. He's such a precious child. How did your buggy ride go with Madeline?"

Timmy wrinkled his forehead. "Who is Madeline?"

"She's my new friend. You'll like her. She's pretty and a sweetheart," Adam said.

"I want to meet her." Timmy leaned against his *daed.*

"I plan to introduce you to her sometime soon. Put your pencil, crayons, and paper away while I talk to Lois." He watched as his son ran to the other room Lois called the playroom.

"Madeline and I have a strong connection, Lois. I can't wait for you to get to know her better. I invited her to your *haus* tomorrow evening. Do you mind?"

Lois shook her head. "I'm glad. She seemed nice when I met her at the ice cream shop. I'd love to have more time to talk with her. Are you ready to introduce her to Timmy? Maybe it's too soon. And does she know about your past?" Lois shook her head. "I'm asking too many questions."

"Yes, I told her about my life in the outside world. I'm not sure how she's taking it, but I'm drawn to her. I don't have much time before she'll return to Berlin. Her aunt's leg will mend, and she'll be gone if I don't entice her to stay. Timmy's an important part of my life. She and he need to get to know each other."

"Timmy will melt her heart."

David joined them. "Staying for supper, Adam?"

"Of course. I can't turn down Lois's cooking, and she's made ham, beans, and cornbread. One of my favorite meals." He set the table. David and Lois hadn't judged him, and they *wilkomed* him and Timmy in their home upon his return. Not all Amish were happy to have him back.

Timmy ran to David and hugged his legs. *"Daed* has a new friend. Her name is Madeline."

"Is that so?" He tousled Timmy's sandy-blond hair. "When do I get to meet her?"

Lois filled their plates with ham and beans and set a basket of cornbread on the table. "She's *kumm*ing to our *haus* with Adam tomorrow evening. Time for supper."

David smiled. "I'll look forward to meeting her." He held out his arms. "Let's join hands, I'll pray." He offered a prayer to God for the food.

Timmy raised his head and opened his eyes. "Does Madeline have any *kinner?"*

"No. She's never been married." Adam cut Timmy's ham in smaller pieces.

"Are you going to marry her?" Timmy sipped his water. "Is she going to be my new *mamm?"*

Lois and David raised their brows. "Good question, Timmy."

"Friends, you are enjoying this conversation way too much." Adam picked up his glass. "I don't know."

CHAPTER TWO

*M*adeline ordered more board games from her aunt's supplier Friday afternoon and gazed at the door often. Adam said he'd show today. Why hadn't he mentioned Sadie? He'd told her about Lisa. His past was a concern and now, Sadie. He'd captured her heart, but her mind said to stay away.

A little boy skipped inside the shop with Adam. "Good morning, Madeline. I'm Timmy."

Her eyes widened at the child standing next to Adam. "It's a pleasure to make your acquaintance." He was adorable.

"*Daed* said you're pretty, and he's right." Timmy gazed at her.

Her cheeks warmed. "*Danki.* You're a little charmer."

Adam smiled. "I hope you don't mind I brought Timmy with me. He overheard me telling Lois about you, and he was eager to meet you."

"How was school? What do you two have planned for today?" She was completely charmed by the boy's smile, his blond hair, and the freckles sprinkled across his nose and cheeks.

"School was fun. I like playtime best. I'd like to go skim flat rocks in the pond." Timmy glanced at Adam. "Will you take me, *Daed*? Please? Madeline, you should *kumme* with us."

She bent to meet him at eye level. "Your idea sounds fun, but I have to work. *Danki* for the offer." She patted his shoulder.

Adam cocked his head. "Have you given any thought to *kumm*ing for supper tonight at Lois and David's with us?"

She hadn't arrived at a decision. Timmy was as irresistible as Adam. He was the friendliest little boy. She was weak when she faced Adam. But she had to put an end to this. Aunt Lydia had a point. Her parents wouldn't consider him the ideal potential husband for her with his past, and she would fall deeper in love with him if she kept spending time with him. It was one of the most difficult decisions she'd had to make. "I appreciate the invitation, but I must decline."

Adam worried his brows. "Tomorrow evening or the next?"

"No. I'm sorry." Madeline wrenched her gaze from his. The disappointment in his eyes made her heart ache. She didn't have a choice in the matter. Her parents would be disheartened if she went against Aunt Lydia's advice and caused dissention between them over Adam. She didn't think God would approve of her and Adam courting under the circumstances.

An elderly gentleman approached them. "Adam, I'm glad I ran into you. And Timmy, *kumme* here and give me a hug. You give the best hugs."

Timmy hugged him. "Mr. Zook, do you have any more jobs for me to do?" Timmy glanced at Madeline. "Mr. Zook paid me to help him feed the chickens and the goats the other day. We played horseshoes and fished in his pond. It was fun."

"I had more fun than you," Mr. Zook teased.

"This is Madeline. She's *Daed*'s new friend." He turned to Madeline. "You're my new friend now, too, right?"

She nodded. "Yes." Timmy made it difficult to disassociate from Adam. She marveled at what a wonderful relationship Adam had built with his son. The child adored him. "Mr. Zook, how may I help you?"

Mr. Zook lifted a jar of strawberry jam off the shelf. "I'll buy this. A little boy named Timmy loves this jam, and I'm out of it." He had a twinkle in his eye.

Timmy rubbed his stomach. "Save some for me."

"I will. You're *wilkom* to my *haus* anytime, young man." Mr. Zook paid for his purchase, tipped his straw hat, and bid them farewell.

Madeline's stomach was in knots. She wanted Adam to leave, and then she didn't want him to leave. It was all so confusing. How foolish she'd been to think this would work, but she had to stick to her decision given their situation.

He took the cedar box. "We have something special, Madeline. Please pray about us." He gestured to Timmy. "Let's go."

Timmy rearranged the wooden animals on the shelf. "I hope you'll visit us soon, Madeline." He clasped his *daed*'s hand, and they proceeded out of the shop.

Adam drove home, and Timmy hopped out of the buggy. "You play in the yard where I can see you while I unharness the mare."

"When can we visit Madeline again? I like her." Timmy picked up a ball he'd left in the yard.

"I'm not sure." Adam's stomach knotted. He'd revealed too much about his past too fast. He'd hoped she'd not listen to her aunt but form her own opinion about him. Lydia hadn't spoken to him since his return. Maybe after Madeline had pondered his past and proposal to court, she couldn't accept him. She tugged on his heart strings each time he encountered her. He prayed God would change her mind.

∼

Sunday, Madeline helped Aunt Lydia into the bed of the wagon. "Are you certain you want to go to church with your broken leg?"

Her aunt winced and groaned as she sat on a wool blanket with her legs outstretched. She had her back to the front bench with crutches beside her. "Yes. I couldn't take this ride every day, but once in a while is something I can manage. I have to get out of the *haus* sometimes.

Madeline drove to the church barn the Amish community had built for services. Buggies were parked off to the side, and she found a spot. She tied her reins to the long hitching rail and put the makeshift wooden stairs at the end of the wagon for her aunt. After supporting her as she got out of the wagon, Madeline handed Lydia the crutches and waited for her to get comfortable with them under her arms. "This is a wonderful idea to have a barn for services. It is great families don't have to take turns and host services in their homes. It's a lot of work."

"Your *daed* wrote me and said you have a barn like ours in Berlin for Sunday services. Both communities are blessed to have such a place." Aunt Lydia waved to her friends.

"It really is a blessing. Our barn for services is about the same size." Madeline scanned the sea of bonnets and black hats for Adam. She met his gaze and then took her seat next to Aunt Lydia. She hadn't expected him to have centered his gaze on her at the same time she spotted him.

The bishop had them sing hymns, and he read scriptures. Out of the messages he delivered, the one she liked best was on not judging others.

Yesterday, she'd waited for Adam to visit her, but he hadn't shown at the shop. She shouldn't expect him to visit her since she'd sent him away with no hope for them. She didn't know whether to accept him as a suitor or stay away from him. Their obstacles were difficult to overcome, but not impossible.

The bishop held his Bible up. "Many verses in the Bible remind us to forgive one another. We're not to hold grudges or gossip about someone's past mistakes."

Madeline glanced at her aunt. It was as if the bishop's message was directed to her aunt.

Aunt Lydia smiled and returned her attention to the bishop.

Her aunt didn't react to the bishop's message the way Madeline wished. She and her parents disagreed at times, but they were short-lived occasions and about nothing as important as her choice for a suitor.

The bishop finished his message. "Please bow your heads and close your eyes." He offered a prayer to God for the food they were about to receive. "Amen." He raised his head and opened his eyes. "Please help yourselves to the delicious food our gracious ladies have provided for us."

After Aunt Lydia introduced Madeline to some friends, she covered her aunt's hand. "I'll fix your plate."

Her aunt grinned. "*Danki*. I like everything, so you can select the same food for you and me."

Madeline stepped to the end of the line.

Timmy skipped over to her. "Madeline, please play with me. I already hurried and finished my sandwich."

She bent and faced Timmy at his level. "I'm sorry, Timmy, but my aunt and her friends will be upset if I don't sit with them. And I need to have something to eat."

Timmy frowned. "All right."

Adam hurried to them. "I hope he didn't say anything to make you feel uncomfortable."

"His innocence is heartwarming." Madeline's stomach fluttered. She would've loved spending more time with Timmy and Adam. It was awkward with her aunt sitting not far from them.

Adam gestured for them to step away out of earshot from her aunt.

She obliged.

"I'm surprised your aunt made it today with her broken leg." Adam cocked his head.

"She's stubborn and determined not to miss the service." Madeline stared at the ground.

Adam lifted her chin so her eyes would meet his. "I'm glad you're here. Madeline, is it my past keeping us apart?"

Timmy tugged on his *daed*'s sleeve. "*Daed*, I'll be with my friends."

"I'll bring your plate to you. We'll sit with your friends at the outside picnic table."

"Yes and no. I'd rather not discuss it here. There are too many eyes and ears."

"May we talk at the shop tomorrow?" Adam held her gaze.

She nodded. "We'll have to be careful and wait until there are no customers."

"Yes. I don't want to interfere with your work. But we must talk again. I don't want to leave anything unsaid between us." Adam glanced at her aunt and her friends. "Your aunt seems impatient. We should take our place in line."

Madeline glanced at her aunt. Her aunt pinched her lips and gestured to the line. It was almost worth her aunt's disdain to gaze into his compassionate light blue eyes and listen to his pleasant voice again.

She stood quietly with him in line, and then they parted. She carried the two plates of food to her aunt. "Enjoy. The ladies made meat spread sandwiches, a fruit salad, and potato salad. There's an assortment of pies and cookies for dessert." She hoped her aunt wouldn't make a negative comment about Adam.

Aunt Lydia scowled. "You took a little longer than necessary. My friends are almost ready to leave."

Madeline bit the inside of her cheek. Her aunt's remark was unnecessary.

Lois approached them. Her timing couldn't have been better. "Lydia, I'd like to invite you and Madeline to supper tomorrow evening."

Lydia patted her broken leg. "It's a chore to travel these days. *Danki* for the invitation, but I'm sure you'll understand we must decline."

Lois nodded.

The ladies greeted Lois, and she chatted with them for a moment. Madeline was pleased they were all kind to each other. Lois placed a hand on her aunt's shoulder. "I have an idea. Madeline can have supper with us, and I'll send home shepherd's pie and bread pudding for you."

Aunt Lydia glanced from Madeline to Lois. "I'm afraid she won't be able to make it. She's leaving tomorrow. Her parents are picking her up. I haven't had a chance to tell her the change in plans. Jonathan came to fix a loose door on my cupboard this past Friday. He mentioned he was going to Berlin. I sent a note with him to my *bruder*. I've arranged for Edwina to take over the store. She quit her job at the dry goods shop, and now she has time to work for me."

Madeline's jaw dropped. She closed her mouth and hoped no one had noticed her reaction. She didn't know what to make of this. Her aunt should've discussed this with her. "Lois, I would've liked to have had gotten better acquainted with you. I'm sorry."

Lois gave her a compassionate smile. "I'm sorry, too. Please have a safe trip home. I hope you'll visit Mt. Hope again soon. If so, please stop by. We don't need any notice. I should join my husband. He was headed to the buggy when I came over here. You ladies enjoy the rest of your day." She hurried to leave.

Madeline had to find Adam. She scanned the grounds for him or Timmy to no avail. He'd go to the shop tomorrow, and she wouldn't be there. She didn't want to leave without saying goodbye.

Aunt Lydia came alongside her on her crutches. "I'm tired. Let's go home."

Madeline followed her aunt to the wagon, got in, and drove home in silence. She was too frustrated to speak.

They arrived home, and once her aunt had made it out of the wagon, she smirked at Madeline before heading to the *haus*.

Madeline ignored her and unharnessed the mare and led her to the stall. She fed and watered the horse and shut the barn doors. She crossed the yard and entered the *haus*. Her aunt sat on her favorite high-backed chair with her leg resting on the footstool. "I meant to tell you the news about the change in plans after we came home from the service, but I had to put a stop to you going to Lois and David's *haus*. She and her husband are close friends of Adam and Timmy. I have no doubt she would have them join you. It would be wrong of me to encourage you to court such a man. His past behavior leaves much doubt about his future."

"You show such disdain for him. I don't agree with it." Madeline stared at her.

"You need a man who has remained Amish. Not a suitor who may take off at any moment for the outside world. He left Sadie. He might leave you. And he couldn't be too committed to the Amish life in the first place since he left and married an *Englischer*."

"He's sincere about his life here. He has no plans to leave." Madeline wanted to believe this was true.

"Don't be gullible. He's proven he can't be trusted. You haven't used good judgment, and you need to make better choices. I appreciate the help here and at the shop, but I'm ashamed of the way you've gone against my advice and talked with Adam more than once. I had to put an end to it for your sake."

"What did you tell my parents?" Madeline hoped her aunt hadn't painted in her a bad light.

"I wrote them a note. I told them I'd explain when they arrived." Aunt Lydia avoided eye contact with her.

Madeline blew out a frustrated breath. "I told Adam no when he asked me to court him. I wish you had talked to me about this first." She sighed.

"You're smitten with each other. My friends agree. It's the endearing looks you give each other. I noticed it today for myself. It's only a matter of time before he'd talk you into believing he's the one for you. I won't have it. Good night." Aunt Lydia managed to stand and place her crutches under each arm. She padded to her bedroom and shut the door.

Madeline plopped on the settee and shook her head. She got in trouble by breathing around her aunt. The woman was impossible.

CHAPTER THREE

$\mathcal{A}$t noon on Monday, Madeline answered the knock at the door. *"Daed!"* She opened the door, and he stepped inside the *haus*.

He hugged her. "I've missed you." He handed her the cedar box. "I found this on the porch."

She opened it and found a note inside. She shut the lid. Her stomach clenched. Lois must have told Adam her parents were *kumming* today to take her home. "It's for me." She put the box in the bag she'd packed and left by the front door. She'd read the note when she was alone. "I've missed you so much. How is everyone?" Madeline gestured to the settee. "I've got coffee heating on the stove. Would you like a cup?"

"Not right now, sweetheart. Your *mamm* is eager for you to *kumme* home. She stayed home to take care of the animals. Your friends have asked about you. Where's Lydia?"

"She's taking a nap. Before we tell her you're here, what did Lydia tell you in her note?" Madeline searched his face.

He removed his straw hat and raked his fingers through his thin brown hair. "She didn't say much. She asked me to fetch you today. She'd made other arrangements for the store."

"What happened?" He lifted his brows.

"I've done everything she's asked of me. She's upset because I met a wonderful man. His name is Adam Coblenz. He visited the store, and we've had straightforward and good conversations. He asked me to court him, so we could find out if our friendship would grow into us wanting a future together.

I declined, but I'll tell you more on the way home. I don't want her to overhear us talking about this."

Aunt Lydia joined them. "How was your drive here?" She gave no immediate sign that she'd overheard their conversation.

Daed rose. "Fine. I don't have much time to visit. I've got a lot of work waiting for me."

"Have dinner before you go, so we have time to talk. It's a shame we don't visit with each other more often. We're just shy of an hour away."

"It may as well be five hours away when I've got a farm to manage. Winters are too cold for travel, which is when we'd be less busy." *Daed* traced the rim of his hat with his fingers. He hadn't been comfortable when he'd left Madeline with her aunt, and he was definitely uncomfortable now.

Madeline warmed chicken noodle soup and made grilled cheese sandwiches. Her hands trembled. She wasn't sure what would *kumme* out of her aunt's mouth. She'd gritted her teeth not to argue. She filled their soup bowls and set sandwiches on plates and served them.

Daed reached for their hands. "Let's pray." He offered a prayer to God for the food.

Aunt Lydia set her spoon beside her bowl. "The reason I had you *kumme* today to take Madeline home is she's been talking to Adam Coblenz, a no good. She's refused to listen to my advice about the man, and so I notified you. I had friends who reported back to me when he went to the store, and when they were out to dinner and a buggy ride together. Trust me. I'm doing Madeline a favor."

"Aunt Lydia, I declined his offer to court. What more do you want from me?" Madeline was so aggravated. Her aunt's authoritative tone set Madeline's teeth on edge.

Daed hurried to finish his grilled cheese sandwich and left half his soup in the bowl. He wasn't in the habit of not finishing a meal. He carried his dirty dishes to the sink. "It would be hard to miss the tension between you and my *dochder*. Maybe it is best I take Madeline home. How will you manage without help, Lydia?"

Madeline hadn't finished her sandwich or soup, but she understood her *daed* was ready to go home. She was, too. She carried her dishes to the counter and waited for her aunt's answer to *Daed*'s question.

"Jonathan, the young man I sent to your *haus*, will check on me. He's tending to my animals and the garden. My friend, Edwina, agreed to manage the store. She's in a position to do that now. I'll be fine. I've mastered the crutches, and it's amazing what I can do on them." Aunt Lydia gave him a smug grin.

"Seems like you'll be fine. We'll be on our way." *Daed* walked to the door and picked up Madeline's bag. "Take care of yourself."

"Drive safe." Aunt Lydia kept her distance from them.

"Goodbye, Aunt Lydia. I pray you have a speedy recovery."

"*Danki*, dear." Aunt Lydia didn't sound sincere.

Madeline left with her *daed* and got in his buggy. Aunt Lydia had already shut the door. *Daed* had always avoided having much conversation with his sister. "Were you and Aunt Lydia ever close?"

He shook his head. "I had misgivings when she asked if we could spare you to help her. She's always been overbearing, judgmental, and a gossip. I shouldn't speak about her this way, but it's the truth. I didn't stay long so she wouldn't have much time to disparage you for one reason or another. I wanted to avoid an argument with her. I'm more interested in your side of this story." He glanced at her. "Tell me about this Adam Coblenz."

Madeline squeezed his arm. "*Danki* for giving me a chance to explain and for rescuing me." She loved the close relationship she had with *Daed* and *Mamm*. "He's a widower raising his son who is five. He left the Amish life to experience the outside world before he became eighteen. He fell in love and married Lisa. He owned a farm, and he worked at the bank for her *daed*. When she died, he returned to the Amish life. He came to the shop, and we went to dinner when I closed the shop for a mid-day break. We also went on a buggy ride. I like him a lot."

"Sounds too soon for him to ask you to court him. I'm relieved you didn't take him up on his offer." *Daed* frowned.

"We had enough discussions for him to ask to court me. He meant well." Her heart hurt knowing she wouldn't speak to him again.

"I don't trust a man who has left our way of life and then returns as a potential husband for you. He may change his mind and want to live in the outside world again. He may also have more modern views than we do about things, and you don't want to have to compromise your beliefs to match his."

She didn't like where this conversation was headed. She wasn't sure if she'd want to contact Adam, and she didn't want *Daed* to forbid her to speak with him again. "It wasn't an easy decision."

"Nonetheless, it was a good one," *Daed* said.

She was sick about not ever looking into Adam's big blue eyes again. She had a lot to ponder.

Mamm was outside hanging laundry on the clothesline when they arrived. Madeline jumped out of the buggy and met her halfway across the yard.

Mamm wrapped her arms around Madeline. "I missed you. I'm glad you're home."

"I missed you, too," Madeline said.

"Tell me about your time in Mt. Hope, and why Lydia insisted *Daed* fetch you." *Mamm* plucked a damp shirt out of the basket, snatched two clothespins from her apron pocket, and hung it on the line.

"I met a handsome gentleman, Adam Coblenz. He's a widower, and he has a five-year-old boy."

"Does it bother you he has a child?" *Mamm* picked up the last piece to hang on the clothesline.

"Absolutely not. I liked his son, Timmy. He's not among the reasons why it would be difficult to court Adam." Madeline was sure she and Timmy would've grown to love each other. She wouldn't mind being a step*mamm*.

"List the reasons."

"We live in two different places. We don't have time to go to our town, let alone Mt. Hope. Aunt Lydia didn't approve of him leaving the Amish life or his marriage to a woman who lived in the outside world, even though he returned to the Amish life when she died. I wasn't sure you and *Daed* would support our courtship given this information."

"I'm not happy about his decision to marry an *Englischer*. I also would rather you marry a man who doesn't have *kinner*. We have plenty of available suitors here. What about Micah? You get along well."

Daed interrupted them. He kissed *Mamm*'s cheek and passed Madeline a bag. "You left this in the buggy."

She accepted it and took out the box. She was curious to read Adam's note, but she'd wait until later. "*Danki.*"

"I'll be in the barn." *Daed* said.

"To answer your question about Micah, he's not the one for me. I care about Adam a lot. I miss him already. I wish things would've worked out for us. Maybe if we'd had more time, we could've had a chance."

"I'm sorry you're hurting, but maybe it is better this way." *Mamm* caressed her cheek and then dropped her gaze to the box. "Did you buy the pretty box at Lydia's shop?"

"Adam bought it at her shop the day we met. He later gave it to me as a gift." She hoped the box wouldn't become the last thing he'd ever give her. She hadn't been home a day, and her heart ached to hear his voice again.

"He has good taste, and his gesture shows he's a romantic. Your *daed* was also. I'm convinced God has the right man for you. You'll just have to be patient. And if Adam is the one, God will work it out for you. I may have my reservations about him, but I trust your judgment. On another topic, how was your stay with Lydia?"

"You were right. She has a tough exterior, and she doesn't look on the bright side of things. I tried to tread lightly around her, but my meeting Adam didn't make her very happy. I apologize if I've caused any trouble. *Daed* seemed to understand, and he wasn't upset with me."

"I had doubts about sending you to help her. She isn't someone we enjoy because she's always looking for the worst in people, as I'd mentioned to you before you left. It's hard to hug a porcupine. We appreciate your efforts. And I don't question your time with Adam. You have our trust in all things."

Madeline let a tear stain her cheek. "I love you, *Mamm*."

"I love you, too. Now, go rest and unwind."

Madeline went inside the *haus* to her bedroom. She opened the cedar box and lifted the note. *"Dear Madeline, Lois said she invited you to supper, and your aunt surprised both of you with the news your parents would arrive tomorrow and take you home. Your aunt is set on keeping us apart. I had one more important matter to tell you. I'd hoped to tell you in person. I'll visit you in a couple of days and reveal this to you. I'll get your address from the post office in Berlin. I'd like to meet your parents, and I have an exciting idea I'll share with you. Love, Adam."*

She read the note a couple of times. He'd said love. She loved him, too. She reckoned most of her friends would say it was too soon. They'd insist she and Adam hadn't had enough time together to know if they loved each other or not. It didn't have to make sense to anyone but them. But she didn't know how any idea he had would change their circumstances. She'd keep praying about their situation.

⁓

A week later on Monday, Madeline rinsed her dirty furniture dusting rag under the water pump in the yard.

Adam drove down the lane.

She gasped and watched him as he and parked his buggy, jumped out, and tied his mare to the hitching post.

Daed met him. *"Wilkom.* I'm Samuel Yoder." He held out his hand.

Adam shook his hand. "I'm Adam Coblenz, Mr. Yoder. I met your *dochder* when she was in Mt. Hope."

Madeline approached them. *"Daed*, this is the man I mentioned to you. Adam, I'm glad you're here." Her heart beat fast with joy at the sight of him.

Daed motioned to the *haus*. "I look forward to talking with you more, Adam. For now, I'm sure Madeline's eager to introduce you to her *mamm*. You two go inside. I'll join you in a couple of minutes after I offer your horse food and water."

"Danki, Mr. Yoder. It's very kind of you." Adam followed her inside the haus.

Mamm was bent over as if looking for something on the floor.

Madeline tapped her on the shoulder.

Mamm startled and gasped.

"I'm sorry, *Mamm*. We didn't mean to scare you. This is Adam Coblenz." Madeline gestured at Adam.

"It's a pleasure to meet you, Mrs. Yoder."

Mamm chuckled and held her hand to her chest. "I thought I'd noticed a spider crawling on the floor, but I couldn't find it. I was concentrating so hard on it that I didn't hear you *kumme* in. Where are my manners? Have a seat, please. Would you like lemonade, coffee, or tea? Are you hungry? I'd be happy to fix you cheese and crackers to hold you over until supper. I hope you'll join us."

Adam smiled and nodded. "I'd be happy to stay, and I don't need anything. I had a biscuit with strawberry jam before I came here. *Danki*."

"*Mamm*, Adam and I will take a walk along the pond's edge in the back. We won't be long."

"Take your time. We'll look forward to getting better acquainted with Adam at supper. You've got a couple hours before then." *Mamm* grinned.

Madeline led him out the back door. "You said you would visit, but I didn't know when you would arrive. I'm shocked you're here this soon."

"Your departure was sudden, so I didn't know how I'd be received by you or your parents." Adam frowned. "I surmised it might have been your aunt's doing."

"I was upset I didn't have a chance to talk to you before *Daed* took me home. Aunt Lydia is determined to keep us apart. She wrote to my parents and asked *Daed* to *kumme* and take me home." Madeline was grateful Adam had not given up on her. She'd longed to see him again to discuss what was on her mind.

"I'm not going to beat around the bush. I love you, and I don't care if anyone thinks it's too soon. What matters to me is how you feel. Where do you stand?" Adam gazed into her eyes.

She heaved a big sigh. "I'm in love with you, but I'm baffled as to why you didn't tell me about Sadie. My aunt said you were heartbroken when you left Mt. Hope and then married Lisa. It's too important a subject to dodge, given we had admitted we care for each other." She searched his face.

Adam's shoulders slumped. "I should've told you. I'm sorry. You had a lot of information to digest about me, and I didn't want to burden you with all my past at once. I had no idea your aunt would shorten our time together like this. I planned to tell you about Sadie."

Madeline had been blindsided by her aunt, and he had too. He had a point. "I need to know everything, Adam."

"Sadie Bontrager and I grew up together. Her parents and mine were best friends. She and I didn't have siblings, and we grew close. Our families and friends expected us to court when we turned sixteen. I liked Sadie a lot, but I was not in love with her."

"Did she want to court you?" Madeline didn't fully understand.

"No. She had met and fallen in love with a newcomer, Ezra Raber. He was ten years older than her, and he had three *kinner* under the age of fourteen.

His *fraa* died in a buggy accident. Her parents didn't approve of the difference in Sadie's and Ezra's ages. Sadie lied to her parents and said we were taking canoe rides or picnicking when she was not with me, but with Ezra. I didn't know this until the day I left. When I told her I was for sure leaving, she confessed to me what she'd done, and she realized it was time to be honest and make it right with her parents."

"Were you angry?" Madeline didn't think Sadie had been fair to Adam.

"I was disappointed in her, but I forgave her. After I left, Lois and David and I kept in touch through letters. They kept me informed about what was happening with Sadie, Ezra, and her family. They had written and told me many of the Amish thought I'd abandoned her, and Ezra was her second choice. The gossips loved this story. Ezra's *bruder* wrote to him and asked if he would move to Lancaster, Pennsylvania, and go in on a dairy farm with him. Sadie's parents grew to like Ezra, and they approved the marriage. Right after Ezra and Sadie wed, they left for Lancaster. Her parents moved there shortly after, and they got involved in the dairy business, too."

"My aunt said you broke Sadie's heart. She made it seem as if you'd had a serious commitment to Sadie. I'm glad you and she were friends and nothing more." Madeline let go of her doubts about him. Her aunt and others had misjudged him. But how could they be together when they lived in two different communities?

"Will your parents agree with your aunt about me? What have you told them?" Adam worried his brows.

"They are fair and loving. I'm proud of the way they both *wilkom*ed you here. I told them I was interested in you and about your past. They would prefer you'd have stayed Amish, but they'll believe you if you tell them you're committed to the Amish life from now on. They'll also trust my judgment." They would appreciate Adam *kumm*ing to talk to them in person. "But how will we court when we're not in the same community?"

"Lois had hired Martha to work at the ice cream shop, and the girl quit to move with her family to Nappanee, Indiana. They need someone to take her place, and I suggested you. They're very much in favor of that solution. They have a small *haus* in the back of their place you could live in. It's furnished, and you'll have everything you need. We can take as much time as we need to court and to find out if we want a future together. What do you say?"

Madeline pressed a hand to her heart. She had to take this leap of faith. She had no doubt he was the man for her. "I'd love to go with you. I've been praying to God about us, and I believe He's answered my prayer."

He reached for her hands. "I believe God put everything we needed into place for us."

"Now my prayer is that our love for each other will grow," she said.

He brushed her cheek with the back of his hand. "I was miserable this past week."

"Me, too." She blushed.

He kissed her gently. After they discussed their future, they headed back to the haus for supper.

Mamm had the table set and the food dishes ready.

"Let's sit, and I'll pray." *Daed* offered a prayer to God for the food. Then he lifted a big spoonful of buttered noodles onto his plate. "Adam, tell us about yourself."

Adam recounted his past and the misunderstanding their aunt, as well as other Amish in the community, had about him and Sadie. "Many of the Amish in Mt. Hope know the real story, and they have no problem with me. When I returned to Mt. Hope, the bishop insisted we have meetings once a week, and he led me through a Bible study and reminded me of our Amish lifestyle and traditions. He and I have a friendship, and I'd be happy to have him vouch for me."

Madeline listened to her parents as they questioned Adam. He'd made it clear he'd never leave Amish life again, and he promised to take good care of her. Then the conversation turned to farming and everyday life in Berlin. She cleared her throat. "Adam has a plan he'd like to discuss with you. I'm in favor of it."

Adam recounted the plan to her parents. "You're *wilkom* to visit anytime. You can stay with me or with my friends, David and Lois. They're like family to me and Timmy."

Madeline's stomach jittered. She couldn't finish her supper. "What do you think?" She centered her gaze on *Daed*, and then *Mamm*.

Daed drummed his fingers on the table. "*Mamm* and I are grateful to have met Adam, and I'm impressed he came to Berlin to talk to us. He's answered our questions, and I'm pleased with his answers. If this is what you want, then we support you."

Mamm dabbed her damp eyes with her napkin. "I'm sad and happy for you, Madeline. I'm used to having you here with me."

Madeline leaned over and circled her arm around *Mamm*'s shoulders. "I'll make every effort to visit."

Adam grinned and reached across the table to shake her *daed*'s hand.

~

Eight months later, Madeline opened the cedar box and placed a handkerchief she'd embroidered for Adam with his initial and the short love note she'd written telling him how much he and Timmy meant to her. Then she shrugged into her new blue Amish dress. "*Danki*, Lois for making this dress for me, and a new shirt and pants for Adam. You're like a sister to me."

Lois pinned the short cape at the base of her neck. "I feel the same. You are lovely inside and out. You are such a blessing to me." She glanced out the window. "David has the buggy waiting to take us to the Sunday service barn where Adam will be waiting for you. I'm thankful your *mamm* let me stay with you while she and your *daed* went ahead of us to make any last-minute touches to the food tables. The sunshine will provide beautiful weather for your wedding. Are you ready to become Adam's bride?"

"I can't wait." Madeline grinned. She and Adam had properly courted, and he'd proposed three months after she'd returned to Mt. Hope. Her family had visited twice, and Adam had won over her grouchy aunt with his genuine charm. Madeline would be a *fraa* and a *mamm* before the end of the day. Her heart soared. She'd prayed for the right man, and God had given her more than she'd requested. She'd was getting a wonderful son, too. She couldn't be happier or more grateful.

ABOUT THE AUTHOR

Molly Jebber is a bestselling and award-winning author. Her Amish historical romance books have made *Publisher's Weekly* Best Ten List, *USA Today*, and have been in featured interviews on newspaper sites and popular magazines across the U.S. She's a national speaker for Women's Christian Connection. She has served as a keynote speaker for writing conferences and as a guest lecturer at libraries and events across the U.S. on writing, publishing, and marketing. She just signed a contract with Sony Pictures/Pureflix to make a movie of LIZA'S SECOND CHANCE. She loves God, her family, and friends. She says yes to cupcakes and no to coconut!

http://www.mollyjebber.com

Amish Charm Bakery Series:
https://www.amazon.com/Molly-Jebber/e/B00NI1CSVC

HOPE BLOSSOMS

RACHEL J. GOOD

CHAPTER ONE

$\mathcal{F}$ury in his eyes, Josiah Miller's brother burst through the door of their family home and headed straight for Josiah, waving a folded paper and an envelope. "This is all your fault," Simon screamed.

"What's my fault?" Josiah stepped back a few steps and held up a hand as his brother barreled toward him, hoping to calm Simon enough to get a coherent answer.

"This." Simon thrust the yellow stationery and envelope at Josiah, sank into the nearest chair, and buried his head in his hands. "What am I going to do?"

Josiah turned over the crumpled and smudged envelope. He could barely read the return address, but the letter had come from Bird-in-Hand, the town in Lancaster County where Simon had worked six years ago. At least he had until Josiah had intervened. The bishop had agreed with Josiah and insisted Simon move back to Gratz. No one but Josiah and the bishop knew the real reason Simon had returned to their community after only a few months at his new job.

Desperation edged Simon's voice. "I don't want Katie to find out. I never told her about this."

"You didn't?" It wasn't Josiah's place to lecture his brother, but surely a husband should have shared his past with his wife.

"I—I didn't think she'd understand. It all happened long before I met her, and I didn't want to lose her."

"Maybe you should tell her now." Josiah's sister-in-law had a sweet, loving spirit. She'd be devastated by the news, but she'd forgive Simon. And now that they were married, Katie wouldn't leave him.

"I can't. I just can't." Simon shook his bowed head. "She'd never look at me the same again."

"I'm not sure that's what matters in this situation. Something needs to be done right away. And you need to take responsibility for—"

Simon cut him off. "Easy for you to say. You're not married or even dating anyone." His voice rose. "Besides, this is all your fault. If you hadn't gone to the bishop, I would have known about this. I could have taken care of it then."

"I did what was right and best for you at the time."

"Maybe for me. But what about that?" Simon waved toward the yellow letter. "Something has to be done. I don't want to upset Katie. Not when she's carrying our first *boppli*."

This was the first Josiah had heard the news. "Congratulations."

"I can't tell her now. But this has to be fixed. Right away."

As he always did when one of his younger siblings had a problem, Josiah took over the role of their deceased parents. "I'll take care of it."

And he would. He just didn't know how.

Lily Bontrager shrugged deeper into her sweater to ward off the chill in the spring air, but neither the sweater nor the scarf she'd tied tightly around her ears could lessen the iciness in her heart. She and *Mamm* should be out here together planting these seedlings. Lily lifted her face to the tiny sliver of sun peeking out from gray clouds, so much like the shadows hiding God's grace in her own life right now.

She squeezed her eyes shut and prayed from the depths of her soul, *Please, Lord, help me find a way to ease this grief.*

Although she accepted *Mamm*'s death as God's will, the ache inside grew stronger with each passing day. Rattling around alone in the big house, once filled with laughing, squabbling siblings and two loving parents, made Lily's loneliness even more acute. And now, she had to face spring planting without *Mamm*.

"Whatcha doing?"

The shrill question startled Lily. She turned her head and spotted two little *Englisch* girls with matching impish grins, tousled hair, and threadbare dresses that had long ago faded to pale blue. They stood a few feet away, staring curiously. They'd tromped through her previously planted rows, mashing fragile seedlings.

Lily tried not to grimace. She'd nursed those plants from seeds over the past weeks. "I'm planting tomatoes."

"No, you ain't." One twin crossed her arms and glared. "Mommy says it's bad to lie."

"'Matoes is round and red." Her sister pointed to the flat of seedlings. "Them things are green and skinny."

Hiding a smile, Lily held up the seedling she'd been about to put in the ground. "If you walk carefully without stepping on the baby plants"—she waved toward the rows between them—"I'll let you sniff this. You'll see it smells like tomatoes. After I plant it, it will get taller, and when the weather is warmer, tomatoes will grow on it."

Both girls gave her skeptical looks. Then, in unison, they shook their heads.

One sister leaned close to the other one's ear. "She's lying." Her loud whisper carried. Then she lifted her chin. "'Matoes come from the store."

"That's true. Sometimes they do. But how do tomatoes get to the store?"

The little girl's defiant look slid into a puzzled frown. Then, a moment later, she crowed triumphantly, "On trucks."

Her twin nodded. "We seen those big trucks dropping off food."

"And how do the tomatoes get on those trucks?"

"They load 'em up."

"Right." Lily had never been around children who didn't know tomatoes grew in a garden. She smiled encouragingly. "Where do the drivers get the tomatoes to put on the trucks?"

The sisters gave Lily the side eye as they put their heads together. After whispering furiously for a bit, one of them admitted, "We don't know."

"They grow from plants like these."

The twins stared at her, their expressions uncertain.

"Do you want to smell this?" Lily held out the seedling. "Just remember to watch where you walk."

With an exaggerated tiptoe, the closest girl started toward Lily.

Her sister grabbed her sleeve. "Mommy says never talk to strangers."

"We already did," her twin pointed out.

"But she could snatch us."

"I promise I won't snatch you." Where had these girls lived that they were so fearful?

Lily waited until both girls had sniffed the leaves and declared they smelled a little bit like a tomato, before she questioned them. "Where do you live?"

"Over there." One sister waved in the direction of a rundown shack near the street, just at the edge of Lily's property.

No one had lived there for years. Did it even have heat, running water, or a toilet?

"Are you sure?"

They both nodded vigorously. "We moved in yesterday," they chorused. Then they giggled.

Uncertain whether or not they were telling the truth, Lily extended her hand—the one without a tomato plant in it. "That means we're neighbors. Nice to meet you. My name's Lily."

"I'm Scarlett, and this is Meryl."

Meryl elbowed her sister. "I can name my own self."

Scarlett glared at her. "It's OK to help someone."

"Not when they want to do it theirselves." Meryl turned to Lily. "We're five years old, and we're twins."

"I could tell. You look alike." Since the girls seemed to want to talk about themselves, Lily asked the question that had been nagging at her ever since they'd shown up. "So, where did you move from?"

"New York City." Once again, Scarlett jumped in first to answer.

"Mommy lost her job, and we got 'victed." Meryl seemed eager to top her sister's information.

"Eee-victed." Scarlett emphasized the beginning of the word. "That's when they throw all yer stuff out on the sidewalk."

Meryl sniffled. "Not all of it. I lost my fuzzy bunny and my baby doll and my . . ."

What had these poor girls been through? Lily's heart went out to them.

Before she could find out more, a panicked voice sliced through the air. "Scarlett? Meryl?" The front door of the shack banged open, and a young woman raced onto the porch. She studied the fields across the street and swiveled her head to glance up and down the street.

A guilty look crossed Scarlett's face.

Meryl looked about to burst into tears. "Uh-oh, Mommy's mad."

Normally, Lily barely raised her voice, but she yelled at the top of her lungs, "Back here." She could only imagine how worried the mother must be.

The young woman whirled around, and spying her daughters, charged in their direction. "Oh, you found them." Relief oozed from her voice, and the tightness in her face relaxed . . . until her gaze settled on her daughters' muddy shoes and the path they'd traveled. "Yikes! They squished your plants."

"It's all right. I can probably replant most of them." Lily wasn't sure about that, but she wanted to lessen the mother's guilt.

"I'll pay for them as soon as I can." The woman rubbed her forehead. "Not another expense," she muttered.

Perhaps she hadn't intended anyone to hear that, but Lily couldn't help feeling sorry for this young mother. Although her strained expression made her appear older, the woman couldn't be much more than twenty-one or twenty-two. Too young to have five-year-old daughters.

"I'm Lily. It's nice to meet you. Your daughters said you just moved in."

"We did. I'm Aliyah." She wrapped an arm around each daughter. "We need to go, girls. Tell Lily you're sorry for messing up her garden."

"Where to? Back to New York?" When Aliyah shook her head, the hope in Meryl's eyes died.

"To work with me."

"Nooo." Scarlett emphasized her moan with a glum expression. "Will we have to hide again?"

Redness seeped into Aliyah's cheeks. "We'll talk about it later." She tried to herd her daughters toward the shack, but Scarlett pulled away.

"Why can't we stay here with Lily?"

Through gritted teeth, Aliyah said in a low tone, "We can't afford to pay anyone. Now let's go."

"You wouldn't have to pay me." The words jumped from Lily's mouth before she had a chance to consider them. "I'd enjoy having company. I could teach the girls to garden and—"

Aliyah waved a hand to cut her off. "Thank you for your kind offer, but we couldn't impose."

"You wouldn't be imposing. My *mamm* passed recently, so I'd be happy for company."

"It wouldn't work. I have an interview shortly. If they take me, I'll be staying and covering the night shift."

Lily had never acted impulsively, but something about these little girls called to her. "I have plenty of bedrooms. Empty bedrooms that used to belong to all my brothers and sisters. Having your girls spend the night would keep me from being lonely."

Aliyah avoided Lily's eyes. "To be honest, I don't really trust the Amish. I had a very bad experience." She kept her head lowered and nibbled on her lips. "Thanks for the offer, though."

"No, Mommy." Scarlett pulled on her mother's hand, trying to drag her back. "Please don't make us go. It ain't easy to sit for hours and not make noise."

With a sigh, Aliyah corrected her. "*Isn't*. Not *ain't*. It *isn't* easy to sit." She gave Lily an embarrassed shrug. "They picked up bad grammar in our old neighborhood. We've been working on it, but . . ."

Meryl added her plea to her sister's. "Let us stay with Lily. We'll be good."

"Why don't we try it this once?" Lily suggested.

Doubt clouded Aliyah's features. "I'm not sure."

"I've taken care of plenty of children. I have a dozen nieces and nephews of all ages. If you want references, you can check with any of the neighbors here. I babysit for them too." Lily gestured toward the houses across the street and next door.

"Please, Mommy." Meryl's eyes swam with moisture.

Maybe her daughter's tears swayed her, but each word came out reluctantly. "Just this once."

Her daughters both cheered.

She bent to look them in the eyes. "Behave yourselves and do what you're told. I'd better not hear about you causing any trouble. And do what you can to fix these broken plants." She stood and brushed off her pants. "I have to go. I don't want to be late."

Lily wanted to reassure Aliyah and remove some of the worry from her eyes. "I'll take good care of your daughters."

With a terse "thank you," Aliyah strode off.

Two eager faces smiled up at Lily. What had she gotten herself into? She'd asked God for a way to get over her grief. Perhaps this had been His answer.

CHAPTER TWO

*J*osiah fidgeted as his driver cruised up and down the Bird-in-Hand country road printed on the envelope. The return address on his brother's envelope had been smudged, and he squinted to make out the name and house number. Four mailboxes stood together on one side of the road. That one looked the closest to the smudged number, but which house did each mailbox belong to?

"Wait," Josiah cried.

Rusty slammed on his brakes, pitching Josiah forward. The seatbelt chafed against his chest, but kept him from flying too far forward.

"Sorry," Rusty apologized. "You startled me. Did you mean for me to stop?"

"*Jah*, I did. Could you pull over somewhere near here? I want to walk along this road a ways." He'd seen a woman with two girls about the right age.

Rusty drew the car onto the opposite shoulder, and Josiah paced back down the road. It had been one of these yards along here. He passed a tiny, rundown house, and then in the spacious backyard nearby, a beautiful blonde Amish woman knelt in a garden.

At the sight of her, Josiah's heart flip-flopped. But what started his pulse racing was not the woman's beauty, but the two small girls staring up at her with enraptured faces. They seemed to be hanging on her every word. What was she saying that held such intense interest? Josiah wanted to find out, but he held himself back.

Those twins had his brother's eyes and features. Simon used to stare at Josiah with that same concentration. This had to be the right house. But Josiah had always believed Simon's ex-girlfriend was *Englisch*. Although maybe she'd been going through *Rumschpringa* too. But several other things didn't add up. The letter-writer claimed to be living in poverty and asked for money. Yet, from this distance, the blonde's dress and black work apron appeared almost new. But the girls faded dresses seemed almost *Englisch* and very bedraggled. No Amish mother in his community treated herself to new clothes while making her children do without. And the girls' hair hung down uncombed instead of being pulled back in bobs. What was this mother thinking?

The garden must belong to the huge house nearby. As if to prove him right, the blonde stood, dusted off her apron, and took the girls' hands. They picked their way through the newly planted seedlings, laughing and chatting. She looked like a kind and loving mother, not one to neglect her children's hair and clothing.

The trio headed for the back porch together and entered the house before Josiah had time to decide what to do. Should he knock on the door? What would he say? He'd planned to offer the girl money, but anyone who lived in that well-maintained farmhouse didn't need it. Besides, with her being Amish, the church would help her.

Josiah went over the letter in his mind. He'd read it again when he returned to the bed-and-breakfast where he was staying. But she'd claimed the roof leaked, they had no heat, and the children were hungry. None of those fit the picture in front of him. Maybe she and the girls had found a room or two to rent in this house? If so, her circumstances weren't as dire as she'd described them.

"Excuse me. Can I help you?" An elderly Amish man hobbled in Josiah's direction. "Are you lost?"

Not exactly. Josiah shook his head and posed a question of his own. "Is tomorrow church Sunday in this *g'may?*"

"It is. You'd like to attend?"

"*Jah*, I would. Can you tell me where it will be held?"

The man introduced himself as Thomas King and gave Josiah directions. "I'll look forward to seeing you tomorrow."

"*Danke.* I'll be there." Josiah headed for the car.

That would give him a chance to study the girls more closely to be sure his eyes weren't playing tricks on him. And perhaps he could find a way to talk to their *mamm.* Or find out her true situation from others.

～

After they'd all cleaned up from gardening, Lily sat on the couch with her heavy encyclopedia of gardening. She flipped to the pages showing the growth of tomatoes from seeds to fruit.

"I planted seeds that looked like this in small containers. I kept them warm even when it was cold outside. And they grew. Here's how tall they'll be in a few weeks."

"They grow flowers?" Scarlett narrowed her eyes. "I don't see no 'matoes."

"After the yellow flowers fall off, you can see the baby tomatoes." Lily turned the page.

Meryl shook her head. "*Unh-uh.* They's green."

"*Jah*, they are. When they turn red, they're ready to pick and eat."

Disbelief on their faces, the girls flipped the pages, studying the life cycle of the tomato plant.

Lily stood. "Why don't you look at this book while I fix us some supper?"

Scarlett looked up. "What we having?"

"Meatloaf, baked potatoes, and corn." Lily hoped the girls would like that. She wanted to fill their stomachs. They looked thin and hungry.

Evidently, she'd made a good choice. After the girls had spent more than an hour poring over the gardening book and exclaiming over oranges and lemons growing on trees and bananas growing upside down, they raced to the table and wolfed down their meals.

When Lily offered them seconds, their eyes widened.

They stayed silent for a full minute, before Meryl said in a tentative voice, "We can have more?"

"Of course. There's plenty left." Lily indicated the rest of the half-eaten meatloaf. She'd also baked extra potatoes. If the girls didn't eat them, she'd slice them for fried potatoes tomorrow.

Meryl nudged Scarlett, then leaned over to whisper in her ear. "We can sneak it in our pockets for Mommy."

Her sister nodded. "Can both of us get more?"

Lily nodded and cut generous slices of meatloaf and halved a baked potato. "This is for you to eat now. I'll wrap up the rest for your mommy."

Scarlett gasped. "All of it?"

"*Jah*. I mean *yes.* Your mom can have everything that's left."

Her eyes filled with wonder, Meryl stared at Lily. Then she breathed out a small, startled, "Thank you."

Scarlett sat, her mouth gaping open, until Meryl elbowed her and hissed, "Say *thank you.*"

Her sister repeated the words, but her brow furrowed. "Is you rich?"

"No, but God has given me more than enough for myself and to help others."

"Can God give Mommy lots of money and food?"

Ach, what had she started? Lily paused to find the best answer. "I don't know God's will for your mommy, but God can do anything."

"You sure?" Scarlett tilted her head to one side and watched Lily closely as she waited for an answer.

"God can give us everything we ask for, but He doesn't always do that. Sometimes He says *no.*"

Scarlett crossed her arms. "That's mean."

"No. We have to trust that God knows best. He has a good reason for whatever He does."

Meryl nodded. "Like when Mommy says, 'Don't eat that, so we have some food for tomorrow.'"

Lily's heart ached. How often had these little girls gone hungry?

Her mouth full of meatloaf, Scarlett declared, "I'm going to ask God for food every day."

Lily suspected God would answer that prayer. She'd already decided not to let this family miss a meal again. She'd talk to people at church about helping too. Some of the men could fix up the shack, and the woman could make sure the children were clothed and fed. The twins might be *Englisch,* but her community would never ignore someone in need, especially not young children.

Scarlett and Meryl helped wash the dishes and clean the kitchen. Evidently, they'd done chores at home, and they seemed happy to help. They relaxed enough to chatter about their past, making Lily even more determined to change their future.

But when Lily wrapped up the food and went to place it in the refrigerator, Meryl tensed up, and Scarlett tugged at Lily's skirt.

"What about Mommy?"

"This is for her," Lily assured them. "Would you like to put it in the refrigerator at your house instead?"

Meryl bit her lip. "We ain't got no fridge."

"That's cause we got no 'lectricity."

"I don't either."

Disbelief was written on both faces.

Then, Scarlett shook her head. "You gots a fridge."

"Mine's gas-powered."

Meryl's face fell. "We ain't got gas neither."

What were they doing for heating? Lily had to get to work right away. Thank heavens, they had church tomorrow. She'd get people lined up to help immediately.

Lily placed a hand on each girl's shoulder. "I hope we can get that fixed."

"You gonna ask God to do that?" Scarlett demanded.

"I am." Lily herded them toward the stairs. "And I'll ask people I know who like to help God."

"Does you know more nice people like you?"

Before Lily could answer, Meryl chimed in, "We knowed nice people in

New York. Sometimes they gived us food. But sometimes they was hungry too. Just like us."

If I have anything to say about it, you'll never go hungry again.

After helping the girls bathe and wash their hair, Lily gave them nightgowns her nieces used when they spent the night. Then she told them Bible stories as she combed the tangles out of their hair and toweled it dry. Before she tucked them into bed, she helped them say their prayers.

Instead of getting into the bed Lily had made up for her, Meryl climbed in with Scarlett. "I always sleep with my sister."

"It keeps us warmer," Scarlett murmured sleepily. "This bed's softer than the floor."

"Is that where you've been sleeping?" Lily couldn't keep the concern from her voice.

"We don't gots no furniture yet," Meryl explained. "Most of our stuff got all broken into pieces. Those men throwed it out in the alley."

"Once Mommy gets a job, we gonna get pretty new things. She promised."

"I see." Lily added another need to her list, which had been growing and sprouting faster than her tomato seedlings. She hoped her requests would bear as much fruit.

She stood in the doorway until the girls' breathing slowed and softened. Then, with tears in her eyes, she tucked the quilt around them.

Lily had spent so much time taking care of *Mamm* she'd never had a chance to date and marry. And now she was the *alt maedel* at the singings. All her friends had paired off, and only boys younger than her attended the singings. Perhaps God had brought these little twins into her life to fill her longing to be a mother—something that most likely would never happen.

CHAPTER THREE

$\mathcal{T}$he next morning at dawn, the girls watched fascinated as Lily combed her long hair and pulled it back into a bob.

Scarlett rushed over when Lily finished. "Do that to me."

"And me." Meryl dogged Scarlett's heels.

Lily combed her out and then had Scarlett place her head down on the table, so Lily could do her bob. Meryl copied her sister, and soon both girls had neat bobs at the back of their heads.

"I rinsed out your dresses last night, but they aren't dry yet. Would you like to wear some of my nieces' clothes?"

"To match you?" Meryl asked shyly.

"They'd be Amish dresses." Lily led them to the closet where her young nieces stored a few things. "You can pick your favorite dress."

Meryl chose pink, while Scarlett picked blue.

Then she twirled in a circle. "*Whee*, I'm Amish."

Her sister followed her lead, and they whirled in circles until they fell onto the floor, giggling and dizzy.

Once they'd calmed down, Lily gave them warm stockings to wear underneath their dresses. The thin ankle socks with holes they'd worn yesterday provided little protection from the chilly spring weather.

"Who'd like some breakfast?" she asked.

They both stopped clowning around and stared at her.

Scarlett found her voice first. "We got a big dinner last night."

"Mommy says if you eat lots at night, your tummy don't need food in the morning," Meryl explained in a solemn tone. "But sometimes my belly hurts."

Lily tried not to let her distress show. These poor little girls. And their mother. "At my house, we have breakfast even if we had a big supper the night before."

She fed them a hearty breakfast of sausage, eggs, and toast. Once again, they gobbled down everything on their plates as well as most of their second helpings.

Meryl pushed aside a portion of each item on her plate.

Lily disliked wasting food and always cleaned her plate. When she'd been greedy as a child, *Mamm* made her sit at the table until she'd finished every bite. But she didn't want to overstuff the girls. They probably had never had enough to eat, so they hadn't learned how much to take when food was unlimited.

She asked, "You're full?"

Meryl shook her head. "I gots to save some for Mommy."

A guilty look crossed Scarlett's face as she shoveled the last bite into her mouth. "I forgot. But she can eat the meatloaf."

"I have plenty of eggs and sausage." Lily didn't want them to worry about eating everything she served them. "I can make more for your mommy if she'd like some."

"You can?" Meryl's concerned expression relaxed into a broad smile, and she picked up her fork and finished up everything except a piece of toast.

"You can eat the toast if you want. There's more bread on the counter."

After checking where Lily pointed, Meryl ate her toast too.

"Now it's time for dishes and chores."

While they washed up and cleaned the kitchen, Lily took care of the horse and barn. She returned to puddles on the floor, but clean plates, silverware, and counters. The twins came out to help her hitch up the horse for church.

They'd never been around a horse before, so they stood far away. And when Daisy snorted and shook her mane, they jumped back and squealed.

"She's scary." Meryl pressed her back against the barn wall.

"Not really. She's gentle. Come on over and feel how soft she is."

With a little encouragement, Scarlett ventured over to pet Daisy's nose. "It's fuzzy, Mer. Try it."

After much coaxing, Meryl let Lily carry her over. With her face buried against Lily's shoulder, Meryl allowed Lily to guide her hand to Daisy's neck. "Ooo, that feels funny." Meryl lifted her head and peeked. "She's so big."

Both girls trailed Lily as she led Daisy out into the driveway and tied the horse to a post. Lily needed to leave soon, but she hadn't asked Aliyah about taking the children to church with her.

Just then, Scarlett screamed, "Mommy!" She ran toward a shadowy figure trudging down the road.

"Wait!" Lily hurried after Scarlett. When the person bent and hugged Scarlett, Lily let out a relieved breath. Meryl joined them, and as the girls and their mother walked over to Lily, the twins chattered away, interrupting and talking over each other.

Just before they reached Lily, Scarlett announced, "Oh, and Lily made us take baths and say our prayers."

At the word *prayers*, Aliyah's eyes hardened. "I don't want my daughters exposed to the Amish religion."

"We just thanked God for His blessings and prayed for your safety."

Aliyah shifted from one foot to the other. "I dislike—" She snapped her mouth shut. "Never mind." Her voice gruff, she added, "Thank you for thinking of me."

"How did the job go?"

"Better than in New York. Bosses and hotel guests in Pennsylvania don't seem as high pressure." Her jaw tightened, though, as she studied the dresses her daughters wore.

"I'm sorry they're in Plain clothes." Lily hadn't thought she'd offend Aliyah by lending her daughters something to wear. "I rinsed out their dresses last night, but they were still damp this morning."

Her eyes flashing lightning bolts of fury, Aliyah spit out her words. "Despite what you think, I'm perfectly capable of taking care of my daughters, and we don't need charity." She whirled around and stalked off.

The girls chased after her, but Scarlett slid to a stop, dragging Meryl back with her. "We forgot the meatloaf."

"I don't know . . ." At the girl's horrified looks, Lily swallowed what she'd planned to say: *I don't know if it'll upset your mother.* Judging from Aliyah's comments, she wouldn't appreciate her daughters bringing gifts of food, but Lily couldn't disappoint the girls. "Let's get the meal, and you can take it home."

She handed them the foil-wrapped bundles and followed them outside. Then she kept an eye on them as they dashed across the lawn, each holding a package.

An unfamiliar buggy slowed, and the driver craned his neck to look at her and the girls. He was too far away for Lily to see his face clearly, but his scrutiny made her nervous. She crossed her arms and stared at him.

Twice in the past two days, she'd had a prickly sensation of someone watching her. But maybe he hadn't been looking at her. Had he had been studying the twins?

Her inspection must have made him nervous because he urged his horse into a trot and disappeared.

Josiah's driver, Rusty, had returned to Gratz last night to be with his family for Sunday School and church. Josiah had arranged to spend a few days here. With his assistant manager in charge, Josiah didn't have to worry about his landscaping business. And he'd brought some of the more complicated designs along with him to complete.

But this morning, he needed to find a way to church. Because it was their off-Sunday, the owners of the bed-and-breakfast insisted Josiah use their buggy. Grateful for the offer, he left early so he could drive past the house he'd checked out yesterday.

As he drove past, the twins, dressed in clean, pressed Amish dresses rushed outside, each waving a foil package. Maybe yesterday they'd only been dressed in ragged clothes for gardening.

Their mother appeared on the back porch ready for church. She kept an eye on the girls as they ran toward an old shack. It looked like they were feeding a poor neighbor.

Suddenly, the woman turned his way and stared directly at him. Josiah turned his face away, so she wouldn't recognize him later in church, and clicked to the horse to make it move faster. He didn't want her to think he was stalking her.

That might be harder to accomplish than he'd expected. After the women filed into church later that morning and he'd picked the right person out in the crowd, he struggled to drag his gaze away. He couldn't let the congregation see him mooning over her like a lovesick teen.

What was wrong with him? How could he possibly be attracted to the woman who'd enticed his brother into sin? He could understand why Simon had fallen for her, but Josiah had better not make the same mistake.

With great effort, he swiveled his head and focused his full attention on the minister. The words of the sermon about avoiding temptation pierced his conscience. God must be sending him a direct message not to stray.

He limited himself to a few brief peeks during the next sermon and tried to sweep his gaze around the women's section in front of her and behind her. But somehow, she always ended up in his line of sight.

After the service and the meal, Josiah set off to find her. But whenever he strolled past the kitchen or the room where the women were eating, trying to appear casual and headed elsewhere, the young mother was always chattering to someone different. She reminded him of a gadfly, flitting about aimlessly, her mouth constantly moving.

A hand descended on his shoulder. "You having trouble finding the bath-room?" Thomas King pointed to the hallway behind them. "It's that way." The knowing look in his eyes revealed he suspected Josiah hadn't been lost.

Heat flooded Josiah's cheeks. *"Danke."* He headed in the direction Thomas had pointed.

The elderly man chuckled. "Lily's right pretty, ain't so? But more than that, she has a good heart."

Josiah pretended not to hear those comments as he scurried down the hall.

Lily? So that's her name. Josiah hadn't been able to read the name on the envelope. There had been an *li*, but it appeared to be part of a much longer name. Maybe Lily was a nickname.

Thomas was right about Lily's beauty, but as much as Josiah was drawn to the sweetness of her features, her talkativeness turned him off. He wouldn't want to be married to a woman whose mouth ran all day long.

Married? Wait, what am I thinking? Josiah reined in his thoughts with a sharp jerk. He hadn't even met this woman yet. The last thing he wanted was to get involved with his brother's ex-girlfriend. What would Simon think if Josiah brought Lily home to meet the family? Everyone would see the twins and know the truth. Or would they suspect the children belonged to Josiah? He and Simon resembled each other.

Josiah shook his head. No matter how pretty and good-hearted Lily was, he had no interest in her other than caring for her children—his brother's children.

As he exited the bathroom, he almost plowed into her and a friend chatting in the hallway.

"You are coming to the singing early tonight, right?" the woman asked Lily.

"Of course, but I have something important to talk about now."

Both of them glanced up and nodded as he edged past, but Lily barely paused in her rapid chattering. "I started to tell you about the twins earlier. I'm really worried about them. I never want them to go hungry again." Her brows drew together.

The other woman laid a hand on Lily's arm. "Don't worry. I'll organize a rotation of people to bring meals every day."

Hmm . . . Not only had Lily come after his brother for money, she also was begging for support from the church. Most likely, she expected Simon to send cash rather than drive all the way to Lancaster County to find her. She'd told him she didn't have enough money to feed the children, but here she was lining up others to bring meals every day. What kind of a scam was she running? He intended to find out and expose her.

CHAPTER FOUR

When Lily arrived home from church, Aliyah dashed out of the house. "Can I talk to you for a minute?"

"Of course, but I need to take care of my horse first. Would you like to come over for tea in half an hour?"

Aliyah shuffled her feet. "You don't have to feed me."

"It's only tea. I'm happy to share my water."

"After the way I treated you?"

Lily waved a hand. "You were upset, but that's all been forgotten. Why don't we start over as friends?"

Aliyah didn't meet her gaze. "You're as generous as my girls claimed." She pivoted and hurried off to her house. "I'll come back in half an hour," she called over her shoulder.

Sure enough, she showed up with the twins in tow. Dressed in too-short pants and tight shirts, they held the folded Amish dresses and stockings Lily had given them. They handed her the clothing and thanked her.

In her hands, Aliyah held a paper plate with four cinnamon rolls.

"Mommy got them at work," Scarlett chirped.

Meryl bounced on her toes. "They're day-old, but we can dip 'em to make 'em soft."

Aliyah's cheeks reddened to the color of ripe tomatoes. "Hush, girls." She tipped her head toward the plate. "These are to thank you for taking care of the girls. And I hope you'll accept my apology for my rudeness. You didn't deserve it after all you did for my daughters."

"Like I said before, let's forget it. Come in, so we can get to know each other. I'm glad we'll be neighbors."

After they'd all settled at the table and finished their tea and rolls, Lily beckoned to the girls and led them to the other end of the large kitchen. "I have a small cabinet here with games and toys for my nieces and nephews. You can choose whatever you'd like to play with while I talk to your mommy."

Lily returned to the table, poured herself and Aliyah another cup of tea, and settled in to discover more about her neighbor. After answering a few questions about her own life, she turned the conversation to Aliyah, and soon the young mother was spilling her life story.

"At sixteen, I ran away from my home in Georgia, hoping to be an actress. I'd gone as far north as Lancaster when I met Simon. He was Amish, but he didn't look it. I guess he was in *Rum*-something."

"*Rumschpringa?*"

"Yes, that's it. We both got small parts in one of the Sight and Sound plays." Aliyah's starry eyes revealed her love for Simon and for acting. She sat silent for a while, staring off into the distance. Lily stayed silent, waiting to hear the rest of the story.

This time, when Aliyah picked up the thread, dark storm clouds descended over her features. "Then I found out I was expecting. I wrote Simon a letter to tell him about the baby." She ran a finger around the rim of her tea cup. "I was too embarrassed and ashamed to tell him in person. Plus, I wanted to give him some time to think about it. He'd asked me to marry him, but I told him we were too young. I hoped with the baby coming . . ."

"He didn't plan to return to the Amish?"

Aliyah shrugged. "I don't know. I guess that's what he ended up doing. When I went to the house where he was staying, the man at the door took my letter and promised to give it to Simon. The next day, I returned to talk to him, but he'd disappeared. Nobody would tell me where he went. I tried to find him, but do you know how many Millers there are?"

Hundreds or thousands. Finding Simon would be like looking for a lost quilting needle in a mountain of fabric. Often, you only found it if you got poked in the finger.

"That day," Aliyah continued, "my dreams crashed and died. I had the girls and made it to New York, but I never made it on stage." She held up her rough, chapped hands. "I spent the best years of my life cleaning toilets and scrubbing floors, trying to keep my girls fed and put a roof over their heads."

"I'm sorry." For Lily, missing out on being an actress wasn't such a bad thing. And Aliyah was still quite young, but her eyes reflected the depths of her loss.

"I even named my girls after famous actresses I admired. But I guess you already figured that out." Aliyah paused. "Or maybe you didn't. You people don't watch TV or movies, do you?" Her hollow laugh held no mirth.

"No, we don't." Lily kept her words gentle. She didn't want Aliyah to feel judged.

"I dragged my daughters with me to work all hours of the day and night. They learned to sit quietly and hide whenever my boss came around. It's no life for kids, but I did what I could until I lost my job."

"What brought you back here?"

Aliyah hung her head. "You'll probably think I'm crazy."

"I think you're a good mom who did what she needed to do to survive."

"At a house I cleaned the week before I lost my job, I saw an article about this Amish garden designer in a decorating magazine. They'd snapped a picture of him from behind, but I could see a bit of his face. He looked so much like Simon, it took my breath away. And his last name was even Miller. I asked the lady if I could keep the magazine, and she let me. When we got evicted—"

"The girls mentioned that. It must have been hard."

Aliyah winced. "I didn't mean for them to see that, but I didn't have any choice. I had nowhere to leave them."

Lily tried to imagine not having anyone to lean on. Being a part of the Amish community meant she always had someone to turn to for help.

"Anyway, I had that magazine with me. And I looked up that landscaping company. When I called and asked about Simon, an employee gave me his address." Aliyah dragged in a deep breath and lowered her gaze. "I lied about why I wanted it."

Although Lily didn't agree with lying, she understood Aliyah's desperation.

"I wrote him a letter, telling him I planned to come here. He never answered me. But I came to Lancaster. Simon and I used to meet in that shack. He said it belonged to one of his relatives, but no one ever used it anymore."

Lily suspected Simon hadn't been truthful about that. When she was young, an *Englischer* owned the farm next door. Migrant workers often stayed in the shack during the harvest. After the man died, most of the land had been sold off to developers, who'd put up new homes, but the shack had stayed empty. Lily kept that information to herself. Aliyah had enough troubles already.

"If Simon's family owns the building, then my girls should have a right to stay in it." She lifted her chin. "Besides, we won't be there long. Now that I have a job, I'll save up enough for a security deposit on an apartment."

Lily would ask Thomas King who owned the property. He'd likely know. She'd contact the owner and pay rent on the shack until Aliyah moved out. Lily never wanted the girls to be evicted again.

~

The owner of the B and B stopped Josiah as he headed to his room after the church meal. "Since you're staying a few more days, I wondered if you'd need a buggy."

Josiah hadn't worked out his transportation issues. Hiring an *Englisch* driver when he knew nobody in the area would be difficult. "A buggy would be great. Any idea where I can rent one?"

"Our neighbor is in Pinecraft until the end of the month. I talked to his son, and you can use his *daed*'s horse and buggy if you'll care for and feed the horse. You're welcome to use our stable while you're here. I can take you over there now to pick it up, if you'd like."

"That would be wonderful. *Danke*." He have to get used to the horse and let the horse get used to him, but that solved his problem of getting to the singing tonight. Now he just needed to handle his brother's problem.

Maybe he'd figure that out at the singing. At least he hoped he would.

~

The girl next to Lily at the singing elbowed her and whispered, "That newcomer is wonderful handsome."

Lily couldn't help but agree. He'd ended up directly across from her, and every time she glanced up, he was studying her, a concerned frown etched into his brow. Did he think she'd done something wrong?

Her friend leaned over again. "He can't keep his eyes off you."

She was right, but an uneasy feeling crept over Lily. Rather than the dreamy expression of a man interested in her, his gaze assessed her, judged her, found her wanting.

~

When they broke for snacks, Josiah still hadn't figured Lily out. She seemed sweet and quiet, so unlike the busybody she'd been that morning at church. Which one was her real personality, or did she go from whirlwind to withdrawn?

A group of younger boys shoved past him to be first at the snack table. Jostling each other, they knocked into a petite girl with Down syndrome and a limp. She teetered, and Josiah dashed over to steady her, but Lily caught the girl before she fell.

"Here, Martha." Lily led her to a nearby seat. "Why don't you sit down? I'll get you a plate."

Martha's eyes welled with tears as she clutched her elbow. As Lily took off, Josiah reached Martha's side.

He knelt in front of her. "Did you get hurt?"

Martha nodded, and teardrops spilled onto her cheeks. "Those boys hit my arm."

"Will you let me see?"

She tipped her arm up. The collision hadn't left a mark or bruise.

"I'm sorry it hurts, but it'll be fine."

"What will be fine?" Lily stood over him, a questioning look on her face.

Josiah gulped. Being this close to her did strange things to his insides. He forced out words and hoped they made sense. "The boys bumped Martha's elbow, but it's better now. Isn't it, Martha?" He turned his attention to the young girl, hoping to get his heartbeat under control.

Martha beamed, joy lighting her whole face. "You're nice."

"*Danke.*" He couldn't help smiling.

"No, *danke* for taking care of Martha." Lily interrupted their exchange. "That was kind of you.

He stood and brushed off his pant legs. "Anyone would have done the same."

Lily shot back. "I didn't see anyone else come to her rescue, did you?"

"*Jah*, I did."

Her eyebrows rose. "You did?"

"I certainly did." He pointed to the plate she'd held. "You did."

"Ah, you." Lily tossed her head. "Very funny." She bent and handed Martha the snacks.

"Not funny at all. Very kind."

"*Danke* for the compliment, but you would have done the same."

"How do you know that?" He flashed her a teasing grin.

"Because you did."

Her bell-like laugh strummed chords deep in his soul. "Would you like me to get you a plate?" He had to do something to take his eyes off her.

"You don't have to do that."

"I want to. Besides, I'm sure Martha would like your company. Wouldn't you, Martha?"

Martha nodded as her gaze bounced from one to the other. "Stay with me, Lily."

~

"Sure." Lily didn't care if she got refreshments. She'd had plenty to eat before she came.

As soon as he walked away, she sank onto the bench next to Martha before her knees collapsed. His smile had given her heart palpitations.

Who was he? And why was he here? He didn't seem to be related to anyone at church. She'd had plenty of opportunity to ask as she'd flitted around after church that morning requesting food and clothing and help for her new neighbors.

A short while later, Martha's rescuer returned bearing two plates. He handed her one.

"I hope you like what I picked. Lily, right?"

"How do you know that?"

"Martha told me."

"I did?" Martha squeaked.

"*Ah-ha.* You called me by name earlier, Martha." Lily grinned at her, but her smile faltered as she turned to face him. "And you are?"

He gave a slight bow. "Josiah."

"No last name?"

"Miller. But there are plenty of people with that name."

Maybe so. But none who looked like him or made her pulse pitter-patter like this.

"And do you have a last name, Lily?"

"Bontrager."

"Mine's Troyer," Martha told him.

"Nice to meet you, Martha Troyer, and you too, Lily Bontrager."

"Nice to meet you too, Josiah Miller."

CHAPTER FIVE

$\mathcal{L}$ ily's sassy tone made him smile. If he wasn't careful, though, he could easily end up falling for her.

"Time for more singing," someone announced.

Neither of them had eaten anything from their plates. But good thing they had to get back to singing before he made a fool of himself. Lily and Martha stayed where they were, so the girls on the other side of the table rearranged themselves. Now that Lily wasn't across from him, Josiah had trouble sneaking peeks at her.

During the next hymn, he decided the only way to find out more about Lily and the twins was to drive her home after the singing. Would she go with him?

As soon as the last song ended, he rushed over to her side of the table. "Could I drive you home?"

"Me?" Martha squealed.

"Of course," Josiah said smoothly. "Why don't you get your coat?"

Martha rushed across the room, yelling at a young man who must be her brother, "I have a ride home after the singing."

He frowned. "With who?"

Martha took his hand and dragged him over. "With Josiah."

"Um, I don't think . . ." Her brother gave Josiah an apologetic smile.

"It's all right. I invited her."

He studied Josiah suspiciously. "You did?"

"*Jah*, if Lily doesn't mind coming along to show me the directions. I'm new here." He turned to Lily and quirked an eyebrow.

She weighed the suggestion for a few moments. "I guess I could do that."

"Martha," her brother whispered, "this is just as friends."

"I know, I know. Josiah is a good friend. He's very nice." She leaned over and whispered in a voice that carried, "I think he wants to be Lily's boyfriend. He looks at her all the time."

Ach! Had he been that obvious? Josiah's face burned hotter than the crackling logs in the nearby fireplace.

Lily laughed uncomfortably. "I'd better get my coat. And I'll need to let Esther know I won't be riding home with them."

Josiah went to find his jacket too. Then he escorted Martha and Lily outside. Martha sat up front, and when she got home, she begged Lily to walk her to the door.

"I think he likes you lots." Martha's words reached Josiah's ears. "Maybe you'll get married."

Josiah shook his head. Absolutely not. It surprised him a girl as lovely as Lily had never married. But then he reminded himself about why he was here. How many Amish men would want to marry a woman who'd had children out of wedlock? Even if she was gorgeous and kind and . . .

Stop right there!

No matter how appealing Lily was, Josiah had only one thing in mind tonight—finding out about the twins.

∼

Lily cringed when Martha announced Josiah wanted to be her boyfriend. Even worse, Martha had mentioned marriage. Lily only hoped he hadn't overheard. And even more, she prayed he couldn't tell how her heart sped up around him.

He'd asked to drive her home. That had to mean something, didn't it? Usually, couples got to know each other first. But she and Josiah had managed to have a fun conversation because of Martha. And Lily admired how he'd jumped right in to help Martha.

"He's nice, isn't he?" Martha asked as she reached her front porch.

"Very nice."

Martha's lips stretched into an even wider smile. "Can I be your sidesitter?"

"Of course. If I ever get married."

"You will. Josiah really likes you." Martha opened the door and went inside, leaving Lily standing on the steps, stunned and embarrassed.

If Josiah had overheard this conversation, what would he think?

She wished she could walk home instead of having to get back in the buggy. Her steps slowed as she neared the passenger side. But Josiah's friendly smile calmed her nerves.

Martha might be right. He did seem to like her. That made her spirits sing a joyous chorus. Maybe God had brought someone into her life after all. Maybe she wouldn't have to live alone. She tried not to get her hopes up, but having someone to date would be a special blessing.

Those thoughts made her so tongue-tied, she couldn't come up with any conversation. Martha had kept the talk lively. Now that she was gone, though, Lily wanted to retreat into her shell. She couldn't do that. Not when she needed to make a good impression on the first man she'd ever been out with. But what could she say?

~

Josiah waited until the horse had moved away from the curb and into traffic to ask for directions to Lily's house. He already knew how to get there, but he didn't want her to know he'd driven by her house. Twice, in fact.

After she'd gotten him onto the main road, he racked his brain for a way to ask her about the twins. He couldn't just come out and say, *Tell me about your twins.* Or she'd know he'd been checking her out.

"So, do you have any children?" he blurted out the question so abruptly, she stared at him as if he were crazy. He should have found a less offensive way to phrase that.

"Me?" She gave him a puzzled look, then her face cleared. "Oh, you mean in my family?"

Of course, he meant in her family. Where else would her children be?

"I have three older brothers and two younger sisters. *Daed* died when we were younger, but *Mamm* died a few months ago."

"I'm sorry to hear that."

"*Danke.* It's been a hard adjustment. I took care of her for more than a year, and so much of my time revolved around her needs, I'm still trying to fill all the empty spots in my days." A shadow crossed her face, and she swallowed hard.

Josiah understood how much it hurt to lose a parent. "It takes a while. Give yourself time."

"You're right. I've been praying for different things to do. That's helped." She turned to him. "Tell me about your family."

This conversation had gotten way off track. When he'd asked if she had children, she'd changed that to children in her family. That hadn't been what he was asking. Had she deliberately avoided the question?

She was looking at him as if expecting an answer. *Oh, right.* She'd asked about his family.

"Not much to tell. My parents died when I was eighteen. Being the oldest, I raised my younger brother and two younger sisters. They're all grown and married now."

"But you aren't?"

Wasn't that obvious? "*Nay*, I'm not." How could he get back to the twins? "When I asked about children, I meant did you have any children of your own."

Lily gaped at him. "If I did, why would I be at the singing?"

"Because you're unmarried?" Interesting. She didn't deny having children. Instead, she'd asked a question.

"*Jah*, I am." Hurt flared in her eyes.

He hadn't meant to make her feel bad or ashamed. So far, he'd reminded her of her mother's passing and brought up her single state. Maybe he should stop avoiding his real question. "I couldn't help hearing you talk about your twins to people at church today."

"*My* twins? *Nay*, they're not mine. I'm concerned about a neighbor's children."

What? He'd offered her a ride home because he'd believed she was Simon's ex-girlfriend and planned to talk about why she needed money for the twins. Now, he couldn't do that. But he might get some information about them.

"You seemed really concerned about these twins. Can you tell me about them?"

"It's heartbreaking. I only met them yesterday, but God has been leading me to take care of them. Their mother is having trouble providing for them, but she's proud and doesn't like to accept help."

That didn't match with the letter she sent to his brother, imploring him to send her money.

Lily described the twin's reactions to meals. "I can't even imagine what their lives have been like. Going to bed hungry or skipping meals. Saving a portion of their food so their mother doesn't starve. No child should have to live that way."

A sick feeling roiled Josiah's gut. These were his brother's little ones. Simon should have been taking care of them. That poor mother. "I hate to think about what they've lived through."

"Me too. The little girls told me about being evicted, seeing their furniture and things thrown out into the street after their mother lost her job. Little Meryl never got her stuffed bunny or some of her other toys back. You should have seen her face when she told me that." Tears sprang to Lily's eyes.

Josiah wanted to reach out to comfort her, but he clenched one hand in his lap and the other on the reins. "Those poor girls."

Even as he said the words, they bounced back and stabbed him straight through the heart. He owned most of that responsibility. He could have checked on Simon's girlfriend over the years. But he hadn't known she was expecting.

Lily kept talking. "*Jah*, the twins have had a rough time. And their mother has been through a lot in her young life. The father of her babies abandoned her."

"Maybe he didn't know about them." Simon had been shocked to learn he had children. If he'd known, he would have taken responsibility.

Lily shook her head. "That's the saddest part. She wrote her boyfriend a letter letting him know and dropped it off at the house where he lived. When she went back the next day, he'd disappeared. He just took off without telling her or giving her any way to contact him. I don't understand how any man could be that cruel, that uncaring."

The nausea swirling in Josiah's stomach traveled to his throat. He swallowed down the bile. He could understand it. Simon had never known.

Josiah had gotten that letter telling about the babies. Afraid Simon might go back to the girl, Josiah had hidden that letter from his brother. He'd torn it into tiny pieces and thrown away. Neither he nor Simon had ever read it.

Everything those little girls suffered over the years has been my fault.

CHAPTER SIX

$\mathcal{L}$ ily regretted going into the graphic details. Josiah's pale face and haunted eyes showed how seriously he took this situation.

"Are you all right?" she asked in alarm.

Josiah didn't answer. He stared straight ahead as if he hadn't heard her, as if he were a million miles away, as if he were reliving all the pain the girls had gone through.

She wanted to comfort him. "Try not to dwell on the past."

His head whipped around, and he stared at her. "How did you guess?"

"From your expression." Lily reached out and laid a hand on his arm. He flinched, and she withdrew it. "We didn't know, so all we can do is make it right from now on."

"I will do that," he said with such fierceness it almost frightened her. "What can I do?"

"The church is helping. They'll provide meals. And a few contractors will renovate the shack to add heat, electricity, and running water."

"The mother and children don't have that? How can they live there during this cold snap? The temperatures go pretty low at night."

"I know. I dropped off some quilts, and the owner of Allgyer's Hardware promised to leave a space heater on the porch. Aliyah doesn't want charity, but if she doesn't see the giver, she can't reject the gift. At least, I hope she won't."

"What if she does?"

"She might deny herself, but she cares too much about her daughters to make them do without."

"You're sure?"

"I can't be positive. Maybe we should pray."

"Good idea."

Josiah closed his eyes briefly, but even after he opened them to concentrate on the road, his lips moved silently. What arrested Lily's attention, though, was his fervent expression. He really seemed to care about this family's needs.

Once again, her pulse fluttered. How had she been so lucky to get asked out by a man with such a loving heart? Lily bowed her head and thanked God for bringing Josiah into her life. She also prayed the two of them could work together to help Aliyah and the twins.

~

Josiah's thoughts pinwheeled out of control. What was he going to do? How could he make up for his past mistake? He'd doomed Simon's girlfriend and her children to a tragic life. He could take care of them now, but how could he ever erase the pain he'd caused?

Lily lifted her head after praying and flashed him the most beautiful smile. Her angelic face and expression twisted the sharp edge of guilt even deeper into his heart.

"Maybe we could work together on this?"

He sucked in a breath at her sweet trusting question and innocent eyes. She gazed at him as if . . . *Ach, no!* She didn't think he'd offered to drive her home because he wanted to court her, did she?

Her shining eyes dimmed when he didn't respond right away. Her full lower lip trembled.

Why did she have to be so appealing? So kind and caring? So . . . so . . .

How could he say *nay?* She ducked her head and looked on the verge of tears. He didn't want to hurt her again or make her cry.

Josiah cleared his throat and, against his better judgment, said, "Let's do that."

After all, she didn't need to know about his connection to the twins' difficulties. Neither did Aliyah. As Lily had counseled earlier, he wouldn't dwell on the past. Maybe he didn't need to mention his brother. No one here knew about that situation. No one but Aliyah, and he didn't need to meet her to assist with Lily's plans.

Although his conscience nagged at him, he pushed away those warnings. And he ignored the alarm bells cautioning him he'd be leading Lily on when he had no intention of offering her a relationship. No way could he risk losing his heart to Aliyah's neighbor.

~

Lily turned to Josiah, startled that he'd turned in the right direction at the crossroads. "You turned here without asking." Maybe they'd become so tuned to each other's thoughts, Josiah had picked up on hers.

He shifted in the seat and tugged at his collar. "I, um, did it without thinking."

She hadn't meant to make him nervous or embarrassed. "Don't worry," she reassured him. "You're going the right way."

He breathed out a relieved sigh. "That's, um, good."

"I'll try to pay more attention to the road." Lily wanted to clap a hand over her mouth. Why had she blurted that out? Now he'd know she'd been watching him instead. She didn't want him to think she was too forward. "I mean, our conversation has been so interesting."

Josiah cleared his throat. His answer came out rather choked. "I agree."

Ach, he really did care deeply about others.

"When you come to the next stop sign—it's about half a mile from here—you'll turn left on my road."

"All right."

Had a chill entered his voice, or was she imagining it? Maybe he regretted the trip ending so soon. She certainly did. But they'd have plenty of time to get to know each other as they helped Aliyah.

Lily wanted to dance with joy. Josiah had sneaked peeks at her during the singing and whenever he wasn't absorbed in watching the road or worrying about Aliyah and the girls. Not only did he seem interested in her, but he also wanted to care for the twins.

They may have started their relationship as almost strangers, but this would give them plenty of time to get to know each other better. Lily didn't have to spend more time with him, though, to know he had a good heart. First, he'd been kind to Martha—even driving her home—and then, he'd been deeply affected by Aliyah's plight. His goodness, generosity, and faith shone through his actions. What more could she ask in the man she hoped to date?

Martha's comment about marriage rang in Lily's ears. Courtship often led to marriage. Although it was much too early to be thinking about weddings, little trills filled her soul in anticipation of the future.

~

Josiah couldn't believe he'd turned toward her house without asking. Finding out the truth about Aliyah and Simon's girls had distracted him. So had being in the buggy with Lily. Her presence had totally disrupted his life.

If only he could stay here and court her . . . But that was much too danger-ous. Sooner or later, he might run into Aliyah. Would she recognize him?

What if Lily heard more of Aliyah's stories and figured out Josiah was related to Simon?

He'd been so lost in thought, Lily's soft question startled him.

"How long have you been in the area?" She gazed at him expectantly, as if she couldn't wait to hear his answer. He'd never been around a woman who seemed so attuned to others like this. Or maybe he'd never been close enough to find out.

Josiah answered with the truth. "Two days."

Lily sucked in a breath. "Only two days?"

"Where are you living?" When he hesitated, she nibbled at her lower lip. "Sorry if that sounded nosy. You don't have to answer, if you don't want to."

"It's all right. I'm at Miller's Bed and Breakfast."

"Are they relatives of yours?"

His laugh came out strained. "Not that I know of."

"But why didn't you go to their church?" Lily clapped a hand over her mouth. "That's none of my business."

"This is their off-Sunday. I really wanted to go to church."

"What brought you to Lancaster?"

Josiah swallowed hard. Lies floated to mind, but he didn't want to add to his earlier dishonesty. He should just admit the truth and lift the heavy burden on his soul. But he liked how Lily gazed at him with admiration in her eyes. A man could get used to that. He mentally shook himself. If he told her he'd been the one who'd caused Aliyah's suffering, she'd never look at him that way again.

"I, um . . ." He hesitated. "Business," he hedged.

"Oh, what business are you in?"

Answering that wouldn't get him in trouble. "I own a landscaping company."

"And you think the Lancaster area will be better for business? Where were you before?"

"I'm from Gratz." Although he spoke the truth, his answer implied he'd moved to Lancaster. He needed to stop Lily's line of questioning before he told any more half-truths. "Have you lived here all your life?"

"I have." Her gentle smile revealed her fondness for her home. "I still live in the house I grew up in. I was the youngest and the only one not married when *Mamm* passed away. My brothers and sisters already had houses and farms, so they let me stay."

"That's nice." So, that large house belonged to her.

"What about you? Did you always live in Gratz?"

Why did she turn every question around, cornering him?

"I stayed in the house after my parents died. That let me keep the whole family together." Before she could ask anything else, he pulled up to the stop sign. "This is where I turn?"

"*Jah.*" She waved in the direction he'd planned to go. "I'll let you know when we get to the next turn."

He smiled at her. A big mistake. Their eyes met and held. Next thing he knew, he was drowning in depths of soft green framed by sweeps of long eyelashes. If a car hadn't pulled up behind them, he might have stayed stuck in that spot all night.

CHAPTER SEVEN

*J*osiah waited for Lily to get in the house before he turned the buggy around in her driveway. He planned to pause beside that small shack.

Were they actually living in that rundown building? His stomach twisted. The blame for this lay with him—and him alone.

A small girl darted from the doorway. "Lily," she yelled, "can we stay with you tonight?"

Lily had been closing the door. She opened it wide and beamed at the child. Not just any child. His brother's daughter. His niece.

Their family should have been taking care of this little one. And her twin. And their *mamm*.

"Of course, Scarlett. Where's Meryl?"

Out of breath, the little girl panted. "She's coming."

Scarlett? Meryl? What odd names for Simon's children. Josiah didn't know any *Englischers* with those names, and he'd spent plenty of time around them when he designed their gardens.

The other twin flew across the lawn hugging her arms around herself. Her too tight top barely reached her middle. Like her sister's shirt, the fabric had frayed from many washings. They'd both outgrown their sweatpants, leaving their bare ankles exposed to the chilly weather. Neither of them wore jackets.

The one Lily had called Scarlett stood shivering on the porch until her sister caught up with her, despite Lily's insistence she come in. When Meryl reached the porch, Scarlett put an arm around her sister and urged her through the door first.

Those two girls needed warm clothes and spring jackets right away. He couldn't do it tonight because stores had closed. Besides, he'd never shop on a Sunday. But first thing tomorrow morning, he'd see to it.

So far, the girls' mother hadn't appeared. Josiah needed to let Lily know his plan. He'd risk Aliyah seeing him, but he had to take a chance.

He hopped out of the buggy and hooked his horse to the nearby hitching post. He headed for the back porch. With Aliyah's house near the front of the property line, he hoped to stay out of sight.

After knocking, he bounced from one foot to the other, praying Lily would come quickly. The longer he stood here, the more likely Aliyah was to glance out the window or come after the girls.

Lily answered, and her eyes widened. "Josiah?" The surprise in her eyes softened into pleasure—and an invitation to enter. She held open the door.

He stepped inside. "Listen, I saw the twins run over here. I'm worried they aren't dressed warmly enough for the weather. Tomorrow morning, I'd like to take them to the store to get clothes, jackets, and shoes."

She sucked in a breath. "That's so kind of you."

The hero-worship in her eyes made him sick. If only she knew the truth. . .

"I, um, don't know much about buying girls' clothes, so if you could come along?" He left the question hanging, hoping her answer would be *jah*.

"Of course. I'd be happy to." Her bubbly, enthusiastic response and the stars shining in her eyes made it clear she'd mistaken his invitation for a date.

He didn't want more guilt added to the burden already on his conscience. "Will tomorrow at nine work?"

At his clipped words, her lips slipped from a wide, generous welcome to a *just-acquaintances* smile. He regretted his curt tone because it hurt her and also because he missed her beaming expression and the admiring looks she'd directed his way.

To prevent himself from trying to bring the spotlight of attention back in his direction, he focused on the neat mudroom. The only thing out of place were four worn shoes, one with the sole completely worn through, lying tumbled on the floor. "Where are the twins?"

Lily laughed, and the melodious sound filled him with longing—for a home, a wife, and a family. He concentrated on the shoe with the hole. Dreams of the future wouldn't be found here.

"Can't you hear them upstairs?"

Josiah had been concentrating so hard on not getting lured in by Lily's sweetness and beauty, he'd missed the scuffling and giggling overhead.

"I told them to put on my nieces' dresses and tights so they'd be warmer. I'll make sure they change out of them before they go home tomorrow. It'll be *wunderbar* for them to have some warm *Englisch* clothes to wear home." She smiled up at him shyly, adoringly.

Josiah's heartbeat galloped like a runaway horse. He drew in a long, slow breath, attempting to rein in his thundering pulse.

Lily's forehead creased into a concerned frown. At first, he assumed she'd noticed his reaction to her, but she went back to talking about the twins and their mother. "Aliyah wouldn't be happy to know her daughters are wearing Plain dresses. She can't stand Amish clothes. Or people."

Lily's words washed over Josiah like a sudden dousing from a freezing hose. He'd caused that.

"I hope she'll change her mind after she gets to know us. Meanwhile, I'm trying to show her God's love."

If anyone could do that, Lily could.

An explosive *One, two, three* came from above, and the girls ricocheted down the stairs.

"I was first."

"*Nuhn-uh.* I beat you. Race you to the kitchen. One, two, three."

The twins burst into the kitchen and skidded to a stop. Josiah's rapid pulse went careening in the opposite direction as he and the five-year-olds locked gazes.

"Who are you?" the winner demanded. The rebellious thrust of her chin and her suspicious squint were a mirror image of her dad's childhood reaction to strangers.

Josiah's eyes stung. For five whole years, he'd denied these little ones time with their father, grandparents, and extended family. He'd also been responsible for their poverty.

When he didn't answer, the miniature copycat of her dad thrust her hands on hips. "I'm Scarlett, and this is Meryl."

From Meryl's pout, she didn't appreciate her sister introducing her. Or maybe losing the race had upset her. But she echoed her sister's question. "Who is you?" She studied him.

"I'm Josiah." He hoped they wouldn't recognize his name. Had Aliyah told them about their father? Luckily, neither girl showed any sign of recognition.

A loud pounding on the front door startled all of them.

Scarlett's triumphant grin disappeared. "Oh, no. Bet that's Mommy."

Meryl sucked on her forefinger. "She said it ain't nice to ask to stay here again."

Ach! Josiah's own internal warning kicked into high gear. "I need to go. See you tomorrow morning."

Could he sneak out without Aliyah seeing him?

~

Lily didn't even get to say goodbye to Josiah because he rushed away so fast. She hurried to answer Aliyah's battering at the door. Lily had hoped to introduce him to Aliyah, so he could meet the person he'd be helping.

But maybe Lily's reaction to him had made him eager to leave. After she'd let her attraction to him show on her face, he'd become stiff and standoffish.

She pulled open the front door. "Hello, Aliyah. Come in."

"No, thank you. I just came to get my girls."

Scarlett and Meryl hid behind Lily's skirt as best they could, but Aliyah's eyes narrowed. Too late, Lily realized the girls had on Amish clothes.

"I told you I didn't want my children exposed to Amish ways." Aliyah glared at Lily.

"I'm so sorry. They looked chilly. I only wanted to warm them up."

"Are you implying that I don't take care of my children?"

"No, of course not."

"Let's go, girls. Get back into your own clothes. I don't have time. I'm going to be late for work."

"They're welcome to stay here again," Lily offered.

"I already told them it isn't polite to ask. They sneaked off while I was bathing."

"I'm glad to know you have water." Lily had expected the shack to have no plumbing.

"We gots to get it at the pump," Meryl volunteered. Despite her mother's scowl and signal to shush, Meryl added, "It's freezing cold." She shivered.

"*Ach*, I'm so sorry. You're welcome to use my bathroom and shower."

Aliyah stuck her nose in the air. "It's only temporary until we get an apartment."

"I understand. It doesn't make sense to hook up plumbing when you don't plan to stay long."

"That's right." Aliyah's face relaxed.

"I'd do the same for any of my neighbors. Please come over any time."

Scarlett sent her mother a pleading look. "Lily's bathroom ain't stinky like the outhouse."

Lily swallowed back a gasp. They were using the old outhouse near the woods? She thought it had been padlocked years ago.

Red crept into Aliyah's cheeks. "Time to go."

"Please let them stay. We had so much fun together last night. And they kept me from being lonely. They're such a blessing."

"A blessing? *Humph*. Wish they were that for me."

"Please, Mommy? Pretty please?"

"Oh, all right. If you're sure they're no bother?"

"I love having them."

"Be good," she warned her daughters.

Both of them let out loud, relieved sighs when their mother turned to leave.

"We going have fun, ain't we, Lily?" Meryl sidled up to her, and Lily put an arm around the small girl's shoulder.

"We are." Having the girls here would keep her mind off the mistakes she'd made with Josiah. She only hoped she could fix them tomorrow.

~

Josiah dashed out the back door. Feeling like a fool, he flattened himself against the side of the house so Aliyah couldn't see him through the kitchen window. Would she recognize him? He couldn't take that chance. He had to get out of here without her spotting him. He jogged to his buggy and kept his face averted as his horse trotted down the driveway.

But he couldn't resist one brief glance in her direction as he turned onto the road. He might have known her face, but from the back, her reddish hair surprised him.

Five years ago, her hair had been a ghastly shade of purple. Why she'd want to cover up the auburn hair God had given her, he'd never understand. At least, she'd gone back to her natural color. He hoped she no longer had piercings in her eyebrows, nose, and lips. The thought of rings through those delicate body parts had turned his stomach the day he'd met her, so he hadn't looked at her closely back then. Plus, he'd been trying to get rid of her before Simon discovered she'd come to visit.

Now, though, that memory made him sick. He'd answered the door, grabbed the letter, thanked her, and slammed the door shut. He'd just let out a major sigh of relief that he'd accomplished his mission when Simon rushed into the room.

"Who was at the door?"

It was the first and only time Josiah had ever deliberately lied. "A delivery person."

Simon glanced at him askance, and Josiah almost—almost—broke down and confessed. With the letter still dangling from two fingers behind his back, Josiah reminded himself his brother's soul was more important than any message the *Englischer* had delivered.

For all Josiah knew, this girl might convince Simon to stay in Bird-in-Hand. That would never do. Josiah had promised to bring his brother home, to get him out of this life of sin.

And Josiah did exactly that. He waited until Simon left the room for his suitcase. Then Josiah ripped the letter to shreds and buried it under garbage in the trash can. Less than an hour later, the driver took him and his sullen brother home to Upper Dauphin County.

After talking with the bishop, Simon confessed what he'd done and agreed to start baptismal classes when they began the following year. He'd started taking Katie out several months after they both had been baptized, and the family never brought up Simon's past again.

Josiah had put that purple-haired girl out of his mind long ago. Until that letter came. Now, though, no matter what he did, no matter how much he gave, he could never make up for the harm he'd caused. Aliyah and the twins would haunt his dreams forever.

CHAPTER EIGHT

*J*osiah tossed and turned all night. As he'd expected, his past and present responsibilities kept him awake, but so did a petite blonde with an enticing smile. He welcomed the dawn with gratitude. Today, he could put things to right. And as soon as he'd done that, he'd hurry home.

When he reached Lily's house a little before nine, the girls had their noses pressed against the window pane.

Scarlett flung open the front door. "That man's here."

Josiah smiled. "Ready to go shopping?"

She nodded and pranced out the door. Meryl trailed behind.

"We gonna ride in that?" Scarlett pointed to the buggy.

"*Jah*, I mean, yes. You'd better get your jackets first."

"We don't have no coats."

"Didn't you need them in New York?"

Scarlett's head swished back and forth. "Mommy din't let us go outside much."

"But we was still cold." Meryl shivered, and her large brown eyes, so like Simon's, flashed with remembered pain.

Each word they spoke lashed Josiah's conscience. How could he ever make this up to them?

"Meryl? Scarlett?" Lily's worried voice floated out to them.

"They're here," Josiah called, "but they don't have jackets." He reached into the buggy and brought out blankets to wrap around them.

He tucked a blanket around Meryl and lifted her onto the backseat of the buggy. The little girl squealed with delight. Josiah wanted to hug her. She reminded him so much of his youngest sister when she was small. But to them, he was still a stranger.

Josiah snuggled Scarlett in beside Meryl and turned to find Lily standing on the doorstep, holding two sweaters. He melted at the tenderness in her eyes. How could he leave her and these little ones to return home?

~

Lily's heart swelled at Josiah's gentleness with the girls. He'd make a *wunderbar daed.* "I brought sweaters, but I think they'll be warm and snug all wrapped up like that."

"Hard to believe they don't have jackets. Let's get those first before we do the rest of the shopping."

The twins squealed as Josiah flicked the reins and the horse started off.

Meryl clung to Scarlett. "It's noisy and bouncy."

"Not as noisy as a train." Scarlett leaned forward. "Is this like them roller-coasters? I ain't never been on one, but on TV they makes people scream."

"I've never ridden one either." And Lily had no desire to.

Riding in the buggy excited the girls, but it couldn't compare to shopping. Wide-eyed, the girls stared at the racks of clothing in the children's section of the large department store.

Scarlett tilted her head and gave Josiah the side-eye. "We each get one jacket? Any one we wants?"

"That's right. Pick your favorite."

She squinted at him. "Where we get the money?" She planted her hands on her hips. "We ain't gonna steal them."

"Don't worry. I'm paying."

"You sure?" Meryl looked him up and down as if to be sure he was telling the truth. "You got lots of money?"

"It's all right," Lily assured Meryl. "Josiah also plans to get you some clothes. He has enough to pay for everything." At least she hoped he did. He had offered, after all. If he didn't, she take care of the rest of the bill.

In less than an hour, Lily had helped the girls select five new outfits each, a pair of sneakers, and a jacket. Their eyes sparkled with awe as they slipped on new clothes, shoes, and jackets in the spacious store restroom. Then, clutching large bags to their chests, they skipped out to the buggy.

After she settled in the back seat, Meryl ran her hand over the fuzzy sleeve of her jacket. "They ain't got nothin' this good at the thrift shop."

"I have one more place to go before we head home." Josiah pulled into the parking lot of a bank. "We should get your mommy a present too." He returned clutching a checkbook that he handed to Lily. "This might help Aliyah rent an apartment and take care of some expenses."

Lily couldn't believe his generosity. And it didn't end there. He stopped at the pretzel shop and bought each of them a warm soft pretzel. As their eyes met over the girls' heads, Lily let hers thank him for all he'd done.

Sparks flew between them, and Josiah's tender smile lit a flame inside her. She'd never been so attracted to a man as she was to him. She poured her deepest emotions and gratitude into the looks she sent him. His gazes returned those feelings. Hope blossomed anew in her soul.

Scarlett tugged at Josiah's hand. He bent down to her eye level, and she threw her arms around his neck. "This was the bestest day ever."

Meryl nodded and hugged him too. Josiah hugged them back, and after he'd untangled himself from their buttery fingers and stood, he studied the girls for a long time. His eyes appeared damp, but maybe it was only a trick of the light.

Then he straightened and stared off into a distance. His lips twisted, and his eyes grew shuttered. He'd blocked Lily out completely.

Josiah could barely speak around the lump blocking his throat. These precious girls should be part of his family, but how could he ever have a relationship with them? Leaving would be so hard. And he could never forget them or Lily.

Lily herded the twins to the buggy. "*Danke* for all you've done for them."

"Don't thank me. Thank God." He deserved no praise. The gratefulness in Lily's expression made him squirm. He'd only just begun to pay down the gigantic debt he owed.

"We should go." He pulled two napkins he'd tucked in his coat pocket and wiped his nieces' faces. "What time is their mother expecting them?"

"I'm not sure. She got home around five this morning. I left a note telling her I'd watch her daughters while she slept. She'll probably sleep until noon or so."

In his joy at outfitting his nieces with necessities, he'd forgotten about avoiding Aliyah. They'd make it home before she awoke. Josiah breathed easier.

He'd drop everyone off, go back to the B and B to collect his things, and then call a driver to take him home. The thought depressed him.

By the time they pulled into the driveway, Meryl had fallen asleep. Scarlett's eyes drooped. They'd had a busy and exciting morning.

Josiah turned to Lily. "If you help Scarlett inside, I'll carry Meryl."

She nodded, but her eyes reflected his sadness. He'd hurt her by turning away. Yet, what else could he do? Cutting it off was for the best. Still, it didn't lessen the pain. How could he have gotten so entangled with two small girls and one lovely woman in such a short time?

CHAPTER NINE

*J*osiah held the door open for Lily and, with his other arm, cuddled Meryl close to his chest. A picture flitted through his mind of him and Lily as parents, bringing their children inside after a family outing.

A sharp pain stabbed through him. That could never be. He'd been living a lie.

Aliyah came charging out of her house, screeching, "What are you doing with my children? Did I give you permission to take them anywhere?" Her words shot out like bullets, each one hitting Josiah in his gut.

But she hadn't been aiming her firepower at him. She hurtled toward Scarlett, and snatched her hand from Lily's. "What have you done to her?"

"She got a little sleepy on the ride home." Lily tried to soothe Aliyah, but the irate mother only scowled.

Then she whirled on Josiah. "Put my baby down this instant. How dare you —?" She froze in place as her gaze reached his face. Her mouth opened and closed, but no sound came out.

Josiah's arm tightened around Meryl. He wouldn't put her down. Not out here. She'd wake up disoriented. He'd set her on the couch.

All the color drained from Aliyah's cheeks. "You. . ." She sucked in a breath, and her whole body expanded like a mother bear ready to fight for her cub. "Give me my baby now," she thundered. "You have no rights to her. Not after abandoning me like that."

"What?" Lily's mouth gaped open. "You know each other?"

Josiah said *no*, as Aliyah said *yes*.

"You're a liar." She hissed her words out through clenched teeth.

"You've mistaken me for someone else."

"Oh, no I haven't. I'd know your face anywhere."

Her brow furrowed, Lily's gaze ping-ponged back and forth between them. Then, Scarlett swayed against her mother.

Lily reached out to support the little girl. "Let's go inside and put Scarlett down for a nap. Josiah can lay Meryl on the couch."

"Josiah?" Aliyah's bitter laugh carried a world of pain. "You lied to her about your name? Why? So you can get another woman in trouble?"

"You've made a mistake." He kept his words low and even. "My name really is Josiah."

∾

Lily ushered everyone into the house and supervised putting the two children on the couch in the parlor. Then she stared at Aliyah and Josiah—if that was his real name—in confusion. What was going on here?

Eyes blazing, Aliyah leaned forward. She jutted her pointer finger inches from his chest. "So, you just pretended your name was Simon?"

Lily sucked in a breath. *Simon?* Had her infatuation with this man blinded her to his lies? Was he the twins' father? The man who'd abandoned his children and their mother?

Part of Lily argued that the man who'd gently tucked the girls into blankets, bought them new clothes, and been kind to Martha would never do that. But he'd hidden the truth of his connection to Aliyah and the twins. That omission made Lily suspicious.

Josiah straightened to his full height, and Lily berated herself when her insides fluttered at his muscular shoulders, his take-charge attitude. He took two firm steps back from the finger Aliyah threatened to poke into his broad chest.

"I'm Simon's brother." Josiah's words fell with a thud.

Aliyah's face crumpled. Her shoulders slumped as the fight leaked out of her.

Lily's mind whirled. If he was related to Simon, why hadn't Josiah said so when she'd told him Aliyah's story? He'd only listened and sympathized. At least she'd assumed he'd been empathizing. He'd been very upset. At the time, she'd thought his reaction was caring. Maybe it had been guilt.

"Simon never knew about the babies. That's my fault."

Aliyah's eyes, narrow and assessing, studied Josiah. Lily did too. He'd been the cause of Aliyah's suffering?

"When you brought the letter, I worried it might change Simon's mind. The bishop and I wanted Simon to return the Amish community. I'd

374

convinced him to go back with me that day. While Simon packed, I ripped the letter to shreds. Neither of us read it."

Aliyah sank into the nearest chair and covered her face with her hands.

Lily's heart went out to both of them. Josiah's story cleared Simon of abandoning Aliyah. The whole situation had been a terrible and tragic misunderstanding.

As Josiah spoke, though, something else became clearer. He'd come into Lily's life under false pretenses. Lily had misinterpreted his interest in her. Josiah hadn't asked her home from the singing because he'd hoped to court her. He'd only wanted to find out about the twins.

The ache in her chest blossomed and spread throughout her body. She'd fallen for him when he had no romantic intentions. How could she have been such a fool?

Josiah cleared his throat. "After hearing about some of the things you and the girls have gone through, I want to do what I can to make things right. I can't give you those years back, but—"

"No, you can't." Aliyah lifted her head and shot him a fiery glare. "And you don't know even a tiny portion of what we lived through."

The lines etched into Josiah's face showed his anguish. "I'm sorry."

"And what are you doing here? Why didn't Simon come?"

"He, um, he's married and—"

"And he doesn't want people to know about his kids." Bitterness dripped from each one of Aliyah's words. "You Amish like to pretend you're goody-goodies, but you're no different from the rest of the world."

Josiah winced. "We sin and make many mistakes, and this is one of them."

"But you like to cover them up. Even if Simon had known, he'd have let me suffer to save his precious reputation."

"That's not true." But Josiah didn't sound too sure of his answer. "And now that we know," he said firmly, "I'll—I mean, we'll—take care of you and the children."

Aliyah angled her chin up. "A bribe for me to stay out of your lives? No, thanks. I don't want your money. I've made it this far without it. Just get out of here and leave me alone."

Josiah turned to Lily as if hoping she'd contradict Aliyah and ask him to stay. But right now, she couldn't deal with her jumbled feelings. She'd trusted him and even built up fantasies about courting him when he had no interest in her. He'd lied to her—maybe not outright, but he'd misled her by concealing the truth.

Lily lowered her lashes because she couldn't look at Josiah as she said the words she needed to say. Each one was wrenched from her. Each one tore off a piece of her heart. "Aliyah's right. You should go."

CHAPTER TEN

*J*osiah had been expecting it, imagining it, dreading it. But when
Lily uttered those words—*You should go*—with such finality, his
heart squeezed into a tight, burning spot in his chest. The ache
pulsed out from there, radiating to every part of his body.

He forced himself to move in mechanical steps to the front door. His
throat had closed, but he managed one heartfelt, "I'm sorry," to both of them
before he opened the door and strode out into the overcast day. A storm was
brewing in the sky and in his life.

Each footfall away from Lily's front porch cut him more deeply. Over and
over, he'd warned himself not to fall for her. But he hadn't followed his own
advice. Somehow, this angelic woman had floated into his life and brought
him peace and joy. And now he'd never forget her sunny, welcoming smile.
Her kindness and caring. Her gentle voice and bell-like laugh. Her womanly
softness. Her love and generosity.

He'd allowed his emotions to sway his common sense. And he'd made not
just one mistake, but two. Falling for her had been his first error, but lying to
her had been even worse.

Be sure your sins will find you out.

The change in her eyes—from adoration as he'd purchased the twins'
clothing to revulsion as Simon's story unfolded—had been fitting punishment
for his deception.

Josiah groaned. He'd covered up his real intentions to avoid facing her
disappointment. But doing that had made everything much worse when the
truth came out. If he'd told her before today, he would have tarnished her

image of him. Now he'd not only done that, he'd also destroyed any chance of a relationship. Lily would never trust him again.

As much as he'd railed against getting involved, his attraction to her had overruled his good judgment. He'd lost his heart to her. And walking away now, he'd leave a huge piece of himself behind.

~

When the door clicked shut behind Josiah with sharp finality, the floodgates inside Lily burst, and pain poured into her, crashing through her in waves, washing away her hopes for the future, drowning her dreams.

"Are you all right?" Aliyah's gentle question penetrated Lily's self-pity.

Lily gripped the chair arms. *Lord, give me strength to cope.* "I will be." *With God's help.*

But now was not the time to focus on her own loss. She turned her attention to Aliyah, who'd been dealing with five years' worth of grief. Hearing the story of Simon had to have cut her deeply. "Does it help to know he didn't abandon you?"

"A little." Aliyah stared down at her lap. "All these years, I blamed Simon for my struggles and poverty. I told myself if he'd stayed, I'd have had someone to help raise the girls, and we'd have a roof over our heads and. . ."

Lily waited quietly as Aliyah struggled with tears.

"I believed Simon was responsible for my loneliness, my grief, my exhaustion. But all along, I brought myself heartache by dwelling in the past. Now I know we wouldn't have made it as a couple. I'd never have agreed to become Amish."

"And I'm guessing Simon never would have left the community to become *Englisch.*" Once his *Rumschpringa* ended, Lily suspected he'd have returned to his home and taken baptismal classes.

Aliyah nodded. "Back then, I'd rebelled against my strict upbringing and run away from home. I wanted nothing to do with God. Now I wonder if returning to the faith of my childhood would have made these struggles bearable."

"I'm sure it would have. God can comfort us through anything." Even losing someone she'd fallen for.

"Would you pray with me?" Aliyah leaned over and reached for Lily's hands. The checkbook Josiah had given Lily tumbled onto the floor, but Aliyah grasped Lily's fingers tightly, so she couldn't pick it up. "I've strayed so far from God, but I need to find my way back. I want to be an example for my children."

Lily prayed first, and Aliyah followed with a halting prayer of her own.

"Dear Lord Jesus, please forgive me for turning my back on you and living a life of sin. And cleanse my soul of all disobedience, anger, and resentment. From now on, help me to live a life that honors you."

When Aliyah lifted her head, her eyes shone with a new light. Lily thanked God for her neighbor's new commitment.

Silently, Lily prayed for her own situation. *Lord, please help me to accept Your will.*

Aliyah's sharp intake of breath drew Lily from her tearful plea. Aliyah had picked up the checkbook and was staring at the open page, her mouth pursed into an *O*.

"What is it?" Lily leaned forward in concern as Aliyah held out the checkbook with shaking hands.

"It—it has my name on it."

"Josiah planned to give you that." Lily didn't want to intrude on the young mother's privacy but the clear, block-printed numbers stood out. Twenty thousand dollars? And Josiah planned to replenish it whenever it ran low?

"I—I don't know what to say." Aliyah hung her head. "I should have thanked him, but I don't have his address. I'm sorry I was so hasty in telling him to go."

"It was for the best," Lily murmured. Josiah's generosity choked her up, but she never wanted to face him again. Her feelings of betrayal were still raw. "I don't want to see him again."

Aliyah cocked one eyebrow. "I had a good reason for wanting him out of my life. But you?"

Lily bit her lip. Should she confess she'd fallen for him? *Nay*, it hurt too much to say the words. "He lied to me. When I told him about you and Simon, he acted as if he'd never heard the story before."

"He hadn't heard some of it." Aliyah swallowed hard. "He didn't know what the letter said. He didn't know about the babies."

True, but he still could have indicated Lily was describing his brother.

Shaking her head, Aliyah ran a hand over the checkbook cover. "I spent years stewing in anger and bitterness. And now, because of this money, I'm willing to forgive. What does that say about my character?"

"It says you just prayed for God's forgiveness, and that makes you willing to forgive others. You would have been fine with a small amount or even nothing at all, wouldn't you?"

The joy lighting Aliyah's face contrasted with Lily's low spirits. "You're right. And this money is a gift from God, not just Josiah. Although I am grateful for the part he played in giving it to me. I still can't believe this."

Then Aliyah's eyes lasered into Lily's. "And you? Have you forgiven him for lying to you?"

If Lily didn't answer truthfully, she couldn't criticize Josiah for lying. She lowered her head. "Not yet."

"I thought you Amish believed in forgiveness."

"We do. It's just that. . ." She couldn't put his betrayal in words. How did she explain it hurt her to know Josiah hadn't trusted her with the whole story? Did he see her as too judgmental and fear he couldn't share his brother's mistakes?

Lily replayed their conversations in her mind, trying to see if anything she'd said or done might have led him to that conclusion. And what had he said to mislead her?

He'd indicated he'd recently moved to this area. *Nay*, that wasn't true. She'd assumed that from his answers. He never came out and said he'd moved. After all, he was at a B and B. He hadn't bought a house or a farm. And when he said he'd come here on business, she presumed he meant landscaping. Instead, he'd been referring to Aliyah and the twins.

But he'd listened to her story about Aliyah without mentioning his part in it. Perhaps in keeping that to himself, he'd been trying to protect Aliyah's privacy. After all, Lily had just met him. Maybe she should give him the benefit of the doubt.

Aliyah studied Lily as she wrestled with her reluctance to let go. "Can't you ask God to give you a forgiving heart?"

Lily didn't answer right away because she had to admit other deeper truths. *Jah*, she could ask the Lord to soften her spirit. But part of her wanted to hang on to her anger at Josiah to avoid facing why she didn't want to forgive.

Josiah should have been honest with her about knowing Aliyah, but the real reason Lily wanted him out of her life had less to do with his actions than with her injured pride. She'd fallen hard for him, but realizing he didn't return her feelings had cut her deeply. She was too embarrassed to see him again.

Their ministers often warned against *hochmut*. And this was why. Her pride stood in the way of surrendering to God.

"Would it help if we prayed together?" Aliyah held out her hands again.

Lily tussled over keeping her secret to herself. But she confessed it to Aliyah, and they both bowed their heads as Lily asked God to take away her pride and shame.

When she opened her eyes, sun peeked through the clouds outside the window, and her spirits lightened. "I know where Josiah's staying. Should we get the girls and head over to see him?"

Aliyah nodded. "Yes, let's do that. I think we both have some apologizing to do."

CHAPTER ELEVEN

*A*s soon as he returned to the B and B, Josiah packed his suitcase and checked out. Then he asked the Millers for the name of a driver to take him back to Gratz. They graciously called several drivers until they found one who was free.

Josiah paced back and forth past the pair of rocking chairs on the front porch while he waited. What was taking the man so long? All Josiah wanted to do was flee. He needed to get away from this area, from the memories haunting him.

He'd learned his lesson about lying. Until now, he'd always tried to be truthful. Except for lying to his brother. And misleading Lily. Both times he'd lied, he'd destroyed something precious.

A buggy pulled into the driveway, but Josiah was so immersed in his thoughts, he didn't look up. Instead, he glanced at his watch, impatient to be on his way.

"Josiahhhh!" two voices yelled.

His head jerked up. Scarlett and Meryl came racing toward him.

"How did you get here?" He prayed they'd come in the buggy that had pulled past the house. And that their driver had been their beautiful neighbor.

"Lily brought us."

Scarlett affirmed Josiah's hope. Maybe he'd get a chance to apologize to Lily. His pulse leaped as she rounded the corner with Aliyah. Unlike the frowns they'd both worn earlier, this time, they both grinned as they chatted. Would their cheerful expressions change once they spotted him?

Aliyah spoke first. "Lily brought me here so I could thank you."

Josiah's spirits plunged. Lily hadn't been coming to see him. Between sneaking peeks at her and trying to frame an apology, he barely heard Aliyah's speech of gratitude.

He tuned in when she described asking Jesus into her heart. "That's wonderful."

"I know." She beamed. "If only I'd done it years ago, I would have had God's help and strength during my trials."

Her words stabbed through him. "I'm so sorry you had to go through all that. I wish I hadn't lied to my brother. I should have given him the letter and trusted God for his future. Instead, I thought I knew best."

"What's done is done, and God used it to bring me back to Him. I suspect He also had another reason for it." She shot Lily a sideways smile. "Listen, I know you two need to talk, so I'll take the girls out back to look at the chickens and horses."

The girls had been competing to see who could rock the fastest. They jumped off the rocking chairs and scampered over to their mother.

"Yay!" Scarlett bounced up and down on her toes.

Meryl took her sister's hand. "We ain't never seen no real chickens."

"We never saw real chickens, Meryl," Aliyah said in a patient voice.

"I know. I said that."

Aliyah sighed and took Meryl's other hand. As she led her daughters away, Aliyah explained the finer points of grammar.

Lily smiled as she followed their progress across the lawn. How Josiah longed to stay in Bird-in-Hand so he could court her. But he'd ruined any chance of a relationship.

Still, he needed to make things right before he went. To break the awkward silence after Lily turned in his direction, he motioned to the rockers. "Want to sit?"

She sank into the closest rocker, but rather than relaxing, she wrung her hands, looking as if she'd rather be anywhere else but here. He might not have much time before she jumped up and hurried to join the twins.

He rushed to get the words out. "Lily, I'm so sorry I didn't tell you the truth about my brother and the real reason I came to Lancaster County. Will you forgive me?"

She avoided looking at him. All Amish been taught from childhood to forgive as God forgave, but Josiah didn't want a dutiful response. He longed for genuine forgiveness. Without it, he had no hope of a future friendship or— what he truly desired—a relationship.

Then she turned to face him. "Of course." The words rang with sincerity, and then her beautiful sunny smile lit up his world. He couldn't believe it.

To his surprise, she hung her head. In a voice so low he could barely hear it, she asked, "Will you forgive me for my unkindness and"—she nibbled at her lip and stared at the wooden floorboards—"and. . . my lie?"

"You didn't lie to me." Josiah couldn't picture Lily ever doing that.

"*Jah*, I did. Back at the house. I told you I wanted you to go. But I didn't."

Josiah's rocker squeaked to a stop. "You didn't?"

"*Nay.* And I wish you weren't leaving."

She sounded so miserable, he wanted to comfort her. If only he could pull her into his arms. He settled on reaching out a finger and tilting her chin so he could look into her eyes.

"If you want me to stay, I will. I can do my business from anywhere."

Her face lit with hope. "You can?"

"I'd do anything for you."

"That's because you have a generous heart. Look at all you've done for Aliyah and the twins."

"I wanted to make up for all their years of neglect. But I have different reason for doing things for you."

The eager light in her eyes gave him courage to tell her what was in his heart. "I fell for you after I met you, but I tried to talk myself out of it."

Her breathless "You did?" gave him hope.

But first he had to admit all the thoughts that had gone through his head. "I didn't see any future for us, especially not with Aliyah being your neighbor. And I'd misled you by pretending I didn't know her story. I assumed you'd never trust me again."

"I already forgave you. And it doesn't change how I feel about you."

Josiah swallowed hard before asking the question burning inside. "How *do* you feel about me?"

"I fell for you too," she said shyly. "I hoped when you drove me home that night you intended to court me."

"I hurt you when I treated you so coldly, didn't I?"

Lily focused on her hands. "*Jah.*"

"*Ach*, Lily, I'm so sorry. I never want to hurt you. Will you forgive me? And can we start over?"

She studied him for a moment. "Are you sure?"

"Very sure."

"Then *jah* and *jah!*"

Lily's enthusiastic agreement filled Josiah with more joy than he'd ever experienced. Not only had the sun overhead chased away all the clouds, Lily's glowing face made hope blossom in his heart and soul. He couldn't wait to plant the garden he and Lily would grow together—a garden of love, joy, and family. A garden where it would always be springtime in their hearts.

EPILOGUE

*wo springs later. . .*

Lily adjusted the black *kapp* on her head and smoothed down her white apron. Ten minutes to go until her wedding.

Loud footfalls pounded up the stairs, and the bedroom door burst open. Scarlett and Meryl bumped each other to be the first through the doorway.

Scarlett, looking sweet in a lilac Amish dress, beat her sister. "Guess what, Lily? I gots—got—to hold the new baby."

Not to be outdone, Meryl, in her favorite shade of pink, elbowed her sister aside. "I held Natty's hand and helped him walk."

"He already knows how." Scarlett's tone held a sarcastic edge.

Meryl glared. "He don't—doesn't--walk too good yet. Katie said he needs help 'cos he's only eighteen months old."

Smiling, Lily bent to hug them. "I'm sure you're both a big help to Katie."

Simon had confessed everything to his wife, and true to her sweet nature, Katie had quickly forgiven him and grown to love the twins. Some weekends, the girls went to stay with Simon and Katie.

Scarlett and Meryl had fallen head over heels in love with their baby brother, Natty, when he was born that first October. Katie and Simon had just had another boy a few months ago. The twins loved spending time with their *daed*, Katie, and the little boys.

Their weekends away gave Aliyah time for her acting. She'd starred in several productions at Sight and Sound. During her weekday rehearsals, the girls stayed with Lily. Some nights, the twins slept over.

Not only had Aliyah reversed her dislike of the Amish, she even allowed Lily to take the girls to church, and Aliyah sent them to the Amish school nearby. She agreed they should learn about their father's faith. On off-Sundays, she took them to her church.

Josiah had purchased the property near Lily for Aliyah, and he'd helped the men of the *g'may* rebuild the house, expanding and modernizing it. He'd also done the landscaping, while Lily helped the girls plant a garden.

Lily still smiled when she recalled the first time Scarlett and Meryl had seen the tomato flowers in her garden that first summer. They'd squealed and waited impatiently for the tomatoes.

"You was right," Meryl crowed the day they'd picked the first one. "'Matoes really do grow on them skinny green stems."

"We has to plant our own garden," Scarlett insisted. She'd been disappointed to learn she'd have to wait until the following year to grow her own tomatoes.

Now, though, the two girls had become seasoned gardeners. They also helped Lily and Katie in their gardens.

Scarlett frowned at Lily's blue dress and white apron. "When you gonna get dressed? Mommy says the wedding's starting soon."

"I am dressed." Lily twirled around so they could see the new dress she'd sewn.

Scarlett looked horrified. "You can't wear that. Where's your white gown?"

Meryl's brow knotted. "And yer veil?"

"That's only for *Englisch* weddings. This is for Amish weddings."

"Lily still looks pretty, doesn't she, Scarlett?" Meryl studied Lily with an anxious look on her face, then she leaned over to whisper in her sister's ear. "We don't want to hurt her feelings. 'Member what Mommy says about being nice to everyone."

"I am being nice. I'm helping Lily look better for her wedding."

Martha peeked into the room, interrupting Meryl's loud huff. "*Ach*, Lily, you look beautiful!"

"See," Meryl said to Scarlett, "that's what yer supposed to say to brides."

A rapturous look in her eyes, Martha wrapped her arms around herself. "I'm so excited to be a side-sitter. *Danke, Danke,* Lily!"

"I'm so glad you're doing it." Lily and Josiah had both agreed Martha should have a special place in their wedding. "You were with us on our first date."

"I know. I told you Josiah would marry you, didn't I? And I was right!"

"*Jah*, you were." How embarrassed Lily had been that night. She'd worried about Josiah overhearing Martha's comments. If only Lily had known what the future held. . .

"We need to head downstairs. It's almost eight," Martha warned. She ushered Scarlett and Meryl ahead of her. "Your *mamm* is waiting for you two."

The girls skedaddled down the steps, and Martha followed more sedately.

The next time Lily saw all three of them, she'd be a married woman. Married to the man she loved with all her heart.

∼

Martha's grin stretched from ear to ear as Josiah, with Lily at his side, made his way to the *eck*, the special corner table that had been beautifully decorated. Josiah's smile most likely matched Martha's because his whole being over-flowed with love and joy for his bride. His dreams had come true today as he'd made his promises before God to take Lily as his wife.

After they sat in their places, Josiah twined his fingers through Lily's under the table. Then he leaned past his beautiful bride to speak to Martha.

"*Danke* for being here with us today. You've been a part of the two most special days of our lives. We might not have met if it weren't for you."

"I know." Martha beamed with pride. "That night, I told Lily you would marry her."

Lily laughed. "I didn't believe you, and I don't think Josiah did either. Neither of us could have guessed what God had planned."

When her eyes met his, Josiah tried to convey all the tenderness and deep love he felt for his sweet wife. "We never know what blessings God has in store for us. And you are the most *wunderbar* blessing I've ever received after God's love and forgiveness."

Lily sniffled and dabbed at her eyes.

Alarmed, Josiah stared at her. "Are you crying?"

"Don't worry. They're tears of joy. I'm so grateful to God for bringing you into my life. Two years ago, I'd hit a low point. I was missing *Mamm* and regretting that I'd be an *alt maedel*."

"You?" Josiah couldn't believe it. A woman as beautiful, sweet, caring, kind. . . His list could go on and on.

"*Jah*. I remember tucking the twins in when they stayed overnight and thinking God had brought them into my life to make up for me not having a family."

"They are your family now, but we'll have some little ones of our own too."

Her watery smile revealed she wanted children as much as he did. He marveled that God had given him such a perfect helpmeet.

Thomas King passed the table and winked at Josiah. "Told you Lily was right pretty and had a good heart. You believe me now?"

"I've always agreed with you." Josiah had guessed it that day, and now he knew it for sure and certain. He'd married the most wonderful woman in the *g'may*. His heart overflowed with gratitude.

"I hope you and Lily will be as happy as Mae and I are after fifty-seven years."

Lily squeezed Josiah's hand under the table and smiled at Thomas. "I hope so too."

"Well, if you keep God at the center of your union, you will be. Now I want to join my blushing bride." With a quick wave, Thomas headed off to join the gray-haired woman who still looked at him with stars in her eyes as if they were newlyweds.

"I want us to be as in love as they are when we're that age," Lily whispered.

"We will be. We'll put God first in our marriage." For the next fifty-seven springs—or however many years the good Lord gave them—Josiah promised to always see Lily as his blushing bride. And if he loved her the way the Bible commanded, he knew in his heart, she'd still look at him with the same adoration as she did today. They'd keep springtime in their hearts forever.

ABOUT THE AUTHOR

USA Today bestselling, award-winning author **Rachel J. Good** writes life-changing, heart-tugging novels of faith, hope, and forgiveness. She grew up near Lancaster County, Pennsylvania, the setting for her Amish novels. Striving to be as authentic as possible, she spends time with her Amish friends, doing chores on their farms and attending family events. Rachel is the author of several Amish series in print or forthcoming – the bestselling *Love & Promises, Sisters & Friends, Unexpected Amish Blessings, Surprised by Love,* and two books in *Hearts of Amish Country* – as well as the *Amish Quilts Coloring Books.* In addition, she has stories in many anthologies, including *Amish Christmas Twins* and *Christmas at the Amish Bakeshop* both with Shelley Shepard Gray and Loree Lough.

Rachel loves to connect with readers at www.racheljgood.com and https://www.facebook.com/people/Rachel-J-Good/100009699285059/.

To read more of Rachel J. Good's books, please visit: https://www.amazon.com/Rachel-J-Good/e/B019DWF4FG/

GLOSSARY OF AMISH WORDS

Because Amish words come from many different areas around the country and Amish is not a written language, the words may be spelled in various ways.

- *ab im kopp*: crazy
- *ach*: oh; *ach vell*: oh well
- *ach, du lieva*: oh, my goodness
- *aendi, aenti*: aunt
- *alt maedel*: old maid
- *appeditlich*: delicious
- *Ausbund*: Amish hymnbook
- *bann*: shunning, excommunication
- *banns*: wedding announcements
- *bensel*: silly, silly child
- *bobli, boppli*: baby; *bopplin*: babies
- *bruder*: brother; *bruderen*: brothers
- *bu*: boy; *buwe*: boys
- *chust*: just
- *cum, kumme, cumme*: come
- *daadi haus, dawdi haus*: A small house next to or attached to a larger Amish house usually used for grandparents
- *Daed, Dat, Datt*: Dad
- *Dawdi*: grandfather
- *dawdihaus*: a small dwelling typically used for grandparents
- *denki, danki, danke*: thank you

- *Der Herr*: The Lord
- *der welt*: the world
- *die youngie*: the young people
- *Dietsch*: Pennsylvania German
- *Dochder, dochter*: daughter; *dochdern*: daughters
- *dumm*: dumb; *dummkopp*: dummy
- *du bischt wilkumm*: you're welcome
- *eck*: corner table where the newly married couple sits at their wedding
- *Englisch, English, Englischer*: non-Amish people
- *fater*: father
- *ferhoodled*: mixed up
- *fraa, Frau*: wife; *fraaen*: wives
- *froh*: glad
- *geh*: go
- *g'may*: the church district, congregation
- *Gott, Gotte*: God
- *Gross sohn*: grandson
- *Guder mariye, Guten morgen, Gut morgen*: Good morning
- *Guder owed*: Good evening
- *Gude nacht, Guten nacht*: Good night
- *gut, gute goot*: good
- *Guten tag*: Good day
- *hallo*: hello
- *haus*: house
- *heartzley*: sweetheart
- *Herr*: Lord
- *hinnerdale*: backside
- *hochmut*: pride
- *jah, ja, ya, yah*: yes
- *kaffe, kaffi, koffee* - coffee
- *kapp*: prayer covering
- *kinna, kinn*: child; *kinner, kinder*: children
- *komm, kumm, kumme, cum, cumme*: come
- *lieb*: love; *liebchen*: sweetheart, darling
- *lieber Vater*: dear Father
- *Loblied*: hymn in the Ausbund, sung as the second hymn in every service
- *maidel, maedel*: girl over twelve; *maed*: plural
- *Mamm*: Mom
- *Mammi*: Grandma
- *maud*: maid, household helper

- *mei*: my
- *meine liebe*: my love
- *mudder, mater*: mother
- *mutza*: black suit worn by Amish men
- *narrisch*: foolish, crazy
- *neh, nae, nee*: no
- *newehockers, neuwesitzer*: "sidesitters," attendants at a wedding
- *nix*: nothing
- *oke*: okay
- *onkel*: uncle
- *Ordnung*: the rules by which Amish church members conduct their lives
- *Rumspringa, Rumspringe, Rumschpringe*: "running-around," a period of freedom when teens decide about joining the Amish church
- *schatzi*: dear
- *schweschder, schwester*: sister; *schweschdern*: sisters
- *seltsam*: weird
- *sohn*: son
- the *familye* way: pregnant
- *Unparteiisches Gesang-Buch*: a German songbook
- *vatter*: father
- *Wie geht's?, Vie gehts*: How is it going?
- *Wilkom*: Welcome
- *wunderbar, wunderbaar*: wonderful
- *ya, yah*: yes
- *youngie*: youth who are running around

Made in the USA
Middletown, DE
17 February 2022